There's only one Thing
To do With a crown.

Ramona saw at once that burs had all sorts of interesting possibilities. She picked two and stuck them together. She added another and another. They were better than Tinkertoys. She would have to tell Howie about them. When she had a string of burs, each clinging to the next, she bent it into a circle and stuck the ends together. A crown! She could make a crown. She picked more burs and built up the circle by making peaks all the way around like the crown the boy wore in the magarine commercial. There was only one thing to do with a crown like that. Ramona crowned herself—ta-*da*!— like the boy on television.

Enjoy all of
Beverly Cleary's books

FEATURING
RAMONA QUIMBY:

Beezus and Ramona

Ramona the Pest

Ramona the Brave

Ramona and Her Father

Ramona and Her Mother

Ramona Quimby, Age 8

Ramona Forever

Ramona's World

FEATURING
HENRY HUGGINS:

Henry Huggins

Henry and Beezus

Henry and Ribsy

Henry and the Paper Route

Henry and the Clubhouse

Ribsy

FEATURING
RALPH MOUSE:

The Mouse
and the Motorcycle

Runaway Ralph

Ralph S. Mouse

MORE GREAT FICTION
BY BEVERLY CLEARY:

Ellen Tebbits

Otis Spofford

Fifteen

The Luckiest Girl

Jean and Johnny

Emily's Runaway
Imagination

Sister of the Bride

Mitch and Amy

Socks

Dear Mr. Henshaw

Muggie Maggie

Strider

Two Times the Fun

AND DON'T MISS
BEVERLY CLEARY'S
AUTOBIOGRAPHIES:

A Girl from Yamhill

My Own Two Feet

Beverly Cleary

Ramona and Her Father

ILLUSTRATED BY

Tracy Dockray

HarperTrophy®

An Imprint of HarperCollins*Publishers*

Chapter 7, "Ramona and the Three Wise Persons,"
originally appeared in *Family Circle* magazine.

Harper Trophy® is a registered trademark of
HarperCollins Publishers.

Ramona and Her Father

Printed in the United States of America. For information
address HarperCollins Children's Books,
a division of HarperCollins Publishers,
1350 Avenue of the Americas, New York, NY 10019.

Library of Congress Catalog Card Number: 2005938680
ISBN-10: 0-380-70916-3 — ISBN-13: 978-0-380-70916-8

Typography by Amy Ryan

❖

Reillustrated Harper Trophy edition, 2006
Visit us on the World Wide Web!
www.harpercollinschildrens.com

CONTENTS

1
payday

"Ye-e-ep!" sang Ramona Quimby one warm September afternoon, as she knelt on a chair at the kitchen table to make out her Christmas list. She had enjoyed a good day in second grade, and she looked forward to working on her list. For Ramona a Christmas list was a list of presents she hoped to receive, not presents she planned to give. "Ye-e-ep!" she sang again.

"Thank goodness today is payday," remarked Mrs. Quimby, as she opened the refrigerator to see what she could find for supper.

"Ye-e-ep!" sang Ramona, as she printed *mice or ginny pig* on her list with purple crayon. Next to Christmas and her birthday, her father's payday was her favorite day. His payday meant treats. Her mother's payday from her part-time job in a doctor's office meant they could make payments on the bedroom the Quimbys had added to their house when Ramona was in first grade.

"What's all this yeeping about?" asked Mrs. Quimby.

"I'm making a joyful noise until the Lord like they say in Sunday school," Ramona explained. "Only they don't tell us what the joyful noise sounds like so I made up my own." *Hooray* and *wow*, joyful noises to Ramona, had not sounded right, so she had

settled on *yeep* because it sounded happy but not rowdy. "Isn't that all right?" she asked, as she began to add *myna bird that talks* to her list.

"Yeep is fine if that's the way you feel about it," reassured Mrs. Quimby.

Ramona printed *coocoo clock* on her list while she wondered what the treat would be this payday. Maybe, since this was Friday, they could all go to a movie if her parents could find one suitable. Both Ramona and her big sister, Beezus, christened Beatrice, wondered what went on in all those other movies. They planned to find out the minute they were grown up. That was one thing they agreed on. Or maybe their father would bring presents, a package of colored paper for Ramona, a paperback book for Beezus.

"I wish I could think of something interesting to do with leftover pot roast and creamed cauliflower," remarked Mrs. Quimby.

Leftovers—yuck!, thought Ramona. "Maybe Daddy will take us to the Whopper-burger for supper for payday," she said. A soft, juicy hamburger spiced with relish,

French fries crisp on the outside and mealy inside, a little paper cup of cole slaw at the Whopperburger Restaurant were Ramona's favorite payday treat. Eating close together in a booth made Ramona feel snug and cozy. She and Beezus never quarreled at the Whopperburger.

"Good idea." Mrs. Quimby closed the refrigerator door. "I'll see what I can do."

Then Beezus came into the kitchen through the back door, dropped her books on the table, and flopped down on a chair with a gusty sigh.

"What was that all about?" asked Mrs. Quimby, not at all worried.

"Nobody is any fun anymore," complained Beezus. "Henry spends all his time running around the track over at the high school getting ready for the Olympics in eight or twelve years, or he and Robert study a book of world records trying to find a record to

5

break, and Mary Jane practices the piano all the time." Beezus sighed again. "And Mrs. Mester says we are going to do lots of creative writing, and I hate creative writing. I don't see why I had to get Mrs. Mester for seventh grade anyway."

"Creative writing can't be as bad as all that," said Mrs. Quimby.

"You just don't understand," complained Beezus. "I can never think of stories, and my poems are stuff like, 'See the bird in the tree. He is singing to me.'"

"Tee-hee, tee-hee," added Ramona without thinking.

"Ramona," said Mrs. Quimby, "that was not necessary."

Because Beezus had been so grouchy lately, Ramona could manage to be only medium sorry.

"Pest!" said Beezus. Noticing Ramona's work, she added, "Making out a Christmas list in September is silly."

Ramona calmly selected an orange crayon. She was used to being called a pest. "If I am a pest, you are a rotten dinosaur egg," she informed her sister.

"Mother, make her stop," said Beezus.

When Beezus said this, Ramona knew she had won. The time had come to change the subject. "Today's payday," she told her sister. "Maybe we'll get to go to the Whopperburger for supper."

"Oh, Mother, will we?" Beezus's unhappy mood disappeared as she swooped up Picky-picky, the Quimbys' shabby old cat, who had strolled into the kitchen. He purred a rusty purr as she rubbed her cheek against his yellow fur.

"I'll see what I can do," said Mrs. Quimby.

Smiling, Beezus dropped Picky-picky, gathered up her books, and went off to her room. Beezus was the kind of girl who did her homework on Friday instead of waiting until the last minute on Sunday.

Ramona asked in a quiet voice, "Mother, why is Beezus so cross lately?" Letting her sister overhear such a question would lead to real trouble.

"You mustn't mind her," whispered Mrs. Quimby. "She's reached a difficult age."

Ramona thought such an all-purpose excuse for bad behavior would be a handy thing to have. "So have I," she confided to her mother.

Mrs. Quimby dropped a kiss on the top of Ramona's head. "Silly girl," she said. "It's just a phase Beezus is going through. She'll outgrow it."

A contented silence fell over the house as three members of the family looked forward to supper at the Whopperburger, where they would eat, close and cozy in a booth, their food brought to them by a friendly waitress who always said, "There you go," as she set down their hamburgers and French fries.

Ramona had decided to order a cheeseburger when she heard the sound of her father's key in the front door. "Daddy, Daddy!" she shrieked, scrambling down from the chair and running to meet her father as he opened the door. "Guess what?"

Beezus, who had come from her room, answered before her father had a chance to guess. "Mother said maybe we could go to the Whopperburger for dinner!"

Mr. Quimby smiled and kissed his daughters before he held out a small white paper bag. "Here, I brought you a little present." Somehow he did not look as happy as usual. Maybe he had had a hard day at the office of the van-and-storage company where he worked.

His daughters pounced and opened the bag together. "Gummybears!" was their joyful

9

cry. The chewy little bears were the most popular sweet at Glenwood School this fall. Last spring powdered Jell-O eaten from the package had been the fad. Mr. Quimby always remembered these things.

"Run along and divide them between you," said Mr. Quimby. "I want to talk to your mother."

"Don't spoil your dinner," said Mrs. Quimby.

The girls bore the bag off to Beezus's room, where they dumped the gummybears onto the bedspread. First they divided the cinnamon-flavored red bears, one for Beezus, one for Ramona. Then they divided the orange bears and the green, and as they were about to divide the yellow bears, both girls were suddenly aware that their mother and father were no longer talking. Silence filled the house. The sisters looked at one another. There was something unnatural about this silence. Uneasy, they waited for some sound, and then their parents began to speak in whispers. Beezus tiptoed to the door to listen.

Ramona bit the head off a red gummybear. She always ate toes last. "Maybe they're planning a big surprise," she suggested, refusing to worry.

"I don't think so," whispered Beezus, "but I can't hear what they are saying."

"Try listening through the furnace pipes," whispered Ramona.

"That won't work here. The living room is too far away." Beezus strained to catch her parents' words. "I think something's wrong."

Ramona divided her gummybears, one heap to eat at home, the other to take to school to share with friends if they were nice to her.

"Something is wrong. Something awful," whispered Beezus. "I can tell by the way they are talking."

Beezus looked so frightened that Ramona became frightened, too. What could be wrong? She tried to think what she might have done to make her parents whisper this way, but she had stayed out of trouble lately.

She could not think of a single thing that could be wrong. This frightened her even more. She no longer felt like eating chewy little bears. She wanted to know why her

mother and father were whispering in a way that alarmed Beezus.

Finally the girls heard their father say in a normal voice, "I think I'll take a shower before supper." This remark was reassuring to Ramona.

"What'll we do now?" whispered Beezus. "I'm scared to go out."

Worry and curiosity, however, urged Beezus and Ramona into the hall.

Trying to pretend they were not concerned about their family, the girls walked into the kitchen where Mrs. Quimby was removing leftovers from the refrigerator. "I think we'll eat at home after all," she said, looking sad and anxious.

Without being asked, Ramona began to deal four place mats around the dining-room table, laying them all right side up. When she was cross with Beezus, she laid her sister's place mat face down.

Mrs. Quimby looked at the cold creamed cauliflower with distaste, returned it to the refrigerator, and reached for a can of green beans before she noticed her silent and worried daughters watching her for clues as to what might be wrong.

Mrs. Quimby turned and faced Beezus and Ramona. "Girls, you might as well know. Your father has lost his job."

"But he liked his job," said Ramona, regretting the loss of that hamburger and those French fries eaten in the coziness of a booth. She had known her father to change jobs because he had not liked his work, but she had never heard of him losing a job.

"Was he fired?" asked Beezus, shocked at the news.

Mrs. Quimby opened the green beans and dumped them into a saucepan before she explained. "Losing his job was not your father's fault. He worked for a little company.

A big company bought the little company and let out most of the people who worked for the little company."

"But we won't have enough money." Beezus understood these things better than Ramona.

"Mother works," Ramona reminded her sister.

"Only part time," said Mrs. Quimby. "And we have to make payments to the bank for the new room. That's why I went to work."

"What will we do?" asked Ramona, alarmed at last. Would they go hungry? Would the men from the bank come and tear down the new room if they couldn't pay for it? She had never thought what it might be like not to have enough money— not that the Quimbys ever had money to spare. Although Ramona had often heard her mother say that house payments, car payments, taxes, and groceries seemed to eat up money, Mrs. Quimby somehow managed to make their money pay for all they really needed with a little treat now and then besides.

"We will have to manage as best we can until your father finds work," said Mrs. Quimby. "It may not be easy."

"Maybe I could baby-sit," volunteered Beezus.

As she laid out knives and forks, Ramona wondered how she could earn money, too. She could have a lemonade stand in front of the house, except nobody ever bought lemonade but her father and her friend Howie. She thought about pounding rose petals and soaking them in water to make perfume to sell. Unfortunately, the perfume she tried to make always smelled like rotten rose petals, and anyway the roses were almost gone.

"And girls," said Mrs. Quimby, lowering

her voice as if she was about to share a secret, "you mustn't do anything to annoy your father. He is worried enough right now."

But he remembered to bring gummy-bears, thought Ramona, who never wanted too annoy her father or her mother either, just Beezus, although sometimes, without even trying, she succeeded in annoying her whole family. Ramona felt sad and somehow lonely, as if she were left out of something important, because her family was in trouble and there was nothing she could do to help. When she had finished setting the table, she returned to the list she had begun, it now seemed, a long time ago. "But what about Christmas?" she asked her mother.

"Right now Christmas is the least of our worries." Mrs. Quimby looked sadder than Ramona had ever seen her look. "Taxes are due in November. And we have to buy groceries and make car payments and a lot of other things."

"Don't we have any money in the bank?" asked Beezus.

"Not much," admitted Mrs. Quimby, "but your father was given two weeks' pay."

Ramona looked at the list she had begun so happily and wondered how much the presents she had listed would cost. Too much, she knew. Mice were free if you knew the right person, the owner of a mother mouse, so she might get some mice.

Slowly Ramona crossed out *ginny pig* and the other presents she had listed. As she made black lines through each item, she thought about her family. She did not want her father to be worried, her mother sad, or her sister cross. She wanted her whole family, including Picky-picky, to be happy.

Ramona studied her crayons, chose a pinky-red one because it seemed the happiest color, and printed one more item on her Christmas list to make up for all she had crossed out. *One happy family*. Beside the words she drew four smiling faces and beside them, the face of a yellow cat, also smiling.

2

Ramona and The Million Dollars

Ramona wished she had a million dollars so her father would be fun again. There had been many changes in the Quimby household since Mr. Quimby had lost his job, but the biggest change was in Mr. Quimby himself.

First of all, Mrs. Quimby found a full-time job working for another doctor, which was good news. However, even a second grader could understand that one paycheck would not stretch as far as two paychecks, especially when there was so much talk of taxes, whatever they were. Mrs. Quimby's new job meant that Mr. Quimby had to be home when Ramona returned from school.

Ramona and her father saw a lot of one another. At first she thought having her father to herself for an hour or two every day would be fun, but when she came home, she found him running the vacuum cleaner, filling out job applications, or sitting on the couch, smoking and staring into space. He could not take her to the park because he had to stay near the telephone. Someone might call to offer him a job. Ramona grew uneasy. Maybe he was too worried to love her anymore.

One day Ramona came home to find her father in the living room drinking warmed-over coffee, smoking, and staring at the television set. On the screen a boy a couple of years younger than Ramona was singing:

Forget your pots, forget your pans.
It's not too late to change your plans.
Spend a little, eat a lot,
Big fat burgers, nice and hot
At your nearest Whopperburger!

Ramona watched him open his mouth wide to bite into a fat cheeseburger with lettuce and tomato spilling out of the bun and thought wistfully of the good old days when the family used to go to the restaurant on payday and when her mother used to bring home little treats—stuffed olives, cinnamon buns for Sunday breakfast, a bag of potato chips.

"That kid must be earning a million dollars." Mr. Quimby snuffed out his cigarette in a loaded ashtray. "He's singing that commercial every time I turn on the television."

A boy Ramona's age earning a million dollars? Ramona was all interest. "How's he earning a million dollars?" she asked. She had often thought of all the things they could do if they had a million dollars, beginning with turning up the thermostat so they wouldn't have to wear sweaters in the house to save fuel oil.

Mr. Quimby explained. "They make a movie of him singing the commercial, and every time the movie is shown on television he gets paid. It all adds up."

Well! This was a new idea to Ramona. She thought it over as she got out her crayons and paper and knelt on a chair at the kitchen table. Singing a song about hamburgers would not be hard to do. She could do it herself. Maybe she could earn a million dollars like that boy so her father would be fun

again, and everyone at school would watch
her on television and say, "There's Ramona
Quimby. She goes to our school." A million
dollars would buy a cuckoo clock for every
room in the house, her father wouldn't need
a job, the family could go to Disneyland. . . .

"Forget your pots, forget your pans,"
Ramona began to sing, as she drew a picture
of a hamburger and stabbed yellow dots across

the top of the bun for sesame seeds. With a million dollars the Quimbys could eat in a restaurant every day if they wanted to.

After that Ramona began to watch for children on television commercials. She saw a boy eating bread and margarine when a crown suddenly appeared on his head with a fanfare—ta-*da*!—of music. She saw a girl who asked, "Mommy, wouldn't it be nice if caramel apples grew on trees?" and another girl who took a bite of cereal said, "It's good, hm-um," and giggled. There was a boy who asked at the end of a weiner commercial, "Dad, how do you tell a boy hot dog from a girl hot dog?" and a girl who tipped her head to one side and said, "Pop-pop-pop," as she listened to her cereal. Children crunched potato chips, chomped on pickles, gnawed at fried chicken. Ramona grew particularly fond of the curly-haired little girl saying to her mother at the zoo, "Look, Mommy, the elephant's legs are wrinkled just like your pantyhose." Ramona could say all those things.

Ramona began to practice. Maybe someone would see her and offer her a million dollars to make a television commercial. On her way to school, if her friend Howie did not walk with her, she tipped her head to one side and said, "Pop-pop-pop." She said to herself, "M-m-m, it's good," and giggled. Giggling wasn't easy when she didn't have anything to giggle about, but she worked at it. Once she practiced on her mother by asking, "Mommy, wouldn't it be nice if caramel apples grew on trees?" She had taken to calling her mother Mommy lately, because children on commercials always called their mothers Mommy.

Mrs. Quimby's absentminded answer was, "Not really. Caramel is bad for your teeth." She was wearing slacks so Ramona could not say the line about pantyhose.

Since the Quimbys no longer bought potato chips or pickles, Ramona found other foods—toast and apples and carrot sticks—to practice good loud crunching on. When they had chicken for dinner, she smacked and licked her fingers.

"Ramona," said Mr. Quimby, "your table manners grow worse and worse. Don't eat so noisily. My grandmother used to say, 'A smack at the table is worth a smack on the bottom.'"

Ramona, who did not think she would have liked her father's grandmother, was embarrassed. She had been practicing to be on television, and she had forgotten her family could hear.

Ramona continued to practice until she began to feel as if a television camera was watching her wherever she went. She smiled a lot and skipped, feeling that she was cute and lovable. She felt as if she had fluffy blond curls, even though in real life her hair was brown and straight.

One morning, smiling prettily, she thought, and swinging her lunch box, Ramona skipped to school. Today someone might notice her because she was wearing her red tights. She was happy because this was a special day, the day of Ramona's parent-teacher conference. Since Mrs. Quimby was at work, Mr. Quimby was going to meet with Mrs. Rogers, her second-grade teacher. Ramona was proud to have a father who would come to school.

Feeling dainty, curly-haired, and adorable, Ramona skipped into her classroom, and what did she see but Mrs. Rogers with wrinkles around her ankles. Ramona did not hesitate. She skipped right over to her teacher and, since there did not happen to be an elephant in Room 2, turned the words around and said, "Mrs. Rogers, your pantyhose are

wrinkled like an elephant's legs."

Mrs. Rogers looked surprised, and the boys and girls who had already taken their seats giggled. All the teacher said was, "Thank you, Ramona, for telling me. And remember, we do not skip inside the school building."

Ramona had an uneasy feeling she had

displeased her teacher.

She was sure of it when Howie said, "Ramona, you sure weren't very polite to Mrs. Rogers." Howie, a serious thinker, was usually right.

Suddenly Ramona was no longer an adorable little fluffy-haired girl on television. She was plain old Ramona, a second grader whose own red tights bagged at the knee and wrinkled at the ankle. This wasn't the way things turned out on television. On television grown-ups always smiled at everything children said.

During recess Ramona went to the girls' bathroom and rolled her tights up at the waist to stretch them up at the knee and ankle. Mrs. Rogers must have done the same thing to her pantyhose, because after recess her ankles were smooth. Ramona felt better.

That afternoon, when the lower grades had been dismissed from their classrooms,

Ramona found her father, along with Davy's mother, waiting outside the door of Room 2 for their conferences with Mrs. Rogers. Davy's mother's appointment was first, so Mr. Quimby sat down on a chair outside the door with a folder of Ramona's schoolwork to look over. Davy stood close to the door, hoping to hear what his teacher was saying about him. Everybody in Room 2 was anxious to learn what the teacher said.

Mr. Quimby opened Ramona's folder. "Run along and play on the playground until I'm through," he told his daughter.

"Promise you'll tell me what Mrs. Rogers says about me," said Ramona.

Mr. Quimby understood. He smiled and gave his promise.

Outside, the playground was chilly and damp. The only children who lingered were those whose parents had conferences, and they were more interested in what was going on inside the building than outside. Bored, Ramona looked around for something to do, and because she could find nothing better, she followed a traffic boy across the street. On the opposite side, near the market that had been built when she was in kindergarten, she decided she had time to explore. In a weedy space at the side of the market building, she discovered several burdock plants that bore a prickly crop of brown burs, each covered with sharp, little hooks.

Ramona saw at once that burs had all sorts of interesting possibilities. She picked two and stuck them together. She added another and another. They were better than Tinkertoys. She would have to tell Howie about them. When she had a string of burs, each clinging to the next, she bent it into a circle and stuck the ends together. A crown! She could make a crown. She picked more burs and built up the circle by making peaks all the way around like the crown the boy wore in the magarine commercial. There was only one thing to do with a crown like that. Ramona crowned herself—ta-*da*!—like the boy on television.

Prickly though it was, Ramona enjoyed

wearing the crown. She practiced looking surprised, like the boy who ate the margarine, and pretended she was rich and famous and about to meet her father, who would be driving a big shiny car bought with the million dollars she had earned.

The traffic boys had gone off duty. Ramona remembered to look both ways before she crossed the street, and as she crossed she pretended people were saying, "There goes that rich girl. She earned a million dollars eating margarine on TV."

Mr. Quimby was standing on the playground, looking for Ramona. Forgetting all she had been pretending, Ramona ran to him. "What did Mrs. Rogers say about me?" she demanded.

"That's some crown you've got there," Mr. Quimby remarked.

"Daddy, what did she *say*?" Ramona could not contain her impatience.

Mr. Quimby grinned. "She said you were impatient."

Oh, that. People were always telling Ramona not to be so impatient. "What else?" asked Ramona, as she and her father walked toward home.

"You are a good reader, but you are careless about spelling."

Ramona knew this. Unlike Beezus, who was an excellent speller, Ramona could not believe spelling was important as long as people could understand what she meant. "What else?"

"She said you draw unusually well for a second grader and your printing is the best in the class."

"What else?"

Mr. Quimby raised one eyebrow as he looked down at Ramona. "She said you were inclined to show off and you sometimes forget your manners."

Ramona was indignant at this criticism. "I do not! She's just making that up." Then she remembered what she had said about her teacher's pantyhose and felt subdued. She hoped her teacher had not repeated her remark to her father.

"I remember my manners most of the time," said Ramona, wondering what her teacher had meant by showing off. Being first to raise her hand when she knew the answer?

"Of course you do," agreed Mr. Quimby. "After all, you are my daughter. Now tell me, how are you going to get that crown off?"

Using both hands, Ramona tried to lift her crown but only succeeded in pulling her hair. The tiny hooks clung fast. Ramona tugged. Ow! That hurt. She looked help-lessly up at her father.

Mr. Quimby appeared amused. "Who do

you think you are? A Rose Festival Queen?"

Ramona pretended to ignore her father's question. How silly to act like someone on television when she was a plain old second grader whose tights bagged at the knees again. She hoped her father would not guess. He might. He was good at guessing.

By then Ramona and her father were home. As Mr. Quimby unlocked the front door, he said, "We'll have to see what we can do about getting you uncrowned before your mother gets home. Any ideas?"

Ramona had no answer, although she was eager to part with the crown before her father guessed what she had been doing. In the kitchen, Mr. Quimby picked off the top of the crown, the part that did not touch Ramona's hair. That was easy. Now came the hard part.

"Yow!" said Ramona, when her father tried to lift the crown.

"That won't work," said her father. "Let's try one bur at a time." He went to work on one bur, carefully trying to untangle it from Ramona's hair, one strand at a time. To Ramona, who did not like to stand still, this process took forever. Each bur was snarled in a hundred hairs, and each hair had to be pulled before the bur was loosened. After a very long time, Mr. Quimby handed a hair-entangled bur to Ramona.

"Yow! Yipe! Leave me some hair," said Ramona, picturing a bald circle around her head.

"I'm trying," said Mr. Quimby and began on the next bur.

Ramona sighed. Standing still doing nothing was tiresome.

After what seemed like a long time, Beezus came home from school. She took one look at Ramona and began to laugh.

"I don't suppose you ever did anything

dumb," said Ramona, short of patience and anxious lest her sister guess why she was wearing the remains of a crown. "What about the time you—"

"No arguments," said Mr. Quimby. "We have a problem to solve, and it might be a good idea if we solved it before your mother comes home from work."

Much to Ramona's annoyance, her sister sat down to watch. "How about soaking?" suggested Beezus. "It might soften all those millions of little hooks."

"Yow! Yipe!" said Ramona. "You're pulling too hard."

Mr. Quimby laid another hair-filled bur on the table. "Maybe we should try. This isn't working."

"It's about time she washed her hair anyway," said Beezus, a remark Ramona felt was entirely unnecessary. Nobody could shampoo hair full of burs.

Ramona knelt on a chair with her head in a sinkful of warm water for what seemed like hours until her knees ached and she had a crick in her neck. "Now, Daddy?" she asked at least once a minute.

"Not yet," Mr. Quimby answered, feeling a bur. "Nope," he said at last. "This isn't going to work."

Ramona lifted her dripping head from the sink. When her father tried to dry her hair, the bur hooks clung to the towel. He jerked the towel loose and draped it around Ramona's shoulders.

"Well, live and learn," said Mr. Quimby. "Beezus, scrub some potatoes and throw them in the oven. We can't have your mother come home and find we haven't started supper."

When Mrs. Quimby arrived, she took one look at her husband trying to untangle Ramona's wet hair from the burs, groaned, sank limply onto a kitchen chair, and began to laugh.

By now Ramona was tired, cross, and hungry. "I don't see anything funny," she said sullenly.

Mrs. Quimby managed to stop laughing. "What on earth got into you?" she asked.

Ramona considered. Was this a question grown-ups asked just to be asking a question, or did her mother expect an answer? "Nothing," was a safe reply. She would never tell her family how she happened to be wearing a crown of burs. Never, not even if they threw her into a dungeon.

"Beezus, bring me the scissors," said Mrs. Quimby.

Ramona clapped her hands over the burs. "No!" she shrieked and stamped her foot. "I won't let you cut off my hair! I won't! I won't! I won't!"

Beezus handed her mother the scissors and

gave her sister some advice. "Stop yelling. If you go to bed with burs in your hair, you'll really get messed up."

Ramona had to face the wisdom of Beezus's words. She stopped yelling to consider the problem once more. "All right," she said, as if she were granting a favor, "but I want Daddy to do it." Her father would work with care while her mother, always in a hurry since she was working full time, would go *snip-snip-snip* and be done with it. Besides, supper would be prepared faster and would taste better if her mother did the cooking.

"I am honored," said Mr. Quimby. "Deeply honored."

Mrs. Quimby did not seem sorry to hand over the scissors. "Why don't you go someplace else to work while Beezus and I get supper on the table?"

Mr. Quimby led Ramona into the living

room, where he turned on the television set. "This may take time," he explained, as he went to work. "We might as well watch the news."

Ramona was still anxious. "Don't cut any more than you have to, Daddy," she begged, praying the margarine boy would not appear on the screen. "I don't want everyone at school to make fun of me." The newscaster was talking about strikes and a lot of things Ramona did not understand.

"The merest smidgin," promised her father. *Snip. Snip. Snip.* He laid a hair–ensnarled bur in an ashtray. *Snip. Snip. Snip.* He laid another bur beside the first.

"Does it look awful?" asked Ramona.

"As my grandmother would say, 'It will never be noticed from a trotting horse.'"

Ramona let out a long, shuddery sigh, the closest thing to crying without really crying. *Snip. Snip. Snip.* Ramona touched the side of her head. She still had hair there. More hair than she expected. She felt a little better.

The newscaster disappeared from the television screen, and there was that boy again singing:

Forget your pots, forget your pans.
It's not too late to change your plans.

Ramona thought longingly of the days before her father lost his job, when they could forget their pots and pans and change their plans. She watched the boy open his mouth wide and sink his teeth into that fat hamburger with lettuce, tomato, and cheese hanging out of the bun. She swallowed and said, "I bet that boy has a lot of fun with his million dollars." She felt so sad. The Quimbys really needed a million dollars. Even one dollar would help.

Snip. Snip. Snip. "Oh, I don't know," said

Mr. Quimby. "Money is handy, but it isn't everything."

"I wish I could earn a million dollars like that boy," said Ramona. This was the closest she would ever come to telling how she happened to set a crown of burs on her head.

"You know something?" said Mr. Quimby. "I don't care how much that kid or any other kid earns. I wouldn't trade you for a million dollars."

"Really, Daddy?" That remark about any other kid— Ramona wondered if her father had guessed her reason for the crown, but she would never ask. Never. "Really? Do you mean it?"

"Really." Mr. Quimby continued his careful snipping. "I'll bet that boy's father wishes he had a little girl who finger-painted and wiped her hands on the cat when she was little and who once cut her own hair so she would be bald like her uncle and who then grew up to be seven years old and crowned herself with burs. Not every father is lucky enough to have a daughter like that."

Ramona giggled. "Daddy, you're being silly!" She was happier than she had been in a long time.

3

The Night of The
Jack-O'-Lantern

"Please pass the tommy-toes," said
Ramona, hoping to make someone in
the family smile. She felt good when her
father smiled as he passed her the bowl of
stewed tomatoes. He smiled less and less as the
days went by and he had not found work. Too
often he was just plain cross. Ramona had
learned not to rush home from school and
ask, "Did you find a job today, Daddy?" Mrs.

Quimby always seemed to look anxious these days, either over the cost of groceries or money the family owed. Beezus had turned into a regular old grouch, because she dreaded Creative Writing and perhaps because she had reached that difficult age Mrs. Quimby was always talking about, although Ramona found this hard to believe.

Even Picky-picky was not himself. He lashed his tail and stalked angrily away from his dish when Beezus served him Puss-puddy, the cheapest brand of cat food Mrs. Quimby could find in the market.

All this worried Ramona. She wanted her father to smile and joke, her mother to look happy, her sister to be cheerful, and Picky-picky to eat his food, wash his whiskers, and purr the way he used to.

"And so," Mr. Quimby was saying, "at the end of the interview for the job, the man said he would let me know if anything turned up."

Mrs. Quimby sighed. "Let's hope you hear from him. Oh, by the way, the car has been making a funny noise. A sort of *tappety-tappety* sound."

"It's Murphy's Law," said Mr. Quimby. "Anything that can go wrong will."

Ramona knew her father was not joking

this time. Last week, when the washing machine refused to work, the Quimbys had been horrified by the size of the repair bill.

"I like tommy-toes," said Ramona, hoping her little joke would work a second time. This was not exactly true, but she was willing to sacrifice truth for a smile.

Since no one paid any attention, Ramona spoke louder as she lifted the bowl of stewed tomatoes. "Does anybody want any tommy-toes?" she asked. The bowl tipped. Mrs. Quimby silently reached over and wiped spilled juice from the table with her napkin. Crestfallen, Ramona set the bowl down. No one had smiled.

"Ramona," said Mr. Quimby, "my grandmother used to have a saying. 'First time is funny, second time is silly, third time is a spanking.'"

Ramona looked down at her place mat. Nothing seemed to go right lately. Picky-

picky must have felt the same way. He sat down beside Beezus and meowed his crossest meow.

Mr. Quimby lit a cigarette and asked his older daughter, "Haven't you fed that cat yet?"

Beezus rose to clear the table. "It wouldn't do any good. He hasn't eaten his breakfast. He won't eat that cheap Puss-puddy."

"Too bad about him." Mr. Quimby blew a cloud of smoke toward the ceiling.

"He goes next door and mews as if we never give him anything to eat," said Beezus. "It's embarrassing."

"He'll just have to learn to eat what we can afford," said Mr. Quimby. "Or we will get rid of him."

This statement shocked Ramona. Picky-picky had been a member of the family since before she was born.

"Well, I don't blame him," said Beezus,

picking up the cat and pressing her cheek against his fur. "Puss-puddy stinks."

Mr. Quimby ground out his cigarette.

"Guess what?" said Mrs. Quimby, as if to change the subject. "Howie's grandmother drove out to visit her sister, who lives on a farm, and her sister sent in a lot of pumpkins for jack-o'-lanterns for the neighborhood children. Mrs. Kemp gave us a big one, and it's down in the basement now, waiting to be carved."

"Me! Me!" cried Ramona. "Let me get it!"

"Let's give it a real scary face," said Beezus, no longer difficult.

"I'll have to sharpen my knife," said Mr. Quimby.

"Run along and bring it up, Ramona," said Mrs. Quimby with a real smile.

Relief flooded through Ramona. Her family had returned to normal. She snapped on the basement light, thumped down the stairs, and there in the shadow of the furnace pipes, which reached out like ghostly arms, was a big, round pumpkin. Ramona grasped its scratchy stem, found the pumpkin too big to lift that way, bent over, hugged it in both arms, and raised it from the cement floor. The pumpkin was heavier than she had expected, and she must not let it drop and smash all over the concrete floor.

"Need some help, Ramona?" Mrs. Quimby called down the stairs.

"I can do it." Ramona felt for each step with her feet and emerged, victorious, into the kitchen.

"Wow! That is a big one." Mr. Quimby was sharpening his jackknife on a whetstone while Beezus and her mother hurried through the dishes.

"A pumpkin that size would cost a lot at the market," Mrs. Quimby remarked. "A couple of dollars, at least."

"Let's give it eyebrows like last year," said Ramona.

"And ears," said Beezus.

"And lots of teeth," added Ramona. There would be no jack-o'-lantern with one tooth and three triangles for eyes and nose in the Quimbys' front window on Halloween. Mr. Quimby was the best pumpkin carver on Klickitat Street. Everybody knew that.

"Hmm. Let's see now." Mr. Quimby studied the pumpkin, turning it to find the best side for the face. "I think the nose should go about here. With a pencil he sketched a nose-shaped nose, not a triangle, while his daughters leaned on their elbows to watch.

"Shall we have it smile or frown?" he asked.

"Smile!" said Ramona, who had had enough of frowning.

"Frown!" said Beezus.

The mouth turned up on one side and

down on the other. Eyes were sketched and eyebrows. "Very expressive," said Mr. Quimby. "Something between a leer and a sneer." He cut a circle around the top of the pumpkin and lifted it off for a lid.

Without being asked, Ramona found a big spoon for scooping out the seeds.

Picky-picky came into the kitchen to see if something beside Puss-puddy had been placed in his dish. When he found that it had not, he paused, sniffed the unfamiliar pumpkin smell, and with his tail twitching angrily stalked out of the kitchen. Ramona was glad Beezus did not notice.

"If we don't let the candle burn the jack-o'-lantern, we can have pumpkin pie," said Mrs. Quimby. "I can even freeze some of the pumpkin for Thanksgiving."

Mr. Quimby began to whistle as he carved with skill and care, first a mouthful of teeth, each one neat and square, then eyes and

jagged, ferocious eyebrows. He was working on two ears shaped like question marks, when Mrs. Quimby said, "Bedtime, Ramona."

"I am going to stay up until Daddy finishes," Ramona informed her family. "No ifs, ands, or buts."

"Run along and take your bath," said Mrs. Quimby, "and you can watch awhile longer."

Because her family was happy once more, Ramona did not protest. She returned quickly, however, still damp under her pajamas, to see what her father had thought of next. Hair, that's what he had thought of, something he could carve because the pumpkin was so big. He cut a few C-shaped curls around the hole in the top of the pumpkin before he reached inside and hollowed out a candle holder in the bottom.

"There," he said and rinsed his jackknife under the kitchen faucet. "A work of art."

Mrs. Quimby found a candle stub, inserted it in the pumpkin, lit it, and set the lid in place. Ramona switched off the light. The jack-o'-lantern leered and sneered with a flickering flame.

"Oh, Daddy!" Ramona threw her arms

around her father. "It's the wickedest jack-o'-lantern in the whole world."

Mr. Quimby kissed the top of Ramona's head. "Thank you. I take that as a compliment. Now run along to bed."

Ramona could tell by the sound of her father's voice that he was smiling. She ran off to her room without thinking up excuses for staying up just five more minutes, added a postscript to her prayers thanking God for the big pumpkin, and another asking him to find her father a job, and fell asleep at once, not bothering to tuck her panda bear in beside her for comfort.

In the middle of the night Ramona found herself suddenly awake without knowing why she was awake. Had she heard a noise? Yes, she had. Tense, she listened hard. There it was again, a sort of thumping, scuffling noise, not very loud but there just the same. Silence. Then she heard it again. Inside the house. In the kitchen. Something was in the kitchen, and it was moving.

Ramona's mouth was so dry she could barely whisper, "Daddy!" No answer. More thumping. Someone bumped against the wall. Someone, something was coming to get them. Ramona thought about the leering, sneering face on the kitchen table. All the ghost stories she had ever heard, all the ghostly pictures she had ever seen flew through her mind. Could the jack-o'-lantern have come to life? Of course not. It was only a pumpkin, but still— A bodyless, leering head was too horrifying to think about.

Ramona sat up in bed and shrieked, "Daddy!"

A light came on in her parents' room, feet thumped to the floor, Ramona's tousled father in rumpled pajamas was silhouetted in Ramona's doorway, followed by her mother tugging a robe on over her short night-gown.

"What is it, Baby?" asked Mr. Quimby. Both Ramona's parents called her Baby when they were worried about her, and tonight Ramona was so relieved to see them she did not mind.

"Was it a bad dream?" asked Mrs. Quimby.

"Th-there's something in the kitchen." Ramona's voice quavered.

Beezus, only half-awake, joined the family. "What's happening?" she asked. "What's going on?"

"There's something in the kitchen," said Ramona, feeling braver. "Something moving."

"Sh-h!" commanded Mr. Quimby.

Tense, the family listened to silence.

"You just had a bad dream." Mrs. Quimby came into the room, kissed Ramona, and started to tuck her in.

Ramona pushed the blanket away. "It was *not* a bad dream," she insisted. "I did too hear something. Something spooky."

"All we have to do is look," said Mr. Quimby, reasonably—and bravely, Ramona thought. Nobody would get her into that kitchen.

Ramona waited, scarcely breathing, fearing for her father's safety as he walked down the hall and flipped on the kitchen light. No shout, no yell came from that part of the house. Instead her father laughed, and Ramona felt brave enough to follow the rest of the family to see what was funny.

There was a strong smell of cat food in the kitchen. What Ramona saw, and what Beezus saw, did not strike them as one bit funny. Their jack-o'-lantern, the jack-o'-lantern their father had worked so hard to carve, no longer had a whole face. Part of its forehead, one ferocious eyebrow, one eye, and part of its nose were gone, replaced by a jagged hole edged by little teeth marks. Picky-picky was crouched in guilt under the kitchen table.

The nerve of that cat. "Bad cat! Bad cat!" shrieked Ramona, stamping her bare foot on the cold linoleum. The old yellow cat fled to the dining room, where he crouched under the table, his eyes glittering out of the darkness.

Mrs. Quimby laughed a small rueful laugh. "I knew he liked canteloupe, but I had no idea he liked pumpkin, too." With a butcher's knife she began to cut up the remains of the jack-o'-lantern, carefully removing, Ramona noticed, the parts with teeth marks.

"I *told* you he wouldn't eat that awful Puss-puddy." Beezus was accusing her father of denying their cat. "Of course he had to eat our jack-o'-lantern. He's starving."

"Beezus, dear," said Mrs. Quimby. "We

simply cannot afford the brand of food Picky-picky used to eat. Now be reasonable."

Beezus was in no mood to be reasonable.

"Then how come Daddy can afford to smoke?" she demanded to know.

Ramona was astonished to hear her sister speak this way to her mother.

Mr. Quimby looked angry. "Young lady," he said, and when he called Beezus young lady, Ramona knew her sister had better watch out. "Young lady, I've heard enough about that old tom cat and his food. My cigarettes are none of your business."

Ramona expected Beezus to say she was sorry or maybe burst into tears and run to her room. Instead she pulled Picky-picky out from under the table and held him to her chest as if she were shielding him from danger. "They are too my business," she informed her father. "Cigarettes can kill you. Your lungs will turn black and you'll *die*! We made posters about it at school. And besides, cigarettes pollute the air!"

Ramona was horrified by her sister's

daring, and at the same time she was a tiny bit pleased. Beezus was usually well-behaved while Ramona was the one who had tantrums. Then she was struck by the meaning of her sister's angry words and was frightened.

"That's enough out of you," Mr. Quimby told Beezus, "and let me remind you that if you had shut that cat in the basement as you were supposed to, this would never have happened."

Mrs. Quimby quietly stowed the remains of the jack-o'-lantern in a plastic bag in the refrigerator.

Beezus opened the basement door and gently set Picky-picky on the top step. "Nighty-night," she said tenderly.

"Young lady," began Mr. Quimby. Young lady again! Now Beezus was really going to catch it. "You are getting altogether too big for your britches lately. Just be careful how you talk around this house."

Still Beezus did not say she was sorry. She did not burst into tears. She simply stalked off to her room.

Ramona was the one who burst into tears. She didn't mind when she and Beezus quarreled. She even enjoyed a good fight now and then to clear the air, but she could not bear it when anyone else in the family quarreled, and those awful things Beezus said—were they true?

"Don't cry, Ramona." Mrs. Quimby put her arm around her younger daughter. "We'll get another pumpkin."

"B-but it won't be as big," sobbed Ramona, who wasn't crying about the pumpkin at all. She was crying about important things like her father being cross so much now that he wasn't working and his lungs turning black and Beezus being so disagreeable when before she had always been so polite (to grown-ups) and anxious to do the right thing.

"Come on, let's all go to bed and things will look brighter in the morning," said Mrs. Quimby.

"In a few minutes." Mr. Quimby picked up a package of cigarettes he had left on the kitchen table, shook one out, lit it, and sat down, still looking angry.

Were his lungs turning black this very minute? Ramona wondered. How would anybody know, when his lungs were inside him? She let her mother guide her to her room and tuck her in bed.

"Now don't worry about your jack-o'-lantern. We'll get another pumpkin. It won't be as big, but you'll have your jack-o'-lantern." Mrs. Quimby kissed Ramona good-night.

"Nighty-night," said Ramona in a muffled voice. As soon as her mother left, she hopped out of bed and pulled her old panda

bear out from under the bed and tucked it
under the covers beside her for comfort.
The bear must have been dusty because
Ramona sneezed.

"*Gesundheit!*" said Mr. Quimby, passing
by her door. "We'll carve another jack-o'-

lantern tomorrow. Don't worry." He was not angry with Ramona.

Ramona snuggled down with her dusty bear. Didn't grown-ups think children worried about anything but jack-o'-lanterns? Didn't they know children worried about grown-ups?

4

Ramona To The Rescue

The Quimbys said very little at breakfast the next morning. Beezus was moody and silent. Mrs. Quimby, in her white uniform, was in a hurry to leave for work. Picky-picky resentfully ate a few bites of Puss-puddy. Mr. Quimby did not say, "I told you he would eat it when he was really hungry," but the whole family was thinking it. He might as well have said it.

Ramona wished her family would cheer up. When they had finished eating, she found herself alone with her father.

"Bring me an ashtray, please," said Mr. Quimby. "That's a good girl."

Reluctantly Ramona brought the ashtray and, with her face rigid with disapproval, watched her father light his after-breakfast cigarette.

"Why so solemn?" he asked as he shook out the flame of the match.

"Is it true what Beezus said?" Ramona demanded.

"About what?" asked Mr. Quimby.

Ramona had a feeling her father really knew what she meant. "About smoking will make your lungs turn black," she answered.

Mr. Quimby blew a puff of smoke toward the ceiling. "I expect to be one of those old men with a long gray beard who has his picture in the paper on his hundredth birthday and who tells reporters he owes his long life to cigarettes and whiskey."

Ramona was not amused. "Daddy"—her voice was stern—"you are just being silly again."

Her father took a deep breath and blew three smoke rings across the table, a most unsatisfactory answer to Ramona.

On the way to school Ramona cut across the lawn for the pleasure of leaving footprints in the dew and then did not bother to look back to see where she had walked. Instead of running or skipping, she trudged. Nothing was much fun anymore when her family quarreled and then was silent at breakfast and her father's lungs were turning black from smoke.

Even though Mrs. Rogers announced, "Today our second grade is going to have fun learning," as she wrote the date on the blackboard, school turned out to be dreary because the class was having Review again. Review meant boredom for some, like Ramona, because they had to repeat what they already knew, and worry for others, like Davy, because they had to try again what they could not do in the first place. Review was the worst part of school. Ramona passed the morning looking through her workbook for words with double *o*'s like *book* and *cook*. She carefully drew eyebrows over the *o*'s and dots within, making the *o*'s look like crossed eyes. Then she drew mouths with the ends turned down under the eyes. When she finished, she had a cross-looking workbook that matched her feelings.

She was in no hurry to leave the building at recess, but when she did, Davy yelled, "Look out! Here comes Ramona!" and began to run, so of course Ramona had to chase him around and around the playground until time to go inside again.

Running until she was hot and panting made Ramona feel so much better that she was filled with sudden determination. Her father's lungs were not going to turn black. She would not let them. Ramona made up her mind, right then and there in the middle of arithmetic, that she was going to save her father's life.

That afternoon after school Ramona gathered up her crayons and papers from the

kitchen table, took them into her room, and shut the door. She got down on her hands and knees and went to work on the bedroom floor, printing a sign in big letters. Unfortunately, she did not plan ahead and soon reached the edge of the paper. She could not find the Scotch tape to fasten two pieces of paper together, so she had to continue on another line. When she finished, her sign read:

NO SMO KING

It would do. Ramona found a pin and fastened her sign to the living-room curtains, where her father could not miss it. Then she waited, frightened by her daring.

Mr. Quimby, although he must have seen the sign, said nothing until after dinner when he had finished his pumpkin pie. He asked for an ashtray and then inquired, "Say, who is this Mr. King?"

"What Mr. King?" asked Ramona, walking into his trap.

"Nosmo King," answered her father without cracking a smile.

Chagrined, Ramona tore down her sign, crumpled it, threw it into the fireplace, and stalked out of the room, resolving to do better the next time.

The next day after school Ramona found the Scotch tape and disappeared into her room to continue work on her plan to save her father's life. While she was working, she heard the phone ring and waited, tense, as the whole family now waited whenever the telephone rang. She heard her father clear his throat before he answered. "Hello?" After a pause he said, "Just a minute, Howie. I'll call her." There was disappointment in his voice. No one was calling to offer him a job after all.

"Ramona, can you come over and play?" Howie asked, when Ramona went to the telephone.

Ramona considered. Of course they would have to put up with Howie's messy little sister, Willa Jean, but she and Howie would have fun building things if they could think of something to build. Yes, she would like to play with Howie, but saving her father's life was more important. "No, thank you. Not today," she said. "I have important work to do."

Just before dinner she taped to the refrigerator door a picture of a cigarette so long she had to fasten three pieces of paper together to draw it. After drawing the cigarette, she had crossed it out with a big black *X* and under it she had printed in big letters the word *BAD.* Beezus giggled when she saw it, and Mrs. Quimby smiled as if she were trying not to smile. Ramona was filled with fresh courage. She had allies. Her father had better watch out.

When Mr. Quimby saw the picture, he stopped and looked while Ramona waited. "Hmm," he said, backing away for a better view. "An excellent likeness. The artist shows talent." And that was all he said.

Ramona felt let down, although she was not sure what she had expected. Anger, perhaps? Punishment? A promise to give up smoking?

The next morning the sign was gone, and that afternoon Ramona had to wait until Beezus came home from school to ask, "How do you spell *pollution*?" When Beezus printed it out on a piece of paper, Ramona went to work making a sign that said, *Stop Air Pollution.*

"Let me help," said Beezus, and the two girls, kneeling on the floor, printed a dozen signs. *Smoking Stinks. Cigarettes Start Forest Fires. Smoking Is Hazardous to Your Health.* Ramona learned new words that afternoon.

Fortunately Mr. Quimby went out to examine the car, which was still making the *tappety-tappety* noise. This gave the girls a chance to tape the signs to the mantel, the refrigerator, the dining-room curtains, the door of the hall closet, and every other con-spicuous place they could think of.

This time Mr. Quimby simply ignored the signs. Ramona and Beezus might as well have saved themselves a lot of work for all he seemed to notice. But how could he miss so many signs? He must be pretending. He had to be pretending. Obviously the girls would have to step up their campaign. By now they were running out of big pieces of paper, and they knew better than to ask their

parents to buy more, not when the family was so short of money.

"We can make little signs on scraps of paper," said Ramona, and that was what they did. Together they made tiny signs that said, *No Smoking, Stop Air Pollution, Smoking Is Bad for Your Health*, and *Stamp Out Cigarettes*. On some Ramona drew stick figures of people stretched out flat and dead, and on one, a cat on his back with his feet in the air. These they hid wherever their father was sure to find them—in his bathrobe pocket, fastened around the handle of his toothbrush with a rubber band, inside his shoes, under his electric razor.

Then they waited. And waited. Mr. Quimby said nothing while he continued to smoke. Ramona held her nose whenever she saw her father with a cigarette. He appeared not to notice. The girls felt discouraged and let down.

Once more Ramona and Beezus devised a plan, the most daring plan of all because they had to get hold of their father's cigarettes just before dinner. Fortunately he had tinkered with the car, still trying to find the reason for the *tappety-tappety-tap*, and had to take a shower before dinner, which gave the girls barely enough time to carry out their plan.

All through dinner the girls exchanged excited glances, and by the time her father asked her to fetch an ashtray, Ramona could hardly sit still she was so excited.

As usual her father pulled his cigarettes out of his shirt pocket. As usual he tapped the package against his hand, and as usual a cigarette, or what appeared to be a cigarette, slid out. Mr. Quimby must have sensed that what he thought was a cigarette was lighter than it should be, because he paused to look at it. While Ramona held her breath, he frowned, looked more closely, unrolled the paper, and discovered it was a tiny sign that said, *Smoking Is Bad!* Without a word, he crumpled it and pulled out another—he thought—cigarette, which turned out to be a sign saying, *Stamp Out Cigarettes!* Mr. Quimby crumpled it and tossed it onto the table along with the first sign.

"Ramona." Mr. Quimby's voice was stern. "My grandmother used to say, 'First time is funny, second time is silly—'" Mr. Quimby's grandmother's wisdom was interrupted by a fit of coughing.

Ramona was frightened. Maybe her father's lungs already had begun to turn black.

Beezus looked triumphant. See, we told you smoking was bad for you, she was clearly thinking.

Mrs. Quimby looked both amused and concerned.

Mr. Quimby looked embarrassed, pounded himself on the chest with his fist, took a sip of coffee, and said, "Something must have caught in my throat." When his family remained silent, he said, "All right, Ramona. As I was saying, enough is enough."

Ramona scowled and slid down in her chair. Nothing was ever fair for second graders. Beezus helped, but Ramona was getting all the blame. She also felt defeated. Nobody ever paid any attention to second graders except to scold them. No matter how hard she tried to save her father's life, he was not going to let her save it.

Ramona gave up, and soon found she missed the excitement of planning the next step in her campaign against her father's smoking. Her afternoons after school seemed empty. Howie was home with tonsillitis, and she had no one to play with. She wished there were more children her age in her neighborhood. She was so lonely she picked up the telephone and dialed the Quimbys' telephone number to see if she could answer herself. All she got was a busy signal and a reprimand from her father for playing with the telephone when someone might be trying to reach him about a job.

On top of all this, the family had pump-kin pie for dinner.

"Not *again*!" protested Beezus. The family had eaten pumpkin pie and pumpkin custard since the night the cat ate part of the jack-o'-lantern. Beezus had once told Ramona that she thought her mother had tried to hide pumpkin in the meat loaf, but she wasn't sure because everything was all ground up together.

"I'm sorry, but there aren't many pump-kin recipes. I can't bear to waste good food," said Mrs. Quimby. "But I do remember seeing a recipe for pumpkin soup someplace—"

"No!" Her family was unanimous.

Ramona was so disappointed because her father had ignored all her little signs that she did not feel much like eating, and especially not pumpkin pie for what seemed like the hundredth time. She eyed her triangle of pie and knew she could not make it go down. She was sick of pumpkin. "Are you sure you cut off all the parts with cat spit on them?" she asked her mother.

"Ramona!" Mr. Quimby, who had been stirring his coffee, dropped his spoon. "Please! We are eating."

They had been eating, but after Ramona's remark no one ate a bite of pie.

Mr. Quimby continued to smoke, and Ramona continued to worry. Then one afternoon, when Ramona came home from school, she found the back door locked. When she pounded on it with her fist, no one answered. She went to the front door, rang the doorbell, and waited. Silence. Lonely silence. She tried the door even though she knew it was locked. More silence. Nothing like this had ever happened to Ramona before. Someone was always waiting when she came home from school.

Ramona was frightened. Tears filled her eyes as she sat down on the cold concrete steps to think. Where could her father be? She thought of her friends at school, Davy and Sharon, who did not have fathers. Where had their fathers gone? Everybody had a father sometime. Where could they go?

Ramona's insides tightened with fear. Maybe her father was angry with her. Maybe he had gone away because she tried to make him stop smoking. She thought she was saving his life, but maybe she was being mean to him. Her mother said she must not annoy her father, because he was worried about

being out of work. Maybe she had made him so angry he did not love her anymore. Maybe he had gone away because he did not love her. She thought of all the scary things she had seen on television—houses that had fallen down in earthquakes, people shooting people, big hairy men on motorcycles—and knew she needed her father to keep her safe.

The cold from the concrete seeped through Ramona's clothes. She wrapped her arms around her knees to keep warm as she watched a dried leaf scratch along the driveway in the autumn wind. She listened to the honking of a flock of wild geese flying through the gray clouds on their way south for the winter. They came from Canada, her father had once told her, but that was before he had gone away. Raindrops began to dot the driveway, and tears dotted Ramona's skirt. She put her head down on her knees and cried. Why had she been so mean to her father? If he ever came back he could smoke all he wanted, fill the ashtrays and turn the air blue, and she wouldn't say a single word. She just wanted her father back, black lungs and all.

And suddenly there he was, scrunching through the leaves on the driveway with the collar of his windbreaker turned up against the wind and his old fishing hat pulled down over his eyes. "Sorry I'm late," he said, as he got out his key. "Is that what all this boohooing is about?"

Ramona wiped her sweater sleeve across her nose and stood up. She was so glad to see her father and so relieved that he had not gone away, that anger blazed up. Her tears became angry tears. Fathers were not supposed to worry their little girls. "Where have you been?" she demanded. "You're supposed to be here when I come home from school!

I thought you had gone away and left me."

"Take it easy. I wouldn't go off and leave you. Why would I do a thing like that?" Mr. Quimby unlocked the door and, with a hand on Ramona's shoulder, guided her into the living room. "I'm sorry I had to worry you. I was collecting my unemployment insurance, and I had to wait in a long line."

Ramona's anger faded. She knew all about long lines and understood how difficult they were. She had waited in lines for her turn at the slides in the park, she had waited in lines in the school lunchroom back in the days when her family could spare lunch money once in a while, she had waited in lines with her mother at the check-out counter in the market, when she was little she had waited in long, long lines to see Santa Claus in the department store, and—these were the worst, most boring lines of all—she had waited in lines with her mother in the bank. She felt bad because her father had had to wait in line, and she also understood that collecting unemployment insurance did not make him happy.

"Did somebody try to push ahead of you?" Ramona was wise in the ways of lines.

"No. The line was unusually long today." Mr. Quimby went into the kitchen to make himself a cup of instant coffee. While he waited for the water to heat, he poured Ramona a glass of milk and gave her a graham cracker.

"Feeling better?" he asked.

Ramona looked at her father over the rim of her glass and nodded, spilling milk down her front. Silently he handed her a dish towel to wipe up while he poured hot water over the instant coffee in his mug. Then he reached into his shirt pocket, pulled out a package of cigarettes, looked at it a moment, and tossed it onto the counter. Ramona had never seen her father do this before. Could it be . . .

Mr. Quimby leaned against the counter and took a sip of coffee. "What would you like to do?" he asked Ramona.

Ramona considered before she answered. "Something big and important." But what? she wondered. Break a record in that book of records Beezus talked about? Climb Mount Hood?

"Such as?" her father asked.

Ramona finished scrubbing the front of her sweater with the dish towel. "Well—" she said, thinking. "You know that big bridge across the Columbia River?"

"Yes. The Interstate Bridge. The one we cross when we drive to Vancouver."

"I've always wanted to stop on that bridge and get out of the car and stand with one foot in Oregon and one foot in Washington."

"A good idea, but not practical," said Mr.

Quimby. "Your mother has the car, and I doubt if cars are allowed to stop on the bridge. What else?"

"It's not exactly important, but I always like to crayon," said Ramona. How long would her father leave his cigarettes on the counter?

Mr. Quimby set his cup down. "I have a great idea! Let's draw the longest picture in the world." He opened a drawer and pulled out a roll of shelf paper. When he tried to unroll it on the kitchen floor, the paper rolled itself up again. Ramona quickly solved that problem by Scotch-taping the end of the roll to the floor. Together she and her father unrolled the paper across the kitchen and knelt with a box of crayons between them.

"What shall we draw?" she asked.

"How about the state of Oregon?" he suggested. "That's big enough."

Ramona's imagination was excited. "I'll begin with the Interstate Bridge," she said.

"And I'll tackle Mount Hood," said her father.

Together they went to work, Ramona on the end of the shelf paper and her father halfway across the kitchen. With crayons Ramona drew a long black bridge with a girl

standing astride a line in the center. She drew blue water under the bridge, even though the Columbia River always looked gray. She added gray clouds, gray dots for raindrops, and all the while she was drawing she was trying to find courage to tell her father something.

Ramona glanced at her father's picture, and sure enough he had drawn Mount Hood peaked with a hump on the south side exactly the way it looked in real life on the days when the clouds lifted.

"I think you draw better than anybody in the whole world," said Ramona.

Mr. Quimby smiled. "Not quite," he said.

"Daddy—" Ramona summoned courage. "I'm sorry I was mean to you."

"You weren't mean." Mr. Quimby was adding trees at the base of the mountain. "You're right, you know."

"Am I?" Ramona wanted to be sure.

"Yes."

This answer gave Ramona even more courage. "Is that why you didn't have a cigarette with your coffee? Are you going to stop smoking?"

"I'll try," answered Mr. Quimby, his eyes on his drawing. "I'll try."

Ramona was filled with joy, enthusiasm, and relief. "You can do it, Daddy! I know you can do it."

Her father seemed less positive. "I hope so," he answered, "but if I succeed, Picky-picky will still have to eat Puss-puddy."

"He can try, too," said Ramona and slashed dark V's across her gray sky to represent a flock of geese flying south for the winter.

5
Beezus's Creative Writing

The Quimby women, as Mr. Quimby referred to his wife and daughters, were enthusiastic about Mr. Quimby's decision to give up smoking. He was less enthusiastic because, after all, he was the one who had to break the habit.

Ramona took charge. She collected all her father's cigarettes and threw them in the garbage, slamming down the lid of the can

with a satisfying crash, a crash much less satisfying to her father, who looked as if he
wanted those cigarettes back.

"I was planning to cut down gradually,"
he said. "One less cigarette each day."

"That's not what you said," Ramona
informed him. "You said you would try to
give up smoking, not try to cut down gradually."

There followed an even more trying time
in the Quimby household. Out of habit
Mr. Quimby frequently reached for cigarettes that were no longer in his pocket. He
made repeated trips to the refrigerator, looking for something to nibble on. He thought
he was gaining weight. Worst of all, he was
even crosser than when he first lost his job.

With a cross father, a tired mother, a sister
who worried about creative writing, and
a cat who grudgingly ate his Puss-puddy,
Ramona felt she was the only happy member

of the family left. Even she had run out of ways to amuse herself. She continued to add to the longest picture in the world, but she really wanted to run and yell and make a lot of noise to show how relieved she was that her father was giving up smoking.

One afternoon Ramona was on her knees on the kitchen floor working on her picture when Beezus came home from school, dropped her books on the kitchen table, and said, "Well, it's come."

Ramona looked up from the picture of Glenwood School she was drawing on the roll of shelf paper taped to the floor. Mr. Quimby, who had a dish towel tucked into his belt for an apron, turned from the kitchen sink. "What's come?" he asked. Although it was late in the afternoon, he was washing the breakfast dishes. He had been interviewed for two different jobs that morning.

"Creative writing." Beezus's voice was filled with gloom.

"You make it sound like a calamity," said her father.

Beezus sighed. "Well—maybe it won't be so bad this time. We aren't supposed to write stories or poems after all."

"Then what does Mrs. Mester mean by creative?"

"Oh, you know. . . ." Beezus twirled around on one toe to define creative.

"What are you supposed to write if you don't write a story or a poem?" asked Ramona. "Arithmetic problems?"

Beezus continued to twirl as if spinning might inspire her. "She said we should interview some old person and ask questions about something they did when they were our age. She said she would run off what we wrote on the ditto machine, and we could make a book." She stopped twirling to catch the dish towel her father tossed to her. "Do we know anyone who helped build a log cabin or something like that?"

"I'm afraid not," said Mr. Quimby. "We don't know anybody who skinned buffalo either. How old is old?"

"The older the better," said Beezus.

"Mrs. Swink is pretty old," volunteered Ramona. Mrs. Swink was a widow who lived in the house on the corner and drove an old sedan that Mr. Quimby admiringly called a real collector's item.

"Yes, but she wears polyester pant suits," said Beezus, who had grown critical of clothing lately. She did not approve of polyester pant suits, white shoes, or Ramona's T-shirt with Rockaway Beach printed on the front.

"Mrs. Swink is old inside the pant suits," Ramona pointed out.

Beezus made a face. "I can't go barging in on her all by myself and ask her a bunch of questions." Beezus was the kind of girl who never wanted to go next door to borrow an egg and who dreaded having to sell mints for the Campfire Girls.

"I'll come," said Ramona, who was always eager to go next door to borrow an egg and looked forward to being old enough to sell mints.

"You don't barge in," said Mr. Quimby, wringing out the dishcloth. "You phone and make an appointment. Go on. Phone her now and get it over."

Beezus put her hand on the telephone book. "But what'll I say?" she asked.

"Just explain what you want and see what she says," said Mr. Quimby. "She can't bite you over the telephone."

Beezus appeared to be thinking hard. "OK," she said with some reluctance, "but you don't have to listen."

Ramona and her father went into the living room and turned on the television so they couldn't overhear Beezus. When Ramona noticed her father reached for the cigarettes that were not there, she gave him a stern look.

In a moment Beezus appeared, looking flustered. "I meant sometime in a day or so, but she said to come right now because in a little while she has to take a molded salad to her lodge for a potluck supper. Dad, what'll I *say*? I haven't had time to think."

"Just play it by ear," he advised. "Something will come to you."

"I'm going too," Ramona said, and Beezus did not object.

Mrs. Swink saw the sisters coming and opened the door for them as they climbed the front steps. "Come on in, girls, and sit down," she said briskly. "Now what is it you want to interview me about?"

Beezus seemed unable to say anything, and Ramona could understand how it might be hard to ask someone wearing a polyester pant suit questions about building a log cabin.

Someone had to say something so Ramona spoke up. "My sister wants to know what you used to do when you were a little girl."

Beezus found her tongue. "Like I said over the phone. It's for creative writing."

Mrs. Swink looked thoughtful. "Let's see. Nothing very exciting, I'm afraid. I helped with the dishes and read a lot of books from the library. The *Red Fairy Book* and *Blue Fairy Book* and all the rest."

Beezus looked worried, and Ramona could see that she was trying to figure out what she could write about dishes and library books. Ramona ended another awkward silence by asking, "Didn't you make anything?" She had noticed that Mrs. Swink's living room was decorated with mosaics made of dried peas and beans and with owls made out of pinecones. The dining-room table was strewn with old Christmas cards, scissors, and paste, a sure sign of a craft project.

"Let's see now. . . ." Mrs. Swink looked thoughtful. "We made fudge, and—oh, I know—tin-can stilts." She smiled to herself. "I had forgotten all about tin-can stilts until this very minute."

At last Beezus could ask a question. "How

did you make tin-can stilts?"

Mrs. Swink laughed, remembering. "We took two tall cans. Two-pound coffee cans were best. We turned them upside down and punched two holes near what had once been the bottom of each. The holes had to be opposite one another on each can. Then we poked about four feet of heavy twine through each pair of holes and knotted the ends to make a loop. We set one foot on each can, took hold of a loop of twine in each hand, and began to walk. We had to remember to lift each can by the loop of twine as we raised a foot or we fell off—my knees were always skinned. Little girls wore dresses instead of slacks in those days, and I always had dreadful scabs on my knees."

Maybe this was why Mrs. Swink always wore pant suits now, thought Ramona. She didn't want scabs on her knees in case she fell down.

"And the noise those hollow tin cans made on the sidewalk!" continued Mrs. Swink, enjoying the memory. "All the kids in the neighborhood went clanking up and down. Sometimes the cans would cut through the twine, and we would go sprawling on the sidewalk. I became expert at walking on tin-can stilts and used to go clanking around the block yelling, 'Pieface!' at all the younger children."

Ramona and Beezus both giggled. They were surprised that someone as old as Mrs. Swink had once called younger children by a name they sometimes called one another.

"There." Mrs. Swink ended the interview. "Does that help?"

"Yes, thank you." Beezus stood up, and so did Ramona, although she wanted to ask Mrs. Swink about the craft project on the dining-room table.

"Good." Mrs. Swink opened the front door. "I hope you get an *A* on your composition."

"Tin-can stilts weren't exactly what I expected," said Beezus, as the girls started home. "But I guess I can make them do."

Do! Ramona couldn't wait to get to

Howie's house to tell him about the tin-can stilts. And so, as Beezus went home to labor over her creative writing, Ramona ran over to the Kemps' house. Just as she thought, Howie listened to her excited description and said, "I could make some of those." Good old Howie. Ramona and Howie spent the rest of the afternoon finding four two-pound coffee cans. The search involved persuading Howie's mother to empty out her coffee into mayonnaise jars and calling on neighbors to see if they had any empty cans.

The next day after school Howie arrived on the Quimby doorstep with two sets of tin-can stilts. "I made them!" he announced, proud of his work. "And Willa Jean wanted some, so I made her a pair out of tuna cans so she wouldn't have far to fall."

"I knew you could do it!" Ramona, who had already changed to her playclothes, stepped onto two of the cans and pulled the twine loops up tight before she took a cautious step, lifting a can as she lifted her foot. First the left foot, then the right foot. *Clank, clank.* They worked! Howie clanked along beside her. They clanked carefully down the driveway to the sidewalk, where Ramona tried to pick up speed, forgot to lift a can at the same time she lifted her foot, and, as Mrs. Swink had recalled, fell off her stilts. She caught herself before she tumbled to the sidewalk and climbed back on.

Clank, clank. Clank, clank. Ramona found deep satisfaction in making so much noise, and so did Howie. Mrs. Swink, turning into her driveway in her dignified old sedan, smiled and waved. In a moment of daring, Ramona yelled, "Pieface!" at her.

"Pieface yourself!" Mrs. Swink called back, understanding Ramona's joke.

Howie did not approve. "You aren't supposed to call grown-ups pieface," he said. "Just kids."

"I can call Mrs. Swink pieface," boasted

Ramona. "I can call her pieface any old time I want to." *Clank, clank. Clank, clank.* Ramona was having such a good time she began to sing at the top of her voice, "Ninety-nine bottles of beer on the wall, ninety-nine bottles of beer. You take one down and pass

it around. Ninety-eight bottles of beer on the wall . . ."

Howie joined the singing. "Ninety-eight bottles of beer on the wall. You take one down and pass it around. Ninety-seven bottles of beer . . ."

Clank, clank. Clank, clank. Ninety-six bottles of beer, ninety-five bottles of beer on the wall. Sometimes Ramona and Howie tripped, sometimes they stumbled, and once in a while they fell, muddying the knees of their corduroy pants on the wet sidewalk. Progress was slow, but what their stilts lost in speed they made up in noise.

Eighty-nine bottles of beer, eighty-six . . . Ramona was happier than than she had been in a long time. She loved making noise, and she was proud of being able to count backwards. Neighbors looked out their windows to see what all the racket was about while Ramona and Howie clanked determinedly on. "Eighty-one bottles of beer on the wall . . ." As Mrs. Swink had predicted, one of the twine loops broke, tumbling Ramona to the sidewalk. Howie knotted the ends together, and they clanked on until supper-time.

"That was some racket you two made," remarked Mr. Quimby.

Mrs. Quimby asked, "Where on earth did you two pick up that song about bottles of beer?"

"From Beezus," said Ramona virtuously. "Howie and I are going to count backwards all the way to one bottle of beer."

Beezus, doing homework in her room, had not missed out on the conversation. "We used to sing it at camp when the coun-selors weren't around," she called out.

"When I used to go to camp, we sang about the teeny-weeny 'pider who went up the water 'pout," said Mrs. Quimby.

The teeny-weeny 'pider song was a

favorite of Ramona's too, but it was not so satisfying as "Ninety-nine Bottles of Beer," which was a much louder song.

"I wonder what the neighbors think," said Mrs. Quimby. "Wouldn't some other song do?"

"No," said Ramona. Only a noisy song would do.

"By the way, Ramona," said Mr. Quimby. "Did you straighten your room today?"

Ramona was not much interested in the question. "Sort of," she answered truthfully, because she had shoved a lot of old school artwork and several pairs of dirty socks under the bed.

The next afternoon after school was even better, because Ramona and Howie had mastered walking on the tin-can stilts without falling off. "Sixty-one bottles of beer on the wall. Take one down and pass it around," they sang, as they clanked around the block. Ramona grew hot and sweaty, and when rain began to fall, she enjoyed the cold drops against her flushed face. On and on they clanked, singing at the top of their voices. Ramona's hair grew stringy, and Howie's blond curls tightened in the rain. "Forty-one bottles of beer on the wall . . ." *Clank, crash, clank.* "Thirty-seven bottles of beer . . ." *Clank, crash, clank.* Ramona forgot about her father being out of a job, she forgot about how cross he had been since he gave up smoking, she forgot about her mother coming home tired from work and about Beezus being grouchy lately. She was filled with joy.

The early winter darkness had fallen and the streetlights had come on by the time Ramona and Howie had clanked and crashed and sung their way down to that last bottle of beer. Filled with a proud feeling that they had accomplished something big, they jumped off their stilts and ran home with their coffee cans banging and clashing behind them.

Ramona burst in through the back door, dropped her wet stilts with a crash on the linoleum, and announced hoarsely, "We did it! We sang all the way down to one bottle of beer!" She waited for her family to share her triumph.

Instead her father said, "Ramona, you know you are supposed to be home before dark. It was a good thing I could hear where you were, or I would have had to go out after you."

Mrs. Quimby said, "Ramona, you're sopping wet. Go change quickly before you catch cold."

Beezus, who was often embarrassed by her little sister, said, "The neighbors will think we're a bunch of beer guzzlers."

Well! thought Ramona. Some family! She stood dripping on the linoleum a moment, expecting hurt feelings to take over, perhaps even to make her cry a little so her family would be sorry they had been mean to her. To her wonder, no heavy feeling weighed her down, no sad expression came to her face, no tears. She simply stood there, cold, dripping, and feeling *good*. She felt good from making a lot of noise, she felt good from the hard work of walking so far on her tin-can stilts, she felt good from calling a grown-up pieface and from the triumph of singing backwards from ninety-nine to one. She felt good from being out after dark with rain on her face and the streetlights shining down on her. Her feelings were not hurt at all.

"Don't just stand there sogging," said Beezus. "You're supposed to set the table."

Bossy old Beezus, thought Ramona. She squelched off to her room in her wet sneakers, and as she left the kitchen she began to sing, "Ninety-nine bottles of beer on the wall . . ."

"Oh, no!" groaned her father.

6
The Sheep Suit

Ramona did not expect trouble to start in Sunday school of all places, but that was where it was touched off one Sunday early in December. Sunday school began as usual. Ramona sat on a little chair between Davy and Howie with the rest of their class in the basement of the gray stone church. Mrs. Russo, the superintendent, clapped her hands for attention.

"Let's have quiet, boys and girls," she said.

"It's time to make plans for our Christmas-carol program and Nativity scene."

Bored, Ramona hooked her heels on the rung of her little chair. She knew what her part would be—to put on a white choir robe and walk in singing carols with the rest of the second-grade class, which would follow the kindergarten and first grade. The congregation always murmured and smiled at the kindergarteners in their wobbly line, but nobody paid much attention to second graders. Ramona knew she would have to wait years to be old enough for a chance at a part in the Nativity scene.

Ramona only half listened until Mrs. Russo asked Beezus's friend Henry Huggins if he would like to be Joseph. Ramona expected him to say no, because he was so busy training for the Olympics in about eight or twelve years. He surprised her by saying, "I guess so."

"And Beatrice Quimby," said Mrs. Russo, "would you like to be Mary?"

This question made Ramona unhook her heels and sit up. Her sister, grouchy old Beezus—Mary? Ramona searched out Beezus, who was looking pink, embarrassed, and pleased at the same time.

"Yes," answered Beezus.

Ramona couldn't get over it. Her sister playing the part of Mary, mother of the baby Jesus, and getting to sit up there on the chancel with that manger they got out every year.

Mrs. Russo had to call on a number of older boys before she found three who were willing to be wise men. Shepherds were easier. Three sixth-grade boys were willing to be shepherds.

While the planning was going on, a little voice inside Ramona was saying, "Me! Me! What about me?" until it could be hushed no longer. Ramona spoke up. "Mrs. Russo, I could be a sheep. If you have shepherds, you need a sheep."

"Ramona, that's a splendid idea," said Mrs. Russo, getting Ramona's hopes up, "but I'm afraid the church does not have any sheep costumes."

Ramona was not a girl to abandon her hopes if she could help it. "My mother could make me a sheep costume," she said. "She's made me lots of costumes." Maybe "lots" was stretching the truth a bit. Mrs. Quimby had made Ramona a witch costume that had lasted three Halloweens, and when Ramona was in nursery school she had made her a little red devil suit.

Now Mrs. Russo was in a difficult position because she had told Ramona her idea was splendid.

"Well . . . yes, Ramona, you may be a sheep if your mother will make you a costume."

Howie had been thinking things over. "Mrs. Russo," he said in that serious way of his, "wouldn't it look silly for three shepherds to herd just one sheep? My grandmother could make me a sheep costume, too."

"And my mother could make me one," said Davy.

Sunday school was suddenly full of volunteer sheep, enough for a large flock. Mrs. Russo clapped her hands for silence. "Quiet, boys and girls! There isn't room on the chancel for so many sheep, but I think we can squeeze in one sheep per shepherd. Ramona, Howie, and Davy, since you asked first, you may be sheep if someone will make you costumes."

Ramona smiled across the room at Beezus. They would be in the Nativity scene together.

When Sunday school was over, Beezus

found Ramona and asked, "Where's Mother going to find time to make a sheep costume?"

"After work, I guess." This problem was something Ramona had not considered.

Beezus looked doubtful. "I'm glad the church already has my costume," she said. Ramona began to worry.

Mrs. Quimby always washed her hair after church on Sunday morning. Ramona waited until her mother had taken her head out from under the kitchen faucet and was rubbing her hair on a bath towel. "Guess what!" said Ramona. "I get to be a sheep in the Nativity scene this year."

"That's nice," said Mrs. Quimby. "I'm glad they are going to do something a little different this year."

"And I get to be Mary," said Beezus.

"Good!" said Mrs. Quimby, still rubbing.

"I'll need a sheep costume," said Ramona.

"The church has my costume," said Beezus.

Ramona gave her sister a you-shut-up look. Beezus smiled serenely. Ramona hoped she wasn't going to start acting like Mary already.

Mrs. Quimby stopped rubbing to look at

Ramona. "And where are you going to get this sheep costume?" she asked.

Ramona felt very small. "I—I thought you could make me a sheep suit."

"When?"

Ramona felt even smaller. "After work?"

Mrs. Quimby sighed. "Ramona, I don't like to disappoint you, but I'm tired when I come home from work. I don't have time to do a lot of sewing. A sheep suit would be a lot of work and mean a lot of little pieces to put together, and I don't even know if I could find a sheep pattern."

Mr. Quimby joined in the conversation. That was the trouble with a father with time on his hands. He always had time for other people's arguments. "Ramona," he said, "you know better than to involve other people in work without asking first."

Ramona wished her father could sew. He had plenty of time. "Maybe Howie's grandmother could make me a costume, too," she suggested.

"We can't ask favors like that," said Mrs. Quimby, "and besides material costs money, and with Christmas coming and all we don't have a nickel to spare."

Ramona knew all this. She simply hadn't thought; she had wanted to be a sheep so much. She gulped and sniffed and tried to wiggle her toes inside her shoes. Her feet were growing and her shoes felt tight. She was glad she had not mentioned this to her mother. She would never get a costume if they had to buy shoes.

Mrs. Quimby draped the towel around her shoulders and reached for her comb.

"I can't be a sheep without a costume." Ramona sniffed again. She would gladly suffer tight shoes if she could have a costume instead.

"It's your own fault," said Mr. Quimby.

"You should have thought."

Ramona now wished she had waited until after Christmas to persuade her father to give up smoking. Then maybe he would be nice to his little girl when she needed a sheep costume.

Mrs. Quimby pulled the comb through her tangled hair. "I'll see what I can do," she said. "We have that old white terry-cloth bathrobe with the sleeve seams that pulled out. It's pretty shabby, but if I bleached it, I might be able to do something with it."

Ramona stopped sniffing. Her mother would try to make everything all right, but Ramona was not going to risk telling about her tight shoes in case she couldn't make a costume out of the bathrobe and needed to buy material.

That evening, after Ramona had gone to bed, she heard her mother and father in their bedroom talking in those low, serious voices that so often meant that they were talking about her. She slipped out of bed and knelt on the floor with her ear against the furnace outlet to see if she could catch their words.

Her father's voice, coming through the furnace pipes, sounded hollow and far away. "Why did you give in to her?" he was asking. "She had no business saying you would make her a sheep costume without asking first. She has to learn sometime."

I have learned, thought Ramona indignantly. Her father did not have to talk this way about her behind her back.

"I know," answered Ramona's mother in a voice also sounding hollow and far away. "But she's little, and these things are so important to her. I'll manage somehow."

"We don't want a spoiled brat on our hands," said Ramona's father.

"But it's Christmas," said Mrs. Quimby, "and Christmas is going to be slim enough this year."

Comforted by her mother but angry at her father, Ramona climbed back into bed. Spoiled brat! So that was what her father thought of her.

The days that followed were difficult for Ramona, who was now cross with her cross father. He was *mean*, talking about her behind her back that way.

"Well, what's eating you?" he finally asked Ramona.

"Nothing." Ramona scowled. She could not tell him why she was angry without admitting she had eavesdropped.

And then there was Beezus, who went around smiling and looking serene, perhaps because Mrs. Mester had given her an *A* on her creative-writing composition and read it aloud to the class, but more likely because she was practicing for her part as Mary. Having a sister who tried to act like the Virgin Mary was not easy for a girl who felt as Ramona did.

And the costume. Mrs. Quimby found time to bleach the old bathrobe in the washing machine, but after that nothing happened. The doctor she worked for was so busy because of all the earaches, sore throats, and flu that came with winter weather that she was late coming home every evening.

On top of that, Ramona had to spend two afternoons watching Howie's grandmother sew on his sheep suit, because arrangements had now been made for Ramona to go to Howie's house if Mr. Quimby could not be home after school. This week he had to collect unemployment insurance and take a civil-service examination for a job in the post office.

Ramona studied Howie's sheep suit, which was made out of fluffy white acrylic. The ears were lined with pink, and Mrs. Kemp was going to put a zipper down the front. The costume was beautiful, soft and furry. Ramona longed to rub her cheek against it, hug it, take it to bed with her.

"And when I finish Howie's costume, I am going to make another for Willa Jean," said Mrs. Kemp. "Willa Jean wants one, too."

This was almost too much for Ramona to bear. Besides, her shoes felt tighter than ever. She looked at Willa Jean, who was clomping around the house on her little tuna-can stilts. Messy little Willa Jean in a beautiful sheep suit she didn't even need. She would only spoil the furry cloth by dribbling apple juice down the front and spilling graham-cracker crumbs all over it. People said Willa Jean behaved just the way Ramona used to, but Ramona could not believe them.

A week before the Christmas program Mrs. Quimby managed to find time to buy a pattern during her lunch hour, but she did not find time to sew for Ramona.

Mr. Quimby, on the other hand, had plenty of time for Ramona. Too much, she was begining to think. He nagged. Ramona should sit up closer to the table so she wouldn't spill so much. She should stop making rivers in her mashed potatoes. She should wring out her washcloth instead of leaving it sopping in the tub. Look at the circle of rust her tin-can stilts had left on the kitchen floor. Couldn't she be more careful? She should fold her bath towel in half and hang it up straight. How did she expect it to dry when it was all wadded up, for Pete's sake? She found a sign in her room that said, *A Messy Room Is Hazardous to Your Health.* That was too much.

Ramona marched out to the garage where her father was oiling the lawnmower so it would be ready when spring came and said, "A messy room is not hazardous to my health. It's not the same as smoking."

"You could trip and break your arm," her father pointed out.

Ramona had an answer. "I always turn on the light or sort of feel along the floor with my feet."

"You could smother in old school papers, stuffed animals, and hula hoops if the mess gets deep enough," said her father and added, "Miss Radar Feet."

Ramona smiled. "Daddy, you're just being silly again. Nobody ever smothered in a hula hoop."

"You never can tell," said her father. "There is always a first time."

Ramona and her father got along better for a while after that, and then came the terrible afternoon when Ramona came home from school to find her father closing the living-room windows, which had been wide open even though the day was raw and windy. There was a faint smell of cigarette smoke in the room.

"Why there's Henry running down the

street," said Mr. Quimby, his back to Ramona. "He may make it to the Olympics, but that old dog of his won't."

"Daddy," said Ramona. Her father turned. Ramona looked him in the eye. "You *cheated*!"

Mr. Quimby closed the last window. "What are you talking about?"

"You smoked and you *promised* you wouldn't!" Ramona felt as if she were the grown-up and he were the child.

Mr. Quimby sat down on the couch and leaned back as if he were very, very tired, which made some of the anger drain out of Ramona. "Ramona," he said, "it isn't easy to break a bad habit. I ran across one cigarette, an old stale cigarette, in my raincoat pocket and thought it might help if I smoked just one. I'm trying. I'm really trying."

Hearing her father speak this way, as if she really was a grown-up, melted the last

of Ramona's anger. She turned into a seven-
year-old again and climbed on the couch to
lean against her father. After a few moments
of silence, she whispered, "I love you,
Daddy."

He tousled her hair affectionately and

said, "I know you do. That's why you want me to stop smoking, and I love you, too."

"Even if I'm a brat sometimes?"

"Even if you're a brat sometimes."

Ramona thought awhile before she sat up and said, "Then why can't we be a happy family?"

For some reason Mr. Quimby smiled. "I have news for you, Ramona," he said. "We *are* a happy family."

"We are?" Ramona was skeptical.

"Yes, we are." Mr. Quimby was positive. "No family is perfect. Get that idea out of your head. And nobody is perfect either. All we can do is work at it. And we do."

Ramona tried to wiggle her toes inside her shoes and considered what her father had said. Lots of fathers wouldn't draw pictures with their little girls. Her father bought her paper and crayons when he could afford them. Lots of mothers wouldn't step over a picture that spread across the kitchen floor while cooking supper. Ramona knew mothers who would scold and say, "Pick that up. Can't you see I'm trying to get supper?" Lots of big sisters wouldn't let their little sister go along when they interviewed someone for creative writing. They would take more than their fair share of gummybears because they were bigger and . . .

Ramona decided her father was probably right, but she couldn't help feeling they would be a happier family if her mother could find time to sew that sheep costume. There wasn't much time left.

7

Ramona and The
Three Wise Persons

Suddenly, a few days before Christmas when the Quimby family least expected it, the telephone rang for Ramona's father. He had a job! The morning after New Year's Day he was to report for training as a checker in a chain of supermarkets. The pay was good, he would have to work some evenings, and maybe someday he would get to manage a market!

After that telephone call Mr. Quimby stopped reaching for cigarettes that were not there and began to whistle as he ran the vacuum cleaner and folded the clothes from the dryer. The worried frown disappeared from Mrs. Quimby's forehead. Beezus looked even more calm and serene. Ramona,

however, made a mistake. She told her mother about her tight shoes. Mrs. Quimby then wasted a Saturday afternoon shopping for shoes when she could have been sewing on Ramona's costume. As a result, when they drove to church the night of the Christmas-carol program, Ramona was the only unhappy member of the family.

Mr. Quimby sang as he drove:

"There's a little wheel
a-turning in my heart.
There's a little wheel
a-turning in my heart."

Ramona loved that song because it made her think of Howie, who liked machines. Tonight, however, she was determined not to enjoy her father's singing.

Rain blew against the car, headlights shone on the pavement, the windshield wipers *splip-splopped.* Mrs. Quimby leaned back, tired but relaxed. Beezus smiled her gentle Virgin Mary smile that Ramona had found so annoying for the past three weeks.

Ramona sulked. Someplace above those cold, wet clouds the very same star was shining that had guided the Three Wise Men to Bethlehem. On a night like this they never would have made it.

Mr. Quimby sang on, "Oh, I feel like shouting in my heart. . . ."

Ramona interrupted her father's song. "I don't care what anybody says," she burst out. "If I can't be a good sheep, I am not going to be a sheep at all." She yanked off the white terry-cloth headdress with pink-lined ears that she was wearing and stuffed it into the pocket of her car coat. She started to pull her father's rolled-down socks from her hands because they didn't really look like hooves, but then she decided they kept her hands warm. She squirmed on the lumpy terry-cloth tail sewn to the seat of her pajamas. Ramona could not pretend that faded pajamas printed with an army of pink rabbits, half of them upside down, made her look like a sheep, and Ramona was usually good at pretending.

Mrs. Quimby's voice was tired. "Ramona, your tail and headdress were all I could manage, and I had to stay up late last night to finish those. I simply don't have time for complicated sewing."

Ramona knew that. Her family had been telling her so for the past three weeks.

"A sheep should be woolly," said Ramona. "A sheep should not be printed with pink bunnies."

"You can be a sheep that has been shorn," said Mr. Quimby, who was full of jokes now that he was going to work again. "Or how about a wolf in sheep's clothing?"

"You just want me to be miserable," said Ramona, not appreciating her father's humor and feeling that everyone in her family should be miserable because she was.

"She's worn out," said Mrs. Quimby, as if Ramona could not hear. "It's so hard to wait for Christmas at her age."

Ramona raised her voice. "I am *not* worn out! You know sheep don't wear pajamas."

"That's show biz," said Mr. Quimby.

"Daddy!" Beezus–Mary was shocked. "It's church!"

"And don't forget, Ramona," said Mr. Quimby, "as my grandmother would have said, 'Those pink bunnies will never be noticed from a trotting horse.'"

Ramona disliked her father's grandmother even more. Besides, nobody rode trotting horses in church.

The sight of light shining through the stained–glass window of the big stone church diverted Ramona for a moment. The window looked beautiful, as if it were made of jewels.

Mr. Quimby backed the car into a parking space. "Ho-ho-ho!" he said, as he turned off the ignition. "'Tis the season to be jolly."

Jolly was the last thing Ramona was going to be. Leaving the car, she stooped down inside her car coat to hide as many rabbits as possible. Black branches clawed at the sky, and the wind was raw.

"Stand up straight," said Ramona's heartless father.

"I'll get wet," said Ramona. "I might catch cold, and then you'd be sorry."

"Run between the drops," said Mr. Quimby.

"They're too close together," answered Ramona.

"Oh, you two," said Mrs. Quimby with a tired little laugh, as she backed out of the car and tried to open her umbrella at the same time.

"I will not be in it," Ramona defied her family once and for all. "They can give the program without me."

Her father's answer was a surprise. "Suit yourself," he said. "You're not going to spoil our evening."

Mrs. Quimby gave the seat of Ramona's pajamas an affectionate pat. "Run along, little lamb, wagging your tail behind you."

Ramona walked stiff-legged so that her tail would not wag.

At the church door the family parted, the girls going downstairs to the Sunday-school room, which was a confusion of chattering children piling coats and raincoats on chairs. Ramona found a corner behind the Christmas tree, where Santa would pass out candy canes after the program. She sat down on the floor with her car coat pulled over her bent knees.

Through the branches Ramona watched carolers putting on their white robes. Girls were tying tinsel around one another's heads while Mrs. Russo searched out boys and tied tinsel around their heads, too. "It's all right for boys to wear tinsel," Mrs. Russo assured them. Some looked as if they were not certain they believed her.

One boy climbed on a chair. "I'm an angel. Watch me fly," he announced and jumped off, flapping the wide sleeves of his choir robe. All the carolers turned into flapping angels.

Nobody noticed Ramona. Everyone was having too much fun. Shepherds found their cloaks, which were made from old cotton bedspreads. Beezus's friend, Henry Huggins, arrived and put on the dark robe he was to wear in the part of Joseph.

The other two sheep appeared. Howie's

acrylic sheep suit, with the zipper on the front, was as thick and as fluffy as Ramona knew it would be. Ramona longed to pet Howie; he looked so soft. Davy's flannel suit was fastened with safety pins, and there was something wrong about the ears. If his tail had been longer, he could have passed for a kitten, but he did not seem to mind. Both boys wore brown mittens. Davy, who was a thin little sheep, jumped up and down to make his tail wag, which surprised Ramona. At school he was always so shy. Maybe he felt brave inside his sheep suit. Howie, a chunky sheep, made his tail wag, too. My ears are as good as theirs, Ramona told herself. The floor felt cold through the seat of her thin pajamas.

"Look at the little lambs!" cried an angel. "Aren't they darling?"

"Ba-a, ba-a!" bleated Davy and Howie.

Ramona longed to be there with them,

jumping and ba-a-ing and wagging her tail, too. Maybe the faded rabbits didn't show as much as she had thought. She sat hunched and miserable. She had told her father she would *not* be a sheep, and she couldn't back down now. She hoped God was too busy to notice her, and then she changed her mind. Please, God, prayed Ramona, in case He wasn't too busy to listen to a miserable little sheep, I don't really mean to be horrid. It just works out that way. She was frightened, she discovered, for when the program began, she would be left alone in the church basement. The lights might even be turned out, a scary thought, for the big stone church filled Ramona with awe, and she did not want to be left alone in the dark with her awe. Please, God, prayed Ramona, get me out of this mess.

Beezus, in a long blue robe with a white scarf over her head and carrying a baby's blanket and a big flashlight, found her little sister. "Come out, Ramona," she coaxed. "Nobody will notice your costume. You know Mother would have made you a whole sheep suit if she had time. Be a good sport. Please."

Ramona shook her head and blinked to keep tears from falling. "I told Daddy I wouldn't be in the program, and I won't."

"Well, OK, if that's the way you feel," said Beezus, forgetting to act like Mary. She left her little sister to her misery.

Ramona sniffed and wiped her eyes on her hoof. Why didn't some grown-up come along and *make* her join the other sheep? No grown-up came. No one seemed to remember there were supposed to be three sheep, not even Howie, who played with her almost every day.

Ramona's eye caught the reflection of her face distorted in a green Christmas ornament. She was shocked to see her nose look huge, her mouth and red-rimmed eyes tiny. I can't really look like that, thought Ramona in despair. I'm really a nice person. It's just that nobody understands.

Ramona mopped her eyes on her hoof again, and as she did she noticed three big girls, so tall they were probably in the eighth grade, putting on robes made from better bedspreads than the shepherd's robes. That's funny, she thought. Nothing she had learned in Sunday school told her anything about girls in long robes in the Nativity scene. Could they be Jesus's aunts?

One of the girls began to dab tan cream from a little jar on her face and to smear it around while another girl held up a pocket mirror. The third girl, holding her own mirror, used an eyebrow pencil to give herself heavy brows.

Makeup, thought Ramona with interest,

wishing she could wear it. The girls took turns darkening their faces and brows. They looked like different people. Ramona got to her knees and peered over the lower branches of the Christmas tree for a better view.

One of the girls noticed her. "Hi, there," she said. "Why are you hiding back there?"

"Because," was Ramona's all-purpose answer. "Are you Jesus's aunts?" she asked.

The girls found the question funny. "No," answered one. "We're the Three Wise Persons."

Ramona was puzzled. "I thought they were supposed to be wise *men*," she said.

"The boys backed out at the last minute," explained the girl with the blackest eyebrows. "Mrs. Russo said women can be wise too, so tonight we are the Three Wise Persons."

This idea seemed like a good one to Ramona, who wished she were big enough to be a wise person hiding behind makeup so nobody would know who she was.

"Are you supposed to be in the program?" asked one of the girls.

"I was supposed to be a sheep, but I changed my mind," said Ramona, changing it back again. She pulled out her sheep headdress and put it on.

"Isn't she adorable?" said one of the wise persons.

Ramona was surprised. She had never been called adorable before. Bright, lively, yes; adorable, no. She smiled and felt more lovable. Maybe pink-lined ears helped.

"Why don't you want to be a sheep?" asked a wise person.

Ramona had an inspiration. "Because I don't have any makeup."

"Makeup on a *sheep*!" exclaimed a wise person and giggled.

Ramona persisted. "Sheep have black

noses," she hinted. "Maybe I could have a black nose."

The girls looked at one another. "Don't tell my mother," said one, "but I have some mascara. We could make her nose black."

"Please!" begged Ramona, getting to her feet and coming out from behind the Christmas tree.

The owner of the mascara fumbled in her shoulder bag, which was hanging on a chair, and brought out a tiny box. "Let's go in the kitchen where there's a sink," she said, and when Ramona followed her, she moistened an elf-sized brush, which she rubbed on the mascara in the box. Then she began to brush it onto Ramona's nose. It tickled, but Ramona held still. "It feels like brushing my teeth only on my nose," she remarked. The wise person stood back to look at her work and then applied another coat of mascara to Ramona's nose. "There," she said at last. "Now you look like a real sheep."

Ramona felt like a real sheep. "Ba–a–a," she bleated, a sheep's way of saying thank you. Ramona felt so much better, she could almost pretend she was woolly. She peeled off her coat and found that the faded pink rabbits really didn't show much in the dim light. She pranced off among the angels, who had been handed little flashlights, which they were supposed to hold like candles. Instead they were shining them into their mouths to show one another how weird they looked with light showing through their cheeks. The other two sheep stopped jumping when they saw her.

"You don't look like Ramona," said Howie.

"B–a–a. I'm not Ramona. I'm a sheep." The boys did not say one word about Ramona's pajamas. They wanted black noses too, and when Ramona told them where she got hers, they ran off to find the wise persons. When they returned, they no longer looked like Howie and Davy in sheep suits. They looked like strangers in sheep suits. So I must really look like somebody else, thought Ramona with increasing happiness. Now she could be in the program, and her parents wouldn't know because they wouldn't recognize her.

"B-a-a!" bleated three prancing, black-nosed sheep. "B-a-a, b-a-a."

Mrs. Russo clapped her hands. "Quiet, everybody!" she ordered. "All right, Mary and Joseph, up by the front stairs. Shepherds and sheep next and then wise persons. Angels line up by the back stairs."

The three sheep pranced over to the shepherds, one of whom said, "Look what we get to herd," and nudged Ramona with his crook.

"You cut that out," said Ramona.

"Quietly, everyone," said Mrs. Russo.

Ramona's heart began to pound as if something exciting were about to happen. Up the stairs she tiptoed and through the arched door. The only light came from candelabra on either side of the chancel and from a streetlight shining through a stained-glass window. Ramona had never seen the church look so beautiful or so mysterious.

Beezus sat down on a low stool in the center of the chancel and arranged the baby's blanket around the flashlight. Henry stood behind her. The sheep got down on their hands and knees in front of the shepherds, and the Three Wise Persons stood off to one side, holding bath-salts jars that looked as if they really could hold frankincense and myrrh. An electric star suspended above the organ began to shine. Beezus turned on the big flashlight inside the baby's blanket and light shone up on her face, making her look like a picture of Mary on a Christmas card. From the rear door a wobbly procession of kindergarten angels, holding their small flashlights like candles, led the way, glimmering, two by two. "Ah . . ." breathed the congregation.

"Hark, the herald angels sing," the advancing angels caroled. They looked nothing like the jumping, flapping mob with flashlights shining through their cheeks that Ramona had watched downstairs. They looked good and serious and . . . holy.

A shivery feeling ran down Ramona's backbone, as if magic were taking place. She looked up at Beezus, smiling tenderly down at the flashlight, and it seemed as if Baby Jesus really could be inside the blanket. Why, thought Ramona with a feeling of shock, Beezus looks nice. Kind and—sort of pretty. Ramona had never thought of her sister as anything but—well, a plain old big sister, who got to do everything first. Ramona was suddenly proud of Beezus. Maybe they did fight a lot when Beezus wasn't going around acting like Mary, but Beezus was never really mean.

As the carolers bore more light into the

church, Ramona found her parents in the second row. They were smiling gently, proud of Beezus, too. This gave Ramona an aching feeling inside. They would not know her in her makeup. Maybe they would think she was some other sheep, and she didn't want

to be some other sheep. She wanted to be their sheep. She wanted them to be proud of her, too.

Ramona saw her father look away from Beezus and look directly at her. Did he recognize her? Yes, he did. Mr. Quimby winked. Ramona was shocked. Winking in church! How could her father do such a thing? He winked again and this time held up his thumb and forefinger in a circle. Ramona understood. Her father was telling her he was proud of her, too.

"Joy to the newborn King!" sang the angels, as they mounted the steps on either side of the chancel.

Ramona was filled with joy. Christmas was the most beautiful, magic time of the whole year. Her parents loved her, and she loved them, and Beezus, too. At home there was a Christmas tree and under it, presents, fewer than at past Christmases, but presents all the same. Ramona could not contain her feelings. "B-a-a," she bleated joyfully.

She felt the nudge of a shepherd's crook on the seat of her pajamas and heard her shepherd whisper through clenched teeth, "You be quiet!" Ramona did not bleat again. She wiggled her seat to make her tail wag.

Beverly Cleary is one of America's most popular authors. Born in McMinnville, Oregon, she lived on a farm in Yamhill until she was six and then moved to Portland. After college, as the children's librarian in Yakima, Washington, she was challenged to find stories for non-readers. She wrote her first book, HENRY HUGGINS, in response to a boy's question, "Where are the books about kids like us?"

Mrs. Cleary's books have earned her many prestigious awards, including the American Library Association's Laura Ingalls Wilder Award, presented in recognition of her lasting contribution to children's literature. Her DEAR MR. HENSHAW was awarded the 1984 John Newbery Medal, and both RAMONA QUIMBY, AGE 8 and RAMONA AND HER FATHER have been named Newbery Honor Books. In addition, her books have won more than thirty-five statewide awards based on the votes of her young readers. Her characters, including Henry Huggins, Ellen Tebbits, Otis Spofford, and Beezus and Ramona Quimby, as well as Ribsy, Socks, and Ralph S. Mouse, have delighted children for generations. Mrs. Cleary lives in coastal California.

Visit Beverly Cleary on the World Wide Web at www.beverlycleary.com.

SEE WHAT RAMONA DOES NEXT IN
Ramona and Her Mother!

1

A Present for Willa Jean

When will they be here?" asked Ramona Quimby, who was supposed to be dusting the living room but instead was twirling around trying to make herself dizzy. She was much too excited to dust.

"In half an hour," cried her mother from the kitchen, where she and Ramona's big sister Beatrice were opening and closing the refrigerator and oven doors, bumping into one another, forgetting where they had laid the pot holders, finding them and losing the measuring spoons.

The Quimbys were about to entertain their neighbors at a New Year's Day brunch to celebrate Mr. Quimby's finding a job at the ShopRite Market after being out of work for several months. Ramona liked the word *brunch*, half breakfast and half lunch, and secretly felt the family had cheated because they had eaten their real breakfast earlier. They needed their strength to get ready for the party.

"And Ramona," said Mrs. Quimby as she hastily laid out silverware on the dining-room table, "be nice to Willa Jean, will you? Try to keep her out of everyone's hair."

"Ramona, watch what you're doing!" said Mr. Quimby, who was laying a fire in the fire-place. "You almost knocked over the lamp."

Ramona stopped twirling, staggered from dizziness, and made a face. Willa Jean, the messy little sister of her friend Howie Kemp, was sticky, crumby, into everything, and always had to have her own way.

"And behave yourself," said Mr. Quimby. "Willa Jean is company."

Not my company, thought Ramona, who saw quite enough of Willa Jean when she played at Howie's house. "If Howie can't come to the brunch because he has a cold, why can't Willa Jean stay home with their grandmother, too?" Ramona asked.

"I really don't know," said Ramona's mother. "That isn't the way things worked out. When the Kemps asked if they could bring Willa Jean, I could hardly say no."

I could, thought Ramona, deciding that since Willa Jean, welcome or not, was coming to the brunch, she had better prepare to defend her possessions. She went to her room, where she swept her best crayons and drawing paper into a drawer and covered them with her pajamas. Her Christmas roller skates and favorite toys, battered stuffed animals that she rarely played with but still loved, went into the corner of her closet. There she hid them under her bathrobe and shut the door tight.

But what could she find to amuse Willa Jean? If Willa Jean did not have something to play with, she would run tattling to the grown-ups. "Ramona hid her toys!" Ramona laid a stuffed snake on her bed, then doubted if even Willa Jean could love a stuffed snake.

What Ramona needed was a present for Willa Jean, a present wrapped and tied with a good hard knot, a present that would take a long time to unwrap. Next to receiving presents, Ramona liked to give presents, and if she gave Willa Jean a present today, she would not only have the fun of giving, but of knowing the grown-ups would think, Isn't Ramona kind, isn't she generous to give Willa Jean a present? And so soon after Christmas, too. They would look at Ramona in her new red-and-green-plaid slacks and red turtleneck sweater and say, Ramona is one of Santa's helpers, a regular little Christmas elf.

Ramona smiled at herself in the mirror and was pleased. Two of her most important teeth were only halfway in, which made her look like a jack-o'-lantern, but she did not mind. If she had grown-up teeth, the rest of her face would catch up someday.

Over her shoulder she saw reflected in the mirror a half-empty box of Kleenex on the floor beside her bed. Kleenex! That was the answer to a present for Willa Jean. She ran into the kitchen, where Beezus was beating muffin batter while her father fried sausages and her mother struggled to unmold a large gelatine salad onto a plate covered with lettuce.

"A present is a good idea," agreed Mrs. Quimby when Ramona asked permission, "but a box of Kleenex doesn't seem like much of a present." She shook the mold. The salad refused to slide out. Her face was flushed and she glanced at the clock on the stove.

Ramona was insistent. "Willa Jean would like it. I know she would." There was no time for explaining what Willa Jean was to do with the Kleenex.

Mrs. Quimby was having her problems with the stubborn salad. "All right," she consented. "There's an extra box in the bathroom cupboard." The salad slid slowly from the mold and rested, green and shimmering, on the lettuce.

By the time Ramona had wrapped a large box of Kleenex in leftover Christmas paper, the guests had begun to arrive. First came the Hugginses and McCarthys and little Mrs. Swink in a bright-green pants suit. Umbrellas were leaned outside the front door, coats taken into the bedroom, and the usual grown-up remarks exchanged. "Happy

New Year!" "Good to see you!" "We thought we would have to swim over, it's raining so hard." "Do you think this rain will ever stop?" "Who says it's raining?" "This is good old Oregon sunshine!" Ramona felt she had heard that joke one million times, and she was only in the second grade.

Then Mr. Huggins said to Ramona's father, "Congratulations! I hear you have a new job."

"That's right," said Mr. Quimby. "Starts tomorrow."

"Great," said Mr. Huggins, and Ramona silently agreed. Having a father without a job had been hard on the whole family.

Then Mrs. Swink smiled at Ramona and said, "My, Juanita, you're getting to be a big girl. How old are you? I can't keep track."

Should Ramona tell Mrs. Swink her name was not Juanita? No, Mrs. Swink was very

8

old and should be treated with courtesy. Last year Ramona would have spoken up and said, My name is not Juanita, it's Ramona. Not this year. The room fell silent as Ramona answered, "I'm seven and a half right now." She was proud of herself for speaking so politely.

There was soft laughter from the grown-ups, which embarrassed Ramona. Why did they have to laugh? She *was* seven and a half right now. She would not be seven and a half forever.

Then the Grumbies arrived, followed by Howie's mother and father, the Kemps, and of course Willa Jean. Although Willa Jean was perfectly capable of walking, her father was carrying her so she would not get her little white shoes and socks wet. Willa Jean in turn was carrying a big stuffed bear. When Mr. Kemp set his daughter down, her mother peeled off her coat, one arm at a time so

Willa Jean would not have to let go of her bear.

There stood usually messy Willa Jean in a pink dress with tiny flowers embroidered on the collar. Her curly blond hair, freshly washed, stood out like a halo. Her blue eyes were the color of the plastic handle on Ramona's toothbrush. When she smiled, she showed her pearly little baby teeth. Willa Jean was not messy at all.

Ramona in her corduroy slacks and turtle-neck sweater suddenly felt big and awkward beside her little guest and embarrassed to have jack-o'-lantern teeth.

And the things those grown-ups said to Willa Jean! "Why, hello there, sweetheart!" "My, don't you look like a little angel!" "Bless your little heart. Did Santa bring you the great big bear?" Willa Jean smiled and hugged her bear. Ramona noticed she had lace ruffles sewn to the seat of her underpants.

"What is your bear's name, dear?" asked Mrs. Swink.

"Woger," answered Willa Jean.

Mrs. Kemp smiled as if Willa Jean had said something clever and explained, "She named her bear Roger after the milkman."

Mrs. Quimby said with amusement, "I remember when Ramona named one of her dolls Chevrolet after the car." Everyone laughed.

She didn't have to go and tell that, thought Ramona, feeling that her mother had betrayed her by telling, as if it were funny, something she had done a long time ago. She still thought Chevrolet was a beautiful name, even though she was old enough to know that dolls were not usually named after cars.

"See my bear?" Willa Jean held Woger up for Ramona to admire. Because everyone was watching, Ramona said politely, "He's a nice bear." And he was a nice bear, the nicest bear Ramona had ever seen. He was big and soft with a kindly look on his furry face and—this was the best part—each of his four big paws had five furry toes. You could count them, five on each paw. Even though

Ramona felt she should be outgrowing bears, she longed to hold that bear, to put her arms around him, hug him close and love him. "Would you like me to hold the bear for you?" she asked.

"No," said Willa Jean.

"Ramona," whispered Mrs. Quimby, "take Willa Jean into the kitchen and sit her at the table so she won't spill orange juice on the carpet." Ramona gave her mother a balky look, which was returned with her mother's you-do-it-or-you'll-catch-it look. Mrs. Quimby was not at her best when about to serve a meal to a living room full of guests.

In the kitchen Willa Jean set Woger carefully on the chair before she climbed up beside him, displaying her ruffled underpants, and grasped her orange juice with both hands, dribbling some down the front of her fresh pink dress.

Mrs. Quimby, assisted by Beezus, set out a platter of scrambled eggs and another of bacon and sausage beside the gelatine salad. Hastily she snatched two small plates from the cupboard and dished out two servings of brunch, which she set in front of Ramona and Willa Jean. Beezus, acting like a grown-up, filled a basket with muffins and carried it into the dining room. Guests took plates from the stack at the end of the table and began to serve themselves.

Ramona scowled. If Beezus got to eat in the living room with the grown-ups, why couldn't she? She was no baby. She would not spill.

"Be a good girl!" whispered Mrs. Quimby, who had forgotten the marmalade.

I'm trying, thought Ramona, but her mother was too flurried to notice her efforts.

Read all of
Ramona Quimby's adventures!

Follow along from Ramona's days in nursery school
to her "zeroteenth" birthday.

**Beezus and
Ramona**
Hc 0-688-21076-7
Pb 0-380-70918-X

Ramona the Pest
Hc 0-688-21721-4
Pb 0-380-70954-6

Ramona la chinche
rayo Pb 0-688-14888-3

Ramona the Brave
Hc 0-688-22015-0
Pb 0-380-70959-7

**Ramona and Her
Father**
Hc 0-688-22114-9
Pb 0-380-70916-3
A Newbery Honor Book

**Ramona and Her
Mother**
Hc 0-688-22195-5
Pb 0-380-70952-X

**Ramona Quimby,
Age 8**
Hc 0-688-00477-6
Pb 0-380-70956-2
A Newbery Honor Book

Ramona empieza el curso
rayo Pb 0-688-15487-5

Ramona Forever
Hc 0-688-03785-2
Pb 0-380-70960-0

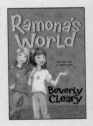

Ramona's World
Hc 0-688-16816-7
Pb 0-380-73272-6

THE SOCIAL STRUCTURE OF A
CAPE COLOURED RESERVE

THE
SOCIAL STRUCTURE
OF A
CAPE COLOURED RESERVE

A STUDY OF RACIAL
INTEGRATION AND SEGREGATION
IN SOUTH AFRICA

BY
PETER CARSTENS

ASSOCIATE PROFESSOR OF ANTHROPOLOGY
UNIVERSITY OF TORONTO

CAPE TOWN
OXFORD UNIVERSITY PRESS
LONDON   NEW YORK   TORONTO
1966

Oxford University Press, Ely House, London W. 1

GLASGOW   NEW YORK   TORONTO   MELBOURNE   WELLINGTON
CAPE TOWN   SALISBURY   IBADAN   NAIROBI   LUSAKA   ADDIS ABABA
BOMBAY   CALCUTTA   MADRAS   KARACHI   LAHORE   DACCA
KUALA LUMPUR   HONG KONG   TOKYO

Oxford University Press, Thibault House, Cape Town

❀ PRINTED IN SOUTH AFRICA BY
THE RUSTICA PRESS, PTY., LTD., WYNBERG, CAPE

CONTENTS

vi CONTENTS

LIST OF ILLUSTRATIONS AND MAPS

LIST OF TABLES

PREFACE

THE FIELD-WORK on which this book is based was carried out between November 1951 and December 1960 although only sixteen months were spent living in the five communities studied. Thirteen months were spent at Steinkopf, the community on which the major portion of this study is focused, and three at Concordia, Komaggas, Leliefontein, and Richtersveld.

In many ways this 'sporadic visit' approach spread out over a period of ten years is unsatisfactory for studies of this kind, but owing to teaching and other commitments it was the only course possible. Some preliminary work was done during vacations (1951-3) while I was an undergraduate at Rhodes University, Grahamstown; a short period was spent in the field at the end of 1954; and it was not until 1956 (owing to a year's absence in Southern Rhodesia, as it then was) that I was able to resume field-work—during vacations—after my appointment as lecturer in social anthropology at the University of Cape Town.

There were, however, advantages to be derived from spreading out my field-work over a decade, since I was afforded the opportunity of studying at first hand some of the processes of social change. Of particular importance were those effected by enforced modifications in the systems of administration and local government of these five peasant communities. These modifications, moreover, in combination with related factors produced a new and distinct period in their history while I was carrying out field-work, and this gave me valuable insight into the other social processes with which I was concerned.

In the writing up of this material I have used, unless otherwise stated, the period 1957-8 as the ethnographic present for all the communities except Richtersveld, which is geared to 1960, when intensive field-work was carried out for one month.

A more detailed account of the ethnography of these communities, especially Steinkopf, is contained in a doctoral thesis accepted by the University of Cape Town in 1962. The present book, although largely based on the thesis, has been both shortened and revised. Permission from the University to quote liberally from the thesis is gratefully acknowledged.

The material for this book (and my thesis) was collected by myself except for certain statistical data, the gathering of which was aided by local school-teachers. Historical data were culled largely from

various manuscripts found at the Steinkopf mission-station, early
government reports, travel and missionary publications, and documents
residing in the Cape Archives, as well as from the unwritten history
told by the people themselves. Certain of the statistics relating to the
economy, population, and marriage were extracted from official
reports.

Quotations from evidence supplied by informants have in most
cases been translated into English. Occasionally I have also given the
original Afrikaans to illustrate local idiom or because the meaning is
obscured by translation. All interviews were conducted in Afrikaans,
which is the home language of the majority of the people studied,
except in Richtersveld, where Nama is generally spoken. In
Richtersveld I had sometimes to use an interpreter.

At all times during my periods of field-work (except in Komaggas
and Concordia) people were friendly and co-operative, and appeared
always to be interested in the problems I was attempting to solve.
Occasionally, however, barriers were raised when we were discussing
those aspects of their religious beliefs which would not be acceptable
to the missionary. And certain people preferred not to disclose details
regarding the numbers of their livestock.

My visits to Komaggas and Concordia, especially the former, were
extremely unsatisfactory from the point of view of carrying out
research. I was treated with suspicion by the people, and in Komaggas
a White church official accused me of subversive political activity
within a few hours of my arrival. These attitudes are significant because
they throw light on the tensions and dissensions which exist in these
two communities.

During my periods of field-work in Steinkopf and Richtersveld
I lived among the people and took part in as many of their social
activities as possible. I attended church services, weddings, funerals,
and meetings of various kinds. And I always ate with the family I was
visiting.

There are many to whom I owe a great deal for their contributions
towards the writing of this book in its various stages. First of all there
are the numerous friends and informants in the communities studied
who gave so much of their time to answering my questions and
patiently instructing me about the complexities of their social life.
Rather than attempt here to thank them individually I do so collectively
in the knowledge that this procedure will be appreciated—though
wryly—by the members of various factions!

I am also greatly indebted to Professor Monica Wilson, who spent long hours reading my material, and discussing aspects of field-work and the formulation of concepts and ideas—especially with regard to the processes of social change.

I must also thank Professor I. Schapera for his invaluable comments on earlier drafts of this work: it was as a result of his stimulation that the material contained in chapters 10 and 11 was developed in its present form.

Dr. Simon Ottenberg of the University of Washington and Dr. Lionel Tiger of the University of British Columbia also read the manuscript and made some valuable suggestions. Mr. Leo Katzen of the University of Leicester, and Dr. Kaye Faulkner of Western Washington State College, both read chapter 3 and gave indispensable advice. I am extremely grateful to all of them.

Finally I wish to thank the Staff Research Fund of the University of Cape Town, the National Council for Social Research, and my parents for financial assistance towards the expenses incurred in the field; Western Washington State College, U.S.A., which provided clerical assistance for the typing of the final manuscript; De Beers Consolidated Mines Ltd. for a generous grant in aid of publication; and Miss Leah Levy of the University of Cape Town for assisting me with the bibliography.

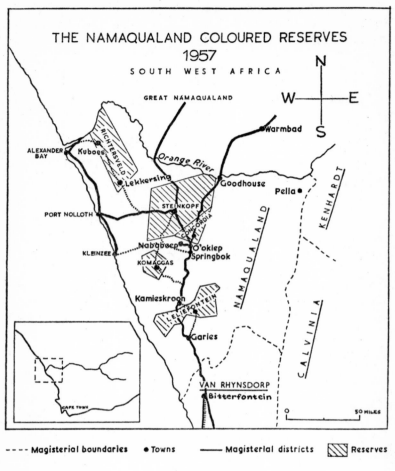

THE NAMAQUALAND COLOURED RESERVES
1957
SOUTH WEST AFRICA

GREAT NAMAQUALAND

N
W — E
S

Warmbad

ALEXANDER BAY
Kuboes
RICHTERSVELD
Orange River
Lekkersing
Goodhouse
Pella

PORT NOLLOTH
STEINKOPF
CONCORDIA

Nababeep
O'okiep
Springbok
KLEINZEE
KOMAGGAS

NAMAQUALAND

KENHARDT

Kamieskroon
LELIEFONTEIN

Garies

CALVINIA

CAPE TOWN

VAN RHYNSDORP
Bitterfontein

50 MILES

- - - - Magisterial boundaries   ● Towns   ———— Magisterial districts   ▨ Reserves

━━━ Main Roads   •••••••• Other Roads   ᴧᴧᴧᴧᴧ Railways

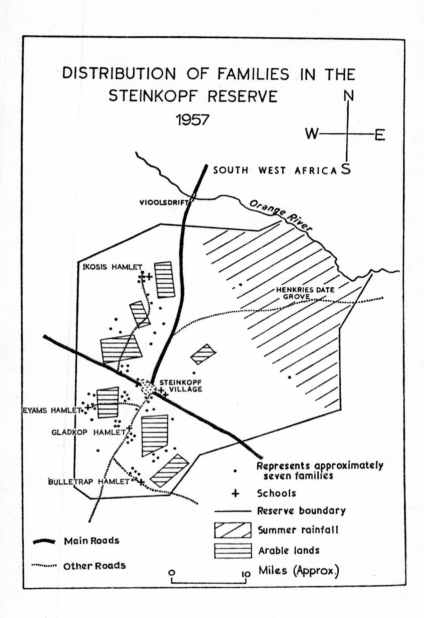

DISTRIBUTION OF FAMILIES IN THE
STEINKOPF RESERVE
1957

N
W   E
S

SOUTH WEST AFRICA

VIOOLSDRIFT

Orange River

!KOSIS HAMLET

HENKRIES DATE
GROVE

STEINKOPF
VILLAGE

EYAMS HAMLET

GLADKOP HAMLET

BULLETRAP HAMLET

•   Represents approximately
    seven families

+   Schools

⎯   Reserve boundary

Summer rainfall

Arable lands

⎯   Main Roads

·········   Other Roads

0   10   Miles (Approx.)

CHAPTER I

INTRODUCTION

THE MAIN focus of this book is an analysis of the social structure of a small peasant community of rural Coloured[1] people who live on a Reserve surrounding the old mission station, Steinkopf, in Little Namaqualand. It has been written primarily as an ethnographic study of one of the constituent communities of a composite society, the Republic of South Africa, although a chapter has been devoted to the comparison of Steinkopf with the four other Reserves in the Namaqualand district. An attempt has also been made to describe and analyse certain of the processes of social change in this area with particular reference to these Coloured Reserves.

Modern Steinkopf provides us with an example of integration or social synthesis. Its present social structure (and culture) is largely the result of contact between, and the subsequent blending of, different traditions—mainly Khoi Khoin (Hottentot) and early Cape Dutch— into one relatively homogeneous community. And the influence of missionaries has been great. Nowadays, however, the inhabitants of Steinkopf, like those living in other reserves in South and South West Africa, must be seen also in terms of their incapsulation in the reservation system which, in its various forms, has been superimposed on certain non-White people. Aspects of the social organization of the Namaqualand Reserves, moreover, resemble many of the contemporary North American Indian Reserves in the United States and Canada. These parallels, it is suggested, can be explained not necessarily in the context of colonial history but more especially by marked similarities in the kinds of administrative systems which have been introduced.[2]

---

[1] Broadly speaking, the term Coloured is used in South Africa to refer to a person of mixed descent. See Appendix: Race Classification in South Africa.

[2] See for example three recent works: H. B. Hawthorn, C. S. Belshaw, and S. Jameson, *The Indians of British Columbia*, Toronto, 1960. J. Gulick, *Cherokees at the Crossroads*, Chapel Hill, 1960. R. W. Dunning, 'Aspects of Indian Policy and Administration', *Anthropologica*, vol. IV, No. 2, 1962, pp. 209-31. During August and September 1962 and March and April 1963 I carried out field-work in the Okanagan, Kamloops, Lytton, and Chilliwack Reserves in British Columbia while on study leave. This research was sponsored by the Leon and Thea Koerner Foundation at the University of British Columbia.

1

I prefer to use the term Khoi Khoin because the word Hottentot has become a derogatory stereotype in South Africa, symbolising the undesirable characteristics attributed to people of Khoi Khoin descent. Furthermore, the origin of the word Hottentot is obscure. The so-called 'Hottentots' referred to themselves collectively as Khoi Khoin (excellent people). They were a linguistic group,[3] who, apart from minor variations, shared a common culture, although they were subdivided into several tribes. On the basis of minor differences and their distribution, we can distinguish three groups of tribes before the White settlers upset their ecological equilibrium. In the north-west, occupying the territories now known as Little and Great Namaqualand, were the Namaqua; in the south were the Cape Khoi Khoin, such as the Goringhaiqua and the Hessequa; east of the Cape were tribes such as the Inqua and the Damaqua, whom we may call the Eastern Khoi Khoin.[4]

One of the most important problems involved in field studies in large modern societies is that of isolating communities or sub-communities of manageable size to be studied in the same way that social anthropologists have studied small-scale societies. It is not as simple as Radcliffe-Brown has suggested to take 'any convenient locality of a suitable size' and 'study the structural system as it appears in and from that region'.[5] For the problem always arises, where does the one community end and the other begin? In the Republic of South Africa, issues such as these are both magnified and complicated by legal discrimination on the basis of certain assumed biological factors, the perpetuation of various rapidly changing ethnic divisions, conflicting nationalisms, and significant religious differences.

'Community' like many other terms used by sociologists, has been variously defined. Here a 'community' refers to a collection of individuals occupying a common territory, held together by some form of local government (or central authority) and common sentiments, and identifiable by the network of social relations connecting them.

[3] For some exceptions see E. O. J. Westphal, 'The Linguistic Prehistory of Southern Africa', Africa, vol. XXXIII, no. 3, July 1963, pp. 237-65.

[4] H. Vedder, 'The Nama', in The Native Tribes of South West Africa, Cape Town, 1928. I. Schapera, The Khoisan Peoples of South Africa, London, 1930, pp. 44-50, et passim. W. Jopp, 'Die frühen Deutschen Berichte über das Kapland und die Hottentotten bis 1750', unpublished Ph.D. thesis, University of Göttingen, 1960.

[5] A. R. Radcliffe-Brown, Structure and Function in Primitive Society, Cohen and West, London, 1952, p. 193.

The reason some form of local government (or central authority) has been included as a criterion for a community is because it provides a convenient focus around which the network of social relations can be observed.

THE COMMUNITY OF STEINKOPF: A SYNOPSIS

The Steinkopf Reserve is situated more or less in the centre of the northern part of the arid magisterial district of Namaqualand in the Cape Province, South Africa. Two-thirds of its surface area of approximately 400,000 morgen[6] are within a mountain belt which receives winter rainfall. The remainder of the country lies in Bushman-land, a low summer-rainfall area in the north-east. There is usually adequate grazing for goats and sheep in the winter-rainfall area from May to December. If sufficient rain falls grain is grown in the valleys and on the slopes of the hills, but even in good years seldom more than 6,000 bags are produced. The north-eastern district provides grazing from January to April if the rainfall has been adequate.

A main road passes through the central village of the Reserve and there are regular transport facilities to Port Nolloth and Springbok. Several telephones are located in the village, and mail is collected and delivered there three times a week.

The Reserve has a population of about 4,000 people, the descendants of Khoi Khoin and Europeans. Their language is Afrikaans, although some of the older people use Nama as well. The majority are mixed farmers; they cultivate the soil and keep sheep and goats and a handful of donkeys. Their success as agriculturists, however, depends largely on the annual rainfall, which is seldom more than seven inches. The donkeys are used as draught animals to pull the ploughs and the small carts which are the main form of transport throughout the Reserve.

Most people are poor. The great majority cannot support themselves by the 'traditional' mixed-farming economy, and as a consequence each family is forced to augment its income by some other means. This is most commonly achieved by sending at least one member of each elementary family to the mines or to the towns as a migrant worker, an occupation which has in recent years become a major source of income.

For economic reasons, therefore, the inhabitants of the Reserve, although theoretically a settled people, are in fact forced to be highly

[6] One morgen = 2·11654 English acres.

mobile. Even within the Reserve itself there are constant seasonal movements of individuals and families. These are extremely difficult to measure, but we can distinguish (in terms of residence) between those who live permanently in the mission village, Steinkopf, and those who live more or less permanently in the small hamlets or in isolated homesteads near their arable lands and livestock.

The majority of the population, however, spends part of the year, when not ploughing, reaping, or herding, or absent as migratory workers, in the village where they have building lots on which some people have erected permanent dwellings. Apart from those isolated conservative people who visit the village only when absolutely necessary, it has in recent years become the ambition of every family to have a *muurhuis* (house with walls) in the village in addition to a mat-house which can be erected near the arable lands.

The mission village, or the *dorp* as it is called, has many of the characteristics of a small town. In the centre stand the church, the mission house, and the church hall—a cluster of fine, white-washed buildings erected during the last century by the missionary and the people of Steinkopf. North of the mission station are the two shops, the butchery, the granary, the police-station, the post-office and telephone, and the offices of the Management Board. South of the church, though somewhat dispersed, are the school buildings—classrooms and hostels. Scattered throughout this zone are the neat houses of the well-to-do *dorpenare* (villagers): teachers, shopkeepers and shop assistants, masons and builders, police, and successful sheep-farmers. In this zone too are the small dwellings of the poor dorpenare and those people who spend only a part of their time in the village. These dwellings are usually crude constructions of rough stone or corrugated iron, each with a detached mat-house used as a kitchen.

In the outer zone of the village are the mat-houses proper, the traditional dwellings of the Khoi Khoin, forming a wide circle of clusters of 'brown bee-hives' around the inner zone. These are the encampments of the farmers who come and go with the seasons. We might well call them the *voor-dorpenare* (pre-villagers) farmers who have not yet made the social adjustments necessary to fit in with the accepted pattern of village life. Thirty years ago nearly all the farmers who owned lands far away from the village followed this semi-nomadic pattern, but gradually more and more families have become attracted to a new life and spend as much time as possible in the village.

In the past there was no attempt to regulate the lay-out of the mission village; as a result there are no defined streets or rows of houses, only the stony tracks which wind through the open spaces between the haphazard array of houses and huts. As the village grew, buildings were erected wherever a convenient site was found near one of the two springs. Few houses are built close to the church, probably because an old rule forbade dancing and parties within a radius of five hundred yards from the mission-station grounds.

Another factor, however, has influenced the ecological pattern of the village. When one looks at the general lay-out of the buildings, it is seen that most of the better residential buildings are in the southern half, while in the northern sector mat-houses and crudely-constructed tin houses predominate. In Steinkopf there are names for these two sections of the village, *onderstraat* and *bostraat*, which are old class-divisions distinguishing the Basters,[7] early immigrants of mixed descent, from the indigenous Khoi Khoin. The interstitial area is the mission-station. These divisions, however, did not refer only to the ecology of the village but applied equally to the social dichotomy found in the rest of the community. And so today, when a family descended from the old Basters comes to the village, he builds his house in *onderstraat*, while those more closely related to the Khoi Khoin build in the *bostraat* zone.

The village is essentially the centre of all the activities of the Reserve. Here is the church and the missionary, the seat of local government where the law is administered and taxes paid; here are the main schools, including the only secondary school for Coloured people in Namaqualand, with its new science laboratory; here are the shops and the granary and the police-station; here you will find a weekly cinema show and the clinic with its trained midwife; it is here that people are baptised, married and buried. Here is the centre of interaction with the outside world, the place where new ideas and fashions are disseminated, spreading outwards to the conservative settlements.

The true dorpenare are those who live permanently in the mission village and co-operate in its social life—the teachers, shopkeepers and shop assistants, the few administrators, the various categories of tradesmen and workers, pensioners and others. But these constitute only about a quarter of the potential village population of approximately 2,000 people; the remainder cannot be classed as true villagers for, although they may spend most of the year in the village, they are engaged also in other activities on their farms. Nevertheless,

[1] See pp. 19 ff. *et passim*.

they do form part of the village community in that they share, if only sporadically, in the social life, making their own contribution to its structure. This applies also to the other people in the Steinkopf Reserve since all have some contact with the mission village, for here they attend church services, pay their taxes, and buy their groceries. These are, of course, the minimum contacts a person can have with the village, and most people like to participate in other activities as well. But there is one small section of the community which visits the village only when it has to. This consists of the conservative farmers proper. Usually, as we have mentioned, they live in small hamlets (some of which have farm schools) near springs and water-holes, ten or twenty miles away from the mission village, or in isolated farm homesteads. They keep a few goats or sheep, a span of donkeys, and a dozen or so chickens. In winter they plough and sow and if the rain is adequate they manage to reap a few bags of grain at the beginning of the summer; and, as happens among the poor dorpenare, at least one member of the family may work on the mines or in the towns to augment the family income.

In Steinkopf there are today three main social classes, membership of which is determined largely by birth. Firstly, there are the registered occupiers, a large class consisting of approximately 90 per cent of the total Coloured population. Registered occupiers have various privileges not enjoyed by the other two classes: they are entitled to vote for members of the local government, to hold grazing rights, to occupy dry lands, gardens, and building sites, in return for their taxes paid to the Management Board. Although membership of this class, as we have said, is largely hereditary, it is subject also to the approval of the Management Board.

Secondly there are the 'strangers', who are a class of newcomers to Steinkopf, consisting mainly of teachers and men who have married the daughters of registered occupiers. Although 'strangers' are not entitled to vote, they may be given, in exceptional cases, privileges similar to those enjoyed by the registered occupiers. But they would not be granted arable lands. Both categories nowadays call themselves collectively *Bruinmense*.

The third hereditary class is that of the *bywoners*. It consists mainly of Namaqua refugees from South West Africa who came to Steinkopf during the Bondelzwart wars, and of servants of some registered occupiers. Bywoners receive few privileges in the community other than temporary building sites in the village, and the right to be employed by the registered occupiers as servants or shepherds, provided the Management Board approves.

To these three we must add here a fourth hereditary class, the Whites, who play a part in forming the pattern of relationships which constitute the social system of Steinkopf: the police, the traders and commercial travellers who make occasional visits to Steinkopf, the neighbouring White farmers who are given annual grazing rights, and the resident missionary and his family.

Formerly the community was stratified according to lineage membership. The basic features of this system, which tends to modify the hereditary class system, are still important and are reflected in the *bostraat–onderstraat* division already mentioned. The hereditary class system is also modified by cleavages in the community which separate groups with opposing attitudes and values. The most prominent of these cleavages is that between the conservative people and the 'new people' who lean towards the cultural tradition of the white Afrikaners, rather than towards the Steinkopf tradition of the last century. Between these groups there is a struggle for power and prestige, particularly in local government. The second major cleavage is a racial one between the light-skinned people, with their straight hair and convex profiles, and the darker-skinned people who have short *korrel* (peppercorn) hair, broad, flat noses, and beady eyes.

Local affairs are dealt with by a Management Board which is subordinate in all its functions to the central government of the Republic of South Africa. The members of the Management Board fit into two categories: those elected by the registered occupiers, and those appointed by the Secretary for Coloured Affairs. The Management Board is concerned mainly with the control and distribution of land, the collection of taxes, and the general administration of local regulations, though it does have some executive functions as well. And criminal and civil cases are usually brought to the notice of the Management Board (though they need not be) before being handed over to the South African Police and the magistrate at Springbok.

The water supply in the mission village and elsewhere in the Reserve is also the concern of the Management Board. In the village, water for domestic purposes is supplied by two concrete dams from which water can be drawn, but people who can afford the costs may apply to the Management Board for permission to lay pipes to their houses. For financial reasons few families are able to take advantage of this concession, and the majority have to walk long distances to draw water.

At the various hamlets scattered throughout the Reserve, water is obtained from springs which have been cleaned and fenced off at the expense of the Management Board. It has also constructed dams in the north-eastern sector of the Reserve to enable stock-farmers to water their animals. It is significant that these dams have been built in the Bushmanland zone, for it is in this area that the wealthy farmers, some of whom are councillors on the Management Board, graze their stock. This tendency to help the *sterk boere* (wealthy farmers) and neglect the poor farmer is widespread in Steinkopf today. The explanation of this relatively recent trend is that political power has shifted from the traditional leaders to the educated and better-off people, who look after the interests of their own class rather than those of the whole community.

Sanitation is also the concern of the Management Board, which employs a local cartage contractor to remove garbage and clean the public and private lavatories in the village. Few people have their own lavatories and those who do are required to pay five shillings a month to the Management Board. Local health regulations are enforced in the mission village only, and not at the other settlements.

Not all figures relating to the revenue of the Management Board are available for the period 1957–8. But in 1961 its income was £6,588, while its expenditure was £7,031. On 1 January 1961 the Board had a credit balance of £857 in the bank.[8]

Medical aid is supplied at a government clinic, where there is a trained midwife. The district surgeon visits the clinic once a week, but his services are not free and he performs his work as a medical practitioner. Not all the inhabitants make use of the available medical services. Many of the conservative people prefer to have their children delivered by an *ouma* (literally, grandmother), the traditional midwife of the Namaqua. These 'midwives' use the techniques which have been passed on from generation to generation, and they are extremely skilful. The trained midwife often calls on an *ouma* to assist her with difficult deliveries such as breech presentations. Those people who do not consult the district surgeon when they are sick, make use of the *bossies dokters* (bush doctors), or treat themselves with traditional medicines prepared from herbs.

Organised entertainment in the village consists of a weekly cinema

[8] See *Report of the Coloured Affairs Department*. RP 11–1963. The Management Board's income in 1958 was £4,916. Personal communication from Department of Coloured Affairs.

show, and occasional concerts given by the school and the women's association, and a tennis club and two football clubs cater for the needs of those interested in sport. But the majority of the population spend their leisure time in other ways: visiting kinsmen and neighbours, gossiping, and attending funerals, weddings, and church services.

Building and construction work is undertaken by local building contractors, carpenters and masons, of whom there are twelve in the Reserve. Their services are used by the Management Board and those people who can afford the costs of employing skilled labour. When work is not available in the Reserve these artisans find employment in the towns or undertake building operations for neighbouring European farmers.

At the beginning of the century the Church was the main force in unifying the diverse sections of the community. This is only partly true today, since its power and influence declined after the Mission Stations and Communal Reserves Act, No. 29 of 1909, effected in theory the separation of church powers from local government. There is only one established Church in Steinkopf, the Nederduitse Gereformeerde Sendingkerk, although a few members of the community do belong to the Roman Catholic and Anglican denominations. The head of the established Church is a White missionary. He is assisted in his duties by deacons and elders, and together with them, he constitutes the *Kerkraad* (Church Council). The functions of the Kerkraad range from purely religious to secular matters: Church services, marriages, baptisms, confirmations, funerals, relief of the poor and sick, the collection of Church dues and thank offerings, and punishing members for immorality and misconduct. Primary education is also a concern of the Kerkraad. Under its jurisdiction are a number of associations, such as the women's association, while closely connected with the Church are five burial-societies.

The elementary family is the basic social and residential unit, and ecologically, as we have shown, the population consists largely of the various categories of villagers and clusters of elementary families surrounding the various springs and water-holes. As residence is often virilocal following a period of uxorilocality immediately after marriage, these clusters are generally subdivided into groups of elementary families containing the male members of a segment of a patrilineage, their wives and unmarried daughters. The span of the segment living in one of these residential units varies throughout the community, depending *inter alia* on the relative distance the *erfs* (arable lands) lie from the settlements; but it is always considered desirable for brothers to own adjacent lands so that they can live near one another.

On the death of a man his property usually passes to his youngest son, or to his widow if the heir is not of age. Marriage is monogamous; close agnatic kin do not usually marry, and there is a tendency to discourage marriages between members of certain lineage categories.

Throughout the community there is a strict rule of separation of the sexes; men keep company with men in work and play, while women co-operate in those activities laid down by custom. Within the elementary family fathers and sons herd and plough together, while mothers and daughters are concerned with housekeeping, hut-building, and other domestic duties. Similarly, in the residential unit of the extended family the men (brothers and their sons) assist each other if co-operation is necessary, as do the women (brothers' wives and daughters). This principle of separation of the sexes is projected into the whole framework of society, and only on certain occasions, such as wakes and marriage parties, do the sexes mix.

Steinkopf can no longer be regarded as an independent and isolated community since it has countless connections with the world outside. In the first place its inhabitants constitute a small section of the 'racial' category in South Africa generally referred to as the Coloured people. Secondly, Steinkopf is part of the magisterial district of Namaqualand, which is a geographical and political division of the Cape Province and the Republic of South Africa. And thirdly, it is a reserve administered in terms of the Mission Stations and Communal Reserves Act, together with certain other Coloured communities. It is essential, therefore, that we see this community within the broader framework to which it belongs while dealing with its internal components, since the form of the latter is inevitably modified by association with the wider society. Moreover, in three most important institutions—religious, educational and governmental—power is invested in groups lying beyond the boundaries of this small community.

NAMAQUALAND

Before the period of European expansion in South and South West Africa the area now known as Namaqualand was inhabited by that broad division of the Khoi Khoin known as the Naman or Namaqua. Geographically it was customary to distinguish between two divisions of this territory, Great and Little Namaqualand, separated from each other by the Orange River. Great Namaqualand extended from the Orange River in the south to the Swakop River in the north, and was bounded in the west and east by the Atlantic Ocean and the Kalahari Desert. Little Namaqualand coincided with what is now the magisterial district of Namaqualand in the Republic of South Africa.

The people who inhabited these two divisions of what was really a common territory were classified by the Dutch settlers as the Great and Little Namaqua.[9] The Great Namaqua are said to have been subdivided into seven tribal groups with one or two offshoots. The Little Namaqua were also made up of several tribes and were the first of the Namaqua to lose their tribal cohesion. Large numbers of these people together with other Khoi Khoin crossed the Orange River into South West Africa during the first half of the nineteenth century to escape from the northerly migration of Europeans and people of mixed descent (the Basters). Here they were known collectively by the Great Namaqua as Orlams. The origin of this name is uncertain but it seems to have been applied to those Khoi Khoin whose culture had been influenced by the colonists with whom they had come in contact. Nowadays the word *oorlam* [sic] is used by the Coloured people of the north-west Cape to refer to sophisticated people, or as they express it, *mense wat 'n klein bietjie slim is* (literally, people who are a little smart).

The other group living in parts of both Little and Great Namaqualand were the Bushmen. Although comparatively little is known about their numbers and movements, archaeological evidence suggests that the Bushmen were scattered over the whole of South Africa before the arrival of the Khoi Khoin and Bantu-speaking peoples. And in Namaqualand small bands of Bushmen seem to have occupied parts of the territory up to 1850 and even later.

In South African history Little Namaqualand as a cultural area must be seen primarily as a buffer or interstitial zone between the bearers of two traditions, the Namaqua in the north and the Europeans (notably Cape Dutch) in the south. This book deals with some of the manifestations of contact between these two groups of people and the Bushmen, although the emphasis is on the contemporary scene rather than on the history.

[9] For details regarding the distribution and culture of the Namaqua see: I. Schapera, *The Khoisan Peoples.* A. W. Hoernlé, 'The Social Organization of the Nama Hottentots of South-West Africa', *American Anthropologist*, vol. 27, 1925. H. Vedder, 'The Nama', in *The Native Tribes of South West Africa.* See also Schapera's bibliography in *Khoisan Peoples*, p. 48.

Little Namaqualand[10] is the most north-westerly district of the Cape Province and has the largest surface area, 18,518 square miles. In the north, it is separated from South West Africa by the last 200 miles of the Orange River, and to the west the coast is washed for about 100 miles by the cold Benguela Current. The easterly and southerly extremities join the arid, thinly-populated districts of Kenhardt, Calvinia, and Vanrhynsdorp. Throughout the year the countryside has a desert appearance, although in exceptional years, when the rainfall is adequate, the desert is transformed into a paradise of wild flowers. There are no permanent rivers apart from the Orange River in the extreme north.

The population is small and scattered and its density is roughly 1·76 persons per square mile. In 1951 according to the official census the total population was 32,635, consisting of 8,500 (26·1 per cent) Whites, 21,018 (64·4 per cent) Coloureds, 3,115 (9·5 per cent) Africans, and 2 Asiatics. Just over half of the White and a quarter of the Coloured population lived in towns where the majority of the African population who are recent migrant workers are employed. Just under half of the total Coloured population live permanently in reserves—Concordia, Komaggas, Leliefontein, Richtersveld and Steinkopf—while the remaining quarter live on White-owned farms or in the small dorps or just outside the boundaries of the towns.

Geographically,[11] Little Namaqualand may be divided into three zones: the *sandveld* or desert coastal belt, the mountain belt, and Bushmanland or the plateau. The social ecology of the territory is largely determined by these natural divisions, thus it is important for us to see them in relation to the people who inhabit each zone.

The White farmers who live in the sandveld are all extremely poor, and have to augment their small incomes made from goats and sheep by other means, such as employment on the mines, where they earn enough to support their families and to save considerable sums. A few Coloured people are found on certain White farms where they herd and do other work in return for very low wages, but in recent years these labourers have tended to leave the farms and find permanent employment, at a better wage, in the towns. The largest groups of people on the sandveld are found on the two diamond mines—Alexander Bay and Kleinzee—and at Port Nolloth, Namaqualand's

---

[10] For a general social survey of the district see P. W. Kotzé, *Namakwaland: 'n Sosiologiese studie van 'n Geïsoleerde Gemeenskap*, Cape Town, 1943.

[11] See *Official Year Book of the Union of South Africa*, no. 19, 1938, chapter 1.

small seaport, where there are two fisheries.

Parallel to the sandveld is the mountain belt, where cultivation, mainly of grain, is carried out in the valleys, and each farmer usually keeps a few goats, sheep and cattle for domestic purposes. The soil is rich in parts where erosion has not set in, but everywhere the shortage of permanent water makes farming precarious. Today the mountain belt cannot adequately support its population on farming alone. As a result the Whites living on farms, and the Coloured people living in reserves, have generally to augment their income derived from farming by migrating for short or long periods to the towns.

Although a large percentage of the population is engaged in farming of some kind, or in some related occupation, mining is the most important economic activity, just as it is in the sandveld. For here are the three copper mines, Concordia, Nababeep, and O'okiep, and the numerous small outcrops of minerals such as beryllium and scheelite which are mined by tributors and small companies.

The third zone, Bushmanland, a summer-rainfall area, stretches eastward from the mountains. Formerly inhabited by Bushman bands, this zone is now the home of the White sheep-farmers and the remaining nomadic trekboers. The trekboers are the descendants of the frontiersmen of the eighteenth and nineteenth centuries. They have no fixed place of abode and spend most of the year moving from place to place in their wagon homes, following their livestock searching for fresh pasture and water-holes. Today there are only a few true trekboer families left; many have been assimilated by the Coloured population in the Reserves, while others have been attracted to the towns by well-paid jobs.

In order to understand the status of the trekboer in Namaqualand it is necessary to distinguish these people from the Afrikaner farmers who are found throughout Namaqualand. The latter may be described as peasants eking out a living usually by mixed farming; many live in crude houses and remote parts of the district. Nevertheless they are a settled people, apart from the fact that individuals and families migrate temporarily to the towns when farming fails. Permanence of residence, however, is not the only characteristic which distinguishes them from the trekboers. The latter, as we have said, are the remnants of the old frontier society, people who lived a life of independence, cut off almost entirely from the rest of the world. And the present-day trekboers have retained the customs and standards of morality of their forebears, and have no regard for authority outside

TABLE I

GROWTH OF NAMAQUALAND'S POPULATION (1921–51)

Year of Census	White				Asiatic			Coloured				Native				All Races			
	M	F	T No.	%	M	F	T	M	F	T No.	%	M	F	T No.	%	M	F	T No.	%
1921	3,227	2,907	6,134	29	—	—	—	7,544	7,595	15,139	70	100	94	194	1	10,871	10,596	21,467	100
1936	4,528	3,807	8,335	32	1	—	1	8,781	8,453	17,234	67	165	112	277	1	13,475	12,372	25,847	100
1946	4,631	3,847	8,478	28	4	7	11	9,950	9,489	19,439	65	2,068	131	2,199	7	16,653	13,474	30,127	100
1951	4,729	3,771	8,500	26	2	—	2	10,583	10,435	21,018	64	2,647	468	3,115	10	17,961	14,674	32,635	100

TABLE II

RACIAL COMPOSITION OF NAMAQUALAND COLOURED RESERVES (1951)

Reserves	White			Coloured			Native			All Races			Density persons per sq. mile
	M	F	T	M	F	T	M	F	T	M	F	T	
Steinkopf	36	19	55	1,402	1,484	2,886	63	56	119	1,501	1,559	3,060	2·4
Concordia	83	71	154	894	962	1,856	141	—	141	1,118	1,033	2,151	10·7
Komaggas	57	46	103	697	735	1,432	—	—	—	754	781	1,535	6·6
Leliefontein	139	113	252	1,510	1,449	2,959	—	—	—	1,649	1,562	3,211	4·3
Richtersveld	349	294	643	424	377	801	240	229	469	1,013	900	1,913	1·6
	664	543	1,207	4,927	5,007	9,934	444	285	729	6,035	5,835	11,870	

the elementary family, or group of elementary families which trek together.

Culturally, Little Namaqualand is predominantly a farming community, although in terms of production, diamond and copper mining and fishing have become dominant economic activities during the past twenty years. As a result of industrial development and consequent urban expansion more and more opportunities are being made available for the employment of both the Coloured and White rural population in the towns and mines.

Yet in spite of the contacts which urbanisation has effected with the world outside, the true Namaqualander, White and non-White, is inclined still to regard his district as an independent country and looks upon all strangers and immigrants as foreigners. Perhaps it is not surprising that this attitude prevails because, as late as 1938, 93 per cent of the White population was Namaqualand-born, while two-thirds of the remainder came from other parts of the western Cape Province, as P. W. Kotzé has shown. Whereas isolation is without any doubt an important factor in the explanation of the attitudes and behaviour patterns in the area, there are other factors which have contributed to the character of the North-West.

When we look into the history of this part of South Africa, we find that the original occupiers were Khoi Khoin and Bushmen, and that it was pioneered by half-breed Voortrekkers (the Basters) and missionaries. The Basters drove out the Bushmen, making it safe and habitable for the Boers and later colonists who followed. Only recently have Bantu-speaking people (Africans), the majority of whom are temporary migrant mine-workers, arrived in the territory. Thus it is the pattern of social relationships and culture which developed mainly out of the Boer–Khoi Khoin complex that has made in Namaqualand and surrounding districts a people separate from the rest of South Africa.

Apart from the clashes with the Bushman bands, the history of the North-West is free of inter-group warfare, although conflicts and rivalries did sometimes occur. The tendency in this part of southern Africa was always towards integration, a phenomenon unusual on the eastern and north-eastern frontiers. In Little Namaqualand today manifestations of this process can be clearly seen. On the one hand there are the Coloured communities, consisting of peoples whose racial and cultural characteristics provide an example of the form of integration which resulted mainly from the contact of Cape Dutch and Khoi

Khoin. On the other hand there are the customs which the predominantly Afrikaans-speaking White peasantry have taken over from the Coloured people, and in former years from the Khoi Khoin. And, of course, there is the tremendous body of European customs that has been passed on in comparatively modern times to the non-White communities. There is no need to elaborate on the latter process, but to illustrate some of the influences which the Khoi Khoin tradition has had on the White peasantry we should realise that twenty years ago roughly 19 per cent of the Afrikaner farmers were living in Namaqua-type mat-houses,[12] and today Namaqua leechcraft and magic play a very important part in their daily lives.

Certain of these processes, which have been arrested in recent years by external forces, have been clearly stated by Dr. T. N. Hanekom in the *Eeufees-Gedenkboek (1850–1950)* of the Nederduitse Gereformeerde Kerk, although the author probably underestimates the influence of the Khoi Khoin and Basters on the cultural tradition of White inhabitants; and he fails to draw attention to the Coloured Reserves as examples of integration:

'Contact with interior native tribes during the northerly movement of our people must be noted as being of special significance [in South African history]. . . . For the history of the North-West, [this contact] was [also] of special significance. It is true that there are records in our frontier history of bloody battles with the notorious Bushmen, but in general we can speak of a peaceful process of conquest—a natural process of development which resulted ultimately in the European and the native inhabitants living together in the same territory. And although we cannot today point to many traces of reciprocal influence in these parts, yet there are indications that the Whites were influenced too in language and customs by the aboriginals, while the latter acquired an endless amount from the former.'[13]

THE COLOURED RESERVES

We have already shown that about half the members of the Coloured population of Little Namaqualand have their homes in the Reserves. These Reserves originated as mission-stations during the first half of the nineteenth century. Formal recognition was given to these mission-stations and the territory around them by the government of the Cape Colony in the shape of 'tickets of occupation' which afforded them

[12] P. W. Kotzé, *Namakwaland*, p. 86.
[13] From p. 21, translated from the Afrikaans.

a sort of guarantee of their lands. Komaggas was recognised in 1843, and the other stations shortly after the territory north of the Buffels River was annexed in 1847.[14]

A system of government developed in all these mission stations (except Richtersveld) in the form of an alliance between the missionary and the *raad* (council), the members of which were elected or appointed from certain sections of the population. The missionary presided over the raad. Although officially under the colonial government after the territory was annexed, these communities tended to rule themselves. Serious offences such as murder, rape, and assault, however, were supposed to be referred to the nearest Civil Commissioner, and towards the end of the nineteenth century field-cornetcies were established on certain of the mission-stations.

This period of relative autonomy in local affairs came to an end in these communities (except in Richtersveld) shortly after 1909, when the Communal Reserves and Mission Stations Act was enforced. This Act, which abolished the secular authority of the missionaries but retained certain features of the old raad, was, as Marais has pointed out, framed on the analogy of the Glen Grey Act of 1894 (and its amendments), applicable to the Bantu-speaking peoples in the eastern part of the Colony.

The 'racial' composition of the five Reserves in 1951 is set out in Table II on page 14. These figures, it must be noted, reflect the number of people in these areas on the day on which the census was taken, 8 May 1951. Thus, as regards the Coloured population we would have to add the number of migrant workers and other persons absent from home on this day if we wished to discover the total number of people claiming residence in these Reserves.[15]

[14] J. S. Marais, *The Cape Coloured People*, 1652-1937, London, Longmans, 1939, pp. 74-84, gives a useful description of the Reserves and their history. See also the Melvill Report (G. 60—1890), pp. 4-5, and Votes and Proceedings of Parliament, Cape of Good Hope, appendix 2, vol. II, A. 7—1896, pp. 1-4, *et passim*.

[15] See pp. 38 ff.

CHAPTER 2

FROM CAPTAIN TO SUPERINTENDENT

THE HISTORY[1] of the Steinkopf Reserve may be divided into four periods: the Khoi Khoin period (1800–40), when the territory was inhabited by a Khoi Khoin tribe and a few bands of Bushmen; the Baster and missionary period (1840–1913), when a more defined area was ruled by a Baster council presided over by a missionary-president; the period of European rule (1913–52); and a fourth period which began a decade ago, characterised also by European rule though in a new form. This period we call *die Afrikaner Kinders* (1952–?).

THE KHOI KHOIN PERIOD (1800–40)

At the beginning of the nineteenth century most of the territory known as Little Namaqualand was claimed by Kupido Witbooi, *kaptein*[2] of the /Hobesen tribe. But his land was too large for him to manage alone, and while he occupied the eastern section of the territory he appointed the heads of two other tribes as *onder-kapteins* (assistant-captains) to look after his interests in the central and western sections. The former he placed under the jurisdiction of Kaptein Vigiland Oorlam (who was later known as Abraham Vigiland), head of an offshoot of the Gei//Khauan, formerly the senior tribe of the Great Namaqua. The western section he put under Paul Links, an immigrant from the south who was acting-captain for a branch of the Swartbois. Later these two areas were named Steinkopf and Richtersveld.

All these Khoi Khoin living in Little Namaqualand at this time were known to the northern tribes as the Orlams.

The small bands of Bushman plunderers who roamed the territory at this time provided a constant threat to the security of Witbooi and his

[1] Cf. G. Meyer, 'Die Gemeente te Steinkopf', unpublished MS. (1927?).

[2] The use of the word kaptein by the Khoi Khoin for their chiefs is very old. Ten Rhyne (1686) tells us: 'Their officers they call, after our fashion, Captains. They differ from the rest, so far as dress is concerned, only in the splendour of their kaross'—William Ten Rhyne, 'A Short Account of the Cape of Good Hope and of the Hottentots who inhabit that Region', in *The Early Cape Hottentots*, Van Riebeeck Society, vol. 14, 1933, p. 135. In a footnote I. Schapera states: 'This term was introduced by the Dutch, who called the headman of every large Hottentot kraal 'kapitein' (a practice later adopted by the Hottentots themselves), and on entering into an alliance with him gave him a copperheaded cane, which henceforth was regarded as a distinguishing badge of authority.'

1   A GENERAL VIEW OF STEINKOPF VILLAGE
The church is in the centre

2   ONDERSTRAAT

3 PART OF BOSTRAAT

4 REPAIRING CARTS AND WAGONS IN A HAMLET

assistant-Captains, for they found the Khoi Khoin easier prey than the
Basters and the Dutch (both of whom possessed guns) in the south.
There were few White men in Little Namaqualand at this time, apart
from a few hunters and explorers who occasionally passed through.

During the first two decades of the nineteenth century two important
events took place in Little Namaqualand, events which were
responsible for remoulding the former pattern of social relationships.
The first was the northerly migration of Baster families who had
hitherto lived mainly in the southern half of the north-western Cape
Colony. The Basters were the descendants of Dutch colonist and
frontiersman fathers, and Namaqua and Cape Khoi Khoin mothers.[3]
Their culture was neither Khoi Khoin nor Dutch but is best described
as a synthesis of the two traditions. They considered themselves superior
to their maternal ancestors and tended to marry amongst themselves,
although some did marry Khoi Khoin women while others again were
absorbed back into the ranks of the Dutch. These Basters, who were
the Voortrekkers of Little Namaqualand,[4] were largely responsible
for defeating and driving out the Bushman, and in certain communities
they also usurped the power of the Khoi Khoin. The vanguard of the
trek in that part of the territory under the jurisdiction of Abraham
Vigiland settled at Besondermeid, a few miles south of the present
village of Steinkopf.

The second event was the arrival in 1805 of the London Missionary
Society (L.M.S.).[5] Operating both north and south of the Orange
River, they began converting the heathen and carrying out those
secular duties usually associated with mission work. Between 1810
and 1816 they established a station at Besondermeid where the Basters
had settled. It is probable that they chose this site because the Basters
had guns and they could protect them from the sorties of the Bushmen,
and also because these 'half breeds' would have been familiar with at
least some of the tenets of Christian teaching; and they spoke Dutch.

The immediate problem that the early missionaries had to solve was
not that of introducing Christian beliefs to a pagan people, but of

[3] Cf. W. P. Carstens, 'Basters', in *Encyclopedia of Southern Africa* (to be published
in 1967). E. Fischer, *Die Rehobother Bastards und das Bastardierungsproblem beim
Menschen*, 1913, p. 41, *et passim*.

[4] J. S. Marais, *The Cape Coloured People*, p. 11. P. J. van der Merwe, *Trek*,
Kaapstad, 1945, p. 207.

[5] Cf. J. du Plessis, *A History of Christian Missions in South Africa*, 1911, pp. 112-19.
J. A. Heese, *Onderwys in Namakwaland*, 1942, pp. 132-3, *et passim*.

keeping in touch with a scattered nomadic population. Conversion appears in fact to have been effected relatively easily. One of the explanations of this phenomenon may be that the Khoi Khoin's traditional conceptions of God and the Devil were close enough to Christian ideas to enable these pagans to grasp the new religious concepts easily. But we should stress the most important factor that traditionally Khoi Khoin chiefs and captains had few ritual functions, so that in the field of religion the possibility of rivalry was unlikely.[6] There were other factors as well. In the first place, the Basters and many of the Khoi Khoin had been in contact with the Dutch tradition in former years when they lived in the southern part of the western Cape. Secondly, the Khoi Khoin tribes had lost a great deal of their former cohesion in the conflicts of the frontier society, and the Baster families were without any form of central authority. Thus the London Missionaries did not have to compete with powerful leaders as did their colleagues in other parts of Africa.

The L.M.S. preached the Gospel periodically in Little Namaqualand until 1838, 'but gave it up as they thought this dry and barren land was not fit for erecting fixed stations in it. And . . . as the Rhenish Mission Society intended to commence mission work in Great Namaqua, Damara and Ovamboland, etc., they (the L.M.S.) left this land and gave it to the Rhenish Society.'[7] This was how the Rhenish Mission Society (R.M.S.) took over the work of the L.M.S.

When the R.M.S. began its work in Steinkopf in 1840, the seeds of a Christian community had already been sown by their predecessors: a scattered 'congregation' existed, but no church, in the sense that there was no cohesive religious institution. Not every inhabitant of the territory was a baptised Christian but the impression given by the early missionaries such as Backhouse, Brecher, and Kitchinman, is that many were active converts.

At this time there were three distinct groups of people living in the territory now known as Steinkopf: the original Khoi Khoin, the Basters, and a few Bushman bands.

The Khoi Khoin were united under the leadership of Kaptein Abraham Vigiland, who, with the aid of his council ruled the territory. Witbooi does not appear to have interfered with the internal government of Steinkopf, although, when he heard that Basters had settled

<hr/>

[6] I. Schapera, *Government and Politics in Tribal Societies*, London, 1956, p. 83.

[7] The Reverend F. Brecher's petition to the Honourable the Speaker and the Members of the House of Assembly (1891).

at Besondermeid, he visited Kobus Engelbrecht, the leader of these Basters, and made it quite clear that Vigiland was his (Witbooi's) official representative in this part of the territory. Vigiland's council consisted of the senior male of each clan, and each clan seems also to have had its own council. Thus in Little Namaqualand at this time there were three main Orlam tribes, and although one of them claimed seniority over the others, each was in practice a separate political community. Witbooi may have claimed to control the whole territory, but in fact he did not, mainly because the area was too large for him to administer, and also because the traditional tribal affiliations south of the Orange River had been reorganised. In Steinkopf, Vigiland was the acknowledged political leader of the Orlam Khoi Khoin who lived in the central part of Little Namaqualand north of the Buffels River. This territory was considered as belonging to the political community (the tribe), though each clan usually had claim to a spring or water-hole. Little is known of Vigiland's powers and duties as kaptein, but they appear, according to local historians, and in the light of certain R.M.S. documents to have been limited to matters which affect the community as a whole: he presided over the tribal council and mobilised the men during Bushman raids. The headmen of the clans were responsible for matters affecting the members of their clans; they settled disputes with the assistance of other senior men, and organised the cleaning of water-holes and springs.[8]

When the missionaries arrived at Steinkopf, the Orlam Khoi Khoin were still a semi-nomadic pastoral people, keeping cattle, sheep, and goats, and their staple diet was meat and milk augmented by *veldkos* (wild vegetable foods). The social structure of the community in general also appears to have resembled very closely the pattern described by Schapera for the Khoi Khoin as a whole. The Basters too were a semi-nomadic pastoral people, but they also grew wheat, a practice they had learnt from the London Missionaries. The ranks of the Bushmen had by this time been greatly depleted by the Basters, but were still a constant source of danger to the latter and the Khoi Khoin.

THE BASTER AND MISSIONARY PERIOD (1840–1913)

Probably the turning point in the history of Steinkopf at this time was the arrival, in 1843, of a very young and energetic missionary,

[8] For a discussion of the powers and duties of other Khoi Khoin chiefs, see: I. Schapera, *The Khoisan Peoples of South Africa*, pp. 328-36, and *Government and Politics in Tribal Societies*, pp. 82-5.

Ferdinand Brecher, who was to play a major role in the social life of the community up to the time of his death in 1902. One of the first things that Brecher did was to move the station's headquarters from Besondermeid to an uninhabited area between the Baster and Khoi Khoin settlements, where there were two good springs. Here he built a church and a mission house with the help of the Christians. He established a proper school and encouraged more extensive agriculture. Here at Kookfontein (later called Steinkopf) were the beginnings of a settled community and village life. Religion and education, which had formerly tended to be confined to the family, now became communal activities. And not only were different lineages brought together, but Khoi Khoin and Basters (and a few Bushmen) worshipped in the newly-constructed church and attended school together. Thus, largely through the establishment of these two institutions, a school and a church, the way was paved for two separate communities, Khoi Khoin and Baster, to become fused together in a common society. Another factor which helped to unite these two groups was their common enemy, the Bushman. But the process of fusion was not without conflicts and jealousies. The Khoi Khoin on the one hand, resented the presence of the Basters whom they saw as political rivals, while the latter were not prepared to remain subservient to an 'inferior' people.

One of the results of the tension was that Kaptein Vigiland left Steinkopf with a large section of his people to search for a new tract of country in South West Africa. It is probable also that, although he was a Christian, he resented the growing power of the missionary as a secular leader in the community.

In his absence, Vigiland was obliged to entrust the territory to the care of Jacobus Engelbrecht, who had risen to senior position on the council. In this connection there is a legend which illustrates very clearly the attitude of the Basters to the Khoi Khoin. We are told that, as Vigiland's wagon moved off in the direction of South West Africa, Engelbrecht turned his back, and tearing up the document authorising him to act as kaptein, muttered, 'Ek sal nie onder 'n Hottentot staan nie!' (I refuse to submit to the authority of a Hottentot.)

Vigiland returned some years later with only a few of the families that had gone with him. He died the same day after drinking a cup of very strong tea, a luxury he was never able to resist. We discussed the cause of the old kaptein's death many times while I was at Steinkopf, and the evidence suggests that he was poisoned by an enemy. This was never actually mentioned, but an old man who has the reputation for being a good and reliable historian said to me one day during my last visit while we were having tea together, 'You know, there is one thing I have not told you: tea alone has never killed anybody yet!'

After Vigiland's death in 1840 Jacobus Engelbrecht became kaptein as the former had no son to succeed him, and Engelbrecht had acted in this capacity during his absence. With the passing of the *kapteinskap* to the Basters, the Khoi Khoin lost not only their power, but also their representation on the community's council. Political power was now in the hands of the Basters and the missionary, who became president of the council.

Four years after Brecher's arrival at Kookfontein, now called Steinkopf, the boundary of the Cape Colony was extended from the Buffels River to the Orange, and the captains of Little Namaqualand became British subjects. This is how Brecher describes the annexation in his petition of 1891:

'The natives of the land were a freed people and were against the extension of the Colony from the Buffel's to the Orange River, but when, in 1846, the Government intended to extend the boundary, the natives were requested by the Civil Commissioner and Resident Magistrate, Mr. Ryneveld of Clanwilliam, whether they would like to become British subjects or not. I advised them to give their consent to this request on account that the British Government was a good Christian Government which would do them no harm but protect them, against anyone who might like to do them wrong. So the Captains[9] of Steinkopf (Jakobus Engelbrecht) and the Orange River (Paul Links) gave their consent to the proposition of the Government, and my Captain at Steinkopf said, "*Wat de groote Baas wil doen, daar kunnen wy niet voor, wy met ons volk onderwerpen ons aan de koningin met deze condisië, dat Harer Majestyds Gouvernement voor ons en ons volk onzen van ouds af bewoonden grond moet beschermen tegen Boeren en anderen die niet van ons zijn, opdat wy een gerust stil en eerlyk leven voeren kannen.*"[10] These words I told His Excellency, Governor Barkly, when His Excellency paid us a visit in August 1873, and which words

[9] Kupido Witbooi had crossed the Orange River with his tribe earlier.

[10] 'What the great Master wishes to do I do not know; I and my people, submit ourselves to the Queen on these conditions, that her Majesty's Government shall protect us and our land, which we have occupied from olden days, from Boers and others who are alien to us, so that we may live peacefully and honestly.'

to hear pleased His Excellency very much. By this opportunity His Excellency, the Governor, said to me, "Mr. Brecher, you must have a good community, as Mr. Boyes, the Magistrate at Springbok, told me that as long as he has been magistrate at Springbok, never a case has come before him from Steinkopf." '

Annexation was proclaimed on 17 December 1847, and Steinkopf as part of Little Namaqualand fell under the sovereignty of Great Britain. But for ten years little if any contact was established between the Government of the Cape Colony and the community of Steinkopf, where Kaptein Jacobus Engelbrecht, assisted by the missionary, still ruled. In 1856, however, a Civil Commissioner and Resident Magistrate was appointed to take charge of the newly created fiscal division of Little Namaqualand, and from his headquarters at Springbokfontein (now Springbok) this official administered the Khoi Khoin, Basters, Dutch and Bushmen inhabiting the territory. Field-cornetcies were established, and as far as Steinkopf and other 'native' areas were concerned, a period of indirect rule began.

Jacobus Engelbrecht, who had held the position of kaptein in his community, was officially appointed field-cornet and received a salary of £12 per year from the Colonial Secretary. This appointment abolished the title of *kaptein* and with it, in theory, if not in practice, the traditional authority of its holder. Through this method of adminis-tration the Civil Commissioner was of the opinion that the 'natives' would gradually 'become subservient to our laws and customs'.

There does not appear to have been much interference in local affairs by the colonial government, except that all regulations for the management of the community were subject to its approval, and the right to search for and mine ores, metals, other minerals, and precious stones was reserved for persons authorised by it. Act 10 of 1870 gave the regulations the force of law, but Act 29 of 1881 repealed it and the regulations officially fell away with it. Thus from 1881 to 1913, when the Mission Stations and Communal Reserves Act was enforced, local regulations existed without the legal backing of any outside authority. Nevertheless, all cases of 'murder, rape, and theft' were required by law to be brought before the Civil Commissioner and Resident Magistrate.

Although Steinkopf, which at this time included Concordia, was proclaimed a Reserve in 1874, boundary disputes have not been satisfactorily settled owing to the fact that the proposals of the numerous surveyors were never accepted by Parliament. Even today the older inhabitants of Steinkopf look at their shrunken boundaries as a reminder of a period in their history when they should have questioned the White man's word.

A separate volume could be devoted entirely to boundary disputes and the period of indirect rule which followed the annexation of Little Namaqualand, but for our purposes we should regard the years between 1847 and 1913 as the period during which the present boundaries of the Steinkopf Reserve were determined, and the then central government prepared the way for the enforcement of the Mission Stations and Communal Reserves Act and its subsequent amendments. This Act, as we shall see later, placed a community which was originally independent under the full authority, though in a disguised form, of the government of the Union of South Africa. The aspirations of the first Civil Commissioner and Resident Magistrate in the area have in fact been fulfilled.

During the years following Kaptein Vigiland's death and the Basters' sudden rise to power, a system of government developed which was characterised by the close co-operation between the Church and the community's council or raad. The missionary, in addition to being the head of the Church, became president of the raad, and carried out his work in this dual capacity until the Mission Stations and Communal Reserves Act effected the separation of power between Church and 'State'. This system of government is of great importance in understanding not only the political system of contemporary Steinkopf, but also many other aspects of its social structure. Further, a large number of the tensions which occur today are the result of enforced legislation which conflicts with established practices and values.

In 1870 some of the laws and regulations enforced by the raad were written down by the missionary-president for the approval of the Civil Commissioner, under the title of 'Short rules laid down for the Rhenish Mission Institution of Steinkopf, Namaqualand'.[11]

The raad consisted of eight people, the missionary-president, the field-cornet or *veldkornet* (the former kaptein) and six councillors, styled corporals or *korporale*. It ruled the whole community and all other people living in the territory of Steinkopf in all matters, having judicial, legislative and executive powers.

'For this object [they chose] the best Law Book in the world as

[11] See Appendix C in W. P. Carstens, 'The Community of Steinkopf', unpublished Ph.D. thesis, University of Cape Town, 1961, for a transcript of these laws and regulations.

[their] adviser and guide, namely the Holy Scripture or Holy Bible, which is the revealed word of God. According to this book [were] judged and decided all cases and differences between parties of the community, however, with the understanding that if any person or persons [were not] satisfied with the decision of the council, such person or persons [were] at liberty to seek their right at the local court of the magistrate or Supreme Court.'

The missionary-president's position on the raad must be seen as the complement to that of the veldkornet. He performed the role of adviser to the latter, but never interfered with any of his decisions or the decisions of the raad. He does not appear to have had a vote on the raad, but always acted as chairman at meetings.

When the colonial government interfered or attempted to interfere in local affairs, the missionary-president advised the raad how best to cope with the difficulty. Hence we find a regular correspondence between him and the Colonial Secretary in Cape Town over questions such as boundary disputes and Boer encroachment. Further, it was he who initiated the agitation and wrote a petition to the Governor after the second assistant surveyor-general had recommended without consulting the raad that a system of individual land tenure should replace the old communal system.[12]

The missionary-president was essentially an integrated member of Steinkopf society and his only face-to-face contacts with members of his own cultural tradition were occasional meetings with other missionaries. Thus, as a member of the community, and as a person who had had experience of the European tradition, he was well-equipped both socially and intellectually for his special role in the political field.

The veldkornet was the senior member of the raad and the traditional leader of the community. His title, as we have already pointed out, was given to him by the colonial government, and replaced the former title of kaptein. His position as senior councillor was an hereditary office but was supposed to be confirmed by a popular vote. This confirmation was required by the colonial government, but it is unlikely that it ever took place. His activities in political affairs were of a dual nature. As veldkornet he was responsible to the Civil Commissioner, to whom he was supposed to refer all cases of murder, rape and theft, and he had power of arrest, a power which he seldom used on his own people. As senior councillor in Steinkopf he com-

[12] Melvill Report. G. 60–1890.

manded great respect and wielded great authority; he was one man whom everyone, old and young, obeyed, and a legend has it that he used to forbid the Civil Commissioner to interfere with his people. The veldkornet's power, therefore, came from two sources, the colonial government and the community of Steinkopf. He retained only some of the power of the traditional kaptein, but the fact that he belonged to the Engelbrecht lineage gave him added prestige. The Engelbrechts resemble in physical type their Dutch rather than their Khoi Khoin forebears; they were the first of the Baster Voortrekkers to reach Steinkopf, and, as we have said, they were largely responsible for killing off or driving away the 'wild' Bushmen with the aid of their guns.

The rest of the raad consisted of six councillors, known as *korporale*, who sat on the council with the veldkornet and the president. Each of these councillors was nominated by the members of a *wyk* (ward), a territorial division, and elected at a general meeting of *burghers*.[13] Korporale once elected held office for life.

Electoral procedure began with general discussions among the members of the *wyk*. This was followed shortly afterwards by an informal local meeting at which a senior burgher would be nominated, but his appointement as korporaal was always subject to confirmation at a general meeting where he would be automatically elected.

Conflicts, we are told, did sometimes arise in the nomination of korporale where the burghers of a *wyk* were divided in the selection of their nominee. But these conflicts were resolved locally, and no case is reported of an opposing candidate being proposed at a general meeting which merely gave its formal approval to nominations.

The Church–State alliance was not characterised merely by the fact that the missionary sat on both the raad and the Kerkraad (Church Council). Apart from its religious functions, the latter body did also have clearly defined judicial functions which were subordinate to the raad. The Kerkraad in fact used also to be known as the *sagteraad* (lenient council) because cases were often brought before it instead of going to the higher court. Of course, when it failed to find a satisfactory solution the matter was automatically referred to the raad. This principle of different levels of authority may be extended still further when we consider the fact that all offences were dealt with first in the

[13] The burghers consisted of the male heads of those elementary families who had full status as members of the community. Newcomers to the community were called 'strangers', and had to apply to the raad for burgher status.

family or lineage, before being handed over to a higher authority. An illustration of the close connection between Church and community affairs is clearly seen in the 'Rules laid down for Burghers and Christians of the Community of Steinkopf regarding the Vice of Fornication or Adultery'.

Whenever Fornication or Adultery in the Community may be committed, which God graciously may prevent, be it done by married or unmarried persons, Members of the Church or Heathens it shall be punished in the following manner viz:

1   When committed by members of the Church it shall be dealt with them according to the Standard Rules of the Church & these Rules.

2   When committed by Heathens with members of the Church it shall be dealt with them as stated above, viz: according to the Rules of the Church & these Rules.

3   When married people, being Heathens or Christians, commit Adultery or Fornication then both shall be flogged by the Councillors, likewise shall be done if one party is a Christian & the other a Heathen.

4   When young unmarried persons being Heathen or Christians commit Fornication or Adultery, they shall marry each other according to the Holy Scriptures Exodus 22, 16, 17 & Deut. 22, 28, 29 and if they do so they shall not be punished bodily, but if they not do so, they shall be flogged by their Parents, or in case of having no more Parents, by their nearest Relations in the presence of Two Councillors.

On behalf of the Council
F. Brecher

Missionary & President of the Council.
Steinkopf
January 1870

Although the Kerkraad and the raad carried out their duties separately, they were not really separate bodies, for the missionary was chairman of both, and familiar with all their activities. Thus he merely changed his role depending on which council he was presiding over: he was one individual but two persons. Further, there was always a duplication of members on both councils. It was customary, as it is today, for one member of the Kerkraad to be represented on the raad, although in practice there were always two or three. These individuals who served on both councils merely changed their roles like the missionary.

The functions of the raad were numerous. Its local duties consisted of the administration of the law, control of land and grazing, the organisation of public services, taxation, finance and welfare. A great deal of its time was taken up with external affairs: settling disputes with the Dutch farmers, who grazed their animals illegally on Steinkopf territory, dealing with boundary disputes, and watching the movements of prospectors who had no regard for private or public property.

Although it had certain obligations towards the colonial government the raad was really an autonomous body, governing an isolated community whose members believed blindly that the Queen would protect them for all time *tegen boeren en anderen*.[14] But they could not know that towards the end of the century their future would be determined for them by the Cape Parliament.[15]

THE PERIOD OF EUROPEAN RULE (1913–52)

The Baster–missionary period came to an end in 1913, when the Mission Stations and Communal Reserves Act, no. 29 of 1909 was enforced, and today the Steinkopf Reserve is administered in accordance with this Act and its subsequent amendments. Even before 1913 the central government began to assert its authority. In 1911 the Civil Commissioner, Mr. D. C. Giddy, received a deputation from the raad concerning his refusal to approve their action of granting Solomon Rabinowitz permission to trade at Steinkopf. Mr. Giddy was requested to withdraw his decision, but he refused.

The provisions of this legislation were the outcome of a number of special reports and proposals which had been submitted to the Colonial Office. The Act was officially designed to 'provide for the better management and control of certain mission stations and certain lands reserved for the occupation of certain tribes or communities and for the granting of titles to the inhabitants of such stations and reserves'. In practice, the immediate effects of the Act were to abolish the former autonomy of the raad, and to recognise boundaries which had never been agreed to by the inhabitants.

New immigrants into Namaqualand in the twentieth century were not interested in farming in semi-desert but in mining and prospecting. As early as 1873, Professor Noble had said that O'okiep was 'beyond

[14] Against Boers and others.

[15] See Votes and Proceedings of Parliament (A. 7—1896).

doubt the richest copper mine in the world'. Companies had been formed, and prospectors and miners had come from all parts of the world in search of new copper deposits and other base metals. The discovery of diamonds in South West Africa had aroused the curiosity of prospectors in Namaqualand. This interest in mining made it necessary for the government to control the territory more effectively in the interests of the mineral hunters. The Act settled for all time the right of outsiders to mine or prospect in any part of the territory, provided they had the permission of the central government. Thus it prohibited the 'natives' of the territory from any legal claim to mineral rights on the land which was reserved for them.

The main effect of the Act in Steinkopf, however, was that it separated the powers of the Church and the raad. The political status and power of the missionary was transferred to the Resident Magistrate who became chairman of the Management Board which now superseded the raad. Nevertheless, in spite of this particular loss of political power, the Church did retain some connexion with local government through the fact that the mission society was required to nominate one of the members for appointment to the Management Board.

The composition of the Management Board was similar to that of the former raad in that six councillors were elected by the people, but in addition to these elected members, the Minister appointed three members, two of whom were regarded as government representatives, and one was nominated by the mission society. Further, the Management Board was to meet under the chairmanship of the magistrate, who had a deliberative as well as a casting vote.

The powers and duties of the Management Board and the procedure for its election were based on the provisions of the Villages Management Act, 1881, and the Health Amendment Act, 1897, in addition to special regulations laid down in the main Act. Briefly, these powers and duties were the distribution of land, the control of grazing, the collection of taxes, public services, trading, public health, prohibition of beer drinks and the suppression of 'heathenish practices' (sic).

The broader sociological effects of the Act of 1909 in Steinkopf can be seen from the events leading up to its enforcement. When the report reached the community that the Act was to be introduced, a message was sent to the Civil Commissioner at Springbok making it quite clear to him that the burghers of Steinkopf were unwilling even to consider the new Act, because they felt that it would interfere with

the rights they had inherited from their ancestors. The Civil Commissioner did not reply, but he called a meeting on 15 November 1910,
for the purpose of explaining the Act. On the day appointed he
arrived at the mission village with a bodyguard of twelve armed
policemen, and we are told that before the meeting began, the police
were ordered out of the hall by Jacobus Engelbrecht, the veldkornet.
The meeting was attended by the missionary, all the raad members and
250 burghers. The Act was explained in the Dutch language, questions
put and answered, and the Civil Commissioner, Mr. Giddy, was
thanked by the burghers for his visit and for explaining the Act to
them. 'Now that they understood the effect which the Act would
have on Steinkopf Reserve, they would meet again shortly and then
request their raad to communicate with the Civil Commissioner.'

This meeting was an important one, for it showed that there was a
tendency in Steinkopf to co-operate with the central government in
spite of their former adamant refusal even to consider the Act. But
more important than this was the effect which the meeting had on
the Khoi Khoin. Steinkopf, it will be remembered, had been ruled by a
Khoi Khoin tribe before the Basters had gained power, and the 1909
Act gave the Khoi Khoin an opportunity to regain some of their lost
power. Within six weeks of this meeting they had sent a deputation
to the Civil Commissioner, which he records in his minutes:

'Carolus Jantjies, Jacob Barlie (*sic*), Gert Jantjies, Jan Barlie, Hermanus
Engelbrecht, Burghers of Steinkopf, visited me this day and expressed
their dissatisfaction at the state of affairs at Steinkopf. They state that they
are the original Namaqua[16] or so-called Hottentots and have no one to
represent them on the raad, that the raad is letting the communal
ground for grazing to outsiders and also certain plough-lands to
farmers.

'The Namaqua request that the Civil Commissioner be their
chairman of council and that the missionary be chairman of the Church
affairs only, but they do not want the 1909 Act proclaimed.'

This deputation was a success, for we find that when a temporary
raad was formed to make arrangements for the enforcement of the 1909
Act, Carolus Jantjies was appointed by the Civil Commissioner as a
government representative; and when the Management Board was
constituted on 14 November 1913, Jacob Balie was elected by the
community as the Namaqua korporaal.

[16] i.e. the descendants of those people who were once united under Kaptein
Vigiland.

What really united the Namaqua with the Basters was their agreement over the principle that the Church should not interfere in local government. Already in 1907 we find some members of the raad objecting to the missionary having similar privileges to burghers, privileges to which he had been accustomed in the past. It appears, therefore, that the *only* reason why the burghers of Steinkopf eventually accepted the Act (although they did so under protest) was because it made provision for the separation of the powers of the Church and the raad. This interpretation is supported by the fact that at a general meeting of burghers in July 1911 'Baster' Jacobus Engelbrecht and 'Namaqua' Nikolas Vries proposed that the new Act be not accepted. This proposal was unanimously agreed to, mainly on the ground that the burghers were not in favour of the transfer of property to the Rhenish Mission Society. In other words, at this stage of development, the society was ripe for accepting the formal separation of Church from 'State', though the Namaqua and the Basters did so for different reasons.

The desire on the part of the Basters to separate the Church from the raad was motivated by their desire for more independence and power. The community had become better integrated, and through the process of social adaptation, more developed; and the Basters no longer felt it necessary to rely on missionary and Church support to maintain their dominant position. They were in fact wrong because thereafter their power in the community declined. On the other hand, the Namaqua burghers desired the separation of powers because they wanted to have the Civil Commissioner as their leader and chairman, since they had been subjected to Baster domination for nearly seventy years and saw him as a sympathetic outsider who would deal with all groups impartially.

Thus the Mission Stations and Communal Reserves Act marked the beginnings of a new era in Steinkopf. It marked the positive inter-ference of the central government in the affairs of Steinkopf, and it largely effected the separation of the powers of Church and State. It also helped to place the Namaqua on an equal political footing with the Basters, and marked the end of the Baster régime and the Engelbrechts' leadership. Finally, it created fresh conflicts and tensions between lineages. Formerly, each large lineage or group of lineages could have only one representative on the raad. Now, government appointments in addition to the elected members made it possible for certain lineages to have more than one representative and, as a result thereof, to wield more power than before. Further manifestations of this redistribution of power is reflected in the class-structure of the present-day community.

We should add here that the tendency of the burghers to support the separation of the powers of Church and State was partly reversed on 4 August 1913 (a few months before the Act was enforced), by which time they had begun to understand fully the implications of the new legislation. At a general meeting of the burghers of Steinkopf, a resolution was unanimously passed stating that they saw 'no chance to adopt any new Management unless the Government of the Union of South Africa' met their wishes, which they laid down. The first of these was 'to appoint *no* Superintendent over Steinkopf and Richtersveld Territory, but to allow the Communities to appoint or elect their own Superintendent or Local Chairman in the person of their Missionary at the time being, as it was the case hitherto since 1842'. Later, however, it is made clear in the same resolution that any future Board will have no right to interfere with Church property which belonged to the congregation.

This resolution, which was a protest against outside interference with traditional rights, was sent to the Governor-General of South Africa. Many of the points raised were reformulated in 1928, fifteen years later, when a memorandum was submitted to the Native Affairs Commission, which was visiting the Namaqualand Reserves. The Commission reported its findings in 1932, pointing out, *inter alia*, 'that the system of government brought into operation under Act No. 29 of 1909 had not been a success'.

Few significant changes were made in the legislation affecting Steinkopf between the years 1913 and 1952, although there were subsequent amendments to the original Act. One amendment, however, did effect the replacement of the magistrate as chairman of the Management Board by a superintendent, another White official.

The R.M.S. continued its religious work in Steinkopf until 1934, when, owing to the fact that it was unable to draw funds from Germany, it had either to find a successor or leave the community without a minister. The first alternative was chosen and the Nederduitse Gereformeerde Kerk agreed to take over the religious work in the Reserve, for this Church adhered to the same theological principles as did the Rhenish missionaries.

The transition from one Church to another was not effected smoothly. There was considerable opposition from the congregation to the religious jurisdiction of the *Boere Kerk* (Dutchmen's Church) in spite of the doctrinal similarities. As an alternative, a few people were in favour of joining the Anglican Church, and some the Roman Catholic, but the bulk of the congregation were too emotionally bound to *the* Church, even to think of alternatives; they were merely opposed on principle to the N.G. Kerk for political reasons.

While matters were being debated, the moving spirit of the Griqua Independent Church, the Rev. Mr. Le Fleur, described in Steinkopf as *'n bruinman met 'n agterstevoor koller* (a Coloured man with a back-to-front collar), appeared at Steinkopf with new promises of eternal salvation—and ways of recovering from the government land which had been expropriated.[17] In spite of the suspicion with which Le Fleur was regarded locally, he attracted a large number of followers from whom he collected considerable sums of money and livestock, but his influence was not strong enough to break down the Rhenish Calvinist tradition. And those people whom he did attract soon rejected his Church and his teaching, not merely because they had lost money and livestock, but, as one man told me, 'because he wanted us to be too familiar with one another; we were not used to his kissing and embracing'. A further deterrent appears to have been that several of his followers died, one suddenly became blind, and many fell sick. It is said that the man who went blind, and the sick, recovered only after they had rejected Le Fleur altogether!

Le Fleur's visit did, however, have one very important effect. It inspired a number of people to become active political agitators by giving impetus to the ill-feeling and antagonism towards the central government which had already been brought about by the 1909 Act, and he made people more conscious of the land that had been expropriated in former years.

Those who wished to have the Roman Catholic Church in preference to the N.G. Kerk were soon deterred by recollections of their Church training, which had always warned them of the dangers and evils of Roman Catholicism.

Although there was this opposition to the N.G. Kerk, the transition from the Rhenish to the N.G. Kerk was eventually successful. The Church has flourished and there are more confirmed members in proportion to the total population than ever before. Apart from the few who still regard themselves as 'Rhenish', most people have overcome their antagonism towards the Boere Kerk by their belief

[17] Cf. Report into the Rebellion of the Bondelzwarts, U.G. 16—1923, p. 26.

5 A POOR MAN'S HARVEST
A single bag of grain brought in to Steinkopf village from an outlying hamlet

6 A BASTER
A member of lineage category A

7 A NAMAQUA
A member of lineage category B

8 'NEW PEOPLE'
A school-teacher and her mother and brother

10 A CONSERVATIVE
HOUSEWIFE COLLECTING
WOOD

9 CHILDREN'S ART AND HANDWORK
An exhibition at the Steinkopf High School

that it is not the man who preaches, but God, who works through him.

DIE AFRIKANER KINDERS (1952–)

On 1 April 1952 Steinkopf entered a new historical period. From this day its control and administration, together with that of the other Namaqualand Reserves, fell under the newly created Division of Coloured Affairs. This transfer from its former controlling bodies, the Department of Native Affairs (1913–44) and the Department of Social Welfare (1944–54), placed the members of the community among the ranks of other Coloured people who inhabit various other parts of South Africa, notably the western Cape Province.

The same day that this change in administration took place, one of the registered occupiers, a former principal of the Steinkopf Primary School, was appointed superintendent in place of the White official who had held the post before him. To the conservative people who still cherish the traditions of the last century (period 2) this appointment was symbolic of a trend which developed after the enforcement of the Act of 1909, namely the growth of a class of 'new people' who have rejected their former heritage and become 'Europeanised'. These 'new people' are known as *die Afrikaner kinders*, because they aspire to associate themselves with the Afrikaans tradition of the Republic of South Africa.

The 'new people' dominate nearly every aspect of social life at the present time. They are a power group that has emerged as the former mission village has developed the characteristics of a small town, where associations based on common interests have superseded the former bonds of kinship. Not only has this most recent period in Steinkopf's history helped to crystallise the trends implicit in a former period, but it has also brought with it more rigid laws and regulations which stem from the central government of South Africa, and which receive the tacit approval of the power group of 'new people' through the Management Board. Thus the phrase *die Afrikaner kinders*, coined by the conservative sages, provides a very apt description of modern Steinkopf.

On 25 October 1957 the Act of 1909 was superseded by the Coloured Mission Stations and Reserves Amendment Act, no. 35 of 1955. The new Act retains the form of the earlier legislation, but one of the subjoined regulations, which is at present being enforced by the Management Board, has curtailed the political and religious freedom of all people in the community. No political meeting of more than five persons can now take place in the Reserve unless special permission is given in writing by the Commissioner for Coloured Affairs or the magistrate. Nor, under the same conditions, can any religious service be held by any person or body, other than those connected with the established Church, Die Nederduitse Gereformeerde Sendingkerk.

CHAPTER 3

THE ECONOMY

THE CHIEF economic activity of the early inhabitants of Steinkopf (both Khoi Khoin and Baster) was, as we have seen, herding. The staple diet was meat and milk, augmented with various kinds of *veldkos*, and locusts during famine. In winter the families were scattered over the western section of the territory, moving east in summer.

The advent of the early missionaries was responsible for many of the changes in the economy in subsequent years. What had been a semi-nomadic pastoral people now rapidly began to take on some of the characteristics of a settled community consisting of mixed-farmers. The establishment of a church and a school by the missionaries stimulated the growth of a village, while the introduction of the plough and cultivation made it possible for people to live more securely in one place than they had before.

The influence of the missionaries, however, must be regarded only as a contributory factor in bringing about the present-day economic pattern. Amongst the other factors, we must include: the diffusion of new ideas through contact with traders and other Europeans; the Anglo-Boer War;[1] the effects of the opening up of the copper, and

[1] Reporting on the changes in the economic and social life in the Namaqualand Reserves, the Native Affairs Commission which visited Steinkopf in 1928 made the following comments:

'The Anglo-Boer War brought about disturbing factors. The residents of the Reserves were employed as transport riders, their oxen, wagons and stock were purchased for military needs, money became plentiful and with a people practically unversed in handling cash, the money received was frittered away. Thus at the close of the war the natural assets of the Reserves—cattle, sheep and goats—had greatly decreased and the cash for them was spent. Then in 1904–1906 came the Hottentot-Rebellion in German South-West Africa, where there was money in transport riding. Cattle and small stock were sold to purchase mules and wagons, money again became plentiful and was easily spent. On the sudden conclusion of hostilities the people were saddled with wagons and mules to them now practically valueless with the resultant effect of greater poverty. This was the common testimony of all the leading residents.

'New needs had been created by this contact with the outside world, new ideas had entered the Reserves, and naturally the patriarchal system began to fail. Poverty also began to appear, so the wants of the people increased and their ability to meet these needs decreased.' (Report of the Native Affairs Commission, U.G. 26, 1932, p. 5.)

later, the diamond mines, i.e. migratory wage-earning labour; natural increase of the population, and immigration; impoverishment of the soil due to bad methods of agriculture and over-stocking; the disappearance of cattle and introduction of donkeys at the beginning of the century; and the effects of legislation, notably the Mission Stations and Communal Reserves Act and its subsequent amendments.

In the contemporary community the economic system may be described as mixed. Some families plough and reap, herd goats and sheep, while one or more of the members of each family may go to work on the mines or in the towns to augment the meagre profits derived from mixed-farming; others keep only a few goats and rely largely on the wages earned by their migrant workers; others rely entirely on the earnings derived from migratory labour. As an alternative to the latter occupations, some people find permanent employment in the village as school-teachers, shopkeepers and shop-assistants, administrative assistants, and labourers, while a few are self-employed as builders, masons, carpenters and transport contractors. And in addition to the occupations mentioned above, some people mine the small outcrops of minerals, such as scheelite and beryllium, in the northerly sector of the Reserve. Nevertheless, in spite of these various occupations, Steinkopf must be regarded culturally as a mixed-farming community. Mixed-farming constitutes the main occupation for the majority of the population, and even those who follow other occupations usually have some interest in stock-farming.

POPULATION

The absence of detailed and reliable official statistical material imposes a major limitation on the analysis of the population of Steinkopf. According to the Coloured Affairs Department the population of Steinkopf in 1953 was 4,400. However, to judge from the 1951 census returns it is clear that this figure of 4,400 reflects the potential and not the actual size of the population, for it includes temporary migratory labourers and possibly some of those young men and women who left home to take up permanent or semi-permanent residence elsewhere in the Cape Province. Furthermore, the natural increase in the population during the years 1946–53 was only 545, and not 900 as official statistics suggest. And there is no evidence that 355 immigrants settled in Steinkopf during this period.

During the period July 1957 to June 1958, approximately 1,000 men and women appear to have been absent from the Reserve as migrant workers. It seems more likely, therefore, that the size of the population resident in Steinkopf in 1953 was only 3,400, although it must always be borne in mind that the majority of people who leave the Reserve as migrant workers do so mainly to earn money for their families, and are therefore in a sense still part of the Steinkopf community. The writer's estimate for 1957 was that the population *including temporary absentees* was only 4,000. This we will refer to as the potential population of the Reserve.

TABLE III

STEINKOPF POPULATION 1890 TO 1957

Year	Population	Source
1890	1,900	G. 60—1890 (Melvill's Report)
1913	2,839	Magistrate's minutes (Springbok)
1945 (October)	3,500	U.G. 33—1947
1951 (May)	3,060*	Census
1953	4,400	U.G. 13—1954
1957	4,000	Carstens's estimate

* includes 55 Whites

The estimate of approximately 1,000 migrant workers absent from the Reserve was based on a sample of 78 domestic families[2] (average size 5·6). In this sample it was found that 58 per cent of the families interviewed had at least one member absent during the year as a migrant worker, but some families had more than one person absent, thus the total number of regular migrant workers was actually 89 (56 men, 33 women). In addition about 30 other persons in these families appear to have been absent for part of the year.

If we assume that the potential Coloured population in Steinkopf in 1957 was 4,000 (males 2,087, females 1,913),[3] and use the small sample as an index, it appears that approximately 30 per cent of the male population and 19 per cent of the female population were absent from the Reserve as migratory labourers for most of the year.

According to this sample 34 per cent went to work at the Anglo-American diamond mine, Kleinzee, and 26 per cent to the State Alluvial Diggings at Alexander Bay; 12 per cent went to O'okiep, Nababeep or Springbok; 10 per cent went to South West Africa; 6 per cent to Cape Town; 6 per cent to Port Nolloth; of the remaining 6 per cent,

[2] A domestic family is used here to refer to kinsmen who usually eat together and generally live under the same roof.

[3] Based on 1951 sex ratios of the assumed potential population.

two persons went to White farms and three to small dorps outside the magisterial district.

It is not possible to comment on the nature of population growth owing to meagre data relating to the number of permanent emigrants and also the number of immigrants. But clearly there has been a steady increase in the potential population since 1890 (see Table III). And as the data relating to natural increase between the years 1946 and 1957 show, there has been in recent years an increase in the number of births, and a striking decrease in the number of deaths (see Table IV).

The crude birth- and death-rates for the community are best left uncalculated. In 1950, however, the Namaqualand Coloured people had a lower crude birth-rate (43·3) than the Cape Province (48·0), while the crude death-rates were about equal (Namaqualand 20·3, Cape Province 20·7).

TABLE IV

BIRTHS AND DEATHS (1946 TO 1957) IN STEINKOPF

Year	Number of Births	Number of Deaths	Natural increase
1946	92	68	24
1947	121	50	71
1948	101	61	40
1949	103	59	44
1950	126	73	53
1951	130	50	80
1952	159	46	113
1953	155	35	120
1954	168	43	125
1955	165	34	131
1956	155	31	124
1957	160	32	128

Although the density of the population is low (roughly 2·4 persons per square mile), large tracts of country are not fit for habitation or even for grazing and cultivation. The majority of the population spends most of the year either in the mission village, or in the hamlets near springs and water-holes at various places in the Reserve. The demographic map on page xiii gives a general impression of the distribution of families, but people do not remain permanently in one place, and the map merely reflects the distribution of families in terms of the places where they reside for the longest periods.

Prior to 1952, Whites were permitted to reside permanently in the

ASYNC1   JPRISM   JBLKJ   JLCKJ   ILL   c   SI

11:4604747

Beginning of record displayed.

ILL   11:4604747

:ILL: 4604747   :Borrower: CGP   :ReqDate: 960220 :Stat:
:OCLC: 259462   :NeedBefore: 960321 :RecDate:
:Lender: *IAR,IBZ,IAH,IAI,IAK   :DueDate: 960520 .
:CALINO:
:AUTHOR: Carstens, W. Peter.
:TITLE: The social structure of a Cape Coloured reserve, a study o
integration and segregation in South Africa,
:IMPRINT: Cape Town, New York, Oxford University Press, 1966.
:VERIFIED: OCLC
:PATRON: FALL,AMY/HWLC
:SHIP TO: CHICAGO PUBLIC LIBRARY / ILL / 400 S. STATE ST., 3N / CHICAGO, IL
60605
:BILL TO: Same
:SHIP VIA: CLS/ILDS/US Mail   :MAXCOST: Postage

Reserve provided they had obtained permission from the Management Board. But in this year all Whites (with the exception of the missionary and the two White policemen and their families) were required to leave the territory as a result of apartheid legislation. Whites, however, may visit the area if they have written permission from the Management Board or the Secretary for Coloured Affairs, and today a handful of prospectors and miners spend short periods in the Reserve during the year. In 1951 there were 55 Whites in Steinkopf but today there are less than 20. Local regulations do not debar Whites from passing through the Reserve without a permit, nor do they prohibit the representatives of commercial firms from carrying out their work.

The sex and age ratios in the community of Steinkopf vary with the time of year and the climate, and we have already shown that approximately a quarter of the population is absent from the Reserve each year. According to the 1951 May census, 1,402 Coloured males and 1,484 Coloured females were living in the Reserve reflecting a masculinity ratio of 94·5, but if we take into consideration that there were approximately 1,000 persons (630 males and 370 females) absent at this time the potential masculinity ratio increases to 109·1. Figures culled from the local Agricultural Census for the period 1956–7 tend to verify this estimate since they indicate that the potential masculinity ratio was 111·3.

During the period 1957–8, it was estimated from a sample of 78 domestic families that 21·9 per cent of these families derived their income from mixed-farming only, 56·4 per cent from mixed-farming plus other sources (migratory labour, local employment, pensions, etc.), 10·2 per cent from migratory labour only, 5·1 per cent from local employment only, 3·8 per cent from local employment plus other sources (migratory labour, pensions, etc.), and 2·5 per cent from pensions and disability grants only.[4]

Apart from mixed-farming and tributing, it was found during the same period that 21 men and 7 women were employed as teachers, 5 men as administrators or policemen, 22 men and 3 women as shopkeepers or shop-assistants, 12 men were self-employed as builders, masons, carpenters, or painters, 4 men in local transport, 1 woman in medical services, and 1 man, the missionary, in religion. There were also 24 men and 10 women employed in unskilled work, i.e. labourers, shepherds, and domestic servants. Approximately 630 men and 370 women were absent from the Reserve as migratory labourers.

[4] See Table XIII on p. 64.

LAND TENURE

Throughout the history of Steinkopf, land has always been of great importance to the community. During the early periods a large tract of country was necessary to carry out effectively the system of nomadic pastoralism, and in later years the territory of Steinkopf became, as it is today, a symbol of the community's unity. Land is symbolic not merely of 'nationality' but also of the past achievements in building up a community life. As an informant once pointed out, 'We pioneered this territory; we drove out the wild Bushmen and animals; we built the church and the schools; and we fostered the Christian tradition.'

The group attitude towards land is reflected also in the traditional system of communal tenure which persists to the present day in a slightly modified form. Furthermore, the collective sentiment associated with land is clearly illustrated by the general complaints of the registered occupiers that in the past the *whole* community has been deprived of land, even though many families have never been directly affected by the expropriation. For example, at the end of the last century, the raad agreed to sell a portion of land in the south-western sector of the Reserve to a White farmer to build a school for his and other children; but it is alleged that the surveyor was bribed, and Steinkopf lost a larger portion of land than was agreed to; the additional piece of land contained a valuable spring.[5] The loss of this land affected only a small section of the community, but as much agitation came from the burghers, who had no use for the spring or the land, as came from those directly affected. The whole community felt that it had lost common property, property which was in addition to its material value a symbol of social unity. As an old resident of Steinkopf once put it: 'The land is our flag and the Church is like the little red pattern [i.e. the Union Jack] in the centre of the flag that flies at the police-station.'

Although the history of Steinkopf reveals many changes in the economic system since the beginning of the nineteenth century, the traditional principle of communal land tenure has remained unaltered, except in administrative detail. The essence of this system is that groups of registered occupiers share certain rights in the land attached to the section of the Reserve in which they reside. Part of the land, the commonage, is set aside for the grazing of stock and the gathering of firewood, while other areas are subdivided into erfs (plots of land),

[5] Report on Coloured Mission Stations, Reserves and Settlements (U.G. 33–1947), p. 52.

which are allocated to individuals to cultivate, and over which they have defined rights provided they fulfil all their obligations to the Management Board. But all land (commonage, and private erfs) is controlled by the Board, and none may be sold. Formerly, the control which the raad had over private land was nominal, but today the Management Board, which represents the central government of South Africa as well as the people of Steinkopf, plays a large part in regulating its use. And in many instances the Management Board's regulations conflict with the customs and wishes of the majority of people.

In addition to the demarcation of commonage and the distribution of erfs, the Management Board assigns allotments on which buildings (including huts) may be erected in the mission village, and if desired, dry garden allotments also. The size and shape of erfs and other allotments, especially the former, vary considerably, but an erf is seldom larger than 8 morgen, and the average area of both building allotments and dry gardens is roughly 600 square yards. There is no discernible pattern in the layout of erfs, although they are sometimes separated by narrow strips of uncultivated ground; some are contiguous, with no perceptible boundary between them. Only a few people have dry gardens which are used for growing vegetables such as pumpkins and watermelons, and they are usually fenced to protect the crops from donkeys and other animals. Gardens are normally situated close to, but separate from the dwellings, although in the mission village they tend to be included in the building allotment. Erfs, on the other hand, may be several miles away from the dwellings, since it is not always possible to obtain arable lands near the springs and water-holes around which people settle. Building allotments are only allocated in the mission village. Thus people who live permanently or seasonally near their arable lands have no defined lots on which to erect their huts.

In spite of the existence of dry gardens, domestic horticulture has never been a significant characteristic of local farming. This is clearly because of the shortage of water (especially fresh water) and the low rainfall, neither of which provide the incentive, nor a satisfactory means, for growing vegetable crops. Similar hazards apply to the cultivation of grain, but grain requires less attention and withstands adverse climatic conditions better.

During earlier periods in Steinkopf's history sons of burghers had no difficulty in obtaining arable lands, since land was plentiful and the population small. Moreover, the procedure for obtaining rights was relatively simple; a person requiring an erf had merely to approach the raad member in his area and ask for a piece of land that was adjacent to his father's. His application would then be referred to the raad, which would authorise two of its korporale to point out beacons, and the request was granted. Newcomers to the territory had to make similar applications, and after their requests had been considered by the raad they were usually granted land and later admitted to the status of burghers, provided they were not of pure Khoi Khoin descent. In more recent times, however, the *kommers* (newcomers) found it more difficult to obtain erfs, and those who were granted land rights and *burgherskap* had sometimes to wait several years before land was available, or until they had served a probationary period of residence, during which time they were granted only grazing rights on the commonage. In the admission of new burghers, preference was usually given to those *kommers* who had married daughters of burghers. Today the allocation of arable lands is reserved almost exclusively for the sons of registered occupiers, although a newcomer who has resided many years in the Reserve, and is considered by the Management Board to have 'earned his right', may be granted an erf and admitted to full status. In all periods, Church membership (i.e. membership of the mission Church) has been considered a most favourable recommendation towards being admitted to the ranks of the registered occupiers.

During the nineteenth century erfs were considerably larger than they are today. Each burgher was allocated up to 'five bags of land' (about 40 morgen), which was generally a larger tract than could be ploughed in any one season, and consequently part of the erf lay fallow each year. These large allotments made it possible for a man to subdivide his land among his sons when he died, if additional land was not available for them. But as the population increased above the optimum size which enabled each burgher to have 40 morgen of arable land, erfs became smaller due to the subdivision of holdings. Today 'one bag' (8 morgen) is considered a reasonable size. The enforcement of the Mission Stations and Communal Reserves Act made further subdivision illegal and erfs have not decreased in size since the Act was applied, except in cases where holdings were considered by the Management Board to be too large by present-day standards for one person.

In spite of the increase in the population in recent years and the consequent shortage of land, there is no evidence to suggest, as might be expected, that internal land disputes among the members of the community are increasing;[6] in fact the opposite reaction is clearly occurring. During the period 1911 to 1937 internal land disputes were dealt with at nearly every meeting of the Management Board. Nowadays internal quarrels over land are rare. There is a strong suggestion, therefore, that migratory labour, which has been increasing rapidly, has tended to reduce the competition for land by providing the major single source of income in the Reserve.

The traditional system of land tenure has in the past been commented on by the authors of various government reports who investigated the Namaqualand Reserves with a view to recommending changes. Although the possibility of a change to individual land tenure was mentioned in the earlier reports, that question was not immediately pursued, and a 'Ticket of Occupation' was issued on 9 December 1874, twenty-seven years after the extension of the boundary of the Cape Colony from the Buffels to the Orange River. This 'Ticket of Occupation', or deed of reservation, certified that the territory of Steinkopf (which was defined) 'shall not for the present be alienated or leased, but shall be held for use jointly of the duly admitted occupants (being Aborigines or Bastards of Aboriginal descent) of Kookfontein alias Steinkopf Missionary Institution, now duly admitted occupants of the said Steinkopf Missionary Institution . . .'. Thus, in spite of the earlier suggestions that a new form of land tenure be introduced, the traditional communal system was retained. But further discussions took place in subsequent years, and in 1889 Mr. S. Melvill, Second Assistant Surveyor-General, was sent to investigate and report on the conditions of the occupants of the mission institutions, and the best way of dealing with 'unoccupied' land without interfering with the rights and requirements of the occupiers or their descendants. The Melvill Report, which was submitted in the middle of 1890, recommended that in order to secure development of land, together with advancement in the prosperity and civilisation of the occupants of land, a change in the mode of occupation was essential. To Mr. Melvill's mind this change should have been in the direction of individual tenure as certain other officials had suggested.

In 1896 a Select Committee was appointed to review the whole question of the Namaqualand Reserves. This committee considered

[6] Cf. G. M. Foster, 'Interpersonal Relations in Peasant Society', *Human Organization*, vol. 19, no. 4, 1960-1, p. 174.

inter alia Melvill's and other proposals regarding the system of land tenure. Some seem to have agreed that individual tenure was unsuited to the type of country and the temperament of the people, the majority of whom, it was felt, would soon be tempted to sell their holdings to Whites. Others (including Mr. Melvill) advocated individual tenure with the right of alienation either to Coloured people or Whites.

Although no immediate action was taken to give effect to the recommendations of the Committee, its findings (including a draft Bill by Mr. W. C. Scully, a former Resident Magistrate of Namaqualand) provided the background to the Mission Stations and Communal Reserves Act. No attention, however, was paid to the proposals concerning individual land tenure.

The Cape Coloured Commission of 1937 agreed that the communal system of land ownership in the Reserve had prevented alienation of the land and was opposed to the suggestions of Melvill and others, made during the last century. Yet they recommended:

'. . . that a system of individual tenure of portions of the land be introduced, with the right of nominating an approved Coloured successor but without the right of alienating except to approved Coloured persons. The portions for individual tenure should be selected according to their suitability for agriculture, as opposed to pastoral stock farming.'

These proposals, however, have never been introduced, probably because it was realised that such a system might interfere with 'the powers of the strict form of government' recommended by the Commission and accepted in later years by the central government.

MIXED-FARMING

Mixed-farming is the economic activity to which most people aspire. The explanation for this ideal, however, is not that mixed-farming is materially beneficial to the majority of these farmers, but because the pattern of mixed-farming is a function of the total network of social activities which occur in the community of Steinkopf. The analysis of the other institutions in subsequent chapters shows how inextricably mixed-farming is bound up with all the facets of social life. The people (even those who have no livestock and do not plough and reap) see themselves as belonging to a farming tradition: they talk about animals and herding, about the quality of grain and the soil, just as men in the city talk about their work. To them farming is 'shop' even though the majority earn more money in other spheres.

Accurate figures are not available to show the distribution of small stock and the number of bags of grain produced annually among the population. This is partly because of the unreliability of the annual Agricultural Census in the area, but especially because of the reluctance on the part of the inhabitants to disclose these details, particularly regarding their livestock (possibly for reasons of tax evasion under the quota system).

The preliminary Agricultural Census figures, however, disclosed by the secretary of the Management Board, based on a sample of 390 families for the period 1953–4, which was a good year, showed that:

> 59 per cent of the families produced 10 or fewer bags of grain or none at all;
> 26 per cent of the families produced 11 to 20 bags;
> 12 per cent of the families produced 21 to 50 bags;
> 3 per cent of the families produced more than 50 bags.

Statistics relating to the distribution of small stock among the population are less reliable. For example, the authors of the Report on Coloured Mission Stations and Reserves (1947) state: 'There are about 400 families who have less than 50 head of small stock or none at all; 17 possess from 500 to 1,000, 36 from 250 to 500, 87 from 100 to 250 and 77 from 50 to 100.'[7] Unfortunately this statement refers to only 667 of the 848 families which the members of the Commission report to be living in Steinkopf; the source of the information is not given, nor is any date mentioned, but the figures probably refer either to 1945, when the Commission visited the area, or to the Agricultural Census of 1938.

For the period 1956–7 (a good year) the secretary of the Management Board supplied the following figures, which refer mainly to the families living in hamlets and farms:

> 12 families possessed more than 500 small stock;
> 30 families possessed 200 to 500 small stock;
> 49 families possessed 100 to 200 small stock;
> 88 families possessed 50 to 100 small stock;
> 226 families possessed 1 to 50 small stock.

No reliable figure for the number of families *not* possessing any small stock during this period was available, though there is a suggestion that it may be a fifth of the total.[8] In addition to these 'rural' families

[7] Report on Coloured Mission Stations, p. 51.

[8] See Table XIII, p. 64.

just mentioned, it is well known that a large percentage of the villagers and pre-villagers also own small stock, but statistics were not available for these people.

Apart from donkeys (which are used as draught-animals) and chickens, the number of other domestic animals is too insignificant to mention when discussing the economic position of the average Steinkopf family. These animals are generally owned by the more successful farmers who do not need to augment their incomes by other means of employment (see Table VI).

The production of grain in Steinkopf varies considerably from year to year, depending on the climatic conditions, notably rain. But according to the Report on Coloured Mission Stations, Reserves and Settlements (1947), an average of 5,000 bags is produced annually. This figure is in agreement with those provided in Table V.

TABLE V

PRODUCTION OF GRAIN IN THE STEINKOPF RESERVE

Year	Number of Bags				
	Wheat	Rye	Oats	Barley	Total Grain
1951	8,600	300	500	200	9,600
1953	3,950	50	400	150	4,550
1954	*	*	*	*	9,500
1955	*	*	*	*	1,500
1956	*	*	*	*	350
1957	*	*	*	*	5,000

* figures not available

All information supplied by the manager of the co-operative store.

The number of livestock owned by the members of the community is more difficult to discern owing to the irregular and wide fluctuations in the Agricultural Census figures, and the discrepancies between these figures and those given in certain official reports. All the available information is given in Table VI.

It is difficult to comment on the discrepancies and fluctuations in these figures, especially as the Reports of the Commissioner for Coloured Affairs do not give the sources of their figures. It is probable, however, that the 1937–8 figures include sheep and goats belonging to Whites living in the Reserve or on its borders. And it is possible that the Commissioner for Coloured Affairs included in his estimates the number of sheep and goats belonging to Whites believed to be grazing on Reserve commonage. Moreover, the stock quota system, which was introduced in 1952, undoubtedly affects the number of sheep, goats, and donkeys declared annually to the Management Board for the purpose of the Agricultural Census. And it is conceivable that the figures are adjusted by officials to correct the low returns submitted by persons whose stock numbers are believed to be greater. But this is mere conjecture.

TABLE VI

NUMBER OF LIVESTOCK IN THE STEINKOPF RESERVE

Year	Sheep	Goats	Cattle	Donkeys	Horses	Mules	Chickens
1937–8[1]	19,099	25,783	266	5,000	28		—
1951–2[2]	6,201	7,311	115	1,078	41	21	1,480
1953–4[3]	10,108	11,865	93	1,251	61	32	1,605
1954–5[4]	16,497	18,156	83	2,190	120	57	—
1956–7[5]	15,403	24,126	237	1,764	265	42	1,391
? [6]	48,455		—	—	—	—	—
1953–4?[7]	17,941	21,604	—	—	—	—	—
1956[8]	17,941	21,604	—	—	—	—	—
1957[9]	18,953	23,851	—	—	—	—	—
1958[10]	12,900	18,050	—	—	—	—	—

[1] Report on Coloured Mission Stations, p. 66, which quotes agricultural census 1937–8.

[2] Agricultural Census forms supplied by the Management Board.

[3] Agricultural Census forms supplied by the Management Board.

[4] Superintendent of Steinkopf Reserve.

[5] Agricultural Census forms supplied by the Management Board.

[6] Commissioner for Coloured Affairs Report 1953.

[7] Commissioner for Coloured Affairs Report 1955.

[8,9,10] Commissioner for Coloured Affairs Report 1960.

Losses of small stock are considerable, to judge from the figures available. In 1957, for example, according to the Agricultural Census, 1,500 sheep died of some sickness, 1,717 as a result of drought, and 842 were killed by wild animals. During the same period 132 goats died of some sickness, 3,177 as a result of drought, and 953 were killed by wild animals. H. A. Kotzè of the University of the Orange Free

State estimated that 15 per cent of the total number of small stock died as the result of the drought in 1958.[9]

Taking the population as a whole, there is a strong suggestion that at least three-quarters of all families are unable to make a living out of mixed-farming alone, and must therefore find other work to augment the family budget. Kotzè has estimated that the net annual income derived from one small stock unit was approximately 7s. 6d., and £1 2s. 0d. for cattle. Grain is normally sold for £2 12s. 6d. per bag.

In the north-eastern corner of the Reserve at Henkries, a date-grove promises to be of great economic importance to the people of Steinkopf. Subterranean water is plentiful and at some places occurs at a depth of one foot. But it is extremely brackish, and only dates will thrive on it.

It is said that the date-grove owes its origin to World War I, when soldiers who were encamped there dropped date-stones which subsequently germinated. In 1943 it was decided to fence in the area to protect the palms against livestock, and cultivate the 100 full-grown date-palms. The experiment was successful and the following year 1,500 lb. of dates were harvested. Since 1943 numerous additional trees have been planted and, under the guidance of the Department of Agriculture, encouraging developments have taken place. In the 1954 season dates were harvested from 203 palms, which included 133 grown from suckers planted in 1948. The total crop consisted of 8,800 lb. of dates, i.e. an average of 43 lb. per tree. The quality and size of the dates are superior, and the demand for them in Namaqualand alone far exceeds the supply, despite the fact that the selling price is 1s. 6d. per lb., as compared with 1s. 2d. per lb. for imported seedless dates.

It has been estimated that there is approximately 60 morgen of additional land on which palms can be planted and grown at a very low cost. In the near future 6,000 selected female palms are to be planted. If development takes place at the present rate, within the next ten or fifteen years an income of between £25,000 and £30,000 can be expected annually from the sale of dates at present prices.

The scheme is controlled by the Department of Coloured Affairs on behalf of the Steinkopf Board of Management. A Coloured official is stationed at the plantation, and manages the scheme under the

[9] H. A. Kotzè, 'Verslag oor Ekonomiese Ondersoek na die Ontwikkeling van 'n Voerbank op Goodhouse vir die Kleurlinggebiede in Namakwaland'. Unpublished report, University of the Orange Free State, 1960, p. 7.

direction of head office, which undertakes monthly inspections.

'As part of the rehabilitation schemes for the Reserves a £5,000 State loan, free of interest, was granted to the Board of Management for a period of 15 years. This fund is utilised for the development of the plantation, which may, however, eventually be taken over by the Board, subject to the redemption of the loan, and with the approval of the Minister. At present all revenue derived from the plantation is credited against the loan. After redemption of the loan the proceeds from the scheme will be devoted to educational purposes, and general improvement of the Reserve.' (U.G. 13—1954, p. 12.)

At present, however, the date-plantation is regarded by the inhabitants of Steinkopf as a government farm from which they will never derive any benefit. In general, people are antagonistic towards its establishment, notably the conservatives and the stock-farmers: the conservatives, because they may enter the area by permit only, when they require rushes for mat-making (Henkries is the main source of these rushes); the stock-farmers, because they can no longer water their animals at the springs.

Unfortunately the possibility of growing dates in other parts of the Reserve is entirely dependent on the discovery of new sources of water, because the existing springs and boreholes cannot even cope adequately with domestic and stock needs at the present moment. It seems certain, therefore, that nothing short of irrigating suitable land with water from the Orange River can make possible the establishment of additional date-groves and the expansion of other forms of cultivation. The central government's proposal to utilise the Orange River for irrigation and hydro-electric power could be of tremendous importance to Steinkopf, should the benefits of the project be extended to the Coloured Reserves.

MIGRATORY LABOUR

The migration of at least one person in each elementary family to the mines and towns outside the Steinkopf Reserve is, as we have stated in an earlier chapter, an economic necessity for a large section of the community. This section consists of those people who do not make a living out of mixed-farming and are unable to find employment locally in the mission village. Thus, it must be stressed that migration of some sort is an essential feature of the Steinkopf economy. Apart from the salaried and wage-earning people in the mission village and settlements, no family can survive unless the whole family, or some of the members spend some part of the year away from home. Even those engaged entirely in mixed-farming have to move after their herds in search of pasture, and migrate to their arable lands during the ploughing and reaping seasons; while the tributers who work small claims have also to migrate to the northerly mountains where the minerals are found. Migration to the towns and mines, therefore, is merely another form of migration that has of necessity become an accepted and integral part of the social system.

In the contemporary community it is necessary to distinguish between three categories of migratory labourers. The first category, *which includes roughly 60 per cent of the total migratory labour force*, finds employment on the two main diamond mines in the area, Kleinzee and Alexander Bay. Both the Church and the Management Board approve of, and encourage, migration to these two mining towns because the compound residential system enables them to maintain contact with their people, and to a certain extent to control their actions as well. The Management Board, for example, realises that it can more easily demand prompt payment of taxes from these migrants since it is in regular contact with the mine authorities as an unofficial labour bureau. And it should also be pointed out that certain members of the Management Board have received payment from the mines for recruiting labour. The Church, on the other hand, appoints officers to look after the spiritual needs of its mine-worker congregation and to collect dues and thank-offerings; bazaars, too are frequently held. Generally the justification for supporting the principle of cheap migrant labour by the Church and Management Board (and often by the wives or parents of the labourers) is framed in moral terms, viz. 'the people are properly cared for and well-disciplined, there is no chance of illicit sex relations with town women', etc. But clearly the economic benefits, in spite of low wages, are seen as paramount, though they are seldom verbalised except by those who control family budgets. They report that institutionalised migrant labour of this kind is most rewarding from their point of view.

In stressing the economic advantages of migrant labour to the mines for the Steinkopf Reserve, it is not intended to convey the opinion that the system is being condoned. On the contrary, this analysis demonstrates the extent to which the Reservation system in its various aspects tends to perpetuate low wages on the mines. In 1952 the modal wage paid to Coloured labourers on the Kleinzee mine was approximately £5 14s. 0d. per month (including overtime). By 1958 this figure had risen to approximately £10, a considerable increase, but only by virtue of the fact that former wages were so painfully low. The 1958 increase, moreover, was the first substantial increase for twenty years, and was not commensurate with the rise in the cost of living for the same period.

The second category of migratory labourers is of a different order. There is no recruitment by an official body, and men and women merely inform the Management Board that they are leaving the Reserve in search of work, or that a job has been secured for them in one of the towns. These people go to various parts of the western Cape and South West Africa; to the fisheries at Port Nolloth, to Springbok, Windhoek or Cape Town, or to the copper mines at O'okiep and Nababeep. It is important to stress here that even when nine or ten people leave the Reserve together, they do so as individuals and not as a recruited group. Wherever they go they must find their own accommodation, which is not easy in urban areas.

Public opinion in the Reserve is usually opposed to this type of migration. The families of these migrants complain that often their children do not return, and when they do, they bring all the 'undesirable' habits of the town with them, and town wives; and further, that when they are away they never send money home as they would do from Kleinzee and Alexander Bay. The Church and the Management Board also stress the 'evils' of the towns and both bodies try to discourage people from this kind of migration, recommending instead the former type. The analysis of kinship genealogies shows that a significant number of these migrants become integrated members of urban communities and return to Steinkopf only to visit their kinsmen. Some never return.

Reference must be made to a third type of migration, though it attracts relatively few people today. White farmers recruit men (sometimes women or elementary families) to work for them as shepherds and domestic servants. Remuneration for their services is always very low—the maximum wage is 10s. per month, plus the scraps from the kitchen—and no housing is provided. Today with the increasing demand for labour in the towns and on the mines, where better wages are paid, very few people are prepared to work for White farmers, but some individuals choose farm work because they prefer a rural life to the noise of the mines or the bustle of the towns.

TRIBUTING

As a result of the development of the mineral wealth of Namaqualand, the inhabitants of Steinkopf have acquired, through their contact with Europeans, a considerable knowledge of certain minerals and mining techniques: some have been prospectors' guides and labourers, while many have been employed by the mining companies. We must not forget, however, that the Namaqua themselves were the first to prospect and exploit the copper deposits of Little and Great Namaqualand.

The type of mining with which we are concerned in this section is the working on a small scale of the patches of mineral deposits, chiefly beryllium and scheelite, which are found in the granite mountains in the remote northern sector of the Reserve. Knowledge of these minerals was derived mainly from contact with European prospectors during the last century.

Tributers work these claims to augment the meagre profits made from mixed-farming, as an alternative to joining the ranks of the migrant workers who go to the towns and White-owned mines. The work is arduous and the profits uncertain, but the life is free: there are no contracts or compound regulations or 'White bosses', and a man can return to his lands immediately the first rains begin, to plough or to reap when the crops are ripe.

It is extremely difficult to estimate the proportion of the population that does this type of mining, since those people who do always 'hush up' their activities. Tributers are very careful not to disclose the whereabouts of their claims, how long they spend there, or what their profits are. Their secrecy is justified because mineral deposits may be mined by any person who carries a prospector's licence. Consequently competition is feared, especially from those Whites who have the capital and equipment to extract large quantities of ore by following the veins in the rock. Steinkopf tributers rely on donkey-cart transport which cannot compete with the trucks and jeeps used by Whites. Their equipment too is crude—generally, only picks and crowbars are used to extricate the ore; occasionally, however, the services of a qualified blaster are employed when the 'traditional' methods of excavation prove inadequate. Very little work is done during the hot months December to February, when the mercury rises on occasions to 110 degrees Fahrenheit.

Normally, men go to their claims without their families, but some are accompanied by sons who are not at school. The usual pattern is for two adult brothers to set off alone and return when they have produced enough to keep their families for several months. We do not know what profits are made, although it is certain that they vary considerably, owing to the fact that deposits occur in patches. Some people claim to make as much as £60 in a month when rich veins are struck. In 1950 and 1951, when the price of beryllium was high, the White shopkeeper who bought the ore estimated that the average tributer made more money out of mining than the most successful farmer made out of grain. This estimate was probably true for this period, but it is unlikely that it applies every year, owing to the fluctuation of prices.

'Owners' of claims do not necessarily work them themselves, but often hire them to neighbours who are remunerated in proportion to the amount of ore produced. The procedure is that the employee 'sells' the ore to the owner, who decides the price. This system, however, does not operate smoothly as there are frequently financial disputes, largely owing to the absence of legal contracts.

Information regarding the purely economic aspect of this type of mining is extremely deficient. But it is evident that mining is most popular when mineral prices are high and when the harvest has failed.

Contact with and reports of tributers show that there is a high correlation between people who resort to this type of mining and poorly integrated members of the community. It is probable, therefore, that there is a tendency for those who deviate from the accepted standards of behaviour to escape the group pressures of the community by retiring to the barren mountains where they are free to live their own lives. As one man, an elder in the Church, put it, 'Mining attracts the godless people;' and then added, 'drinkers and Roman Catholics'!

TRADE AND MARKETS

The transition from a semi-subsistence and barter economy to a monetary economy has been a slow process. During the first half of the nineteenth century the people of Steinkopf lived mainly on the meat and milk of their cattle and other livestock, augmented by veldkos. Coffee, tea, and sugar were obtained from *smouse* (pedlars) in exchange for livestock and hides. Money appears to have been introduced about 1855 with the opening up of the copper mines where people migrated for work, although it is probable that before this date, some were already selling livestock to the Boers and other colonists. But the real change from a semi-subsistence and barter economy to a semi-subsistence and money economy began only in 1887 when trading licences were issued for the first time. According to local historians this event was the main factor responsible for the break with the subsistence–barter tradition, and we are told that the veld-kornet Moses Engelbrecht admitted on his death-bed that the granting of this concession was the greatest mistake he had made during his period of office. The effect which it had was, of course, to create a permanent business centre in the mission village and to encourage the members of the community to adopt the practice of buying luxuries. As a result, many people found themselves heavily in debt and this had usually to be repaid in livestock and grain.

Today barter is practically unknown, and apart from a few items such as water, firewood, building material for huts, a little goatsmilk, all families purchase their commodities from the local shops. And some families do slaughter their own animals for meat, and grind their own corn. The former practice is common on the farms and settlements, while the latter is found only among a few conservative families. But there are many other factors which have contributed towards, or helped to accelerate, this change in the economic system, and attention has already been drawn to them.

Nearly all local trade is centred nowadays in the Namakwase Ko-operatiewe Handelsvereniging (NKHV), a consumers' co-operative society, registered under the Co-operative Societies Act, No. 29 of 1939. Formerly, two European-owned stores served the community's needs, but in December 1945 one of these stores was bought by a group of Steinkopf people, the founders of the present co-operative society; and in 1952 the Management Board refused to renew the trading licence of the other store and granted exclusive trading rights to the NKHV, which had proved itself successfully during the first seven years of its existence.

The reaction to the NKHV's monopoly of local trade was viewed at first with suspicion. Most people said they preferred the European shopkeepers with whom they had dealt for more than half a century, and disliked seeing 'a Coloured man behind the counter'! Their attitude, however, was not merely one of ardent conservatism, because in the past they had benefited in times of financial want from the credit facilities granted by these shopkeepers, who in this regard performed the important function of the money-lender. But with no other shops in the Reserve from 1952 to 1956, they were obliged, in spite of their attitudes, to patronise the NKHV. Today, notwithstanding the initial opposition, membership is large and business flourishing.[10] Membership increased from 484 in 1946 to 937 in 1957, while the annual turnover increased from £13,000 to £92,359 during the same period. Not only is the measure of its success reflected in its annual turnover and large membership, but also in the fact that a recently established grocery shop and café organised by private enterprise has made an unsatisfactory start. No figures are available concerning its turnover, but the owners have acknowledged their inability to compete with the co-operative society.

The NKHV sells nearly all of the commodities which are in demand — groceries, drapery and footwear, hardware (including building materials) and meat.[11] Membership is open to *any* individual or co-operative society provided application is made to, and approved by, the board of directors. In addition, each member must buy at least one £1 share, but he is entitled to buy an unlimited number. Annual dividends and bonuses are paid on shares and cash purchases.[12] Comparatively high wages and salaries are paid to the twenty-five employees. In 1957 they totalled £5,570.

Apart from its purely economic functions, the NKHV provides (as did the European shops in former years) an important informal rendezvous in the village. At all times of the day it is crowded with people, young and old. Not all are customers; some, notably old men, congregate to gossip and cadge a cigarette or a piece of plug from a friend or relation. Not only local gossip is disseminated at the shops, but here also news of the 'outside world' is passed on from motorists, sales-representatives, and neighbouring European farmers.

The NKHV must also be regarded as a large association with a membership that includes the majority of the elementary families in the Reserve. Whereas it is doubtful whether all members are at the present time moved by a spirit of co-operation, nevertheless, the existence of an institution of this kind has provided the basis for the development of such sentiments.

We have seen that the Reserve has to import nearly all the material commodities required by the members of the community. We have now to ask from what source the exchange comes to pay for these imported commodities.

[10] See Table VII, p. 58. The figures for 1957 have been used to facilitate comparison with other data, e.g. Table X on page 59.

[11] See Tables VIII and IX on page 58.

[12] See Table VII on page 58.

TABLE VII

FIGURES RELATING TO MEMBERSHIP, ANNUAL TURNOVER ETC. OF THE NKHV (1946–58)

Year	No. of members	Value of shares £	Turnover £	Total value of bonuses £	Dividends (approx.) £
1946	484	—	13,000	—	—
1950	518	—	16,000	373	—
1954	843	2,951	53,276	1,290	109
1955	882	3,255	86,739	2,410	122
1956	897	6,459	87,605	6,794	152
1957	937	8,620	92,359	7,362	314
1958	973	10,043	114,300	5,153	489

TABLE VIII

THE APPROXIMATE CASH VALUES OF CATEGORIES OF GOODS SOLD BY THE NKHV (1954–7)

Year	Groceries £	Drapery and footwear £	Hardware £
1954	24,937	18,646	13,319
1955	34,695	30,358	21,684
1956	35,042	30,661	21,901
1957	36,943	32,325	23,089

TABLE IX

MEAT SALES BY THE NKHV (1954–7)

Year	Number of sheep	Number of goats	Goats and sheep Cash value (approx.) £
1954	480	720	2,700
1955	540	900	3,240
1956	600	960	3,510
1957	660	1,080	3,915

TABLE X

SOURCES OF INCOME TO THE STEINKOPF RESERVE (1957)

(Where statistics are lacking, symbols have been inserted for convenience)

Source	Estimated amount £	%
EXPORTS:		
Migrant labour	47,000 (approx.)	42·0
Grain		
(5,000 bags)	13,125	11·7
Livestock		
39,529 small stock		
237 cattle	15,278[1]	13·7
Minerals	a	
	£75,403 + a	

	£	%
GOVERNMENTAL INSTITUTIONS:		
Teachers	16,000 (approx.)	14·3
Other Government occupations	2,500 (approx.)	2·2
Old-age pensions and disability		
grants	4,800[2]	4·3
	£23,300	

	£	%
LOCAL TRADE PROFITS:[3]		
Salaries paid to NKHV employees	5,570	5·0
Bonuses and dividends paid by NKHV	7,675	6·9
	£13,245	

	£
MISCELLANEOUS:	
Services rendered to Europeans outside the Reserve by builders, masons, carpenters, etc.	b
	£b
TOTAL	£111,948 + a + b

[1] This figure includes income derived from local sales of livestock.

[2] In 1951. Information from Social Welfare Officer, Springbok.

[3] These figures are slightly affected by sales to people living outside the Reserve, and exclude benefits derived from the privately owned shop.

In Table X on page 59, the various sources of income have been indicated and, where statistics are available, the revenue derived from each source in 1957. From these figures two important phenomena should be noted. The first is the relative importance of migratory labour and the teaching profession to the income of the Reserve, and secondly, the benefits derived from the NKHV in the form of salaries paid to its employees, and bonuses and dividends paid out to its members. Bonuses and dividends have been included as sources of income, since the recipients visualise them as such.

Unfortunately it is not possible to indicate exactly the degree to which the Reserve is financially dependent on institutions outside its boundaries. But it seems that we can safely state that approximately 60 per cent of the Reserve's income is derived from external sources, viz. migratory labour, teaching and other government-paid occupations, old-age pensions, disability grants, and services rendered to Whites living outside Steinkopf by builders, masons and carpenters.

All grain is marketed at Springbok, 40 miles from Steinkopf; and apart from goats and sheep which are sold to the NKHV for slaughter, livestock, hides, and wool are usually taken there to be sold, although neighbouring European farmers do buy livestock from the people at Steinkopf. Base metals used formerly to be sold to the local White storekeepers, but today, in their absence, tributers usually sell to an agent in Springbok.

INCOME AND EXPENDITURE

We have already shown that, culturally, Steinkopf is essentially a farming community even though this activity is by no means the most rewarding for the majority of the population. The basic unit in the realm of mixed-farming is the elementary family, which, although it may obtain external assistance in this connexion, carries out much of its work as an independent group. But its economic activities do not end with herding, ploughing, reaping and selling its produce. We must include also the concomitant activities which form part of the working routine. Huts and houses have to be built and repaired; water fetched from the dam or spring; firewood collected; wagons made and repaired; clothes made, if they are not bought, and mended; and of course there are the long hours spent preparing and cooking food and doing the household chores. A few conservative families still grind their corn, and collect veldkos and honey to augment their diet, while a large number slaughter their own animals.

The elementary family, however, is not the only economic unit found amongst these farmers. We shall see in the next chapter the extent to which groups of elementary families co-operate in their work as extended families, and the extent to which hired labour is used.

In the light of what we have said in earlier sections, it is clear that the majority of families are unable to subsist on the profits derived from mixed-farming alone, as well as pay their taxes, fulfil their financial obligations to the Church, and spend money on 'luxuries'. We see, therefore, how essential it is for them to augment these meagre earnings. Even in the absence of any statistics whatsoever, the fact that people so wedded to mixed-farming leave the Reserve sporadically to work in the towns and on the mines, furnishes us with evidence to suggest that traditional economic activities do not provide sufficient income for all the needs of the people. There may be other factors which encourage people to migrate, but none is comparable with that of economic necessity.

For the unsuccessful farmer, the other ways of making a living are to leave the Reserve permanently and settle in a town, or to abandon farming (perhaps continuing to keep livestock and employing a shepherd to do the herding) and take up a profession such as teaching, or a trade such as building, or start a business, or find permanent employment as a shop-assistant or labourer in the mission village. Teaching is extremely popular, and nearly all pupils who receive secondary education aspire to qualify in this profession.

An analysis based on an estimate of the incomes of 78 domestic families (average size 5·6 persons) and the amount spent at the co-operative store, was made for the period July 1957 to June 1958. (See Tables XI to XIV.) The occupations of the *heads* of these families at the time of investigation were given as:

Mixed-farmers—61·5 per cent.

Migrant labourers—16·6 per cent.

Pensioners—8·9 per cent.

Locally employed (teacher, clerk, painter, lorry-driver, labourer) —7·9 per cent.

Housewives (widows)—5·1 per cent.

The following conclusions may be drawn from the information contained in these Tables:

(a) During that year the gross income of the average family was approximately £143. Just under £54 of this money came from the earnings of migrant workers, while nearly £90 was derived locally from salaries, farming, old-age pensions and disability grants, etc. (Table XI).

(*b*) People living permanently in the Steinkopf village were better off than those living in the hamlets and on the farms (Tables XI and XII).

(*c*) Although the average family in Steinkopf village obtained more money from migratory labour than did the average family in the hamlets and farms, a higher proportion of the latter's gross income was derived from migratory labour (Table XI).

(*d*) The average family in the Steinkopf village with its higher income spent considerably more money at the co-operative store than the average hamlet and farm family did. But the average village family spent only a slightly higher proportion of its gross income at the store than the average hamlet and farm family did (Table XI).

(*e*) The distribution of the annual incomes among these 78 families is set out in Table XII. This analysis suggests that approximately 60 per cent of the families in the community earned £140 (or less) per annum, while only 9 per cent earned more than £220 per annum.

(*f*) According to the sample of 78 families, the families with the highest incomes are those who are locally employed (see Table XIII). This Table shows, moreover, that apart from the families who live entirely on government-aid, the poorest section of the community are the mixed-farmers who do not rely on other sources of income. And by comparing the incomes of these mixed-farmers with those families who devote all their time to migratory labour, it can be seen how much more rewarding migratory labour is. This sample of the population suggests also that when mixed-farming is combined with other occupations, as usually happens, the result is financially less rewarding than the pursuit of one of the other occupations or a combination of them.

(*g*) Table XIV shows that migratory labour was the main single source of income for the families as a whole. 'Source uncertain', refers to income whose source could not be accounted for with reasonable certainty. A portion of this money appears to have come from casual migrant workers, some of it may have come from tributing, from stock in excess of the quota, from services rendered to other people, or from dividends and bonuses from the co-operative store. And we must not rule out the possibility of inaccurate information having been given by the people interviewed. Compare Table XIV with Table X on page 59.

Compare Table XIV with Table X on page 59.

TABLE XI

MEAN AVERAGE ANNUAL INCOMES AND EXPENDITURE AT THE NKHV OF 78 DOMESTIC FAMILIES (AV. SIZE 5·6 PERSONS) (1957–8)

Locality	Average annual income per family			Average annual amount spent at NKHV per family
	Total income	From migratory labour	From other sources	
	£	£	£	£
Steinkopf village	169·7	58·8	110·9	131·5
Hamlets and farms	116	48·7	67·3	94·4
Both localities	143·5	53·9	89·6	113·1

TABLE XII

DISTRIBUTION OF ANNUAL INCOMES OF 78 DOMESTIC FAMILIES (1957–8)

Annual income £	A Steinkopf village		B Hamlets and farms		A + B	
	No.	%	No.	%	No.	%
60 or less	3	7·5	8	21·0	11	14·1
100 or less	9	22·5	9	23·7	18	23·1
140 or less	8	20·0	10	26·6	18	23·1
180 or less	8	20·0	7	18·4	15	19·2
220 or less	5	12·5	4	10·5	9	11·5
more than £220	7	17·5	0	0·0	7	9·0
	40	100·0	38	100·2	78	100·0

It is not known just how the average family manages to balance its household budget, but the evidence suggests that this is extremely difficult, since the income of most families falls below the Poverty Datum Line (PDL) or very close to it. The PDL is 'an estimate of the income needed by any individual household if it is to attain a defined minimum level of health and decency'.[13] In 1957 it was estimated

[13] Edward Batson, *The Poverty Line in Salisbury*, 1945.

that any family consisting of five persons (husband, wife, and three children aged 5, 7 and 15 years respectively) needed an annual income of approximately £169 to be just above the PDL, when the husband was absent from home, and £230 when he was not.[14]

These figures were based on the assumed minimum needs of a

TABLE XIII

DISTRIBUTION OF ANNUAL INCOMES AMONG 78 DOMESTIC FAMILIES IN TERMS OF SOURCES OF INCOME (1957–8)

Source of income	Families		Total annual income[1] £	Average annual income per family £
	No.	%		
Mixed-farming only ..	17	21·9	1,757	103·3
Mixed-farming plus other sources (migratory labour, local employment, pensions, etc.)	44	56·4	6,003	127·3
Migratory labour only ..	8	10·2	1,356	172
Local employment only ..	4	5·1	1,312	328
Local employment plus other sources (migratory labour, pensions, etc.)	3	3·8	640	213·3
Pensions and disability grants only	2	2·5	129	64·5
All sources	78	99·9	11,197	143·5

[1] It is not known how many families included 'income' derived from bonuses and dividends paid out by the NKHV in these figures. Assuming, however, that no family did, we would have to add £10 8s. 0d. to the average annual income per *average* family to arrive at a figure approximating to the amount of cash available for spending each year. Similar adjustments would have to be made to Tables XI, XII, and XIV.

[14] W. P. Carstens, 'The Community of Steinkopf'. Appendix F.

TABLE XIV

SOURCES OF TOTAL ANNUAL INCOMES OF 78 DOMESTIC FAMILIES (1957–8)

Source	Total income	
	£	%
Migratory labour ..	4,202	37·5
Mixed-farming ..	2,413	21·5
Local employment ..	1,852	16·5
Pensions and disability		
grants	345	3·1
Source uncertain ..	2,385	21·3
All sources	11,197	99·9

family which purchased all its commodities locally, and make no allowance for the use of home-grown vegetables, veldkos, or wild honey which is plentiful after a good flower season. The income of the majority of families appears to be less than £140 in a *good* farming year (£150 8s. 0d. if bonuses and dividends are included; see Table XIII).

Moreover, in addition to money spent on food and clothing, we must also add £4 10s. 0d. a year to the family's expenses; for taxes (£2 10s. 0d.), Church dues (30s.), excluding the thank-offering which is also expected, and school books (10s.), plus all the other expenses excluded in the calculation of the Poverty Datum Line.

We may now ask how families whose annual incomes fall in the vicinity of the PDL manage their domestic economies, especially as the incomes derived from mixed-farming are frequently less than in 1957, which was considered a good year. The logical answer is that they have to eat less, and spend less on clothes, lighting material, fuel, 'luxuries'. But this is not entirely satisfactory, since it does not explain how people live when their crops fail, or how nominally destitute families survive. Part of the answer lies nowadays in the opportunities that are open for migratory labour, though it cannot be statistically demonstrated that migratory labour increases when farming fails. In theory, as Table XIV suggests, resorting to migratory labour in favour of mixed-farming could increase the income of the average family, provided there was an adequate demand for labour.

But there are other factors which must be taken into consideration. In the first place, little information regarding the income derived from

66

tributing was obtained, and this may be more significant than is generally realised. Secondly, we must also take into consideration the fact that part of the wheat harvest is sometimes stored for domestic consumption, though most families are forced to sell the whole of their crop because they need cash; and meat and milk may be obtained from the family herd. Thirdly, other factors which help people to bridge the gap between destitution and poverty are the collection of veldkos, home-grown vegetables, domestic chickens and eggs, presents and tips from Whites, sharing food with kinsmen and sometimes neighbours, and doing odd jobs such as collecting firewood and rushes for more prosperous neighbours. Fourthly, we must draw attention to the fact that in former years share-cropping with Whites (which is now illegal) was an important source of income for many families. This practice used to take two forms. In the first, a White farmer would supply the seed, the plough, and draught-animals, and cultivate with his Steinkopf partner, who would receive half of the harvest. In the second, a registered occupier would agree to herd a White farmer's livestock on the commonage in return for a number of animals and a specified percentage of the lambs born during the year. The latter type of share-cropping is reported to have been extremely profitable to the inhabitants of Steinkopf, and many well-to-do registered occupiers are said to have been 'made' by the system; and it is possible that it is still continued illegally by certain persons when conditions are favourable. Finally, we should note again that prior to the establishment of the NKHV the White shopkeepers readily gave credit to local registered occupiers. Debts were sometimes repaid in cash when money was available, but more often they were settled in kind after the harvest.

On the basis of the data collected, it is possible to state some general principles regarding the home economy of Steinkopf. By placing these principles in a sociological setting, some light is cast also on the values attached to 'luxuries' in a changing community.

The basic requirements are, of course, food and shelter. Thus, assuming that a hut has been constructed, consideration is given first to food, but not necessarily to sufficient food, or good food, because there are other essentials to be provided for out of the family income. The first of these is the annual tax which must be paid to the Management Board. If the tax is not paid, a person may be evicted from the Reserve, or have some of his property seized by a government official. Among the very poor, therefore, a balance has to be found between food and the annual tax of £2 10s. 0d. which is almost enough money to feed two adults and a young child for a week. The basic diet (if you are very poor) is home-made bread,[15] and tea with sugar, and perhaps a little goatsmilk. To the basic requirements of living, therefore, we must add tax money.

It is, of course, paradoxical that one of the most important components of a poor man's diet should be tea, an extremely expensive item. Nevertheless, tea is regarded as an essential commodity, and with bread has for many years been regarded as one of the symbols of the post-Khoi Khoin era. This was very neatly phrased by one of the few remaining Namaqua who joined the community of Steinkopf as a bywoner at the beginning of the century. Comparing the new life he found at Steinkopf with the old Nama tradition existing at that time in South West Africa whence he came, he said: 'Toe ek die vleis en die melk gelos het, en by die brood en die tee ingekom het, het ek geweet dat die ou lewe klaar was.' ('When I left the tradition of meat and milk and joined that of bread and tea, I realised that the old life had disappeared.')

A family's income varies with the seasons and rainfall, but when it rises above the amount which is needed for the minimum requirements of day-to-day living, the additional sum does not go towards food, but to the Church in the form of membership fees and Sunday collections. Church fees and donations are high, and a large family with five or six confirmed members will pay a minimum of £2 to the Church annually, or be ostracised by the missionary, Kerkraad and devout church-goers.

Next in importance, after the Church dues have been paid, are education (primary) of the children, clothing, and better food, the order of preference varying from family to family. Conservative people tend to attach least importance to the education of their children, while clothes are becoming more and more of an important item amongst all people. Those, for instance, who go to work on the mines and the towns spend what is left of their wages on clothing after they have sent money home. And even amongst the conservative people, one good set of clothing is considered essential for Sundays, weddings and funerals. These are known as the *kispak* (coffin clothes) because after death the body is usually dressed in them before being placed in the coffin.

Next we may rank the owning of a proper house, a *muurhuis*. The simplest type that is constructed when money is available is made of

[15] Generally made of unsifted meal.

corrugated iron and is erected adjacent to the mat-house. Tin houses are unsuited to the heat of summer and the cold of winter, and are therefore seldom used as dwellings, but rather as store-rooms. A tin house is regarded as a symbol of advancement and is not built to provide a more comfortable abode. *Muurhuise* are usually erected on the family's building plot in the mission village, even though the owners may spend most of the year on their farms. Professional people and well-to-do farmers usually build comfortable houses, similar in design to White homes found in the small rural towns of South Africa. There is a tendency, however, for some farmers to provide for the higher education of at least one child before building a European-type house; and there is evidence to suggest that the parents are influenced and aided by their children (after they have qualified) to build better-type houses as symbols of high status.

The relation between needs and income is important in every society and it is only by looking at the utility of commodities in their social setting that family budgets have any significance for the sociologist. Thus, in Steinkopf, the relationship between size of income and the order of preference given to the purchase of commodities does not merely reflect individual tastes but gives us a good idea of the responses that the members of groups make to the social forces acting upon them.

CONCLUSIONS

There are three general conclusions which can be made about the economy of the Steinkopf Reserve. First, the territory is not at present economically self-sufficient and is unable to support the whole of its potential population. Furthermore, it seems unlikely, even if better techniques of stock-keeping and grain-farming were adopted, that the potential population would be able to exist without the practice of migratory labour. On the other hand, if the Henkries date-grove is fully developed, and the proposed Orange River scheme incorporated, and the mineral resources of the Reserve exploited in the interests of the community, the present economic pattern may be completely transformed.

H. A. Kotzè's suggestion that the establishment of a lucerne fodder-bank at Goodhouse could, if properly planned, place animal husbandry in Steinkopf and the other Reserves on a healthy footing, is theoretically interesting.[16] But for this scheme to be effective, lucerne production at

[16] H. A. Kotzè, op. cit.

Goodhouse will have to be increased and loans will have to be made available to stock-farmers in these Reserves.

Secondly, although mixed-farming as at present practised is economically unprofitable when compared with the semi-skilled jobs available in the towns and on the mines, most people consider it desirable to maintain their interest in the land. To say that they do so merely because it is traditional, is to disregard the fact that living in a Reserve gives them greater security, especially in old age, than other Coloured people in the district or in the Republic of South Africa. The Reserve has become a sort of social refuge-area for some. If a person is unemployed in a town, it is difficult for him and his family to survive; but in the Reserve, housing and land are free (apart from taxes), and mixed-farming does provide some income, even if it is erratic, and local employment is open to a few people. Further, there is always the *possibility* of making a living out of tributing.

Finally, we should not underestimate the growing importance of the NKHV which marks a new phase in the economic life of the community. Apart from the benefits which the members of the NKHV and Steinkopf as a whole enjoy, it has provided a focus for the greater part of local trade, and through it stronger links have been created with the outside world in spite of the fact that it is locally controlled.

CHAPTER 4

KINSHIP AND MARRIAGE

IN THE community of Steinkopf we can distinguish five main kinds of kinship groups:[1] elementary families, residual families, rejuvenated families, extended families of various types, and lineages. The first three belong to one category, since residual and rejuvenated families are really modifications of the elementary family pattern. With the exception of a few residual families and the inclusion of a few extended families, the families constituting this category are the nuclei of the social structure. They may be termed nuclei, not merely because they comprise the simplest groups into which the community can be divided for convenience of analysis, but because each of these groups is the kernel of family life, economic activities, Church membership, and local politics.

Broadly speaking, there are two kinds of homesteads in Steinkopf: the elementary family type and its variations, and the extended family type, usually (but not always) consisting of a number of elementary families.

In Table XV a comparison is made of these homesteads drawing attention to important variations in their form. The differences between the homesteads in Steinkopf village and its environs, and those found

[1] *An elementary family* consists of husband and wife plus unmarried dependent children (including adopted children and illegitimate children of kinsmen). A childless couple in which the wife has not yet passed child-bearing age may also for convenience be classified as an elementary family (cf. M. Wilson, *et al.*, *Social Structure*, Keiskammahoek Rural Survey, vol. III, p. 55).

A residual family refers to a family consisting of a widowed spouse with dependent children. It also refers to an elementary family when all the children have married and established families of their own, leaving a wife who is past child-bearing age, and her husband. For convenience I have classified widows living alone in this category, as well as widows with dependents (ibid., p. 55).

A rejuvenated family refers here to a couple (or widow) who acquire the children of other parents after their own children have married (ibid., p. 55).

An extended family refers either to an elementary family containing additional categories of kinsmen or to a number of genealogically connected domestic families who live in the same homestead. The most common form of extended family in Steinkopf is the patrilineal extended family, consisting of a number of closely related male agnates, their spouses, and their children (cf. A. R. Radcliffe-Brown and D. Forde, *African Systems of Kinship and Marriage*, pp. 5-6).

TABLE XV

TYPES OF HOMESTEADS IN STEINKOPF

Type of homestead	A — Steinkopf village and environs				B — Hamlets and farms				A + B			
	Number of homesteads	% homesteads	Total persons	Av. size of homesteads	Number of homesteads	% homesteads	Total persons	Av. size of homesteads	Number of homesteads	% homesteads	Total persons	Av. size of homesteads
Elementary families	22	50	145	6·6	9	42·8	63	7	31	47·7	208	6·7
Residual families	9	20·5	23	2·5	1	4·8	2	2	10	15·4	25	2·5
Rejuvenated families	3	6·8	12	4·0	—	—	—	—	3	4·6	12	4·0
Patrilineal extended families	7	15·9	64	9·1	11	52·4	136	12·3	18	27·7	200	11·1
Extended families containing affines	3	6·8	34	11·3	—	—	—	—	3	4·6	34	11·3
All types	44	100·0	278	6·3	21	100·0	201	9·6	65	100·0	479	7·4

13·6% of homesteads contain some affinal kin

No homestead contains affinal kin, but see note below

9·1% of homesteads contain some affinal kin in Steinkopf.

Note: The sixty-five homesteads on which this table is based do not constitute a perfect random sample of the homesteads in Steinkopf. But they are considered to represent an adequate cross-section. Subsequently, however, I did locate one extended family containing affines in the !Kosis hamlet.

in the hamlets and on the farms, are also shown. The most important feature reflected here is the high percentage of patrilineal extended families found in the hamlets and on the farms, as compared with the village and its environs. Secondly, except for one known case no type of family living in the hamlets or on the farms contains affinal kin (apart from the wives of agnates), whereas certain families living in the village and its environs do. Thirdly, we must stress the fact that there is a higher percentage of residual and rejuvenated families in the Steinkopf village and its environs than in the hamlets and on the farms. And finally, we should note that there is a greater variety of family type in the village and its environs.

The contemporary kinship system is by no means homogeneous, and we can observe a number of kinship types, ranging from a modified form of the Nama type to the Afrikaner type[2] found amongst Whites in many of the dorps and farms in South Africa, particularly in the Cape Province. The differences in these kinship types are due to the impact of distinguishable cultural traditions and the processes of social change. In this analysis, however, we are concerned mainly with the Baster system, although we do refer also to the variations.

Marriage is monogamous and often virilocal after a short period of uxorilocality; descent is patrilineal, though status is modified by that of the maternal patrilineage; inheritance is mainly patrilineal with a tendency towards ultimogeniture. The largest residential unit of kinsmen is the patrilineal extended family, usually consisting of a husband and his wife and their unmarried children, and the elementary families of their married sons. Each elementary family lives in its own hut or house.

THE ELEMENTARY FAMILY[3]

The traditional dwelling and residential unit of the elementary family and residual and rejuvenated families is the mat-house. Here food is prepared and eaten, and from it members of the elementary family group co-operate with one another and with other kinsmen in various

---

[2] S. Patterson, *Colour and Culture in South Africa*, pp. 147-51, 303-5, and *The Last Trek*, pp. 189-90, 216-17, 239-50, 260-2. P. W. Kotzé, *Namakwaland*, pp. 62-77, *et passim*. H. G. Oxley, 'Wyksdorp', unpublished M.A. thesis, University of Cape Town, 1961.

[3] I have avoided using the term 'domestic family' here because a few domestic families can also be classified as extended families in terms of their members. See p. 39.

economic and social activities.

Today roughly two-thirds of the population still live in the traditional type of dwelling, while the remaining third occupy *muurhuise* which vary from rudely constructed tin shanties to comfortable cottages. But whether an elementary family lives in a Nama hut or in an attractive Dutch cottage, it has much the same degree of independence as one of the nuclei of the community, even though the type of architecture may symbolise certain important social differences.

In addition to its own hut or house, each elementary family usually has its own erf and livestock, manages it own household budget, and to a large extent plays its part independently in political and religious affairs. But in certain aspects of these activities its members co-operate with those of wider kinship groups to which they also belong. This is, of course, most marked among those elementary families which form part of extended families, sharing a common homestead.

The main activities in the elementary family are: for women, housekeeping and its ramifications throughout the year;[4] and for men, ploughing, reaping, herding, and periodical visits to the mines and towns as migratory workers. Thus the common dwelling of each elementary family is not indicative of mutual co-operation among its members in *all* activities. When a man marries, he does not aim to give his wife a home (*tuis*) but a house (*huis*): a place where women work and enjoy the company of women, and which the husband can use when he is not doing other things.

Division of labour and the separation of the sexes

As in most other peasant communities, there is sexual division of labour, and it is important for us to be acquainted with local ideas underlying this division in order to understand the behaviour patterns within the elementary family. There are three fundamental factors which determine a person's socio-economic position in the family: sex, seniority of birth, and marital status. Sex determines the nature of one's work, while the latter two factors determine the role one performs. Most important in family affairs is the contribution made towards its 'economy', and it is not until a person is actually doing the work laid down for him by custom that he can be regarded as a fully integrated part of the family system. Young children tend to

[4] In recent years migratory labour has become common among young women (see p. 39).

form separate groups and are seldom seen with either of their parents when the latter are working. Work begins at an early age (between 6 and 7) but it is a social requirement not necessarily based on the economic value of the service it renders, since much of the labour carried out produces uneconomic results. The cultivation of grain, for instance, results more frequently than not in a total failure of the crop or an annual yield of less than one bag. Yet, in spite of this knowledge, several months are wasted each year in unfruitful pursuits. Such 'economic' practices, therefore, cannot be regarded as having any significant material value for the elementary family and must be seen rather as highly socialised responses to the demands of tradition. We find also that some children of conservative parents are taken out of school, as soon as they can read and write, so that they can assume the roles laid down for them by custom.

In the elementary family the father and his unmarried sons are regarded as the breadwinners. Ideally this should be achieved by stock-raising and agriculture. But overstocking, bad methods of cultivation, and change in the standard of living, preclude a family from subsisting on farming alone. As a result, other occupations are sought; but mixed-farming is the ideal. Herding is carried out by the sons, usually in rotation, while all the sons help the father during the ploughing and reaping seasons. During the year, however, one or more of the members of the family may migrate to the mines or towns. At some time during his life a married man will have cultivated, herded, worked as a migrant labourer and, in some cases, carried out local small-scale mining; and it is part of a young man's general education to acquire all these 'skills', and to learn to adapt himself to a life of occupational alternatives.

The approved way of quickly finishing the major economic activities, such as ploughing, threshing and reaping, is for the closely related male agnates to co-operate with one another, moving as a team from erf to erf. But even when an agnatic plough team has been organised, father and sons still retain their family unity, in spite of the fact that they may be under the leadership of a more senior kinsman. Today, agnatic plough teams are rare owing to the absence of so many men in the towns, and their place has been taken by hired labour —individuals who work for a wage. However, the males of many elementary families still offer their services collectively to people who are unable to complete their work alone. These men have retained the old practice of working in kinship groups, but operate within the framework of the local wage economy. The wages paid vary, but the average is 2s. 6d. per day per person with the midday meal supplied. In the contemporary community, groups of neighbours or affines sometimes constitute a team, but most commonly teams consist of agnates only.

It is a full-time job to be a wife in Steinkopf, even though a woman is helped in her daily chores by her unmarried daughters, and in some of her tasks by her husband's brothers' wives, and sometimes by her mother-in-law. Her duties are many; she has to cook, fetch water, collect firewood, weave mats for hut repairs, make clothes, and do all the other chores of housekeeping. In addition she is responsible for weaving the mats and constructing the mat-houses for her sons when they marry. All these activities are known as women's work. Normally, as we have said, she is assisted only by her unmarried daughters, but in bigger tasks such as hut-building she is helped by her mother-in-law, and her husband's brothers' wives.

Unlike the economic co-operation of fathers and sons, a far more uniform pattern is found among mothers and daughters. We have seen that the stability of the father–sons group depends on co-operating in numerous activities, and conforming to a pattern of allegiance outside the home, whereas cohesion and co-operation between mother and daughters stem from the common activities centred in household duties.

Women are essentially hut-builders[5] and hut-keepers, and in her home a wife has very definite rights and privileges. It is proper always to display great respect towards a woman in her own hut or home. Wives not only get a housekeeping allowance from their husbands, but are also entitled to any money that a son or daughter working away from home sends to the family. Women are very quick to complain if their privileges are not respected by their husbands.

Milk and meat used to be the basic elements of the diet, but with the deterioration of pasture, during the past sixty years fresh milk has become an occasional luxury and meat is eaten only a few times a week. Nevertheless, when milk is available, its supply is still controlled by the women who do the milking of the animals, although the herding is done by men. Generally a family which has cowsmilk or goatsmilk has only enough for its own needs, but should a housewife have milk to spare after she has catered for her own family's requirements, she is expected to give away the surplus to some other family which has

[5] Houses are always built by men only.

none. Failure to observe this custom is thoroughly disapproved, and greedy people who hoard milk are generally looked down on. A case which illustrates very clearly the sanction imposed on people who keep more milk than they require can be cited. I was waiting one morning for my breakfast to be served at the house where I was boarding, when the milk boiled over. My hostess removed the pot and said to herself as she looked out of the window, 'And who has not got milk today?' When I inquired about the significance of her remark, she explained that whenever milk boils over it is believed that someone who is in need of milk caused it to do so; and added that the person responsible could not have known that she had a guest who took milk with his porridge!

The control of the crops and livestock is the prerogative of the head of the household who, with the help of his sons, slaughters the animals needed for meat, handing the carcasses over to his wife. Chickens belong to the wife, who also has control of the eggs.

Once these principles of division of labour and property have been understood, it is easier to grasp the basic behaviour patterns of the elementary family, for it is the proper participation in family economic affairs that gives form to social relationships within the family.

It is not true to say that a wife occupies an inferior status in the elementary family, but it does not follow that husbands and wives are equals, since each occupies a different status: husbands and wives are complementary. A wife, however, must always obey her husband, but it is seldom necessary for her to act against her will because custom demands that each has separate tasks. A husband can merely insist that his wife does her own work properly. It is not surprising, therefore, to find that tensions between husbands and wives very rarely occur, and that divorce is practically unknown. Temporary separations do sometimes take place, but there has been only one divorce during the past ninety years. This was an unusual marriage between a registered occupier and a Cape Town girl who deserted him after six months and refused to return.

We have stressed the importance of the separation of the sexes in the elementary family, but the principle applies to all other social relationships in the community. The general rule is that boys play with boys, girls with girls, men work and keep company with men, women with women. On formal occasions, in church, at funerals, at meetings, there is always rigid separation of the sexes, although at wakes and parties the sexes mix freely. The only time husbands and wives are seen together in public is on their wedding-day, and when they are travelling.

Marriage

The relationship between husband and wife is made clearer by examining the process of getting married.

Marriage begins with courtship (*vryery*) and a young man wanting to court a girl must first obtain the permission of her parents (normally her father). It is not until permission has been granted that he can visit her or 'take her out'. The young man must also inform his own parents of his intentions; this he does out of courtesy and respect, and also to test their reactions to his choice of a lover. Should the parents of the girl disapprove of the young man or even of his family, they will not normally consent to the courtship. On the other hand, if the parents of the young man disapprove of the girl or her family, they will not forbid him to visit his lover, but will make it quite clear that they will never consent to his marrying her. Formerly a young man would never have visited his lover openly unless his parents had expressed their approval first, and even today this practice is observed by the conservative people. But conflicts with parents frequently occur when young men reject the old custom because they wish to be free to select their own lovers. In the traditional community these conflicts between parents and their children were less likely to occur, not merely because young men and women were more obedient and respectful, but also because the attitude of the parents of one party towards the proposed courtship generally received the support of the other, since they always discussed the matter beforehand.

It may be asked why it is necessary for young men and women to obtain special courting sanctions from their parents. In the first place, it may be argued that intimate association between people of the opposite sex is inconsistent with the custom of separation of the sexes, and that a special licence has, therefore, first to be obtained to permit a breach of custom. This explanation is probably true, but it is based on inference only. On the other hand, the popular explanation is that, should a girl become pregnant, it is easy for parents to establish who the genitor is, and arrange a marriage between the couple or mete out suitable punishment for their 'sin'. This explanation is certainly consistent with the facts. We find, for example, that during the period 1947 to 1954 more than 90 per cent of all first babies born after marriage were conceived out of wedlock.[6]

But when we compare these figures with the reports of premarital intercourse in the traditional community, it seems unlikely that the present-day explanation of the courting licence applied also in former times. Formerly there were rigid sanctions against premarital sexual intercourse applied by the family, Church, and local government, and if a girl became pregnant she and her lover were severely flogged by their parents or members of the raad. As a further punishment the couple were made to attend Church and sit in the *sondebank* (sinner's pew) for a specified period of time.

A reliable informant who is well acquainted with the old law and custom informed me that, when he was a young man, nobody dared sleep with a girl before marriage, and that the courting licence in those days had nothing to do with premarital conception. His explanation was: 'No marriage can be successful unless it is preceded by a proper courtship, for it is during courtship that a couple get to know each other. When a couple get to know each other they either fall in love and stay together, or they find that they are incompatible and they separate. It is not good for people to fall in love and learn to understand each other, and then find that one or other pair of parents, or both pairs, disapprove of a marriage between them. For this reason we parents like to approve or disapprove of our daughters' and sons' lovers before they get emotionally involved [*te goed mekaar verstaan*]. It saves a great deal of unhappiness and trouble later on.'

When a couple decide to marry they must again inform their parents, who will give the suggestion considerable thought before official negotiations begin. Should there be no objections at this stage, the young man must select a *vrou-vraer* (go-between) from his father's lineage, preferably one of his father's elder brothers, but his paternal aunt may be chosen if she is a good spokeswoman. The role of the *vrou-vraer* is to speak on behalf of the young man and the young man's family at the first formal meeting with his future wife's family. On this occasion the young man and his *vrou-vraer* are accompanied by his parents and some other senior members of his family. The event takes the form of a party, and the young man is expected to provide food and tea, as a symbol of his ability and intention to look after the girl he wishes to marry. As soon as the gathering has

[6] Statistics were obtained from the missionary and members of the Kerkraad, and confirmed by reliable informants, some of whom said *all* first-born children were conceived out of wedlock.

assembled, the *vrou-vraer* says to the parents of the girl: '*Oom en tante*,[7] this man' (here he gives the man's full name) 'and this girl are engaged. It is my duty to ask you whether you are prepared to give her to us.'

If the parents of the girl agree to the marriage, they will, before giving their consent, ask the members of the young man's family to help their daughter with any difficulties she may encounter during her married life, particularly those problems concerned with housekeeping and the family budget. In some conservative families the girl's parents may refuse on principle to consent to the marriage at first, to test the enthusiasm of the young man, who may have to wait several months before he can arrange or afford another party.

There is no 'bride-price' in the community of Steinkopf, and not even the oldest inhabitants can recall the Nama custom of the gift of a cow by the spouses to their respective mothers-in-law.

After the marriage has finally been consented to by the parents of both the young man and his future wife, the banns of marriage are published in the mission church, and the wedding takes place according to Christian rites. Immediately after the ceremony the couple go to the house of the husband's parents, where they are formally congratulated by the members of both their families. There is a small celebration and a meal is eaten. This is the first formal meeting of the young wife with her in-laws but, as soon as the meal is over, the couple depart to the wife's parents' house, where the wedding feast is held. At this celebration there is much revelry and it is considered to be a time of great rejoicing. When this celebration is over, the husband is alone with his wife amongst her kinsmen, and residence is uxorilocal for a period lasting from a few days to a few months, sometimes until the first child is born. Only at the end of this period does marriage become permanently virilocal. If the period of uxorilocality is a short one, the newly married couple will sleep in the mat-house together with the girl's former elementary family, but should it last for several weeks or months, their new hut will be erected next to the wife's parents' hut and removed again when residence is finally changed. We should draw attention here to the fact that the practice of uxorilocal residence is dying out; today it is found only amongst the conservative people, although the 'new people' often spend one night with the wife's parents. Uxorilocality is essentially a practice confined to the people

[7] *Oom* and *tante* (uncle and aunt) used in this context are formal terms of address and are more or less the equivalent of 'Sir' and 'Madam' in English society.

who still live in mat-houses which can be easily moved.

The temporary changes in residence, the patrilocal meal, uxorilocal before virilocal residence, help to confirm the new status of the couple as married people and to establish a new pattern of relationships between the kinship groups. The couple visit the house of the husband's parents immediately after the marriage ceremony to acknowledge their allegiance to the group to which they will ultimately belong. The meal is given by the members of the man's family who are to be the guardians of the new member, the girl, in her position as a married women; it symbolises, if we may offer this interpretation, the promise of protection, the guarantee that was given by the young man's family to the family of the girl when the *vrou-vraer* asked for their consent to the marriage, and their agreement to transfer the girl to his own kinship group.

Formerly, neither the religious ceremony nor the first meal with the man's family constituted the full recognition of the marriage. This is still true today amongst the conservative people who regard the period of uxorilocality as an essential part of the process of getting married. In Steinkopf everyone is agreed that the purpose of uxorilocality is threefold. First, it is said to be the way in which a man gets to know and understand his wife's family. Secondly, it is said to be a way in which a man shows his respect for his wife's people: the longer the period of uxorilocality, the greater is his respect for them. Thirdly, it is said to help the wife to adjust herself to married life, since her parents are able to advise her should any difficulties arise in her relationship with her husband.

A good husband will always do his utmost to please his wife's family, especially his father-in-law, for whom he does odd jobs, and whom he tries to impress. We are told that many of the difficulties and tensions which inevitably arise in marriage are prevented by the custom of uxorilocality. The conservative people say that the complete process of getting married must be observed if proper and healthy relationships are to exist in kinship contacts. As one informant said, 'Our community is good and stable only where there is good fellowship and love; both these essentials are lacking in marriages among these modern people who maintain that a Church service or a civil marriage is sufficient for a successful marriage.'

The process of marriage, as in all societies, must be looked upon as a transitional rite or a series of transitional rites, whereby two individuals from different groups change status. Any change in status necessarily involves a dislocation of former social relationships and it is one of the functions of marriage rites to restore social equilibrium. In Steinkopf this is achieved not merely by a Church service and a reception, but by the whole process we have described, that is to say, from the day that the courting sanction has been obtained until permanent virilocal residence is assumed. Thus it is not until the couple finally move to take up virilocal residence that each receives the full status of a married person. The process of marriage makes a *vrou* (wife) out of a *meisie* (girl) and a *grootman* (adult man) out of a *jongman* (bachelor). When virilocal residence is established, the wife is admitted to the ranks of another group of women (the wives of her husband's male agnates and the unmarried women in her husband's patrilineal extended family), with whom she will be in regular close association, but she is mistress in her own house and is free to entertain *her* family at any time without the consent of her husband. The husband, on the other hand, returns with his new status to the company of his menfolk.

The majority of men marry in the mid-twenties, while 85 per cent are married by the time they are thirty-five. Women usually marry four or five years earlier; 83 per cent are married by the time they are thirty, and most marry in their early twenties. Closely connected with marriage age are the factors related to the selection of spouses. Men do not marry until they reach the age of twenty-one and become registered occupiers, or in the case of bywoners and 'strangers', until they achieve similar status in their respective classes. They must also be in a financial position to support a wife, which, as we have seen, means providing her with a hut and ensuring her, in theory if not in practice, an allowance to manage her household. Amongst those entitled to arable land, an erf is considered essential for marriage, which may be delayed if land is not available. These are economic factors which apply to all men, though not necessarily equally. But just as important perhaps in determining the age of marriage are the social factors which operate on a man when he begins to consider matrimony.

First, a man is not free to marry whom he pleases, and when he chooses, since all marriages are subject to the parental approval of both families as well as to the rules of endogamy and exogamy. But even when a man's choice of a wife does not violate the community's rules of preferential marriage, he has still to consider his parents' personal attitudes towards his prospective spouse. Older informants tell us that their fathers used to say to them, 'Son, go and court that girl for me!' Such sentiments are no longer expressed and sons are able to select their wives from a much wider circle of girls than in former years. Nevertheless, when parents express their disapproval of a son's choice of a wife, they usually say, 'Don't marry that girl, she is no good for us', implying first of all that she is not worthy to be associated with their family, and secondly that she will not fit in with the circle of women in their family, on whose members she will have to rely for company. Today many sons complain that their parents abuse their authority in this regard by threatening to leave them out of their wills if they disobey. On the other hand parents argue that this is the only way to get their sons to help them with their farming, since a son whose wife is unable to adjust to her new circle of women, when marriage is virilocal, usually leaves his extended family and sets up neolocal residence. Once a son has established himself away from his father most forms of co-operation between them are impossible.

Secondly, there is the emotional and physical maturity of the man; parents say they never allow a son to marry unless they are confident that he will be able to carry the full responsibilities of married life, for it is through a married son that they may achieve prestige, especially if their son marries 'up', or lose prestige if the marriage proves a failure. A marriage in which a man fails in his obligations means that the promises which the *vrou-vraer* made to the girl's family have been broken, and this, in addition to being an unpardonable breach of etiquette, creates tensions and bad relationships between two kinship groups.

Thirdly, no 'respectable' person is considered fit for marriage until he has been confirmed, because a fully integrated member of the community must also be a full member of the Church. We shall see later that common Church membership is the main factor which unites people with conflicting allegiances into a common community.

Generally it is the ambition of every man to marry as soon as he can, for marriage confirms a status, that of maturity and the right to associate with adults. Old age without marital status is viewed with ambivalent feelings, pathos and ridicule, and an old bachelor is still regarded as a child and has no alternative but to submit passively to the authority of his senior siblings and other relations. One old bachelor aged 86 years, for example, is forbidden to take part in adult conversation by his elder brother, aged 89 years. He is allowed to listen to adult conversation, but always remains seated on the ground holding his hand over his mouth and looking at the ground. This posture is said to be characteristic of a well-brought-up child of the last century.

The old bachelor is quite normal physically and has a clear mind; his elder brother attributes his continence to selfishness.

Women marry four or five years younger than men, and their marriage age is governed by most of the same factors. They are trained at home to be good wives, and are not permitted to marry unless their parents approve of their prospective spouses. The difference in the marriage ages of men and women can be attributed to the fact that, in order to marry, women do not require the economic backing that men do, although nowadays brides are expected to provide kitchen utensils and other articles needed for housekeeping. Formerly, a husband provided everything, including the wedding clothes for his wife.

The people of Steinkopf base their rule of exogamy on kinship, while endogamy is essentially class endogamy. In the contemporary community, custom prohibits marriages between siblings, first cousins, and brothers- and sisters-in-law. These prohibitions are based on the belief that such marriages produce physical deformities and intellectual deficiencies in the offspring, and create tensions in the kinship system. Throughout the ranks of the 'new people', the former belief is stressed as being the more important reason for the practice of exogamy, while the conservative people tend to attach equal importance to both. In the old community of a century ago marriages were also prohibited between people of the same lineage, while fifty years ago this prohibition extended only to members of the same major lineage segment.

During the past hundred years, therefore, there have been two changes in the rules of exogamy. First, the range of agnates whom a person may *not* marry has been reduced, although some conservative people still maintain that it is improper for a person to marry another belonging to the same major lineage segment as himself. Second, the incest taboos prohibiting marriage between brothers- and sisters-in-law and first cousins are no longer rigidly enforced, with the result that some 'new people' have begun to marry cross- and maternal parallel-cousins; in all these marriages neolocal residence is assumed directly after marriage, indicating a complete break with tradition necessitated by the violation of the incest taboo.

The rules of endogamy are not as precise as the rules of exogamy, but are implicit in the class structure,[8] which is partly reflected in the four lineage categories described later.[9]

[8] See chapter 6.   [9] See pp. 106-15.

One of the main functions of marriage is economic partnership. A single man is unable to participate in the mixed economy unless he has someone to look after his farming interest when he is absent from the Reserve as a migrant worker. Thus, apart from the fact that marital status gives prestige to the spouse, it is an economic necessity, and it is not surprising, therefore, to find that re-marriage is common; in fact, there are very few widowers who do not re-marry. A widower who does not re-marry cannot be said to be head of an elementary family, for if there are no children the family has ceased to exist; if there are young children they are distributed amongst members of the late wife's and husband's families; if all the children are married they are members of other elementary families. However, if there is a daughter old enough to keep house she will do so, but only until she marries, when she is expected to leave, although occasionally her husband may adopt uxorilocal residence to enable the father to remain under the domestic care of his daughter. Most commonly, the only practical solution is for the man to re-marry. If he is still young he will probably look for a suitable spinster; if he is an older man, it is considered proper for him to find a widow.

Statistics suggest that widows do not re-marry as frequently as widowers. For apart from the obvious factor that widows are less attractive than spinsters (except perhaps in the eyes of elderly widowers) it is easier for a widow to remain unmarried. A widow has a household which is her work place, and it is practicable for her to carry on her former duties and be head of the household (her new status) provided that she has children who are old enough to support her, or is eligible for a government pension.

Inheritance

The rules of inheritance are extremely flexible, and the procedure followed by any one family in the transmission of property from one generation to another depends largely on the size of the family and the age and marital status of each member. Generally, however, provided there are both sons and daughters, and the parents do not die before their children marry, the youngest son inherits his father's stock, tools, lands[10] and the family mat-house, while the daughters receive equal portions of their mother's property (cooking utensils, etc.). Male ultimogeniture is explained by the fact that the other sons

[10] The inheritance of arable lands has, of course, to be approved by the Management Board.

are helped materially by their father before he dies. A.E., for example, is a widower, and has five sons and three daughters. All are married except the youngest son, who is the heir to all his father's property including his lands. In this case male ultimogeniture is the rule because older sons have already received livestock from their father, and have been granted lands by the Management Board. The 'Benjamin' is 30 years of age, and, although he would like to marry, he has not yet received his father's permission to do so. Nevertheless, he knows that he will be rewarded for looking after his old father by the inheritance he will receive. Should he marry against his father's wishes, it is likely (and his father has told him so) that he will have to share his inheritance with his brothers.

It will be seen from this system that, although the youngest son is the heir to his father's property, the other sons have in fact also received property. Thus ultimogeniture is not an accepted rule but merely the logical manifestation of particular circumstances. Primo-, secundo-, or tertio-geniture would be quite normal, depending on the age, maturity and marital status of the sons at the time of their father's death. If the father dies before the eldest son is old or mature enough to receive property, it is customary for his widow to 'look after' his possessions as nominal head of the elementary family, until the son marries and sets up his own household.

In recent years there has been a tendency to modify this pattern. It is said by some people that all sons (and sometimes daughters) must inherit a portion of their father's property. Under these circumstances it is usual for a married man to decide with the help of his family how his property will be divided when he dies. But equal subdivision is often difficult, especially when there is fixed property. And in such cases it is usual for one son to acquire the property and pay each of the others their share in cash.

Disputes over property are common today, and this is attributed to the fact that the Management Board has no powers of arbitration in these matters, whereas the old raad did. Legally recognised wills are seldom made and most agreements are verbal. A recent case provides an example of some of the difficulties which can arise. D.B. owned a large five-roomed house, and it was agreed that when he died his eldest son J (son of his first wife) would inherit the house and pay each of his brothers (sons of a second wife) their share. The agreement was fulfilled and J occupied the house until he was an old man, when he 'gave' it to his youngest son, who paid his older brothers their shares of the property. But no sooner had the new owner moved into the house than his father's half-brothers claimed that they had never received their shares of the value of the property when it was first sold, and threatened legal action unless they were given compensation immediately. The owner wanted to keep the house at all costs—had the means to pay the additional sum and, therefore, complied with his uncles' demands. The informant who described the case explained to me that this *verneukery* (humbugging) would never have taken place in the days when verbal contracts (*toe mense net met die mond gepraat het*) were valid, because a few witnesses would have satisfied the raad that the initial payment had been made. But, since there was nothing in writing, the Management Board refused to interest itself in the case, and for the same reason legal assistance could not be sought.

Illegitimacy

Statistics are not available to assess the number of children born out of wedlock but in sixty-five homesteads studied, approximately 4 per cent of the children under twenty years of age were illegitimate in the sense that their biological mothers were either unmarried or, although married, had not kept their illegitimate children.

In Steinkopf there is no formal arrangement by means of which legitimate status is bestowed upon such children. Although the official adoption laws applying to Whites apply also to the community of Steinkopf, they are never utilised, nor are there customs involving the payment of material considerations such as are found, for instance, among the Bantu-speaking people.

But in spite of the absence of any legal ramifications in the practice of adoption, or the granting of legitimate status to children born out of wedlock, all such children nowadays eventually have social 'parents'. This is achieved by private arrangements either between individuals or between families. Probably the most common way in which legitimate status is acquired is through the marriage of the mother to another man. Such children are known as *voorkinders*. Though they are generally treated without prejudice by their fathers and siblings, they never enjoy the same status as first-born children in other families. On the other hand, should the mother marry, and she or her husband decide against incorporating the child into their elementary family, the child will normally be adopted by some other family (usually closely related) that has no children, or, in the case of elderly foster-parents, no unmarried children. This practice may be regarded as adoption, while the former may not, since the mother always remains the same. Frequently the child will be adopted by its 'grandparents' (i.e. the parents of its mother). In these cases the child is taught to regard his foster-parents as parents proper (even though genealogically they are grandparents) and to use the term of address *ma* instead of *ouma*, but to retain the term *oupa*. In cases of adoption by people other than grandparents, the terms of address *ma* and *pa* are always used.

Most adopted children know who their biological parents are, and their attitude towards them is familiar rather than deferential, especially with regard to the genitor, who is sometimes known as *boeta* (brother). The biological mother is usually called *antie* or *tante* or *nana*.[11] I cannot give any explanation for this relationship, but two alternative possibilities may be suggested. First, the tendency towards familiarity may be a joking relationship fulfilling the function of easing the tension between a person and his biological parents; alternatively, the fact that so many illegitimate children are adopted by their maternal 'grandparents', or families belonging to their grandparents' generation, means that through adoption they 'move up' a generation. This, therefore, places them in the same generation as their biological mothers, and in all probability in that of their genitors as well.

Formerly, when illegitimacy was extremely rare, and greatly disapproved of, both parties responsible for illegitimate children were severely thrashed by their respective parents or in special cases by members of the raad. Today, however, corporal punishment is not inflicted, nor does illegitimacy arouse much social disapproval.

Corporate nature of the elementary family

To summarise the nature of the elementary family, in terms of its corporate characteristics, we can isolate five factors which weld its members together. Firstly, the elementary family is the smallest residential unit in the society. All its members live together in a mat-house, except those who leave the Reserve temporarily as migrant workers, and those who are stationed at the cattle posts. Secondly, it is the unit of procreation and informal education of the offspring. Thirdly, it is a unit of economic co-operation in accordance with the principles of division of labour by sex. Fourthly, it is a political unit the head of which is the father. Formerly only the father had political rights, but recent legislation extends political rights to all male

[11] A term sometimes used for sister.

registered occupiers, which includes a number of single men. Fifthly, it is a religious group. Baptism and confirmation are not individual but family matters, since they are privileges which can be refused by the Kerkraad if the conduct of the parents is unsatisfactory. Similarly, parents are held responsible for their sons' and daughters' conduct by the Kerkraad, which may in certain circumstances summon both parents and erring child to its 'court'. Church dues are paid by the family and not by individuals. Prayers are 'family' prayers offered by individuals when the family is assembled together at home. Occasionally an *ouderling* may be invited to say special prayers if the family, or one of its members, is in great danger or difficulty—when the crops fail, when there is sickness, or in the event of a deceased relative's appearance at night in the guise of an evil spirit. In all family activities, co-operation, mutual respect and love among its members, are demanded by custom, and failure to practise these demands is strongly deprecated.

KINSHIP TERMINOLOGY AND BEHAVIOUR PATTERNS[12]

Before we begin our analysis of the extended family and other kinship groups, it is necessary to examine the nature of the kinship terminology and the behaviour patterns which are implicit in the terms.

Any system of kinship terminology is the formula which expresses an institutionalised pattern of behaviour amongst people who claim family relationships. That is to say, kinship terms are the set form of address used by people when speaking to or about their relatives. But kinship terminology provides no reliable index as to the nature of the residential grouping of kin, nor does a classificatory term necessarily indicate that the kinsmen to whom it is applied constitute a corporate group.

General principles of kinship behaviour patterns in Steinkopf

In Steinkopf there are four interacting factors on which the general principles of kinship behaviour depend: sex and marital status (already discussed), parental authority and respect, and seniority and age.

The members of the community generally hold that there is only one way to behave towards another person (whether he be a kinsman or a stranger), and that is respectfully. It is not surprising, therefore, that the ideal in all kinship relationships is mutual respect, a condition which is largely achieved, although to a lesser degree in recent years than in the past. The degree of respect, of course, varies, some people

[12] See p. 89 for table of kinship terminology.

TABLE XVa

STEINKOPF KINSHIP TERMINOLOGY

Description of kin	Terms of address used (man or woman speaking)
3rd ascending generation	
great grandparents, their siblings, and their siblings' spouses	ougrootjie, or oupagrootjie, or grootjie (men) / oumagrootjie (women) / Christian names and surnames are sometimes used to distinguish between them.
2nd ascending generation	
grandparents, their siblings, and their siblings' spouses	oupa (men) / ouma (women) / Christian names and surnames are sometimes used to distinguish between them.
1st ascending generation	
father and father-in-law	pa or tata
mother and mother-in-law	ma or mama (sometimes moeder)
father's and mother's brothers and their wives (arranged in order of seniority according to their sibling groups). The terms for their wives are given in brackets.	grootoom or oompa or grootpa (grootante or grootantie or grootma) / oomtjies or oom + name, if necessary (antiena or tante + name, if necessary) / middeloom or oom + name, if necessary (annekie or tante + name, if necessary) / oompietjie or oom + name, if necessary (tantekie or tante + name, if necessary) / kleinoom or kleinpa (kleintante or kleinma)
The terms for father's and mother's sisters and their husbands follow the same principles. Thus the terms in brackets apply also to father's and mother's sisters.	Christian names or an appropriate sibling term may be used if the age difference is slight.
sons and daughters of grandparents' siblings and their spouses	oom + name, if necessary (men) / tante or antie + name, if necessary (women) / Christian names or an appropriate sibling term may be used if the age differences are slight.
Contemporary generation	
brothers, in order of descending seniority / sisters, in order of descending seniority / cousins	ouboetie, boeta, Christian name, kleinboetie or kleinpa or oompies / ousus or adda, sussie, antietjie or lala or nana or Christian name, kleinsus / appropriate sibling terms or Christian name; the terminology used being determined by the status of the parents and age differences.
brothers- and sisters-in-law	appropriate sibling terms, or swaer (brother-in-law), sometimes ouswaer or suaerie, and skoons (sister-in-law), sometimes ouskoons
husband and wife	husbands call their wives ma or mama or by their Christian names / Wives call their husbands pa or by their Christian names
1st descending generation	
parents addressing their children, married or unmarried	Christian names, but frequently they use the sibling terms which their children use in addressing each other, e.g. ouboetie, for eldest son
children of other kinsmen	Christian names or seun (boy) and dogter (girl)
2nd descending generation	
grandchildren	as for own children

being afforded more than others, but custom demands that all should be shown it, and one of the first lessons given by parents to their children is instruction in the proper modes of respect.

Respect in Steinkopf is not merely the expression of deferential esteem towards one's kinsmen and neighbours. It must be shown to others for the sake of one's parents, who are to be honoured and obeyed. Thus disrespect towards a person is not simply an indication of bad manners, but one of the most unseemly ways of insulting one's parents. Traditionally, a child who failed to respect one of his father's contemporaries would be thrashed by the person he had insulted, and again by his father when he returned home, for the dishonour his misconduct had brought to his family. But if the initial thrashing was unjustified the child's father would demand an apology, failing which he could bring a case against the person, not for beating the child, but for insulting the father and his family.

Authority in the family, although linked with respect, implies also obedience and honour (*eer*). As with respect, obedience and honour are parentally determined. Thus a man must honour and obey his mother's eldest brother in the same way as his mother does, but in addition he must show his maternal uncle the deference he already displays towards his mother. On the other hand, although he will respect his mother's youngest paternal uncle's son, he will not be expected to honour and obey him, because that person (especially if his mother was the daughter of an eldest sibling) would be considerably junior in status to his mother.

In all relationships with kinsmen the rule is, 'Take your cue from your parents' behaviour'; and it is customary for children to ask their parents how they behave towards a relative if they have not previously had an opportunity of observing their parents' behaviour towards him. Today difficulties often arise because a section of a family may have developed a different set of kinship terms and the corresponding behaviour patterns, and to overcome these difficulties some parents advise their children to ask these kinsmen how they wish to be addressed.

Bearing in mind the principles we have already established, we turn to seniority and age, which (especially the former) are the factors which determine an individual's actual social position in the family. In each sibling group, order of birth (i.e. seniority) is expressed in the kinship terminology, the eldest son (*ouboetie*) and the eldest sister (*ousus*) being considered senior to their junior siblings. Thus the seniority of siblings varies according to the order of birth; the greatest difference in status occurs where there is the greatest difference in age.

The principle of seniority applies generally to kinship behaviour patterns, so that the relation between two people of different sibling groups is the synthesis of their respective sibling statuses as linked through their parents; this relationship is also modified by age. For example, a man's behaviour towards his father's eldest brother's eldest son (when his father is the youngest sibling of his group) is always one of deference: (a) because his parallel cousin is the senior sibling in his group, and (b) because the parallel cousin's father is the senior sibling in his group. In fact, he is linked to his senior parallel cousin through his own father, who is junior to the father of his cousin. On the other hand, the father's eldest brother's youngest son would be treated as an equal if ego was the eldest sibling in his group and their respective ages were the same.

The importance of differences in age and seniority became clear from the very first days of field-work, as the greatest difficulty was always experienced in obtaining any kind of information from junior kinsmen when their seniors were present in the neighbourhood or even in the Reserve. Indeed, many young people stated quite emphatically that they were too stupid to answer even the simplest question. The usual reply to a question from a young kinsman was, 'Ek wil sê, maar ek mag nie sê nie, ek is nog te dom'. ('I want to answer, but I may not, I am still too ignorant.') He would then suggest that I went to see his father who might be able to answer the question. Father would reply in much the same terms, adding that his understanding of the problem was not as good as his elder brother's. Consequently a great deal of time would be spent until the most senior relative in the lineage could be found. On some occasions I went to as many as six different people, members of three generations, before a definite answer to a problem would be given. Then, while the senior man spoke, the others sat round quietly, seldom venturing to make a comment unless asked directly by their senior kinsman. Even then their replies would be apologetically given only after considerable hesitation.

Moreover, when asked for information about the past, many very senior men evaded the answer, because, they said, they had not received their 'understanding' (*verstand*) at that time. In such cases it was quite obvious that they knew the answer but were not prepared to give it because they had been minors when the event took place.

Children and parents

Children address their fathers by the terms *pa* or *tata*, and their mothers by the terms *ma* or *mama* (sometimes *moeder*). They also use these terms when referring to them individually. The term *ouers* (parents) is sometimes used when referring to parents jointly, but it is more common to use the phrase *pa en ma*, which, I suggest, reflects the fact that they perform very different roles in the elementary family, and cannot therefore be referred to jointly.

Generally *pa*'s or *ma*'s word is considered final and there should never be any argument with them or questioning of their orders, although today, amongst the 'new people', disobedience to parental authority has become common, and corporal punishment (which is not as severe as it was in former times) has ceased to be an effective means of instilling discipline. Parents attribute this to school education, which they maintain has undermined their authority, encouraging children to show more respect to their teachers than to them. As alternatives to the traditional forms of punishment, children are sometimes taken to an *ouderling* or the missionary, and older children may even be brought before the Kerkraad. The inability of some parents to discipline their children effectively on their own is demonstrated by the fact that unruly children are often threatened by their parents that they will be taken to the schoolteacher; but these threats are never carried out.

Although many parents still insist that their children are deferential to the point of being obsequious, it does not follow that their attitude towards them is lacking in affection. There is always great tenderness and attachment between a mother and her young children, and both parents tend to behave informally towards all their children when the day's work is completed and the elementary family is, as it were, 'off-duty'. It is difficult to describe precisely all the facets of parent–child relationships, but we may say that the relationship is formal only when there is work to be done, and when there are other people present; on such occasions children should be neither seen nor heard.

During the first part of a child's life, up to the age of five years, its main parental contact is with the mother, but soon after the boys begin to be admitted into the ranks of men, and the girls into the ranks of women, for the purpose of sexual division of labour.

The bonds between parents and their children are retained throughout childhood and adolescence into maturity, although the relationships are modified at marriage when daughters leave home to join their husbands, and men become heads of new elementary families. But respect and honour remain.

Siblings

To complete our analysis of behaviour patterns in the elementary family, we turn to a discussion of the terminology used to distinguish between siblings. The eldest siblings of each sex are honoured by the titles *ouboetie* (eldest brother) and *ousus* (eldest sister), the latter sometimes being called *adda* (derived from *abba*(?), the person who carried her brothers and sisters on her back), if she was old enough to look after her siblings when they were very small. *Ouboetie* and *ousus* are treated with great deference by their younger siblings. When parents are absent from home, *ouboetie* and *ousus* take charge of the family, performing the roles of *pa* and *ma* among their younger siblings. Nowadays, after the death of both parents, *ouboetie* is sometimes responsible for dividing the family property amongst his siblings.

Respect must also be shown to the other brothers and sisters, and not only the second but even the third eldest may be honoured. For example, in a sibling group consisting of three brothers and three sisters, each will be given a title indicative of his social position: *ouboetie*, *boeta* and *kleinboetie*; *ousus*, *sussie* and *kleinsus*. *Ouboetie*, *boeta*, *ousus*, and *sussie* are terms of honour (*eer*) and respect, while *kleinboetie* and *kleinsus* are terms of respect only.

Sibling terminology in Steinkopf can best be described as a substitute for personal names indicating the order of birth and status of the members in each sibling group. In some families personal names are never used either by the parents or by the siblings, and a child will often be rebuked or punished if he fails to honour his eldest brother and sister with their descriptive titles. Thus, if *kleinboetie* is told by *mama* to call *ousus*, he must say to his eldest sister, 'Ousus, mama het gesê dat ousus moet mama-toe gaan'. ('*Ousus, mama* wants to see *ousus.*') In giving the command, *mama* would have said, 'Kleinboetie' (or his Christian name), 'roep vir ousus'. ('*Kleinboetie*, call *ousus.*')

The fundamental rule in sibling relationships, therefore, is that, although all siblings must respect one another, the first and second born must always be honoured, honour being greatest where there is the greatest difference in age.

The position of the youngest son in the family must receive further elaboration. As an alternative term of address to *kleinboetie*, the youngest son is sometimes called *kleinpa* (little father) though normally this term is not used until he is married. *Kleinboetie* is given a great deal of attention and is treated with much affection by his siblings and parents, who nowadays often call him by the English term 'darling'. ('Darling' is a new word in Steinkopf vocabulary and I have never heard it used as a term of affection for anyone besides the youngest son.) One woman explained to me that her youngest son was called *kleinpa* because 'he is really a small edition of his father. We love him and treat him just like father, except that he hasn't got father's position and authority.' *Kleinboetie* is a sort of Benjamin: he often remains in the mat-house with his parents until his brothers have married (he is normally the last to marry) and, as we have seen, in some families he is the heir to his father's property.

The closest and most permanent bonds in all kinship relationships are those between brothers. As children they are playmates, and as they grow up they work together with their father. All brothers are said to 'ape their fathers'. Even when, for practical purposes, the potential extended family unit is divided, brothers try to live in the same district or ward because they need each other not only for economic co-operation but also for companionship.

Sisters, on the other hand, do not display the same fellowship after marriage, although the bonds of companionship between them before marriage are probably stronger than those between brothers. This is because virilocal residence separates them geographically, making regular companionship impossible.

Uncles and Aunts

Two very important categories of kinsmen are parents' siblings and their spouses. Both categories are afforded the same degree of respect, and no terminological distinction is made between paternal and maternal siblings. Where terms overlap, Christian names are used as well to distinguish between them. Mother's and father's eldest brothers are addressed as *grootoom*, *oompa*, or *grootpa*, the last term being used mainly by the conservative people. Mother's and father's youngest brothers are usually known as *kleinoom* or *kleinpa*, although many nephews nowadays use Christian names or the term *boeta*. The siblings in between these two extremes are most commonly called *oom* plus their Christian names, but in many families terms such as *oometjies*, *oompie*, *middeloom*, *oompietjies*, are used to give a more accurate description of their kinship positions. The wives of all these kinsmen are given the corresponding feminine forms of the terms used for their husbands, namely *grootma* or *groottante*, *kleinma*. The conservative people always use this system of terminology, but in recent years the 'new people' tend not to honour all their uncles and aunts, and we find that, where age differences are slight, Christian names are sometimes used in place of terms such as *oompietjies* and *kleintante*.

Terms for father's and mother's sisters follow the same terminological scheme as those used for the parents' brothers' wives, while their husbands are classified as though they were father's and mother's brothers.

The most important characteristic of these categories of kinsmen is that no distinctions, other than those based on age and sex, are made in the terminology between maternal and paternal siblings, and their spouses.

Other bilateral kinsmen in this generation (sons and daughters of grandparents' siblings) may also be addressed as *oom* or *tante*, but they are not regarded as belonging to the same category as paternal and maternal siblings. Thus, the terms *oom* and *tante* in this context are only used to honour senior kinsmen who are much older than oneself. Where the difference in age is insignificant, Christian names are used.

In comparison with modern English terminology and behaviour patterns, we may say that the conservative members of the community have no uncles and aunts, and mother's and father's siblings are best described as uncles and aunts (junior and senior) with a tendency towards being regarded as parents; hence terms such as *oompa*, *kleinpa*, *antiema* and *kleinma* in the terminology.

Grandparents, great-grandparents, their siblings and siblings' spouses

The classificatory term *oupa* is applied to both maternal and paternal grandparents and their brothers. Similarly *ouma* is used for maternal and paternal grandmothers and their sisters. Further, the spouses of all those called *oupa* and *ouma* are known respectively as *ouma* and *oupa*. The term also applies to all old people whether they are related or not.

The same principles apply to great-grandparents and to people of their generation. The men are called *oupagrootjies* or *ougrootjies*, the women *oumagrootjies*. Collectively they are referred to as *grootjies*, but *onse ougrootjies* (our great-grandparents) refers only to agnates. Ancestors above the third ascending generation are referred to as *oorgrootjies*, a term which also applies only to agnates.

Grandparents and great-grandparents are always greatly honoured and admired for their wisdom (*verstand*), experience and knowledge.

But they are far more indulgent towards their grandchildren than parents are towards their children, and as senility sets in, parents usually overlook the horseplay which high-spirited children indulge in towards their grandparents, provided they do not overstep the mark of respect.

Cousins

Just as both paternal and maternal uncles and aunts tend to be regarded as quasi-parents, so also are cousins regarded as quasi-brothers and -sisters. To marry a cousin, either cross- or parallel-, is said to be the same as marrying a brother or a sister, and the principles governing forms of address tend to reflect this, but since cousins derive their status from their parents, they fall into different categories. For example, it is the practice for cousins to use Christian names when addressing each other, except when children of a junior brother or sister address the children of a senior brother or sister. In this case the junior cousins will use titles of honour such as *ouboetie* or *ousus*.

There are two factors which determine relationships among cousins. First, as we have already shown, is the status of their parents: the children of senior siblings being afforded more respect than those of junior siblings except where age differences are slight. Secondly, there is the kinship category of the cousins: agnatic ortho-cousins are considered to be closer kin (that is, more like brothers and sisters) than others, owing partly to the fact that there is a tendency towards father-right, but more especially because agnatic ortho-cousins are welded together through the extended family by common residence and common participation in economic and other activities.

Affines

Parents-in-law are addressed by the same terms as ordinary parents, namely *pa* and *ma*, but the relationship of a man with his parents-in-law differs considerably from his wife's relationship with hers. In the first place a man's formal and regular contact with his wife's parents ceases after the period of uxorilocality. For a woman, the position is different because after virilocal residence has been taken up she enters into regular association, formal and informal, with her husband's parents, and often other kinsmen as well.

But marriage does not deprive the members of the woman's family of the whole of their jurisdiction over the girl they are losing. Custom demands that a married woman should obey her husband and his senior agnates, but the authority which they have over her is a privilege, which, if abused, entitles her to complain to her own kin and so bring her husband's family into disrepute in the community.

The form of address for brothers- and sisters-in-law varies from family to family and either a sibling term, or the terms *swaer* (brother-in-law) and *skoons* (sister-in-law) are used. Sibling terms are generally used by the conservative people, but not always, and the difference between the two forms is mainly a linguistic one, although it has other significance also. In the first place *swaer* and *skoons* are classificatory terms which include as brothers- and sisters-in-law the spouses of husband's and wife's siblings, whereas the sibling terms refer only to husband's and wife's siblings. Secondly, the fact that the conservative people generally use the sibling terms, and the 'new people' the extended terms, suggests that the *swaer-skoons* terminology is of recent development. Nevertheless, in spite of these differences, the behaviour patterns of the conservative and the 'new people' towards *their* brothers- and sisters-in-law are very similar: both groups regard them as quasi-brothers and sisters, and marriage with quasi-siblings of deceased spouses is regarded as incestuous.

The brother- and sister-in-law relationships and the difference in the terminology used are best understood by examining the historical development of this aspect of the kinship system. Although the historical data is meagre, it gives us a clue as to the origin of these changes in the system, as well as a better understanding of its sociological significance.

Mrs. Hoernlé, in a study of the Namaqua,[13] tells us that a man behaved towards his wife's sisters 'much as he would towards his own wife' and that 'a woman considered her husband's younger brothers as her husbands and used, in the old days to be inherited by one of them'. She points out that in the *Berichte der Rheinischen Missionsgesellschaft* (1856 and 1860) numerous instances of a younger brother taking over his eldest brother's widow are reported. She does not tell us whether a man ever married (or was allowed to marry) his deceased wife's sister, but two old Namaqua living in Steinkopf agreed that this was allowed in their traditional society. Mrs. Hoernlé reminds us further that the practice was condemned by the missionaries who report it, and there is a strong suggestion, therefore, that it was partly owing to missionary influence that the practice of the sororate and the levirate became

[13] A. W. Hoernlé, 'The Social Organisation of the Nama Hottentots', *American Anthropologist*, vol. 27, no. 1, 1925, p. 23.

regarded as incestuous, although clearly this was not the only factor.

After the missionaries had established themselves as religious and political leaders in Steinkopf and other communities, we find that the relationships between people and their brothers- and sisters-in-law changed considerably. What had formerly been a potential husband–wife relationship now became a sort of sibling relationship, with marriage between them regarded as incestuous. Accompanying this change in relationships there was a corresponding change in the terminology: brothers- and sisters-in-law were now addressed by appropriate sibling terms. Thus my eldest brother's (*ouboetie's*) wife was called *sussie*;[14] my second eldest brother's wife was also called *sussie*, or perhaps called by her Christian name if she was the same age as myself or younger; my youngest brother's wife (*kleinboetie's* or *kleinpa's* wife) was called *kleinma*. The terms for brothers-in-law also followed this pattern but the rule was even more complicated by the factors of age and seniority. Thus, when my eldest sister married, her husband was usually older than any of her brothers (and, of course, older than my sister), and would normally be addressed as *ouboetie* too. Occasionally, however, if he was much older and belonged to the first ascending generation he could be addressed as *oom* to acknowledge his more senior status.

Nowadays the pattern we have just described is still found amongst some conservative people, although most people use the Afrikaans classificatory terms *swaer* and *skoons*. The terms *ouswaer*, *swaerie* and *ouskoons* are sometimes used to distinguish between people of different ages. But the preference for these Afrikaans terms is, as we have already pointed out, mainly linguistic.

The use of kinship terms outside the family

A study of kinship terminology and behaviour patterns would be incomplete if mention was not made of the use of kinship terms outside the family. For, in spite of the existence and development of class divisions, the people of Steinkopf still regard their community as 'one big family', although the older generation insist that this fellowship used to be stronger than it is today.

The fact that these sentiments, which are still found at the present time, exist side by side with rules and customs which keep families apart, is merely an example of one of the common paradoxes of social

[14] Not *ousus* because she was normally younger than the sibling who was called by that term.

life: conflicting allegiances may help ultimately to produce social cohesion. Cleavages between groups need not necessarily produce social disequilibrium in society as a whole, and in many instances they may help to effect solidarity.[15]

In Steinkopf there are many examples of jealousies, conflicts and cleavages in the various social institutions, but in the wider framework of society bonds exist which override, as it were, these differences and unite people in 'one big family'. And we find that terms of address used within the family are also extended outside it.

Male registered occupiers (but not bywoners) or sons of registered occupiers of the same age-groups, when addressing one another, unless they use Christian names or nicknames (the latter are very common), will call each other *broer* (brother) or *ou broer* (old chap). Children, however, always use Christian names and nicknames.

Older men to whom respect must be shown are normally addressed as *oom* (uncle), or *oupa* (grandfather) when the difference in age is great, and they address younger men and boys as *seun* (son) or *my seun* (my son).

With a few important differences, women follow much the same pattern when speaking to members of their own sex. But generally women are more formal and distant than men in their manner of address and behaviour. Christian names are common amongst friends of the same age-group, but strangers and acquaintances always behave towards one another more respectfully; married women in particular are always afforded respect by acquaintances and are addressed by their surnames with the prefix *Missis* (Mrs.). Sometimes they are called *antie*.

Older married women are addressed as *ouma* though they may be referred to as *ou Missis A*, and older women call girls and young women *dogter* (daughter). If two women friends have the same Christian name they will usually avoid it and call each other *mieta*,[16] although sometimes only one will be termed *mieta* and the other will retain her own name. In Steinkopf *mieta* is no more than a nickname used to avoid the embarrassment of calling somebody else by one's own name.

We have discussed elsewhere the principle of the separation of the sexes, but it is important to realise that this separation does not necessarily imply mutual avoidance; young people of a different sex use

[15] Cf. M. Gluckman, *Custom and Conflict in Africa*, 1955.
[16] Cf. N. Mansvelt, *Proeve van een Kaapsch — Hollandsch Idioticon*, 1884, p. 103. *Meta = naamgenoot* (namesake).

Christian names freely, and occasionally outside the family the terms *broer* and *suster* are used.

Adult men call all young girls *dogter*, unless they are relatives. They reciprocate with *oom* and *oupa* depending on the difference in age, and married women call all young boys *seun*, who reciprocate with *Missis A* (sometimes *antie*) or *ouma*.

Married women are usually addressed by men as *missis* (more commonly without their surnames) or *ouma*: conversely, women use the terms *oom* and *oupa*. Christian names are, of course, used among intimate friends.

In addition to these terms of address used among unrelated people, various titles are given to people holding special positions in the community. All teachers and former teachers are addressed as *Meester*, the postmaster is called *Posmeester*, and all elders and former elders of the Church are called *Ouderling*, while the various members of the Management Board are addressed by the titles corresponding to the office which they hold: *Superintendent* (sometimes called *Meneer*), *Sekretaris*, *Korporaal* (nowadays called *Raadslid*, i.e. Councillor). The manager of the co-operative store is known as *Bestuurder*. It is customary for these people to reciprocate the respect shown them with terms of address such as *oom* and *oupa* for older men, and *missis* and *ouma* for married women, although contemporaries are addressed by their Christian names, surnames or nicknames.

The variability of kinship terminology

In all societies, kinship terms do show some degree of variability: i.e. alternative forms of address are sometimes used for the same categories of kin. In some societies these alternative forms of address indicate different behaviour patterns while in others they do not. In contemporary Western society, for example, a boy may call his father *dad* in ordinary conversation, but when he asks his father for extra pocket money may address him by the more affectionate term *daddy*.[17]

The Steinkopf kinship system provides us with examples of variations in kinship terminology which reflect not only different behaviour patterns but also indicate the existence of minor differences in kinship types. We have already drawn attention to these variations, but for the purposes of this discussion we need merely bear in mind

[17] Cf. D. M. Schneider and G. C. Homans, 'Kinship Terminology and the American Kinship System', *American Anthropologist*, vol. 57, no. 6, Dec. 1955.

that these differences do exist, in order to avoid the misconception
that the kinship pattern is uniform throughout the community.

THE EXTENDED FAMILY

In contemporary Steinkopf the largest residential family unit ever
achieved is the patrilineal extended family, generally comprising a
husband and wife, their unmarried children, and the elementary
families of their married sons. Formerly, patrilineal extended families
were much larger but by the beginning of the century, owing to
population increase and expropriation, shortage of land made it
necessary for large extended families to fragment so that each family
could live close to its erfs. Nevertheless, male agnates tried to secure
adjacent lands in order to make some degree of economic co-operation
possible. Elsewhere we have shown how rivalry between brothers also
led to residential fragmentation.

During recent years two additional factors have influenced residential
grouping: the growth of a village community and a new system of
administration. Amongst other things the village community is
characterised by association and co-operation among people, not on
the basis of kinship but on that of class, occupation, and common
interests. And closely linked with the growth of the village (which
resembles a small town) are the changes which have taken place in
local government. The present-day administration recognises only the
elementary family as a kinship group, and discourages by its legislation,
co-operation among a wider circle of kinsmen (see pp. 139 ff.). Further,
the steady change in the economy from mixed-farming to wage-
earning in the Steinkopf village and outside the Reserve has led to
the greater economic independence of each elementary family, which
tends to make large residential units functionally superfluous. Nevertheless, the extended family persists strongly amongst the conservative
people, and still exists to a certain extent among the 'new people'.

Homesteads consisting of patrilineal extended families are found
mainly in the hamlets and the farming districts which are scattered
throughout the Reserve, and on the periphery of the mission village,
where their presence is marked by clusters of mat-houses which
stand out clearly against the haphazard array of white-washed cottages
and corrugated-iron dwellings. The huts in each homestead are
usually arranged in a straight line facing the east, and are separated
from one another by a distance of fifteen or twenty yards. On the
left (facing outwards) of the main hut (the hut of the father and his

elementary family) stands the hut of the eldest son, while on the right, arranged in order of descending seniority from the main hut, are the huts of the other sons.

In the following description of the corporate activities of the extended family, the independence of each elementary family must be borne in mind in order to distinguish clearly between the functions of each group. The differences in these functions are of degree rather than of kind.

The most important activities of the extended family are economic, and are usually complementary to those of the elementary family. Thus, when the elementary family is unable to achieve a task alone, the extended family comes into operation. Ploughing, reaping, and threshing, for instance, call for the co-operation of all available male agnates. In the contemporary community this means, in practice, all the male members of the extended families, and often neighbours and other kinsmen, when help is needed for major tasks. Earlier we discussed this type of co-operation in our account of the agnatic plough teams (see pp. 74–5). Herding, too, sometimes calls for co-operation amongst extended family members, especially among families who send some of their members regularly to the mines and towns. Thus, one agnate, or a pair of agnates, will look after the livestock of several elementary families while the other men are absent from the Reserve, and after a period of six months or a year will themselves go out as migrant workers while the herding is committed to the charge of other members of the extended family. When the crops are ripening, it is always considered the mutual obligation of all members, men and women, of the extended family to guard the lands and protect them from livestock and donkeys.

Brothers and their sons sometimes pool their resources and carry out small-scale mining activities on the base-mineral deposits in the remote parts of the Reserve. Although there are only a few families who take part in tributing, the existence of this type of co-operation is indicative of solidarity amongst the members of the extended family.

Women members of extended families do not co-operate as actively as men because their work is of a different nature. Yet, whenever a new mat-house has to be built or an old one repaired, it is customary for all the women to co-operate in the extremely arduous task of weaving new mats. Nowadays neighbours tend also to co-operate in these tasks.

Although each elementary family prepares its own food, eats

together and manages its own budget, in times of need or after a drought or blight or unemployment it is customary for each family to assist the other in every possible way. Thus, a family which is penniless can always rely on assistance from the other members of its extended family group, and sometimes from other kinsmen.

As tokens of affection and mutual respect, 'reciprocal meals'[18] are occasionally sent by women to some member of another elementary family, and in former times this was a regular practice. The meal consists of a plateful of choice, carefully prepared food, delivered usually in the middle of the day. After a time the gesture is returned. Most commonly these meals are initiated by a daughter-in-law who sends a plate of food to her mother-in-law, but there is no fixed rule and neighbours are sometimes included. It is clear that the function of these meals is to create good fellowship and friendship between individuals and families, although the 'new people' maintain rather cynically that they are just excuses to show off good cooking. The conservatives, on the other hand, insist that 'reciprocal meals' are symbols of love and respect, and they draw attention to the fact that the infrequency with which they are sent today is but one of the many examples of the lack of charity evident in the new tradition. We pointed out that the sending of 'reciprocal meals' was most common between mothers and daughters-in-law, thus the absence of tension between these two groups of kin among the conservative people, and the marked existence of tensions between them amongst some of the villagers, seem significant.

Leadership amongst the members of an extended family rests with the senior male, who is normally the father of a group of married brothers. But in common tasks, which affect only women, his wife, the senior woman, assumes the position of superordination.

As senior male, the father is often called upon to settle disputes which arise between members of his extended family, and, after his death, although his wife becomes head of his elementary family, his position of authority over the other members passes to his eldest son. Formerly, and amongst some conservative people today, the eldest son was afforded all the respect his father enjoyed; but nowadays, with the weakening of authority in the family, the extended family disintegrates or fragments soon after the death of the father, because *ouboetie*'s leadership is not effective.

[18] There is no special name for these meals today but one informant reported that they used to be known as *liefde male* (meals to show affection).

Earlier we drew attention to the religious functions of the elementary family. On Sundays, if circumstances or distance prevents worship in the mission church, the members of the extended family may meet for corporate worship and prayer in the hut of the senior male, who will lead the service unless he is very old or one of his sons holds a church office.

To summarise, it may be said that the functions of the extended family are auxiliary to those of the elementary family. The larger family group has no special functions of its own other than providing a more effective system of social control, and a wider range of kinsmen for companionship than the elementary family.

In the mission village, where extended family relationships have been weakened, these mechanisms of social control, which formerly stemmed from extended family bonds, have been taken over by other groups such as the Kerkraad, the Sustersbond, Kinderbond, etc. But these associations must not be regarded merely as institutions for the maintenance of good conduct, but also as groups which provide for companionship and good-fellowship, both of which are functions of the extended family as has already been shown.

Thus, conduct is 'good' in the village; there are no delinquent gangs, practically no drunkenness (except on days when people return from the mines and the towns), only an occasional theft, and there were only two assault cases during the years 1951–6. In the *elementary* family, however, discipline (according to conservative standards) is considered 'bad'. Children no longer obey their parents all the time — boys sometimes refuse to leave school to herd for their fathers, and schoolgirls refuse to learn the art of mat-making from their mothers, because 'educated people do not do this kind of work'. But, viewed sociologically, this disobedience and failure of discipline is merely the manifestation of the fact that the functions of parents have been taken over by other individuals, such as teachers, and modified accordingly.

In the changing community of Steinkopf, therefore, we find two systems of social control and association: the extended family of the conservative people found mainly in the farming districts, and the new associations in the mission village. Although their structures differ, they cater for similar needs and fulfil similar functions. Each system works 'efficiently' in its own sphere, though, during the process of change from one to the other, conflicts sometimes occur between the leaders of each. Hence, in the conflicts that exist between teachers and parents, parents who have not yet adapted themselves to the new traditions despair at the values and aspirations of their children, to whom they refer cynically as the *Afrikaner kinders*. The teachers and their followers, on the other hand, who are the champions of learning and change, reject the old values and traditions and tell their pupils that *outyd is dom tyd* (old customs are stupid customs). Although the conflicts are strong, they are always openly expressed, and their manifestations are generally harmless: arguments are good-humoured and though they end with the conservative parents issuing dire warnings that everyone who challenges the values of the old order is likely, sooner or later, to fall out of favour with the Almighty, neither party takes the other seriously, and respect is always shown to older people and those with 'position'.

CHAPTER 5

LINEAGES

IN STEINKOPF there are ten major lineages of varying size, and roughly thirty to forty smaller ones. Today, lineage organisation varies considerably, since not all people attach the same importance to lineage membership. We may, however, classify the population into four broad lineage categories on the basis of their origin:

Category A: The Baster Pioneers, or Voortrekkers, who can trace descent back for six or seven generations.

Category B: The Namaqua, and short-haired Basters, some of whom can trace descent back to the period before the Baster Pioneers entered the territory. The people of this category consist mainly of the descendants of the Gei//Khauan and certain Oorlam tribes.

Category C: The *kommers* (newcomers), Basters who joined the community after the Baster Pioneers, some comparatively recently, and a few Cape Coloured. The majority in this category are able to trace descent back for three or four generations only.

Category D: The *bywoners*, who are a small group of people, consisting mainly of Bondelzwart refugees, who joined the community after the wars in South West Africa.

Categories A and B coincide more or less with the class division known as *onderstraat* and *bostraat* (see chapter 6), while the members of category C overlap with each of these class divisions. In terms of kinship, however, certain rules of endogamy are a distinguishing feature between these categories: members of category A should never marry members of category B; a person from category A may marry certain persons from category C, but not others, while a few people in category C marry persons from category B; and members of category D tend to marry persons in their own category. Marriages with approved aliens are generally permitted. These rules, however, are usually modified by other phenomena already alluded to. Thus, all other factors being favourable, a potential spouse with 'European' physical characteristics will be selected for marriage in preference to a person with 'Khoi Khoin' features, though this is less true for members of category B than for categories A and C, and there is no evidence to suggest that

106

it applies to category D. Active church members, moreover, tend to marry one another. And when a person in category C marries a person in category B, the siblings of the former 'lose caste', and would as a consequence, be unlikely to marry into category A.

The Pioneer Basters (category A)

Elsewhere we have described the part played by the Baster families in the development of Steinkopf. The first of these families to settle permanently in the territory were the Engelbrechts, who established themselves to the south-east of the present mission village. The founding ancestor of these Engelbrecht Basters was a Hollander who had married a Namaqua woman from South West Africa. Engelbrecht was a trader whose business covered the stretch of country known as the Bokkeveld. From time to time members of his wife's clan used to visit him to barter giraffe and gemsbok karosses for tobacco, coffee, sugar and other provisions. During one of these transactions, Engelbrecht is said to have violated the law of the Colony by exchanging a gun and ammunition for the karosses brought by the Namaqua clansmen. Later he was arrested by a field-cornet, found guilty and imprisoned by the landdrost at Clanwilliam. He died while he was in gaol, and as a result of these events his three sons, wishing to escape from the 'unjust' laws of the Colony, crossed the boundary (the Buffels River) into Little Namaqualand which was at this time ruled by Kaptein Kupido Witbooi. After crossing the border the three brothers parted and each selected his own tract of country. Paul chose part of the Pella district near the kraal of Kupido Witbooi, Jan went westward to the sandveld; and Gert set up his mat-house at Karakhoes, now called Besondermeid and situated close to Steinkopf village.

We are told that Witbooi objected strongly to the presence of these strangers but was unable to take any action against them since they were in possession of fire-arms. On the other hand, it is certain that the Engelbrechts, who were Basters and considered themselves superior to the Namaqua, were not prepared to submit to the jurisdiction of the Khoi Khoin ruler, or his captains.

Gert had two wives, each of whom had a son. Willem was the younger of the two sons, but was the son of the first wife, who was also a Baster like her husband. The second wife, however, was a Namaqua and, although her son Pieter was older than Willem, he was not accorded the respect usually shown to a first-born son in

Baster society.

After a period of time, our historians[1] tell us, 'Gert Engelbrecht rose from the position of a patriarch (*familie hoof*) to that of Captain over both his own kinsmen and other (Basters) who had joined them. When he died, his son Willem succeeded him as kaptein of the Steinkopf Basters. At this point in the history of the lineage, as a result of the rivalry which had occurred between the two brothers, Pieter and his family left Karakhoes and settled ten miles south at Witwater, where his descendants live to this day. Here they form a major segment of the Engelbrecht lineage, a segment which still retains the family jealousy that originated during the generation of Willem and Pieter.

Willem had only one son, Jacobus (also called Gous), who succeeded him, and five daughters. Jacobus married the famous Ryk Jasper Cloete's father's sister, a Baster from Springbok, while the five daughters married other Basters who had joined the Engelbrechts at Steinkopf.

The first daughter married one of the Cloete Haals from the Bokkeveld. They were so called because they were fetched (*gehaal*) by the Engelbrechts to strengthen the ranks of the Basters, who feared that they would be overpowered by the Khoi Khoin. The second daughter married Willem Meyer, a Komaggas Baster, and a nephew of the Reverend J. H. Schmelen of the London Missionary Society. The third married a Klaase, a Baster who had also joined the Engelbrechts. The fourth married Jacobus Cloete /aba, a Baster from Springbok; and the youngest married Nicholas Cloete Teekappa, also a Baster from Springbok.

When Jacobus Engelbrecht died, he was succeeded not by his eldest son Willem but by Gert, the third eldest. The second son had trekked to South West Africa before he married and did not return. This, as could be expected, complicated the lineage structure still further. Under normal circumstances, as we have said, it was the custom for the eldest son to succeed his father, but the father was at liberty, after consultation with his family (or, as in this case, the raad), to choose another person as his heir. The historians tell us that Jacobus chose Gert as his successor because 'Willem lacked intelligence'. This may be true; but when we inquire into Willem's history we find information which allows an alternative explanation. Before his father's death, Willem

[1] G. Meyer, 'Die Gemeente te Steinkopf'. Gert Engelbrecht, an elder of the N.G. Kerk, confirmed the statement.

married Lydia Klaase, whose mother was closely related to the kaptein of the Bondelzwarts, Willem Chrisjan, with whom Willem Engelbrecht was on friendly terms. Willem used to spend a great deal of his time in South West Africa on hunting expeditions with, and bartering cattle from, the old kaptein. It could be argued that the marriage was socially acceptable, for Lydia Klaase was a respectable Baster. But for political reasons it was a bad match, and it is highly probable that Jacobus and his advisers saw danger in Willem's association with the Bondelzwarts. In other words, it was not in the interests of the Baster supremacy to have a political leader who was so clearly connected by marriage and friendly association with a tribe of the Namaqua. Moreover, this alliance would have been a violation of the traditional attitude of the Basters towards their 'inferiors'.

In other ways too, Gert was the more desirable leader. He looked more like a European than his elder brother: he had straight hair, a long nose, green eyes and a fair skin. Willem was dark and had Khoi Khoin features. Moreover, Gert had married Anna Cloete from Springbok, a Baster whose family, like the Engelbrechts, regarded themselves as infinitely superior to people of pure Namaqua descent. Further, Gert was an active member of the newly-formed Church, one of the missionary's right-hand men, and he had adapted himself well to the new pattern of mixed-farming. Willem was essentially a pastoralist and a hunter.

When Gert, instead of Willem, was selected to succeed their father, the latter's descendants moved eastwards to a farm now known as 'Klein Besondermeid'. Today these Engelbrechts form a major segment of the maximal lineage retaining the old jealousy that originated in this breach of the rules of succession.

When Gert died, his elder son, Jacobus, was too young and inexperienced to succeed him, and Moses Engelbrecht, Gert's younger brother, was appointed as regent. Some years before, Moses had married a Van Niekerk girl, the daughter of a Kamiesberg Dutch farmer and a Baster woman. We are told that he had a strong personality and was a strict disciplinarian, characteristics which earned him great respect among his own people, the Basters, and the Khoi Khoin over whom he also ruled. Moses carried the title of *veldkornet*, not *kaptein*, for during his period of office the latter title was abolished by the colonial government. He held office until his death in 1891, when Jacobus succeeded him and retained the title of *veldkornet* until 1913. In this year, however, the Mission Stations and Communal Reserves

Act was enforced and the *veldkornetskap* was abolished. Jacobus was now styled *hoofkorporaal* by his people to distinguish him from the other councillors who were known as *korporale*. Also a disciplinarian, he followed in the steps of his uncle and was greatly respected by both his people and the White officials (magistrates and superintendents) under whose authority he and his people were placed. He died in 1932.

Although the political leadership of the Engelbrechts had ceased altogether to be recognised by the central government and by many people in Steinkopf, Joseph Engelbrecht, Jacobus's son and heir, was styled *hoofkorporaal* too by his supporters.[2] Joseph's new position, for reasons we shall discuss now, was responsible for a further cleavage in the Engelbrecht lineage.

Jacobus's first wife was a Losper. She was a Baster from Bushmanland, and she died after bearing him two sons, Gert and Jacobus, and two daughters. He then took a second wife, a Brits woman whose lineage came originally from Buchuberg near the coast. She bore him one son, Joseph, the last of the hoofkorporale. The explanation of Joseph's succeeding to his father's office instead of Gert or Jacobus is twofold. First, Joseph's physical characteristics were more 'European' than those of his two half-brothers. Secondly, both Gert and Jacobus married women from the //are Cloete lineage, while one of their sisters married David //are Cloete, the senior male of his lineage segment. These kinship ties would have placed the Engelbrechts in an even more unfavourable position in the field of local government, had either Gert or Jacobus succeeded their father, for in Steinkopf the status of lineages, and especially small segments of them, is modified by marriage. Several informants pointed out, in fact, that had Joseph not succeeded his father, the //are Cloetes, through marriage, may have assumed a superior position in the political hierarchy of the community. Nevertheless, the recognition in 1932 of Joseph as hoofkorporaal by his followers weakened the unity of the lineage still further: not only are there rivalries between the Groot Besondermeid, Klein Besondermeid, and Witwater segments, but a new conflict has been created in the Groot Besondermeid segment as well.

We may now turn to a brief discussion of the Cloete Pioneer Basters of whom there are four main lineages. We saw that, in the Engelbrecht lineage, descent was traced agnatically from the founding male

[2] The term *hoofkorporaal* was seldom used in 1957, the last year in which the Engelbrechts were represented on the Management Board. And occasionally it was used in jest by the 'new people'.

ancestor, but we observed how important marriage was in influencing lineage segments. We saw, for example, how the status of a wife's lineage could disrupt the customary rules of succession. These factors apply also to the Cloete lineages, but, as we shall see later, each Cloete lineage differs from the Engelbrechts in that they acknowledge a founding ancestress as well as a founding ancestor.

The origin of the Cloete lineage goes back to the eighteenth century, when, we are told, three Cloetes, Jan, Pieter and Hendrik, arrived in Cape Town from Holland. Shortly afterwards Hendrik left Cape Town and trekked north to Little Namaqualand. There he married four Namaqua women and had a number of Namaqua concubines, who, like his wives bore him children. In order to distinguish them on the basis of their maternal parentage, the children of each Namaqua mother took their mother's name as well as their father's surname Cloete. Today the Cloetes have four main lineages and a number of lesser ones, which may be distinguished from one another by the name of the founding maternal ancestor. Thus, each Cloete has three names: a Christian name, the surname Cloete, and the name of the Namaqua ancestress, e.g. Jan Cloete /aba.

Although the Cloete lineages recognise a common ancestor, each lineage is quite separate from, and independent of, the others. Three of these lineages, the //are, /aba, and the Tseyma Cloetes, came to Steinkopf shortly after the Engelbrechts and are also recognised as Baster Pioneers of the community. The four Cloete lineages who came later are regarded as *kommers* (lineage category C), and two Cloete lineages are classed with category B because the physical characteristics of their founders approximated more to that category than to category C.

The Namaqua, and the short-haired Basters (category B)

The Namaqua and the short-haired Basters live mainly in the north-western zone of the Reserve. The distinction between categories A and B in the contemporary community is one of strict class, verging on racial endogamy. The members of category B not only differ in physical characteristics from the Baster pioneers, but also many have retained certain Namaqua customs long ago rejected by the Basters.

The origin of these people is more difficult to trace than the origin of the Baster pioneers. We can, however, make three generalisations about them. First, some are direct descendants of the original Khoi Khoin, united under Kaptein Vigiland. Second, those who do have

White 'blood' are largely the descendants of a few isolated Baster men and a trekboer, who came as individuals to Namaqualand virtually unattached to any tradition of their own, and since they settled in the north-western part of the territory they did not immediately come in contact with the Baster pioneers or the missionaries. Men of this sort soon became completely integrated with their new community, and marriage was uxorilocal. In these situations, then, the Nama language and tradition were dominant over the alien. Thirdly, the members of lineage category B were not concerned (and to a certain extent still are not concerned) with 'breeding out' their Khoi Khoin features. In that respect, therefore, they also differ from members of category A who pride themselves on their greater infusion of white 'blood'.

In category B there are three lineages of largely Khoi Khoin descent: the Balies, Jantjies and Gertzes. The remaining lineages may be classified as short-haired Basters, such as the De Klerks, Vries, Saals, various branches of Cloetes, !uru Engelbrechts and others.

The Vries lineage provides us with a good example of a lineage category B. Descent can be traced back five generations to a Kootjie Vries who was an elder in the Church, but local historians point out that the first Vries was the *touleier* (leader of a span of oxen drawing a wagon) of one of the early missionaries.

As far as the Vrieses themselves (and most other people) are concerned, the Vries lineage began with *Ouderling* Kootjie (nobody appears to know whom he married) who, as a result of his services to the Church, achieved a relatively high status in the community. He was greatly opposed to the intrusion of Whites in the territory and refused to give his consent to the laying of the railway line over the Klipfontein area of Steinkopf by the Cape Copper Company in 1869. And he was not prepared to support the Company's application to use the water at Klipfontein since the Vries lineage claimed usufruct of the springs and arable lands in this area. Unfortunately for Kootjie, the Vries lineage had no representative on the raad at the time and documents granting permission to the Company were signed without his knowledge.

Kootjie's eldest son, Jacob, who married the daughter of Ryk Jasper Cloete of Richtersveld, taught at the mission school as an unqualified teacher. His other three sons married women of Khoi Khoin stock, one of whom came from Great Namaqualand. He had one daughter but nothing is remembered of her.

Certain features of the lineage established in the first and second generation were retained in the third generation. The men tended to marry women with Khoi Khoin physical characteristics, the second senior man and one other became elders in the Church, and the sons of Dawid, who had married a woman of Great Namaqualand, also found their wives across the Orange River. Later Dawid's sons left Steinkopf and settled in Great Namaqualand with their wives. One of the men in the third generation of Vrieses became a korporaal on the raad, probably because he married a kinswoman of the Witwater segment of the Engelbrecht Baster Pioneer lineage. In theory this was an unusual marriage at this time but it was condoned in practice because his wife's mother was a Nama from Great Namaqualand.

The fourth and fifth generations of Vrieses have tended in the main to retain the practice of marrying in lineage category B, and in the low-status section of lineage category C. But a section of the new generations have become very class-conscious and have tried, some with success, to marry up. These Vrieses are progressive 'new people'. Some have become teachers and clerks in the village, while others have left the Reserve to escape from class pressures and have married town girls. The 'leader' of the local progressive Vrieses is a prominent man in the community. He is principal of a farm school and a member of both the Kerkraad and Management Board, and a few years ago legally changed his name to De Vries to symbolise his new position. He is married to a woman whose lineage has high status in category C.

The De Klerk lineage has also tended to follow the Vries pattern, and a section of the last two generations have acquired high status among the 'new people'. This has been achieved by education, hypergamy, the acquisition of wealth, and in two cases through membership of the Management Board. The 'leader' of the progressive De Klerks is the principal of the Steinkopf primary school and one of the Government-appointed members of the Management Board.

The /ono Cloetes are also classified as belonging to lineage category B although in terms of their origin they should really be kommers (lineage category C). The founding ancestor of this lineage in Steinkopf was Klaas Cloete who came to Steinkopf from Komaggas as an evangelist in 1840 (?) to assist in the mission work. Klaas Sendeling, as he was called, was probably more Khoi Khoin than Baster and for this reason was considered by the Basters to be of inferior stock. Neither he nor his descendants married into lineage category A, and the majority tended to marry into lineage category B. But just as certain of the Vrieses and the De Klerks have in recent years acquired high status in the community as 'new people', so also have the /ono Cloetes. For example, the present superintendent of the Reserve before he was appointed to this post was principal of the Steinkopf primary school. He is an elder in the Church, a director of the consumers' co-operative store, and he has other sources of income. One of his brothers was secretary of the Management Board until his death in 1957, another brother is an elected member of the Management Board, and the late secretary's son took over his father's position.

Kommers (the newcomers) (category C)

Contrasted with the former two lineage categories are the *kommers*, so called because in comparison with the early pioneers they are newcomers to Steinkopf, or as the Engelbrechts say, 'Hulle is mense wat van 'n kant afgekom het' (literally, people who came in from the side).

The *kommers* are by no means a homogeneous group of people in origin, social status or physical characteristics. Some are considered to belong to a higher class than others and when they marry outside their own lineage category, tend to marry into category A. A few marry into category B.

As regards origins, there are five types of *kommers*: those descended from English pedlars (*smouse*) who had concubines in Steinkopf; those Cape Basters who migrated slowly from the south near Cape Town; those Basters who came from Bushmanland; those unmarried Basters who gained admission to, and rights at, Steinkopf by marrying the local women; and those composing a miscellaneous collection of people whose origin is uncertain, but who bear well-known Dutch and English names. The social status of all these lineages in category C does not necessarily coincide with their type of origin.

The Van Wyks constitute the largest *kommer* lineage. Their founding ancestor, Cornelius, came to Steinkopf with his wife from the 'direction of Cape Town' about the middle of the nineteenth century. He appears to have spoken good Dutch and had some knowledge of the Khoi Khoin language. It is said, moreover, that his father was a Dutchman and his mother was of slave stock. His wife was probably a Baster. Cornelius was a carpenter by trade and was one of the builders of the new mission house. He had seven sons and three daughters all of whom married either *kommers* or the descendants of the Baster Pioneers. His eldest son, Jakobus, became a member of the raad.

The Van Wyks acquired arable lands in the district known as Annenous and have largely retained these lands to the present day. They have high status in the community and tend to marry either in lineage category A or in the high-status section of their own category.

The bywoners (category D)

The majority of bywoners came to Steinkopf as refugees from South West Africa during the disturbances between 1903 and 1907, and during the Bondelzwart rising in 1922,[3] when they were permitted to join the community on condition that they worked for the burghers in the capacity of servants. This category is discussed in detail in the next chapter.

LINEAGE SOLIDARITY

In the preceding section we stated that the origin of the lineage to which a person belongs was the main factor in determining his social class. Nevertheless, although there is this connexion between lineage and class, the correlation is irrelevant to our analysis of the kinship system, except in so far as members of some lineages stress their lineal relationships in order to increase their social prestige; and by using this technique to boost their personal esteem, tend also to strengthen existing lineage bonds.

We turn now to lineage groupings as a phenomenon of kinship, emphasising the factors which make for group solidarity. Broadly, we may describe these factors as leadership and membership, collective ownership and control of property, and collective action among lineage members.

One of the most important features of the unilineal principle in kinship systems is that provision is made for kinship groups to extend beyond the life of an individual or family. Thus, instead of a group consisting only of living people, most lineage systems also include deceased members and, by implication, those not yet born. Often, an ancestor cult is a concomitant of lineage systems, but in Steinkopf lineage extension is characterised by a line of heroes of varying importance, heroes who are *not* ancestral spirits. Ancestral spirits do exist, but their ranks are made up only of people who lived 'wicked', unrepentant lives; of people who resisted death on their deathbeds;

[3] Cf. Report on the Bondelzwarts Rising, 1922 (U.G. 30–1922). Commission on the Rebellion of the Bondelzwarts (U.G. 16–1923). H. Vedder, *South West Africa in Early Times* (1938). R. Freislich, *The Last Tribal War* (1964).

and of people who died suddenly before they had prepared themselves for death. Active ancestral spirits are, therefore, always evil spirits and, as we shall see in chapter 9, they are few in number and are seldom active for more than a generation after death. The idea that a great and revered ancestor can influence another person's life is abhorrent to the people of Steinkopf, and it is the aspiration of every man and woman 'to die peacefully, to remain in the grave, and never to trouble anybody again'.

The ancestors who are acknowledged are essentially lineage heroes, that is to say, former leaders who are remembered for their noble qualities and great deeds. Although the only memorial to them are the narratives and legends told about their lives, we must look upon these heroes as the personalities who symbolise the unity of their respective lineages or lineage segments in particular historical periods.

A further illustration of the unilineal principle is the rule of succession to senior positions in each lineage or lineage segment. The rule, which is fairly flexible, follows the usual agnatic principle, that is to say, office or rank passed from father to senior[4] son or to father's younger brother, if the senior son is very young or unmarried. In practice, however, the rule is not strictly adhered to; this flexibility is made possible because a father always has the right to nominate any one of his sons to succeed him, if he considers his senior son incompetent or unworthy to hold the position. The fact that senior sons do not always succeed their fathers is important to the lineage organisation for, as we have seen, the rivalries that have been created by deviations from the standard rule have been responsible for the formation of new lineage segments. This segmentation is no violation of the unilineal principle, since the cleavages are necessary to preserve the cohesion and equilibrium of the lineage. Without them the rivalries and jealousies, which are minimised by partial residential separation, would be greatly exaggerated. On the other hand, however, the existing tensions between lineage segments do help them to achieve a large measure of unity. For it is a well-known sociological principle that social cohesion is often achieved by one group uniting against another considered to possess undesirable characteristics. The same principle operates also in these cleavages between lineage segments, though in a slightly modified context.

During the mid-nineteenth century, leadership in the major lineages

[4] I have used the term senior instead of eldest to avoid the confusion of including a *voorkind* as a potential heir (see pp. 86–7).

coincided with political leadership because the senior male member of each lineage automatically represented his people on the raad. In later years, when members of the raad were elected for the first time, these major lineages were similarly represented, since the electoral divisions (*wyke*) usually coincided with areas each of which was inhabited by members of the same lineage. Today, however, owing to the fact that the larger lineages have segmented and become spread out, it has become possible for a member of a minor lineage to be elected to the Management Board. Such people are chosen, not necessarily because they hold senior positions in their lineages or families, but because they possess qualities such as wealth or education. We should add that this modification of the former patterns of political representation is due not only to the fragmentation of lineages but also to the fact that people are nowadays looking for new qualities in their leaders.

In Steinkopf, lineage solidarity is greatly reinforced by collective ownership and control of property. Here I use the term ownership to mean 'the sum total of rights which various persons or groups of persons have over things owned'.[5] All land and water in the Reserve is officially controlled by the Management Board which is responsible for allocating arable lands to the registered occupiers, defining commonage, and making provision for the upkeep of water-holes and springs. But some tracts of land, and water-holes and springs, have always been regarded as 'belonging to' certain lineages, although the registered occupiers of these lineages pay the usual tax levied by the Management Board. These 'privileged' lineages claim their *stamregte* (lineage rights) from the fact that their ancestors were the original occupiers of the areas which they now inhabit, before the community of Steinkopf existed. Their claim to these areas has, however, never been one of exclusive ownership, for in all periods other families have been granted usufruct to springs and water-holes, commonage, and any arable land that is available. Today it is still customary to regard these areas as 'belonging to' the lineages who claim jurisdiction in them, but in recent years the Management Board has to a large extent ignored their claims. An indication of the rights that these lineages used to enjoy in their 'own' section of the territory can be illustrated by the fact that the Van Wyk lineage used to receive £12 per year from the Cape Copper Company in return for the use of a certain spring to fill their locomotives with water on their journeys to Port Nolloth and O'okiep. During the period that the Van Wyks received payment from the Cape

[5] *Notes and Queries on Anthropology* (6th ed.), p. 148.

Copper Company for the use of their water (1869 to 1913), the money was paid to the raad, who in turn paid it to the Van Wyks.

The claim to land and water by certain lineages is the most important illustration of lineage collective ownership, but we must bear in mind the fact that lineage solidarity is also maintained by the rules of inheritance. As we have seen earlier (pages 84–6), the unilineal principle in each minor lineage segment is reinforced by these rules, though they do not directly unite the members of major lineage segments.

In the lineage organisation there is an almost complete absence of ritual objects—heirlooms which have no economic value—except in the Engelbrecht lineage. The Engelbrechts have preserved three muzzle-loading guns, Sterloop, Uitersman and Sierland. These weapons were used by their early ancestors during their pioneering days in Steinkopf to exterminate dangerous animals and to drive the 'wild' Bushmen out of the territory. In short, these guns are regarded as symbols of the power and sophistication of the Engelbrechts, who consider themselves superior to their neighbours through the authority which they commanded during the formative period of the community. The importance of these symbols to the members of the contemporary generations is evident whenever a dispute or argument develops between the Engelbrechts and other Pioneers as to whose ancestors contributed most towards the making of Steinkopf. On one occasion, when I was present, some members of the //are Cloete lineage were insisting that the evidence for their contribution towards the community lay in the number of their ancestors who had lost their lives in sorties against the Bushmen. 'Go to the Orange River or to Henkries and you will find the graves of our ancestors who were murdered by the Bushmen,' said a //are Cloete spokesman. 'Can you' (pointing to his Engelbrecht audience) 'show me the graves of any one of your ancestors who was killed by the Bushmen?' 'No,' replied the Engelbrechts' spokesman, 'our ancestors were much stronger and more civilised than yours. We Engelbrechts, who had guns, shot the Bushmen before they shot us.'

The corporate activities of lineage members are few in the contemporary community. Some form of economic co-operation does take place during the ploughing and reaping seasons in those areas where the arable lands are near enough for agnatic plough-teams to operate. The greatest amount of formal co-operation takes place between the male members of minor lineage segments, but this co-operation is really based on the co-operation of several extended families and is not necessarily a function of the lineage.

When a senior member of a lineage dies, it is considered important, though not essential, for his agnates to attend the funeral. Those who attend these (and other) funerals do so for several reasons. First, they come to hear the details of the deceased person's death, so that they will know whether he suffered great pain while he was dying or died peacefully. Secondly, people attend funerals to hear the sermon and addresses, which deal mainly with the life of the deceased person. The details of these obituaries are long remembered and handed down from generation to generation. Thirdly, people come to pay homage to the dead whom they will never see again, if the deceased has been a good man.

Some of the smaller lineages, or lineage segments, are characterised by the fact that they tend to constitute occupational groups. For example, the Oorlam lineage, before it became extinct, used to be makers of serpentine pipes, the Oppels are masons and builders, as are the Jacobs, while a segment of the Van Wyks have been carpenters for four generations.

CHAPTER 6

SOCIAL CLASSES

THE TERM 'social class' is a loose one and has been variously defined. Here we use it broadly to mean an aggregate of individuals having more or less the same status in a community. By status is meant the prestige enjoyed by a person, not because of any individual peculiarities but by virtue of the social roles which he performs. It is true that some social classes may be characterised by the fact that membership is determined largely by birth, but to stress this factor only in a sociological analysis and to ignore the status of the individuals who constitute each class, is of little value, and even misleading. Hereditary social classes are sometimes confused with castes, but castes are essentially occupational groups, each enforcing strict rules of endogamy among its members. There are similarities between hereditary social classes and castes, but to include both under the same definition is to oversimplify the concept of the latter.

One reason why the concept 'social class' has defied precise definition is implicit in the nature of social classes. In every class-system are reflected the main facets of the social structure of the community or the society in which the class-system occurs. We may say therefore that any class-system provides sociologists with a system which is really the synthesis of the various social groupings found in that society; and it follows that each class-system reflects to a large extent the attitudes (concordant and discordant) and the values which emanate from the various social groups which constitute the social structure.

CLASS AND LINEAGE

Fifty years ago the class-structure of Steinkopf was relatively easy to define because status was largely determined by the lineage category into which a person was born. Men always remained members of their parents' lineage category, although it was possible for a woman after marriage to change her status if she married out of her lineage category and joined her husband's extended family. But today, as the importance of lineage decreases, and the village community develops, a new class-hierarchy is emerging.

In the last chapter we described the main features of the old class-system in terms of lineage membership. In each of the four lineage categories, however, other factors—physical characteristics, lineage and family reputation, legitimacy of birth, wealth, occupation, and standards of education—tend to modify the status of individuals, families, and sometimes lineages. Thus, instead of seeing the old class-system merely as a hierarchy of lineage categories, today we must see each category as containing sub-strata, which, although not always clearly defined, provide the bases of the new class hierarchy.

We have already seen that European characteristics are linked with high status; and in the Engelbrecht lineage we saw that the status of each segment coincided very largely with the physical characteristics of its members. Since 'White' physical characteristics are symbolic of superiority, and in a sense good character in an individual, it is the ideal of each family, notably those belonging to lineage categories A and C, to breed out (*uitbaster*) Khoi Khoin features through selecting spouses with European features. A man from lineage category C once refused to allow his son to marry a girl from lineage category B because of her Khoi Khoin features, and when he was approached by the girl's father to comment on his decision he stated: 'I am sorry, but we never trust people with peppercorn hair, because, like their hair they always talk in circles. We people [with straight hair] speak straight [*praat reguit*] and honestly.' To which the girl's father replied: 'That's not at all true, but I'll tell you something about you people with straight hair; you don't know how to keep things to yourselves; you are always talking out of turn. We, with short curly hair, know how to keep things to ourselves!'

As the above illustration shows, it is not necessarily a person's skin colour which influences his status, but also hair-form and the shape of the nose, the colour and shape of the eyes, and other bodily character-istics. The most 'desirable' physical characteristics, however, are a combination of fair skin, straight hair, and straight nose, light oval eyes, and the absence of such traits as steatopygia and wrinkled skin, both of which are typically Khoi Khoin. Whereas dark pigmentation is considered a disadvantage, it does not necessarily lower a person's status if his other physical characteristics conform to the ideal type. The Van Wyks, for example, carry a relatively high status, in spite of the fact that they tend to be dark, because their 'hair and noses are good'. Conversely a lightly coloured person who has typically Khoi Khoin features tends to carry a lower status. Owing to the great diversity in physical and cultural types the inconsistent use of certain terms is unavoidable. It seems less confusing, however, to use the words 'White' and 'European', 'Baster' and 'Coloured', 'Khoi Khoin' and

'Bushmen', rather than introduce terms such as 'Caucasoid' for 'White', or 'Kakamas' for 'Khoi Khoin'.

A person's status may also be affected by the reputation of his lineage and family. For example, a family may acquire a bad name because a significant number of its members are drunkards, or are antagonistic towards the Church or have become Roman Catholics. On the other hand, a lineage, or a segment of it, may gain a good reputation through the virtues of a section of its members. The Vries family, for instance, are greatly respected not only by the members of lineage category B to which they belong but by the whole community because of their devotion to, and active membership of, the Church.

Related to family and lineage reputation is legitimacy of birth of the founding and subsequent ancestors. The Y's and the Z's, for example, have European features (many resemble Europeans very closely) and other qualities which give them high status in their lineage category, but the fact that they are descended from the illegitimate sons of two White pedlars, who had Baster concubines in Steinkopf, has a damaging effect on their status. As the people say, 'Dit tel teen hulle in die gemeenskap'. ('This counts against them in the community.') I once heard an argument between an Engelbrecht and a Z over some petty affair. The Engelbrecht was losing the argument when suddenly he struck a winning blow, saying: 'Wat weet jy in die besigheid, jy wie die afstammeling is van 'n hoerkind wat gebore is in my oumagrootjie se kombuis?' ('What do you know about this matter, you who are the descendant of a whore's child born in my great-grandmother's kitchen?')

In addition to these factors we must also consider wealth, occupation, and education. During the Baster-missionary period and earlier, very little importance appears to have been attached to wealth, and a common occupation (mixed-farming) was shared by all. Formal education was underdeveloped, elementary instruction in the three R's being given by the missionary's wife with the help of a few untrained teachers, to those who wanted it. But the growth of a village community, and the change to a money economy, gave rise to new activities and values, and provided opportunities for new kinds of people: farmers working for personal gain rather than for collective subsistence, migrant labourers, and people with trades and professions. It is these factors that are moulding the class-structure of contemporary Steinkopf, by modifying the system which grew up during the last century.

When we look at the ecology of the mission village, we can see very clearly the broad features of the old class-system reflected in the population grouping. South-east of the mission-station is a zone commonly known as *onderstraat* (lower street) in which the members of lineage category A, and the upper stratum of lineage category C, reside; while north-west of the mission-station is the zone inhabited by the rest of the population. This zone is known as *bostraat* (upper street). Traditionally marriage within each zone tended to be strictly endogamous, but today individuals do sometimes marry across the line.

In terms of the old class-structure, people from onderstraat paradoxically have a higher status than those in bostraat. Thus onderstraters look down on bostraters and are always ready to assert their superiority. The relationship, however, is by no means perfectly symmetrical since a bostrater will never admit his inferiority in this connection. In fact their general opinions concerning onderstraters tend to be facetious and uncomplimentary. As one informant expressed it, 'Onderstraters think they are more human than us, but as far as I can see all they have to commend them is the fact that they talk more—and their straight hair!' Yet in spite of their refusal to admit their inferior status the majority do in fact accept it in practice; and those individuals from bostraat who nowadays reject their traditional status are well known for their boisterousness, forwardness, and general disregard for convention. These overt gestures can, I think, be interpreted as compensatory activities felt necessary by those who display them because of their unconscious feelings of inferiority in relation to onderstraters.

In the previous chapter we mentioned that a teacher from a well-known bostraat family added a prefix to his surname to symbolise his break with his lineage category and the conservative people. Viewed in the present context the complementary interpretation to the former interpretation is that the advent of a Mr. De Vries (formerly Mr. Vries of bostraat) coincided with his appointment as principal of a farm school attended by children belonging to lineage category A, who, when in the mission village, are classed as onderstraters.

A further illustration that may help to explain the present attitude of bostraters to onderstraters is the reaction of the former to seeing one of its men talking to a girl from onderstraat. On several occasions I heard onderstraters say to one of these young men, 'O, ek sien jy vry nou met 'n meisie van onderstraat' (literally, 'Oh, I see you are now courting a girl in lower street'). The full meaning of this sentence is difficult to convey since the tone of voice and facial expression play almost as important a part as the words themselves. The nearest English equivalent, however, would be the reaction of lower-class people to a social climber, 'Oh, I see you are hobnobbing with the uppity-ups.'

Serious conflicts seldom occur between onderstraters and bostraters, and usually the tensions are amicably resolved in the manner which I have shown. Many said that the reason why Steinkopf people seldom have serious quarrels is because in the event of a disagreement it is customary for the one party to 'cool down as soon as the other gets heated'. But it is unlikely that this is the complete explanation, since our discussion has suggested that there is an institutionalised way of averting the result of serious tension and conflict in the form of joking-relationships, the safety-valves which help to let off steam in situations of social disjunction.

During my period of field-work I did not observe violent aggression arising out of the tensions existing between onderstraters and bostraters, but my informants did provide me with information regarding a few such instances. For example, it is said that some years ago at a Christmas Eve church service B.J. (a bostrater) deliberately sat in F.W.'s (an onderstrater's) place, whereupon the latter muttered, 'Look at this! A bostraat Hottentot sitting in my seat.' B.J. (who was drunk) replied audibly: 'I thought there were only Basters in onderstraat.' After the service there was an argument outside the church between the two men, each of whom received support from certain of his relatives and friends.

Later that night F.W. assaulted C.J. (a bostrater who had taken B.J.'s side in the argument outside the church) in a fit of anger, hitting him in the face with a bicycle-chain.

Why, we may now ask, did this unusual and violent situation develop? The reason offered here is that a bostrater (probably because he was drunk) publicly and in church—the institution which in Steinkopf expresses the unity of the community—overstepped the limits of his class, not just by sitting in an onderstrater's pew but by the insulting reply he had made: for a bostrater to imply that an onderstrater was not a Baster (i.e. was a 'Hottentot') is an unpardonable insinuation which could not be settled by an approved means.

When we look at the main components of onderstraat and bostraat in terms of their origin, it is seen that the former consists of Baster

Pioneers plus those *kommers* whose physical characteristics lean towards the European type and whose cultural background resembles that of the Baster Pioneers. Bostraat, on the other hand, consists of Namaqua and short-haired Basters, bywoners, and those *kommers* who, in earlier periods, owing to their 'inferior' physical characteristics and leaning towards the Khoi Khoin tradition, were afforded a lower status than the other members of their lineage category. Thus the nucleus (or *élite*) of bostraat consists of the descendants of those people who were united under Kaptein Abraham Vigiland during the Khoi Khoin period, while the nucleus of onderstraat is made of the descendants of the Baster Pioneers, who under the leadership of the Engelbrechts usurped the power of the former, and later, together with the missionaries, tended to dominate the political life of the community from 1840 to 1913.

A further subdivision of the village constituting part of the bostraat zone known as *Boesmansdraai* (Bushmen's corner) is also spoken of sometimes, but its real significance is lost for most people. Boesmansdraai refers to that sector of the village where a few descendants of the 'tame' Bushmen and some other families (who may well have Bushman ancestry) live. The residents of Boesmansdraai have the reputation of being rather crafty. A well-known legend indicating a joking-relationship between Basters and Bushmen is told of a certain Piet Prins, whose grandfather is said to have been a pure Bushman captured as a child by the Basters during a Bushman hunt. In his younger days Piet Prins was employed by the raad as cook and honey-beer brewer on occasions when the korporale went out to visit the distant hamlets. At night when they had eaten and drunk, the korporale would remind Piet that he was a Bushman whose stock had once been their enemies in Steinkopf:

Korporaal: 'Piet Prins, you are eating all our minerals' [implying You Bushmen have been stealing our scheelite and beryllium].
Piet Prins: 'I eat my own minerals' [implying, This is my country, I was here first].
Korporaal: 'Piet Prins, you are stealing our honey.'
Piet Prins: 'I gobble my own honey.'
Korporaal: 'Piet Prins, you are eating up our livestock.'
Piet Prins: 'And who shot all the game?'

And so the repartee would continue until Piet Prins relieved the mounting tension with a clever and humorous verse by which he would argue that although he is only a Bushman, he is pretty smart, adding with his tongue in his cheek that only Basters are fair-minded:·

> *Skraal mannetjie van Brakfontein;* [i.e. Piet Prins]
> *Een wonder van Leliefontein;* [i.e. the Basters]
> *Oulik;*
> *Lelik;*
> *Basters vir billik!*[1]

THE NEW CLASS–SYSTEM

In contemporary Steinkopf we can distinguish also four hereditary social classes: registered occupiers, 'strangers' or permanent residents, bywoners, and Whites who live in or visit the Reserve from time to time. In 1957 the secretary of the Management Board supplied the following statistics:

Registered occupiers	801 families	89%
Strangers	36 families	4%
Bywoners	54 families	6%
Whites	9 families	1%

These hereditary divisions are structurally significant because of the legal rights which the members of each class share, although the basis on which they have been formed depends largely on the old class–system we have already described.

Registered occupiers, both in terms of their numbers and the privileges which they enjoy, comprise the dominant hereditary social class. All the members of lineage categories A and B, and the majority of members of lineage category C, are registered occupiers. Those members of lineage category C who are not registered occupiers are classed as 'strangers', but are eligible to become registered occupiers.

When the Mission Stations and Communal Reserves Act was enforced, the Resident Magistrate of Namaqualand was required to determine which persons were entitled to be occupiers of land within the Steinkopf and other Reserves. In terms of the Act, he had also to draw up a register of these persons, and of the number and extent of the holdings and lots which they occupied. These persons were then regarded as registered occupiers, and in Steinkopf they corresponded to the burghers of the Baster-missionary period.

Each registered occupier is entitled to the following privileges

[1] Translated literally: Wiry little man from Brakfontein; The great wonder of Leliefontein; A smart little man; Ugly people; Basters for fair play!'

provided he pays his taxes: (*a*) an allotment on which buildings may be erected; (*b*) a dry-garden allotment; (*c*) arable lands; (*d*) the right to graze his livestock on the commonage; (*e*) the right to vote for new members of the Management Board, provided he has reached the age of 21 years. Although it is customary for the sons of registered occupiers to acquire similar legal status to their fathers when they marry, in terms of the Mission Stations and Communal Reserves Act, no person can become a registered occupier unless his status is approved by the Management Board. New regulations promulgated in 1957 make it possible for unmarried men who have reached the age of 18 years to become registered occupiers. Marriage, as a requirement for registered occupancy, has never been legally necessary, though in practice, prior to 1957, married men were not normally admitted to this status. Widows, provided they do not re-marry, may, subject to the approval of the Management Board, take over their late husbands' positions as registered occupiers, but have to relinquish their positions when their eldest sons are eligible to succeed their fathers.

This class of registered occupiers are in effect the 'citizens proper' of the community of Steinkopf. As with the other hereditary classes, it may be regarded legally as a homogeneous aggregation of people, but, as we have seen, each hereditary social class has a composite structure. The status of registered occupiers is implicit in the privileges which distinguish them, as a *legal* group, from the other hereditary social classes in the Reserve.

The second hereditary social class consists of people, who, although they may have the personal qualities of many registered occupiers, have not been granted the legal status of the latter because they have not resided in the Reserve long enough, or have not proved themselves as desirable members of the community. Thus they form part of the *kommers* (lineage category C). During the Baster-missionary period, all newcomers to the Reserve, before they became burghers, were described as 'strangers' in the written laws of 1870, and we shall use this term to distinguish the second hereditary social class from the bywoners whom we discuss later. 'Strangers' are nowadays called permanent inhabitants by the Management Board.

The privileges which 'strangers' enjoy are limited. They may be granted temporary building allotments where they can construct houses if they wish, but generally they rent a dwelling or, if single, a room from either the Management Board or a registered occupier. They are not entitled to arable lands but may be granted grazing rights on the commonage for a limited number of stock in return for fees laid down by the Management Board. The privileges which they enjoy are superior to those granted to bywoners, and in general the registered occupiers and the Management Board are tolerant of their presence in the Reserve, and the latter is prepared to condone antisocial behaviour for which a bywoner may be evicted. The key to the understanding of this tolerance lies in the fact that many 'strangers' are teachers and are endowed with European-type physical character-istics. 'Strangers' are occasionally admitted to the status of registered occupier. Those eligible, however, must be married to the daughters of registered occupiers, be active members of the Church, and conform generally to the Steinkopf 'way of life'.

Within this hereditary social class we must also include a handful of Whites who, although not regarded as permanent inhabitants, are permitted to enter the Reserve, where they are granted grazing rights for a part of the year, but no building sites. In recent years, owing to the stricter administration of the Reserve their numbers have decreased, but there are still a number of families who constitute an integral part of the social structure. These people mix freely with the inhabitants of Steinkopf and are thus to be distinguished from those other Whites whom we discuss later. These White 'strangers' are an offshoot of the trekboers of the old frontier society, and are probably the modern counterpart of those individuals who intermarried with the Khoi Khoin during the eighteenth and early nineteenth centuries to produce the Baster Pioneers we have already described. Some have legally married the daughters of registered occupiers while others have a White as well as a Coloured wife.

As an example of these White 'strangers' we can take the case of X, who, prior to 1951, had lived the greater part of twenty-five years in the Reserve. Provided grazing was good, he used sometimes to spend several consecutive years as an internal trekboer, but when rains fell in Bushmanland he would trek with his livestock in search of better pasture. At present he lives at Vioolsdrift on the border of the Reserve because under local apartheid regulations he may not reside in Steinkopf. X is a polygynist. He is legally married to a White woman who has borne him five children, but he has also a *bruin vrou* (brown wife), the daughter of a registered occupier of Steinkopf. The latter has borne him four children, His wives live in separate but adjacent mat-houses, each with her own children. Both are treated equally and all his children have received a good education. His first wife, to whom he is legally married, is apparently agreeable to being a member of a compound family and says that her husband 'still treats her as he did before he took the second wife'. Two of his White daughters are married to registered occupiers of Steinkopf, as is one of his Coloured daughters. His Coloured son is married to a Coloured woman in the Cape Peninsula. Whenever X visits Steinkopf he stays with his Coloured father-in-law, with whom he unofficially co-operates in farming.

The bywoners, sometimes known as *Hottenots* [*sic*] or *bediendes* (servants), constitute the hereditary social class whose members enjoy the fewest privileges in the community. Although formerly they enjoyed a number of privileges, today they are granted only building sites for their huts in the mission village, and rely almost entirely on employment as domestic servants and *veewagters* (shepherds) by the better-off registered occupiers for their livelihood. Bywoners may also join the ranks of the migrant labourers if they wish. But this is often difficult; first, because the Management Board tends to recruit only from the registered occupiers, and, secondly, should they leave the Reserve as individuals, they run the risk of losing their building sites when they return.

The status of the bywoners is best illustrated by a case which is typical of the majority of people in this hereditary social class. Gert Chrisjan was the son of Willem Chrisjan, a Bondelzwart kaptein of Warmbad, South West Africa. He came to Steinkopf in 1903 shortly after the first Bondelzwart war and worked for a member of the //are Cloete lineage. As remuneration for his services, he received a few goats and for some years was allowed to plough part of his master's (*baas*) land, from which he reaped the crops for his own use. But today he owns no livestock, for he does not have grazing rights, nor has he any land. Although he has applied for the status of registered occupier, this has always been refused. He is too old to work full-time, but his family subsists on the money which his son, a migrant labourer, sends home, and on the casual earnings he and other members of his family derive from the odd jobs they do for the registered occupiers.

Chrisjan explains that the reason he cannot acquire registered occupancy is because of his Khoi Khoin name and ancestry. He says that his son was lucky to have been selected by the Management Board to go to Alexander Bay as a migrant labourer, but fortunately there was little competition for employment at the time. The fact that his son is employed is the only real security that Chrisjan has, but should he and his family be evicted from the Reserve he will have to migrate to a town where, owing to the higher cost of living, he will find it difficult to exist on his small income.

The position of bywoners in Steinkopf at the present time is characterised by social and economic insecurity. In the first place they lack the security of a permanent building allotment, quite apart from the absence of other privileges granted to registered occupiers and 'strangers'. Secondly, they lack the security of being accepted members of a community, owing to the prejudice—race prejudice—which exists against them because they are Khoi Khoin. Thirdly, the fact that they are essentially conservative rural people makes it difficult for them to leave the Reserve to join an urban or semi-urban community.

The fourth hereditary social class is a somewhat nebulous aggregation of Whites who live in or visit Steinkopf from time to time. These Whites hold various positions in White society outside the Reserve. Thus their only significance as an hereditary social class in the community of Steinkopf is the fact that they are integrated members of the White racial group of South Africa, who, for periods of varying length, interact according to their respective professional roles. The roles which they perform in Steinkopf are secondary, in the sense that they are not fully integrated members of the community. The members of this hereditary social class include the missionary and members of the South African Police and their families, who live in the Reserve, and the various medical practitioners, sales representatives, prospectors, and government officials, who occasionally visit the area.

The process of assimilation of new ideas and customs, and their impact on existing traditions is a common feature of social change in Africa and other parts of the world where two or more cultures have come into close contact. In Steinkopf this process has manifested itself broadly in two different ways. On the one hand it has resulted in the blending or synthesising of various ideas and customs; on the other hand it has resulted in one section of the population consciously grafting itself on to the contemporary Afrikaner tradition of the Republic of South Africa. As a consequence of this latter tendency, a social cleavage, which has the characteristics of a dichotomous class-structure, has developed. The two main elements which constitute the cleavage are the conservative people who cling to the synthetic cultural tradition of the Baster-missionary period, and the 'new people' known cynically as *die Afrikaner kinders* by the conservatives.

11   BUILDING A MAT–HOUSE

12   GRAVES AT STEINKOPF
Note baby's bottle and tea cups and saucers

13   A DWELLING-HUT AND COOKING-HUT IN STEINKOPF
The distance between them is approximately fifteen yards. Note shelter and
preparations for new hut in the foreground.

14   A DWELLING-HUT AND COOKING-HUT IN RICHTERSVELD
Note their proximity. This is the homestead of a *patrilineal* extended family.
The husband's brother's hut is in the background.

The 'new people' tend to reject the old way of life (*ou tyd se goed*).

In terms of occupation and wealth the conservatives are mixed-farmers and generally poor, while the *élite* of the 'new people' consist of teachers, government officials, shopkeepers, shop-assistants, tradesmen, and well-off capitalist farmers.

Thus the cleavage can be seen as constituting a conflict between incompatible customs and ideologies. The conservative people look back on the old days as characteristic of their notion of the ideal society. The 'new people' are progressive. They are trying to sever their ties with the past, openly rejecting the 'ideal' society revered by the conservatives. They are champions of wealth, education, better housing, and are even favourably disposed to the new form of government, which they consider typically European and civilised.

In Steinkopf today, political, economic, educational, and, to a certain extent, religious powers, are in the hands of the 'new people'. They derive their group solidarity not from the fact that they belong to any particular hereditary social class or lineage, but because they share the same aspirations of becoming 'like the Afrikaner', though separate from them. Physical characteristics are important to them, but provided a person does not lean too much towards the Khoi Khoin type he will be recognised as a 'new person' if his social characteristics and aspirations are in the 'right' direction. In fact many of the leaders of the 'new people' are members of lineage category B.

No one factor alone can explain the emergence of the 'new people' as the group that wields the most power in the community, but the dominant factor is their acceptance of and willingness to co-operate with the central government. In the next chapter we discuss this relationship in the realm of local politics. Here we need only add that whereas the early Baster Pioneers achieved their political dominance through their close association and co-operation with the missionary, coupled with the fact that they had guns and confidence in their assumed superiority, the 'new people' have achieved power through their co-operation with the central government and a positive desire to emulate the Afrikaner. This power, moreover, is strengthened by the part which they play in the schools and in the Church, and the support which they receive from these institutions.

CONCLUSIONS

In our discussion of the class structure of Steinkopf we have seen that no one set of criteria provides us with a complete picture reflecting the manner in which the community is stratified. We have analysed differences in status based on lineage membership (the old class-system which is still present though in a modified form); we have described the stratified components (hereditary social classes) based on differences in legal status; and we have drawn attention to the cleavage between the 'new people' and the conservatives. Thus there may be said to be three different class-systems in existence,[2] depending on the criteria selected to evaluate the status of the individuals constituting each class. In other words, in terms of class-affiliation the majority of the population perform at least three roles, corresponding to the prestige they enjoy in each class. For example, one registered occupier may be a member of lineage category A, and a conservative person, while another may be a member of lineage category C, and a 'new person'. Thus, apart from the bywoners, all of whom belong to lineage category D, and are conservative, there are numerous combinations of roles. We must, however, stress that all 'strangers' belong to the lineage category C and are 'new people'; that the majority of the members of lineage category B are conservatives, although this category contains some of the most prominent leaders of the 'new people'; and that lineage categories A and C each appear to have slightly more 'new people' than conservatives.

In conclusion let us attempt to answer the question, what combination of characteristics attributed to an individual gives him high status in contemporary Steinkopf? First, he must be a registered occupier (or a member of a registered occupier's elementary family) because this entitles him to full citizenship in the legal sense; this is the basic requirement. Second, he must come from good stock, that is to say, he should be a member of an old and respected family that has lived in Steinkopf for at least four generations. I use the term family and not lineage because the latter implies that lineage membership in itself is important. Thirdly, he should have received secondary education. Fourthly, he should be a professional person (e.g. a teacher), or a tradesman, or a wealthy farmer; that is to say, he should have money, and display the hallmarks of a wealthy person; he should live in a European-type house and own a motor-car or lorry. Fifthly, he should be an active member of the Church and at some time in his life should hold, or have held, the office of *ouderling* (elder) or *diaken* (deacon). Finally, he should have European physical features and stature. All

[2] Cf. J. Pitt-Rivers, 'Social Class in a French Village', *Anthropological Quarterly*, vol. 33, no. 1, January, 1960.

these characteristics typify the ideal 'new person' in modern Steinkopf. Of course the conservative people should, in theory, look down upon such a person, but whatever attitudes they may express about the *Afrikaner kinders*, a 'new person' with prestige in his own circles is always treated with respect by the majority of the population. Thus, although the old class-pattern is still clearly present, social forces foreign to the golden age of the conservatives are moulding a new class-hierarchy in which those conforming most closely to the ideal type we have described will constitute the dominant stratum. As one conservative Baster Pioneer put it, 'Ons het nou oorgegaan na die Afrikaanse tyd' ('We have now moved into a new period—the heyday of the Afrikaner').

CHAPTER 7

GOVERNMENT AND LAW

THE GOVERNMENT of modern Steinkopf must be seen against the historical background outlined in chapter 2, where we described the transition from a tribal council to a Management Board. The tribal council was an autonomous body; the Management Board is subordinate to the central government of South Africa.

The Management Board was first constituted in 1913, when the Communal Reserves and Mission Stations Act was enforced. It thus superseded the raad of the Baster-missionary period, and although there are certain similarities between the structures of the raad and the Management Board their functions are vastly different. Theoretically, of course, the raad was also subordinate to a higher political authority, the colonial government of the Cape, but as we have already shown, it operated largely as an autonomous body.

Apart from the differences and similarities between the raad and the Management Board, we must emphasise the fact that the Mission Stations and Communal Reserves Act was accepted by the *burghers* of Steinkopf under protest. Nevertheless, in spite of the opposition to the Act in 1913 and subsequent years, nowadays a large part of the community, especially the 'new people', not only tolerate but openly support the Management Board which administers the law.

THE CENTRAL GOVERNMENT

Contemporary Steinkopf is a community within the social structure of the Republic of South Africa, and in this section we are concerned with its direct relationship to the central government, bearing in mind, as we shall see later, that all the activities of the local government are indirectly connected with the central government through the Coloured Affairs Department. In this latter respect Steinkopf must be regarded as a colony within the framework of the Republic of South Africa.[1]

The legal institutions representing the central government in respect of laws and regulations not handled by the Management Board are the magistracy and the South African Police, who have a station in the mission village. In practice the police have to deal with only a small range of offences, and most breaches of the law are uncommon. For

[1] Cf. L. Marquard, *South Africa's Colonial Policy*, 1957.

example, during the period 1955 to 1956 there were only three cases of petty theft and one case of assault, and a few people are convicted each year for not being in possession of dog or bicycle licences. Murder and rape appear to be unknown. But there are two offences which need regular attention by the police; they are contraventions of the Immorality Amendment Act (1950) and the Children's Act. Under the Immorality Amendment Act it is an offence for a White person to have sexual intercourse with a non-White person. The police stationed at Steinkopf devote a great deal of their time and energy attempting to convict people of this offence and to prevent cohabitation. During the first two years after the Act was enforced, these police investigated 134 cases. Most of the allegations concerned White males from Vioolsdrift, a neighbouring White farming community, and Coloured females, many of whom were inhabitants of Steinkopf.

The practice of cohabitation, and to a certain extent intermarriage, has been a common characteristic of race contacts in the Cape Province since 1652. In Namaqualand the extent to which it has occurred in the past has been shown in earlier chapters. The extent to which cohabitation still occurs today, in spite of legislation forbidding it, is shown in the police records. We have an example, therefore, of a law which is incompatible with existing social tendencies in the area.

Violation of the Children's Act is the second major problem with which the police have to deal. The parents of unmarried mothers frequently complain that the illegitimate children of their daughters are not receiving the support of their genitors. These men, however, are generally townsmen who seduce girls while they are away from home and refuse to take responsibility for the consequences. The reason why legal action is seldom resorted to when girls fall pregnant by local men is because the parents are said to be 'too proud' to accept money to support a child, the genitor of whom they know. Further, of course, there is always the probability that the couple will marry, but even when the parents of the girl refuse an offer of marriage by their daughter's lover, they prefer to support the child themselves rather than receive the man's assistance.

LOCAL GOVERNMENT

Local government is centred in a Management Board which, as we have said, is subordinate to the central government of the Republic of South Africa, but is immediately responsible to the Coloured Affairs Department. The community is administered under the

Communal Reserves and Mission Stations Act, No. 29 of 1909 as amended. The following are the main regulations subjoining the Act:

those promulgated under Government Notice No. 461 of 13 March 1913;

those promulgated under Government Notice No. 2601 of 3 December 1948; and

those promulgated under Government Notice No. R. 1866 of 18 November 1960.

The Management Board consists of nine ordinary members, known as *raadslede* or unofficially as *korporale*, a non-voting secretary, and a chairman (a registered occupier, who is also the superintendent of the Reserve and a well-paid government official). Meetings are held once a month in the council room of the Management Board offices, but the chairman may convene special meetings provided he gives previous notice within seven days of his intention to do so. Minutes, copies of which are sent to the Coloured Affairs Department in Cape Town, are kept of all meetings. Of the nine ordinary members, six are elected by those registered occupiers who are over 21 years of age, while three are appointed by the Secretary of Coloured Affairs. Two of the appointed members are nominated by the superintendent, while one is nominated by the *Kerkraad*, with which the superintendent is closely associated.

Each of the six elected members represents a *wyk* (ward), but these are voted for by registered occupiers who have the franchise. Elections are held during the second half of July each year, when two of the ordinary members go out of office. Prior to 1957 the ordinary members were re-elected and re-appointed every twelve months. Extraordinary elections may be held to replace members who, for various reasons, have ceased to hold office before their term expires. There are numerous conditions under which a member is required to vacate his seat. These include insolvency, failure to pay taxes, and absence from three consecutive monthly meetings without leave of the chairman. But perhaps the most significant of these is that a man may be forced to vacate his seat on the Management Board if, in the opinion of the Minister, he 'refuses to subject himself to the provisions of the Communal Reserves and Mission Stations Act or any regulation promulgated under it or to comply therewith'. The significance of this clause is that it reveals very clearly the extent to which the Management Board is subjected to the control of the central government. A further manifestation of this fact is reflected in the composition of the Management Board. Although the majority of members are elected by the voters, it is nevertheless possible for a minority opinion to have a majority vote in the Management Board. Four members are appointed by the central government, but the chairman, who is one of these members, has a deliberative as well as a casting vote. This means that only one of the six elected members need vote with the appointed members to carry a motion designed to further government interests. Thus one of the chief reasons why the 'new people' are so strong politically in contemporary Steinkopf is because the government-appointed members are normally selected from the 'new people', who also return about half (sometimes less than half) of the elected members to office. As a result of their inability to gain power, many conservative voters have tended not to vote at elections because it is realised that the opinions of their representatives on the Management Board are seldom of any consequence; some successful conservative candidates have resigned their seats.

In spite of the limitations imposed on the Management Board by the central government, it does have some of the characteristics of a legislative body. It has authority to frame certain local regulations to assist it in its administrative duties, but the central government always has the right to alter or revoke them. The Mission Stations and Communal Reserves Act states that the Management Board may, 'subject to the approval of the Minister, make regulations in the prescribed manner' for 48 purposes, ranging from the prevention and suppression of all nuisances to providing for licences or permits for making bricks.

Traditionally, when the raad was an autonomous body which exercised its powers in accordance with the local customs, new laws and regulations unacceptable to the majority of burghers do not appear to have been made. Hence, nowadays many of the conservative registered occupiers still regard the Management Board in the light of the old raad, and direct their attacks for all unpopular legislation not against the central government but against the Management Board, which is held responsible for violating the wishes of 'the people'.

Strictly speaking, the Management Board has no judicial functions; it is not a court of law and has no power to punish offenders, but it does have some of the features of a judiciary. First, any individual who contravenes any local regulation or fails to fulfil any obligation under these regulations commits an offence. Such a person is liable on conviction to a fine not exceeding £25, or, in default of payment, to imprisonment with or without hard labour for a period not exceeding thirty days. Offenders are tried at the magistrate's court at Springbok, but usually appear before the Management Board before a charge is made. In practice not all those who appear before the Management Board are committed for trial, since many receive only a warning from the superintendent. It must be pointed out, however, that the new regulations issued in 1957 omit the clause whereby the Management Board has the right to call upon a registered occupier (or other person) to appear in person at a meeting. This is an important omission for it reduces the possibility of settling cases without a formal trial by a magistrate.

Secondly, should a registered occupier fail to pay his taxes, the Management Board can request the resident magistrate to issue a warrant for their recovery. In the event of the person concerned being unable to pay the required amount or refusing to pay, the court messenger is entitled to seize his property. In 1955 a registered occupier objected to the increase in taxation and refused to pay his dues. As a result the Management Board applied to the resident magistrate to issue a warrant to enable a messenger of the court to seize some of his furniture.

Thirdly, bywoners and 'strangers' who are not in government employ in the Reserve may be given notice by the Management Board to leave the Reserve if they undermine its authority, or misbehave, or violate local regulations. A few years ago an African[2] who was married to a registered occupier's daughter and had been granted permission to reside in the Reserve was suddenly ordered to leave within twenty-four hours. No reasons were given to him, but when the girl's father asked for an explanation he was told that it was the policy of the Management Board to protect the community from the infiltration of 'primitive blood' which was detrimental to the stock. So the couple left the Reserve and settled at Port Nolloth.

Fourthly, there is always the power of a threat which the Management Board uses to enforce regulations. With the police station next door to the Management Board offices, and the magistrate's court only an hour's journey by car, threats by the Management Board carry a great deal of authority and provide an effective means of social control.

[2] To my knowledge this is the only African who has ever been permitted to reside in the Reserve.

In spite of the judicial elements present in the Management Board, the tendency in recent years, notably since 1951, has been for the local government to concern itself merely with the administration of the Reserve and to some extent with the framing of regulations in accordance with its subordinate legislative powers. As a result civil cases are seldom brought before the Management Board as was the practice under the Baster-missionary régime, when both criminal and civil cases received the attention of the raad. Even before 1951, during the period of European control, civil disputes were handled by the Management Board, but nowadays little time is devoted to the settlement of disputes, correcting disobedient children, drunkards and adulterers. Any interest that the Management Board does take in civil disputes is purely a cultural retention, for it is under no legal obligation to concern itself with matters outside its official jurisdiction. As a result civil cases are usually handled by the Kerkraad, but if no solution is reached the Management Board or some of its councillors may be asked to arbitrate. When they fail, the police may be called in and the cases may be referred to the magistrate.

The main function of the Management Board therefore is the general administration of the Reserve in accordance with the Communal Reserves and Mission Stations Act, and as such it is the mouthpiece of the central government through the Coloured Affairs Department. The main conflicts which exist between the Management Board and the conservative people are found in these executive activities. When the superintendent says, 'It is our duty to administer the law', the reply is, 'We do not accept that law'. Nevertheless, in spite of their opposition, only a few conservative people have blatantly defied the law, and in practice people are subservient to its demands. Here we deal only with the general principles of the local regulations and their sociological significance.

The control of farming activities, the distribution of land, the granting of building sites, the collection of taxes, the organisation of public services, health, the admission of registered occupiers to their status, and the control of labour and migration, are the main executive duties of the Management Board.[3] When we examine these regulations in their broad sociological perspective, it becomes clear that they acknowledge the elementary family as the only form of kinship grouping, and in doing so tend to contribute towards the dissolution of wider kinship groups.

[3] See also pp. 7–8.

In the first place, every male reaching the age of 21 years is required to obtain written permission from the Management Board to remain in his father's house, and must also apply for registered occupier's rights. Whereas the purpose of this regulation is to increase the revenue of the Reserve through the additional taxes paid, its effect is to hasten the creation of independent elementary families.

Further, registered occupiers and other people are not allowed to have visitors (from outside the Reserve) or their dependants as lodgers or guests in their homes without written permission of the Management Board; nor may they employ domestic servants or shepherds without first obtaining the consent of the Management Board; and residents of Steinkopf may be compelled to make improvements on their buildings, should the Board consider that these buildings disfigure the mission village.

All these restrictive regulations are new to Steinkopf and are symbolic and indicative of the development towards a village community. In a sense they are designed to enable the Management Board to administer the affairs of the inhabitants of the Reserve through the individual family without consideration of wider associations of kinsmen. The view that these regulations are functions of recent social developments is borne out by the fact that where the lineage is strongest and the range of kinsmen greatest, there is the most marked conflict between the individual members of kinship groups and the Management Board.[4] Thus the people most antagonistic towards the modern trends in local government are the conservatives. Conversely, we find that co-operation between individuals and the Management Board is most marked where the elementary family, rather than the extended family, is stressed in kinship relationships.

In terms of their functions, therefore, local regulations, notably those we have mentioned, tend to lay stress on the elementary family by strengthening its bonds and weakening kinship ties outside it. A registered occupier is legally obliged in certain matters to concern himself with his own personal rights and those of his elementary family, but not with the affairs of his wider circle of kin. A man may inherit his father's lands and building plot, but he must first be legally acknowledged as a registered occupier and have his inheritance approved by the Management Board, before he takes possession of them. Further a young man, as we have said, must, on reaching 21

[4] Cf. L. A. Fallers, *Bantu Bureaucracy*, Cambridge, 1956; and 'The Predicament of the Modern African Chief', *American Anthropologist*, vol. 57, no. 2, 1955.

years of age, apply for permission to remain in his father's house and must also (if he is the son of a registered occupier) apply for a similar legal status to that of his father. This means that fathers and sons are regarded as equals by the Management Board. As a result of this legal equality, young men are beginning to claim social equality also, a claim which contributes towards the rebellion of the younger generation against parental authority, and provides the basis for the breakdown of extended family ties.

In 1957 the Management Board tried to compel owners to brand donkeys, horses, and cattle with the numbers shown on the owners' certificate of occupation. The purpose of this regulation was to assist the Management Board to control the stock quota of each registered occupier and also to enable it to recognise animals belonging to outsiders and grazing illegally on the commonage. Farmers, especially the conservative members of the community, objected to branding their animals, on three different grounds. Firstly, it was claimed that the Management Board had no right to make such a law, because it would never have been made by the old raad. Secondly, they maintained that it would be inconvenient especially when animals were sold, exchanged, inherited or given as a present. The third objection, which was given to me independently by two different informants, was astutely sociological. One of these informants said: 'By branding our animals we are breaking away from our old tradition of good-fellowship and love [saamwerking en liefde]. Everyone knows his animals by their markings, and it is very seldom that disputes occur. Now we are being told to brand our animals, and to brand them with the same number by which we now occupy our lands which no longer belong to us. First they took our land away, now they are trying to steal our animals.' To which he added, 'The number divided our extended families, now they are trying to take our animals away—by that same number.'

The first two objections to the branding of animals are natural enough, and the sort of reactions that could be expected in any community. The third objection, however, is of a different order for it explains the disrupting effect which certain regulations are felt to have on wider kinship relationships. Thus we must infer that the control of stock tends also to fulfil the function of stressing the importance of the elementary family to the 'detriment' of certain wider kinship ties.

LOCAL POLITICS AND LEADERSHIP

During the periods of field-work in Steinkopf two major difficulties were experienced. The first, to which attention has already been drawn, was to persuade younger men to speak freely in the presence of older men. The second was to get people to stop talking politics. Local politicians—everyone in Steinkopf is a politician—are divided into two camps; those who support the Management Board on most issues, and those who oppose it on principle. The former category consists mainly of 'new people', while the latter consists mainly of conservatives.

Political power is at present in the hands of the 'new people', because their leaders constitute a majority on the Management Board. These leaders, five of whom belong to lineage category B, have derived their power from two sources. Firstly, through winning the support of the central government, and secondly by giving expression to those aspirations implicit in their followers. The leaders of the conservative people on the other hand derive their power from only one source—their followers.

Leaders and their followers are the basic components of every group. In fact when we speak of a 'group' we necessarily imply these two categories of people (leaders and followers) fulfilling complementary roles. As Homans, referring to small 'autonomous' groups, points out:

'The leader is the man who comes closest to realizing the norms the group values highest. The norms may be queer ones, but so long as they are genuinely accepted by the group, the leader, in that group, must embody them. His embodiment of the norms gives him his high rank, and his rank attracts people; the leader is the man people come to; the scheme of interaction focuses on him. At the same time, his high rank carries with it the implied right to assume control of the group, and the exercise of control itself helps maintain the leader's prestige. This control he is peculiarly well equipped to wield by reason of his position at the top of the pyramid of interaction. He is better informed than other men, and he has more channels for the issuing of orders. He controls the group, yet he is in a sense more controlled by it than others are, since it is a condition of his leadership that his actions and decisions shall conform more closely than those of others to an abstract norm. Moreover, all these elements, and not just one or two of them, come into leadership; all are related to one another and reinforce one another for good or ill.'[5]

[5] G. C. Homans, *The Human Group*, 1951, pp. 188–9.

The chief political leaders of the 'new people' in Steinkopf are, amongst other things, products of higher secondary education. That is to say they are teachers or former teachers. It is not surprising, therefore, that they derive most of their support from the younger men and women, *die Afrikaner kinders*, who have passed through their hands at school. Earlier, we have shown how important schoolteachers are as leaders in the community where they have superseded, as it were, traditional leadership in the family.

As a result of the material benefits of their profession, teachers are economically better off than the majority of people. Thus they are able to display the hall-marks of wealth in their dress, the type of dwellings in which they live, the food they eat, and the mode of transport they use. Not only are they economically superior but through their knowledge (*deur die boeke*) they are better able to command the respect of those who place a high premium on Western learning and its concomitant values.

The 'new people' as a political group first began to crystallise in 1945, when the present superintendent, then principal of the primary school, was appointed to an advisory council by the central government. In this year he presented a memorandum to the Inter-Departmental Commission of Enquiry into the Conditions of Coloured Reserves. Although the memorandum is devoted largely to a general description of the administration of the Reserve, he concludes by stating: 'With the help and stricter, yet sympathetic supervision, of our respected Government, the economic conditions in the Reserve ought to improve.' This was his first attempt to ingratiate himself and his followers with the central government. A year later, in a letter to the secretary of the Management Board he drew attention to the poverty and backwardness of the people, and made some suggestions about how these conditions could be improved. It was this letter, quoted below and translated from Afrikaans, that stamped him as the leader of the 'new people', and made him the obvious candidate to fill the post of superintendent in 1952:

Every newspaper, magazine, and church publication (English and Afrikaans) reports daily of the shortage of food throughout the whole world, and the disasters that follow. Everywhere people are being warned against the irresponsible wasting of food, and certain governments are taking precautionary measures. Our Department, for example, is planning to provide for people of all classes and walks of life.

Will *we* alone continue to be irresponsible? No, we may not, we cannot.

Our people are already in dire poverty and are not even conscious of the dangers of malnutrition and pestilence about which we read so much.

What can we do to try and avoid these miseries and disasters? We can do a great deal.

1. We have ploughed and sown but the grain has not yet been protected even though certain lands are beautifully green. Cannot the pound be opened at once, to help protect our valuable grain?

2. The commonage can be protected and reserved for the flocks of our own people and not leased out to strangers. When all other food runs out, then at least we will have meat and milk. Every district and country must take care of itself; we cannot expect others to look after us.

3. Although it is dangerous to mention the 'crimes' of offenders who have not been caught red-handed, yet we are conscious of the fact that many of our people, even though they are poor already, are becoming poorer (economically, spiritually, morally, and in terms of health) through the misuse of Hottentot beer, various 'patent medicines', and other strong drink. Should we tolerate this situation any longer?

   Surely it would be in the interest of our people to fight the imminent disaster by prohibiting the brewing of Hottentot beer, with the assistance of the Government, and by not selling patent medicines? If such medicines are really needed for the treatment of patients, then surely provision can be made for them to be stored at the local clinic?

   Hottentot beer is a waste of time and money; it disrupts domestic peace and destroys self-respect, and promotes poverty; it is demoralising, as is the misuse of patent medicines and ordinary strong drink.

What are we going to do? Shouldn't we ask the Government to put a stop to beer-brewing? Instead of this waste of time, energy, and money, we could then do other things with our lives. Our Council could for instance serve as a Labour Bureau, and organise all available manpower so that all job-opportunities in Namaqualand can be taken advantage of.

I would oppose sending our people to work outside of the district of Namaqualand because I have estimated that there is enough work locally for everyone. The Copper Company gives preference to our local Coloureds provided they have the proper attitude towards their work, and 3s. 3d. to 15s. 6d. per day plus cost of living can be earned. Should we not encourage our people to accept this offer and so prove to the Company that it can rely on our supply of labour? For when these employers are satisfied with the trustworthiness of our people, then they will not have to import Natives [*Naturelle*] from other parts of the country. If we are successful, moreover, we will avert the situation of an earlier period when our people did relief work for 1*s*. 6*d*. or 9*d*. per day.

According to governmental plans it appears that provision will be made for: old-age pensions, disability grants, pensions for the blind, military pensions, allowances for needy children, and hospitals. For those who do not fall under these categories, there is only one solution, and that is work, i.e. farming or mining, etc.

For those who refuse to work, provision has already been made in the form of *Work Colonies*. And loafers [*onwilliges*] can be forced to work. Are we going to wait until the Government on account of our dire need is obliged to threaten our people, or are we rather going to act now after our own fashion and speak to our people personally? Please don't let us waste any more time. The problem of protecting our people is very serious, and they are looking to us who are their champions for leadership and advice. We will have to account for them.

27 May 1946   (*Signed*) G. CLOETE

The power and prestige of the 'new people' as a political group and as a quasi-social class can best be seen from the part they play in various institutions. Firstly, for reasons we have already given, the 'new people' dominate the activities of the Management Board. Secondly, they are linked through their leaders with the central government. Thirdly, they have close connexions with the teaching profession. Fourthly, they have a powerful influence in Church affairs both through their representation on the Kerkraad and through the missionary, who supports not only their aspirations but also the activities of the Management Board and the central government. Fifthly, they receive also the support of the wealthy stock-farmers who, although they may have conservative tendencies, find it in their material interests to ally themselves with the 'new people' in order to derive benefits, such as additional bore-holes, from the Management Board. To these we must add also the fact that their main leader, the superintendent, and their secondary leaders (other Management Board members and school-teachers) hold positions in the community which are favourable to effective leadership. They use established channels to give their 'orders' and to fulfil their roles. These channels are the law, which is respected by the 'new people', and their authority as respected members of the community. Finally, their unity as a group is achieved not only by the common sentiments which they share, but also by the fact that the actions and norms of behaviour of the conservatives are regularly criticised by their leaders. In a sense, therefore, the conservatives, the 'out' group, are regarded as a common enemy who are a danger to the power of the 'new people' and the progress of the community.

The conservative people are in a less favourable position to maintain their solidarity. In the first place their numbers are gradually decreasing as the processes of social change remould the community. In the second place their leaders carry little weight in local government and they do not have the support or the sympathy of the Coloured Affairs Department. Their political activities are, as a result, negative. They attack the Management Board, the members of which they call traitors, and some refer to the superintendent and his wife in libellous terms. Thus they too regard their political opponents as enemies.

The leaders of the conservative people are members of two old and respected lineages in Steinkopf, the //are Cloetes and the Van Wyks. They are 'new people' in the sense that they have wealth, more than the average amount of education, 'desirable' physical characteristics, and live in European-type houses; but they differ from the leaders of 'new people' in that, with one exception, none are teachers. Further, Barnabas Cloete, their chief leader, is antagonistic towards the Boere Kerk and says that he will not enter the church-building until the N.G. Kerk leaves the Reserve or some other denomination is established. Both the //are Cloetes and the Van Wyks were the chief opponents of the N.G. Kerk's appointment as the established Church when the Rhenish Mission Society was forced to abandon its work in 1934. It is significant also that both the //are Cloetes and the Van Wyks, notably the latter, have tended to become tradesmen and not teachers.

No adequate explanation can be offered as to why these two families have reacted against the 'new people' and assumed leadership among the conservatives. But there is a suggestion that the //are Cloete leaders have hoped to revive the traditional pattern of leadership which the Engelbrechts have gradually lost. The evidence for this assumption is the fact that in recent years the //are Cloetes have tried to prove to the community that *their* ancestors, and not the Engelbrechts', were the first Baster Pioneers to establish themselves in the territory now known as Steinkopf. In order to strengthen their ranks the //are Cloetes through their leader, Barnabas, have set themselves up as champions not only of the conservative registered occupiers but also of the bywoners.

15 STEINKOPF: THE HOMESTEAD OF A PATRILINEAL EXTENDED FAMILY

16 RICHTERSVELD: THREE HOMESTEADS
The two huts in the foreground and their (scarcely visible) adjoining kitchens
constitute the homestead of a matrilineal extended family

Photo by C. Cloete

17   BROTHERS THRESHING IN STEINKOPF

18   A YOUNG GIRL HERDING IN RICHTERSVELD
Note also the proximity of the dwelling- and cooking-huts in the background

Having realised that they will never achieve power through the Management Board, the leaders of the conservative people have attempted to by-pass the local government and appeal to the central government to restore the system of administration which existed prior to the enforcement of the 1909 Act. A large sum of money has been collected, legal advice has been sought, and letters have been written to the Commissioner for Coloured Affairs, and to a former leader of the United Party.

On 7 February 1955, Barnabas Cloete wrote a letter to the Commissioner for Coloured Affairs complaining about the 1909 Act. This letter, quoted in part below and translated from Afrikaans illustrates the approach which the conservative people have adopted through their leaders to assert themselves in the political arena of contemporary Steinkopf. It shows too that the protests which the Management Board used to make against the enforcement of the 1909 Act before the advent of the 'new people' to power, are being carried on by the conservative people today:

My great-grandfather and his brothers lived at this place Kookfontein, later called Steinkopf, after the year 1700; they drove the wild Bushmen out of this territory; they were the Pioneers here in Little Namaqualand and so the land belonged to them until they died, when it was inherited by their children.

In 1812 the first Whites made their appearance; these were the London Missionaries, who later in 1838 handed over their work to the Rhenish Mission Society, which began to operate here in 1840. Soon afterwards the Basters and the Hottentots, who were living here together, built the church.

Up to 1840 we did not fall under the jurisdiction of any [foreign] government. But in 1842 the British invited us to become British subjects, as you can read in the Reverend Mr. Brecher's petition. In that period a Council was established to look after the domestic needs of the community and a tax was instituted; at first it was regarded as a sort of tribute, and later it was called Burgher Tax.

In 1912 we were informed that the Government was about to introduce a new Act in Steinkopf. Our people did not want to accept it; so they consulted a certain lawyer, J. Frank, of Springbok. He advised them that should the Act be forced on us, we ought to accept it under protest only.

In 1913 on 14 November the magistrate arrived with 12 armed policemen, and the magistrate told us that unless we elected a council, the Government would appoint strangers [*Vreemde mense*] over us. Under the circumstances we were obliged to submit and accept the Act under protest. From 1913 the tax continued to be called Burgher Tax until 1949, when the certificate was

11

changed to 'Lot', later to dwelling and dry lands. In 1954 it was just called tax and we do not know what all this means. All these changes go under the name of the Law.

Our rights of ownership are being violated by these new names and documents. This is why there have always been protests against the Act, by which our church and school lands are being surveyed without our permission.

For more than 100 years we have lived peacefully with the White farmers and they always respected our traditional Council. But today this is not the case. By this Act owners of land and property have been chased [off the Reserve] and their rights given to others. There have been many such instances. And all this is done under a Democratic and Christian Government. This Act is of no use in our territory owing to natural phenomena such as droughts, etc.

We can show that for over 100 years we have been law-abiding citizens. . . . And now our rights are being taken away from us and it is said that we do not wish to be subjected to any law. This is nonsense, nobody can prove it. All we ask for are those rights and privileges that are ours.

In terms of the Act the Council is not elected by the majority but by a small group of people.

For more than 100 years our territory was not classified as Crown land or Reserved land. Further, we were not referred to as occupiers but as burghers. These names are all foreign to us. It is about time the Government realised how indecently we have been treated under this Act. Three-quarters of our land has been lost and now through legislation our last rights are being taken away.

We respect our Government which must protect our rights and we hope and trust that it will never be necessary for us to complain elsewhere. I am willing to provide any further information that may be required, either in writing or personally in an interview.

7 February 1955   (*Signed*) BARNABAS CLOETE

CONCLUSIONS

In spite of the opposition and antagonism towards the local government by certain sections of the community, we must see the Management Board, as at present constituted, as a firmly established institution. On the one hand it is unlikely that the existing opposition forces will be able to break the solidarity of the 'new people' under their powerful leadership. Moreover, a regulation enforced in 1957 forbids all political meetings, not convened by the Management Board, from being held in the Reserve if more than five people are present. On the other hand there does not seem to be any possibility that the central government will modify the composition and organisation of the Management Board.[6]

At the present time the main functions of the Management Board may be stated as follows. Firstly, it is an instrument of the central government used to enforce the Mission Stations and Communal Reserves Act and its subjoining regulations. Secondly, it provides an outlet for leadership particularly among the 'new people', and for those conservatives who, after election, are able to withstand being opposed and outvoted on nearly all major issues. It is significant that in 1954 two conservative councillors resigned because they realised that they could not hold their own against the 'new people'. Finally, the Management Board provides the official link with the mines, the neighbouring Reserves, the Coloured people in general, and the rest of the outside world. Nearly all external contacts, both formal and informal, have first to be sanctioned by it. When one leaves the Reserve for a period longer than three months the Management Board must be informed; before a visitor enters the area he must first receive its permission to do so; when government officials inquire into local conditions, it is the Management Board that discusses the community's problems.

The position of the Management Board in the community can be summed up by stressing again its attitude towards those people who either oppose the laws it administers, or attempt to undermine its authority. Many times the superintendent (who belongs to lineage category B) and his right-hand councillors have been heard to say to their opponents: 'We must all respect the government. The Management Board must administer the law efficiently, and you must be obedient. The old and ignorant periods in our history are behind us and we must continue to make progress in the building up of our community. The government has given us schools and other amenities. We must be grateful for these things. How can we oppose those who have saved us from the primitive ways of our forebears?'

[6] Cf. Report of Commissioner for Coloured Affairs. U.G. No. 13—1954, pp. 12–13.

CHAPTER 8

THE CHURCH OF STEINKOPF

THE CHURCH of Steinkopf is the Nederduitse Gereformeerde Sendingkerk (Mission Church)[1] which ministers to approximately 95 per cent of the population. The remainder belong to the Anglican and Roman Catholic communions. Strictly speaking, therefore, the Church is not a 'Mission Church', for all members of the community call themselves Christians and the majority are regular church-goers, though not all are confirmed. We shall see in the next chapter, however, that many pagan beliefs do exist side by side with the Christian beliefs, but the fact that the missionary is largely unaware of these deviations makes the phrase 'Mission Church' a misleading one, until it is remembered that most South African churches regard their work among non-Whites as part of the tradition of missionary endeavour. In the Nederduitse Gereformeerde Kerk this pattern is clearly reflected in the separation of the Mission Church from the Mother Church.[2]

Ordained ministers, White and non-White, serving mission congregations are known as *Eerwaarde* and they have a lower status in the church than their colleagues the *Dominees* who minister to White congregations, although they hold the same rank. Only under special circumstances may a White *Eerwaarde* serve the needs of a White congregation. Nevertheless, in spite of this distinction between ministers and congregations, the organisation of church affairs is largely the same for both the Mission and the Mother Churches. As the title of the latter suggests, however, the administration of mission churches is directed mainly by officers of the Mother Church, although each mission congregation has its own local governing body, the Kerkraad.

Subsidiary to the Kerkraad of Steinkopf are the Sustersbond, the Christelike Jongedogtersbond, the Kinderbond, and the Studente Christelike Vereniging, while various burial societies co-operate with it in their activities.

Since the majority in the community belong to the Church we are describing, people who speak about 'going to' Church or 'belonging to' the Church are referring to the N.G. Sendingkerk, the official

[1] See *Wette en Bepalings vir die Bestuur van die Nederduitse Gereformeerde Kerk in Suid-Afrika.*

[2] *Wette en Bepalings,* art. 297.

and only recognised religious institution. The Anglicans and the Roman Catholics hold occasional services in private houses, and the Anglicans occasionally attend Sunday worship in the mission church.

Here attention must be drawn to the new regulation issued by the Minister of the Interior on 25 October 1957[3] to subjoin the Mission Stations and Communal Reserves Act of 1909. Under Regulation 88 any religious body, other than the established Church, has to apply for permission to hold a service which is to be attended by more than five people. Failure to do so is a punishable offence, and five people have already been found guilty of breaking this law in a neighbouring Reserve.[4] And in Steinkopf the Anglicans and Roman Catholics were at first prevented by the new regulation from holding services if these were to be attended by more than five people. Both these Churches applied for permission to continue the work they had been doing for over a hundred years and after a long delay were eventually granted permission to hold services once a month only.

There are various grades of membership of the Steinkopf Church, and these must be distinguished. They are:

(a) Those who have fulfilled all the requirements to become full members of the Church, the lidmate (confirmed members).

(b) Those who are members through baptism.

(c) Those born of parents who have been baptised or confirmed.

(d) Those who are baptised and confirmed members of the other Reformed churches.

These four categories of members together constitute the congregation, that is to say, the members of each category fall under the official jurisdiction of the Church, which is bound by the constitution of the Mother Church.

As with all associations, active membership is the criterion of the Church's strength; belief is of secondary significance, provided the rules are obeyed and the rituals observed. The social solidarity of any part of a community does not necessarily depend on people believing the same things, but rather on their performing together, either voluntarily or involuntarily, common activities in accordance with certain rules. In an earlier chapter we drew attention to the opposition from the congregation in the 1930's to the proposal that Steinkopf should be placed under the religious jurisdiction of the N.G. Sendingkerk, but it was pointed out that the majority of people later accepted the new

[3] Government Gazette (Union of South Africa), vol. CXC, no. 5962, p. 13.
[4] See W. P. Carstens, 'The D.R. Church Militant', Africa South, January 1959.

Church. Those former members of the Rhenish Mission Church who have not fully accepted the authority of the N.G. Sendingkerk assert that they were baptised and confirmed 'Rhenish' and that they would remain 'Rhenish' until they died. In this connection it is important to point out that investigations revealed that the majority of these 'Rhenish' Christians belong to two lineages (see pages 146–8). We have shown, moreover, that certain members of these two lineages are the chief opponents of the N.G. Sendingkerk and the local government, which suggests that the desire on the part of these people to remain 'Rhenish' is a function of their political attitudes rather than their doctrinal preference for the old Church. It must be pointed out, however, that in spite of their failure to co-operate with the N.G. Sendingkerk, those Rhenish Christians who have died during the past twenty-five years have all had funeral rites administered to them by the present Church.

For example, when Dawid Cloete died in October 1955 at the age of 102, the missionary preached a special sermon and Oupa Dawid was buried in the old cemetery which is used nowadays to inter only distinguished people. Moreover, the scribe of the Steinkopf Church wrote a long obituary in *Die Ligdraer*, the official journal of the N.G. Sendingkerk of South Africa. After extolling Dawid Cloete's virtues the scribe stated: 'His mind and eyesight remained good to the moment of his death. As he was bodily strong so also was he spiritually strong. He never strayed from the word of God, but remained Rhenish. Just before he died he sang Hymn 299 . . . loudly and clearly. At the end of the last line he reached out for his daughter's hand with the words, "I am going". Then, holding his hand high above him he called out, "Come my God, I see You now!" And with a smile on his face he passed away.' The writer concludes the obituary saying that Oupa Dawid was visited regularly a few days before he died by the missionary and members of the Kerkraad.[5]

It appears, therefore, as the case of Oupa Dawid illustrates, that the conflicts between the old 'Rhenish' Christians and the new Church of Steinkopf are resolved when the former die. From the point of view of the individuals in the community, the importance of resolving this conflict before death will become clear in the next chapter when we discuss the death rituals in Steinkopf.

[5] *Die Ligdraer*, vol. 17, no. 1, January 1956, pp. 25–6.

THE KERKRAAD

In Steinkopf the Kerkraad consists of the missionary, who is its chairman, fifteen *ouderlinge*, and sixteen *diakens*, of whom one is elected as the scribe and another as the secretary–treasurer. Employed by the Kerkraad is a verger. Not all the *ouderlinge* and *diakens* live permanently in the Reserve; some are migratory workers who look after members of the congregation in the mine-compounds.

The missionary is appointed by the Kerkraad from a list of three names submitted by the Kerkraad of the Mother Church. The procedure is as follows. When the names are submitted to the local Kerkraad the qualifications and desirability of the three nominees are studied, and the members pray for divine guidance in their selection of the most suitable candidate. As soon as a decision has been reached, a letter is written to the selected candidate 'calling' him to take up the new post. When the candidate receives the 'call', he considers the pros and cons of the invitation and also prays to God for guidance in making his decision. Should he accept, he automatically becomes the missionary-designate of Steinkopf. But, as frequently happens, if the 'call' is not accepted, the procedure begins afresh. In 1947, for instance, it took three years to replace the missionary who had been 'called' to another district, and in 1956 after the resident missionary had accepted a 'call' to another congregation, over a year passed before his place could be filled, five people having rejected the 'call'.

The duties of a *sendeling* (missionary) comprise:

(*a*) Preaching the gospel in general; preaching about the Heidelberg Catechism and the Leyden History of the Lord in particular; holding the usual preparation services before, and the meditations after *Nagmaal* (Communion); and preaching about the meaning of baptism.

(*b*) Administering the sacraments of baptism and Nagmaal.

(*c*) Conducting divine services.

(*d*) Blessing marriages.

(*e*) Catechetical instruction of young and old.

(*f*) Witnessing, together with one or more elders, confirmation candidates' acceptance of the creed of the Church.

(*g*) Carrying out regular *huisbesoek* (house-to-house visiting); visiting the sick; and further, everything that belongs to the pastoral care of the congregation.

(*h*) Presiding over Kerkraad meetings.

(*i*) Deciding with the help of the *ouderlinge* and, where there is a divergence of opinion, on the advice and with the permission of the

Kerkraad, whether or not a visiting preacher should be allowed in the pulpit, or to hold services outside the church in the name of the Kerkraad.[6]

In addition to these duties, which are formally laid down in the Church constitution and apply to all missionaries both in South Africa and in other parts of Africa, the missionary of Steinkopf is also the manager of the primary and farms schools and with his Kerkraad runs the secondary school hostels. The school board scrutinises all teachers' applications and as far as possible only active members of the N.G. Kerk are appointed. As a minister of religion he is also the marriage officer for Steinkopf.

In all his activities the missionary (except when he assumes the role of preacher) must co-operate with the Kerkraad, and Church affairs are controlled, not by the missionary, but by the Kerkraad. However, in spite of the ties between him and this body, the missionary must be considered as a special person in the community, whose status is determined both by his official role, and by the role which is determined by his personality, his attitudes towards his congregation, and his ability as a preacher. Thus he plays his part as a leader in the community first through his office, but his success will depend on the way he carries out his work. He must be strict, insisting on good behaviour, regular attendance at church services, and payment of church-dues; but he must exercise his authority in terms of the accepted norms of the community.

Thirty years ago this was relatively simple because these norms were more or less homogeneous but today the role of religious leader has been complicated by the appearance of new social cleavages; values, moreover, are no longer absolute for all sections of the community and it is not possible for him to be uniformly accepted as he used to be with certain notable exceptions already alluded to.

Although he is still leader of the Church, the esteem with which the missionary is regarded varies from group to group and from individual to individual; and the relationship is further complicated by the fact that he is a White Afrikaner, which for many in the community, as elsewhere in Africa, has become a symbol of domination and oppression. But in general all these differences appear to be outweighed by a common loyalty towards the community's Church.[7]

In the N.G. Sendingkerk a missionary who carries the title of

[6] *Wette en Bepalings,* Art. 35(i).

[7] See also pp. 33–5.

Eerwaarde (Reverend) is usually said to be the *Leeraar* (teacher of the Word) of his congregation. At Steinkopf he is addressed by most members of the congregation as *Meneer* (Sir). Some educated people, however, prefer the term of address Eerwaarde, which respects the office rather than the individual. When speaking about the missionary, these educated people always retain the term Eerwaarde, while the others retain the term of address Meneer, when referring to personal matters, e.g.: 'Meneer gave us a packet of sugar.' But they use the term Leeraar when referring to him in his official capacity as a minister, e.g.: 'The Leeraar will punish you if you don't stop swearing.' These differences are important for, in the first instance, they illustrate the attitudes that different classes have towards him: educated people are concerned mainly with his role as a minister of religion, while the less educated and more conservative people see him as an individual playing different roles.

The term of address Meneer is used only for missionaries: to address any White man as Meneer is considered too familiar and therefore impertinent, the principle being that for a Coloured man to call a White man *Meneer* admits equality—Meneer being the conventional way in which a White Afrikaner addresses a stranger of his own stock. But Whites condone the term of address *Meester* (Master or teacher) if Coloured people refuse to use the term *Baas* (Boss).

The missionary's wife is addressed and referred to as *Juffrou* (Madam or Lady-Teacher) by all people. She does not take part in the same church affairs as her husband, but apart from her duties as a housewife, concerns herself mainly with the women and their problems, and is chairman of the Sustersbond, Christelike Jongedogtersbond and the Kinderbond.

The official duties of the *ouderlinge* and *diakens* are various, but broadly speaking, the *ouderlinge* are concerned with the spiritual activities of the Church, while *diakens* are responsible for Church finance and its routine administration. Article 36 of the Church constitution states that *ouderlinge* are entrusted with:

(*a*) The welfare of the congregation.

(*b*) The purity of the doctrine.

(*c*) The supervision of the congregation, especially *huisbesoek*, with the missionary.

(*d*) Zealous co-operation with the missionary in all matters concerned with the spiritual development of the congregation.

Diakens, on the other hand are charged with:

(a) The collection of alms (*liefdegawes*).

(b) The distribution of alms to destitute members of the congregation (with the approval of the Kerkraad).

(c) Finding ways and means of increasing Church funds.

Half the members of the Kerkraad retire each year and new members are elected at a joint sitting of the Kerkraad and former Kerkraad members. Normally the retiring members are not re-elected for three years for it is the policy of the Church to give as many suitable people as possible the opportunity of becoming Kerkraad members (*ampdraers*) during their lifetime.[8] Apart from its psychological significance, this practice of giving a large number of people an outlet for their energies and qualities of leadership is extremely important sociologically because it makes for a strong system of group leadership and social control, since former *ampdraers* retain the respect that they earned while they held office.

The procedure for the election of new Kerkraad members is as follows. Each retiring member prays independently to God to point out to him the right person to succeed him. When his prayer is answered he goes directly to the person revealed to him and informs him of what has happened; the 'revealed' person then considers the matter, talks it over with his family, and asks God in his prayers to indicate to him whether or not he should accept. In the meanwhile the retiring member will have submitted his candidate's name to the Kerkraad, which normally accepts the nomination. The names of all the nominees are then read in church on three consecutive Sundays and if there are no objections from the congregation they are automatically elected. Should a nominee decide not to accept nomination, he must inform the Kerkraad by the third Sunday on which his name is called, giving reasons for his withdrawal. On the other hand those who accept nomination must inform the Kerkraad personally as soon as their minds are made up.

All church activities, services, *huisbesoek*, etc., fall under the jurisdiction of the Kerkraad, although, as we have seen, the various church officers have specially allocated tasks; but all are united through the missionary in a common association. It is necessary, therefore, to look at all church activities in terms of the activities of the Kerkraad, pointing out, where necessary, any special duties assigned to the various categories of members. According to Calvinist theology, all law, all power,

[8] *Diakens*, however, may be elected as *ouderlinge* if they are eligible. No person under the age of 40 may be elected as an *ouderling*.

all authority spring from God: the Kerkraad is the institution representing man but carrying out the will of God.

The primary duty of the Kerkraad is the organisation of ordinary
church services, which are the usual Sunday morning and afternoon
services, the Wednesday prayer meeting (*biduur*), and Holy
Communion (Nagmaal). There are two services on Sundays in the
mission Church, in the morning and afternoon. The main service
begins at 10.15 a.m. and is centred on the missionary's sermon, which
is usually based on an Old Testament text. If the missionary is away
administering Nagmaal at other centres, his place is taken by an
ouderling who preaches from a table in front of the Church and not
from the pulpit. Every member (full or otherwise) of the Church is
expected to attend the main Sunday service, and some travel up to
thirty miles by donkey-cart. Attendance is considered a social as well
as a religious obligation.

Men sit on the left- and women on the right-hand side of the
church and the singing is led by the women. Sermons are always
relevant to Steinkopf, and the prayers deal mainly with those problems
that especially concern the people: drought, fornication and adultery,
disobedience and irresponsibility. The service, therefore, contributes to
the social cohesion of the community through the common act of
worship, which concerns only Christians of Steinkopf and nobody else.
Sunday morning service, too, is an opportunity for the superintendent
of the Reserve to read notices issued by the Management Board, and
often a short address is given to explain a new piece of legislation.
These notices follow immediately after the church notices, and it is
often difficult to decide whether they have been issued by the authority
of the Church or of the Management Board.

The afternoon service is of a different order. It is attended mainly by
young people for whom there was no accommodation at the morning
service, by the very devout adult Christians, and by members of the
Kerkraad.

The quarterly celebrations of Nagmaal are great occasions at
Steinkopf. These are not merely celebrations of the Lord's Supper but
also times when all confirmed members of the Church living on the
settlements trek to Steinkopf for a social week-end: for family reunions,
friendship, gossip, and courting (including love-making). The trek
begins on Friday or Saturday and most people remain until Monday
morning when they return home early. We might say, therefore, that
Nagmaal performs a dual function in that it unites all the confirmed

members of the Church through their common religious activity, and also helps to renew and cement the bonds of kinship and friendship.

Each Wednesday evening at 8 p.m. a *gemeentelike biduur* (corporate prayer meeting) is held. The church calendar of Steinkopf states that at this service, 'every professing Christian is awaited by God and the community', but in practice Wednesday services are attended by local Kerkraad members, other devout members, and a handful of adolescents. The *biduur* is conducted by either the missionary or an *ouderling*; there is a short address and a hymn followed by extempore prayer begun by the leader of the service, who is followed by those others present who are inspired to pray aloud. The service is of great emotional importance to the very devout, and one can observe the pent-up expressions of the suppliants gradually relax as they pray. Collections are taken at all services.

It is incumbent also upon the Kerkraad to organise special services for marriages and funerals. Marriage, although not considered a sacrament in the N.G. Kerk, can be blessed only by an ordained minister, by the resident missionary, or in his absence by any other missionary or minister who is prepared to visit the village for this purpose. The service is a short one and is attended by relatives and friends, the number attending being determined by the status of the couple.

Funerals are a different matter, for it is not essential for an ordained minister to conduct the religious service, although the service itself is always necessary. A short service in the mission church precedes the graveside burial rites, unless the corpse has started to decay or the person has died from some infectious disease, when the church service is usually omitted.

Much of the Kerkraad's time and energy is spent in arranging baptisms and preparing people for confirmation. Apart from the fact that baptism is always a necessary prelude to confirmation, there is in the religion of Steinkopf a more subtle connexion between them. In the first place we must remember that the Church law lays down that: 'When parents, who are not members of the N.G. Kerk wish to have their children baptised, the case is left to the minister to decide whether they will be baptised or not, with the proviso always that two members of the N.G. Kerk are appointed as witnesses.' The matter is complicated further by the fact that 'confirmation status' alone is not sufficient to entitle them to have their children baptised. Parents must also be regular Sunday church-goers, and attend Nagmaal at least twice a year. Further, their conduct must be 'satisfactory', the drunkenness of one parent being sufficient justification for depriving a child of the sacrament of baptism, with the proviso that reputable members of the Church may stand for the legal parents if they have the religious education of the child concerned under their immediate control and personal supervision. As a result some people are never baptised because they had (in the opinion of the Kerkraad) wicked parents who had nefarious relations and friends and as a consequence there were no suitable persons to look after their welfare; and by the time they were able to approach the Church themselves to receive the sacrament, their backgrounds were held against them and their requests were refused.

Catechetical classes are held every Sunday after morning service and many people spend years in the class before they are admitted to the status of confirmed members of the Church, and to the ranks of the *lidmate*.

Regular huisbesoek is an important duty of the Kerkraad members, who are expected to keep in contact with personal and family affairs. The purpose of huisbesoek is to see to the moral and spiritual life and the welfare of the people, and to ensure that they pay their church-dues. For administrative convenience the Reserve is divided into six wards, coinciding roughly with the political *wyke*, each under the care of an *ouderling* and a *diaken*, both of whom are supervised in their work by the missionary, whose duty also is to visit all members of his congregation at least once a year.

When the missionary carries out his annual huisbesoek rounds, he is usually accompanied by a senior *ouderling* and *diaken* who are resident in the Steinkopf village. But before visiting the inhabitants of a ward, it is customary to contact the local *ouderling* and *diaken*, who accompany them.

During these visits the missionary finds out who have been baptised, confirmed, admitted to the catechetical classes, whether there are regular family prayers, whether there is a Bible in the household, how often people attend Sunday services and Nagmaal, etc. He also makes inquiries into the welfare of the people, especially the aged, and whether people away from home are in touch with the Church. Moreover, he rebukes people for misconduct that has been brought to his notice, warning them to mend their ways. He may reprimand people for not paying their church-dues if he has received word from the *diaken* that they have been neglectful of these financial obligations.

During the huisbesoek rounds, *ouderlinge* and *diakens* may also raise problems which, though they have been raised before, can be more effectively dealt with in the company of the missionary. The people visited, too, are free to state their criticism of the Church and Kerkraad, and many complain bitterly of neglect by their *ouderlinge* and *diakens*.

In general there is an ambivalent attitude towards members of the Kerkraad and indeed towards the missionary; on the one hand there is the genuine desire to conform to and satisfy the demands of the Church, and please the members of the Kerkraad, but on the other hand there is the feeling of antagonism towards them for the many demands made that are often in conflict with their own inclinations. Conformity to the Church is desirable and pleasing because it gives a feeling of social security, and spiritual security for the life after death, but at the same time it is irritating to have to pay church-dues and to abstain from dancing and drinking. Individuals, however, tend not to express their feelings in terms of the institution, the Church, but rather they project them on to the personalities who constitute the Kerkraad.

Huisbesoek also provides a means of finding out about the conduct of other families. It is not the *diakens* and *ouderlinge* alone who volunteer information about members of the congregation, for the members themselves are always ready to justify their own purity by disclosing and exaggerating the sins of their neighbours. Information is volunteered, ranging from the number of times Oom Jacobus has taken the Lord's name in vain, to who has been sleeping with 'Missis X' since her husband died.

The missionary's annual visit to each member of the congregation has a profound influence on the whole community: beer-brewers and *buchu-drinkers*[9] dispose of their supplies, dusty Bibles appear in homes where no one can read, and people put on pious looks which last for several weeks after the visit; church-dues 'just happen' to be produced, and those who can afford them pay their thank-offerings to the missionary's right-hand *diaken* as though they had been waiting for him for a long time.

Apart from the missionary's annual visit, there are regular visits from the local *ouderlinge* and *diakens*. These visits are made sometimes jointly but more often independently, depending largely upon the personal relationship between the two officers. Usually the *ouderlinge* belong to a much higher age-group than the *diakens* and prefer, therefore, to carry out their duties separately.

⁹ People who drink patent-medicines containing alcohol.

The main task of the *diaken* in his ward is the collection of church-dues—the monthly subscriptions of the members and family thank-offerings after the harvest. This is perhaps the most difficult duty of any church officer and requires not only considerable tact and persuasion but that quality found in business men of knowing intuitively when people have got money and when they are in the right disposition to part with it. *Diakens* are the least popular of the Kerkraad members.

In addition to collecting money, *diakens* are charged also with distributing it to needy persons on the recommendation of the Kerk-raad, and alms are occasionally distributed to the sick and aged, and to widows who have no children to support them.

The duties of *ouderlinge* differ from those of the *diakens* since they are entrusted mainly with the spiritual welfare of the congregation. Men are elected to the office of *ouderling* for their 'spiritual' qualities and their knowledge of Church-teaching and the Scriptures. They are expected to assist individuals and families in all their problems; to help solve petty disputes between husbands and wives; to rebuke children who are disobedient at home; to reproach people for their sins; and to remind them of their duties to the Church. *Ouderlinge* are, in other words, the spiritual fathers of Steinkopf. Occasionally on Sundays, and on Wednesdays, they hold services at the settlements for those people who are unable to travel to Steinkopf to worship; many are renowned for their effective preaching and their competence in extempore prayer, and a bad preacher, or one with an inaudible voice, will often be criticised by his congregation.

Another important duty of an *ouderling* is to visit the sick and help prepare people for death. At the sick-bed he will read passages from the Bible and pray, exhorting God to spare the person, 'if that is His will', and help him to be restored to health. In the case of a dying person the *ouderling*, if the missionary is not available, will spend the last hours with the sick man and his family, praying and helping him to 'find' God as death overcomes him.

The Kerkraad has various sources of income: Sunday collections, membership dues, thank-offerings, and baptismal, wedding and confir-mation fees. Sunday collections are voluntary but most people try to put a penny or two, sometimes more, in the collection tray each time they go to church. Membership dues are 6s. a year, payable in advance, or 6d. a month, per member. Thank-offerings are expected from all families after the harvest but very few are able to pay the traditional tithe. The Kerkraad also levies the following rates: registration of baptism 3s. plus 2s. 6d. for a certificate, registration of confirmation 6s., registration of marriage 15s. 6d.

The *diakens* arrange annual bazaars in their own wards to raise extra funds for the Church. Members of the congregation are asked to make cakes and sweets and ginger beer, while those who can, donate meat, or live sheep and goats. A large bazaar is held annually in the Steinkopf village, and this is one of the great social occasions of the year.

In addition to the various social sanctions, both positive and negative, which the Church in general and the Kerkraad in particular impose on members of the congregation, the Kerkraad is also a court of law. Within the framework of its spiritual jurisdiction it can impose punishments ranging from the total exclusion of members from all benefits offered by the Church to formally rebuking wrongdoers. Offenders against whom action is taken may be handled by the missionary alone or by the missionary and one or more *ouderlinge*, or by the whole Kerkraad. Most minor offences are dealt with by the reduced Kerkraad, but serious offences always receive the attention of the full council. Formal punishments are of three kinds:

(*a*) The refusal of the sacraments of baptism and confirmation to children whose parents have violated Church law. In these cases both the parents and the children suffer, although the punishment is directed against the parents.

(*b*) The refusal of the sacraments of baptism and confirmation to sinful adults who wish to become Church members.

(*c*) The exclusion of members from Nagmaal for a fixed period for breaking Church rules.

The most frequent offences for which people are brought before the Kerkraad are fornication and drinking. A couple, for example, who have an illegitimate child or a child conceived before marriage (see pages 77–8) are likely to be excluded from Nagmaal, if they are both confirmed, for a period of six months or a year depending on the circumstances. A couple, however, who have been courting with the intention of marriage are likely to get off with a warning should the girl conceive before marriage, and if both voluntarily confess to the missionary they may not be summoned to appear before the Kerkraad. On the other hand girls who fall pregnant by casual suitors are treated severely, together with the genitors. If no proof can be established as to the paternity of the child, the girl will be punished alone. One girl, for example, has produced three illegitimate children, and for each she was brought before the Kerkraad. She was a full member of the Church and her punishment was meted out accordingly. For the first, she was excluded from Nagmaal services for six months, for the second, a year, and for the third, two years and warned that should she commit a similar offence she would lose her confirmation privileges permanently.

CHURCH ASSOCIATIONS

Under the jurisdiction of the Kerkraad are various women's and children's associations, the Sustersbond, the Christelike Jongedogters-bond, the Kinderbond, and the Studente Christelike Vereniging.

The Sustersbond is a women's association, membership of which is open to all confirmed married women in the Church. The president of this association is the missionary's wife. The activities of the Susters-bond include poor-relief in Steinkopf, the rendering of financial support to charitable organisations in Cape Town (such as Nazareth House) and the holding of regular prayer-meetings. The members of the association always lead the singing at Church services and funerals, and occasionally sing an anthem or hymn at morning services on Sundays. Funds are raised by holding bazaars, organising concerts, and from the sale of clothing made at the weekly work-party meetings. Work-parties play a very important part in establishing and cementing the bonds of friendship among the members of the Sustersbond. They are both secular and religious in nature: people sew and knit and have an opportunity to chat and gossip, but prayers are also said.

The committee forms the nucleus of the Sustersbond and, apart from the administrative routine which its members carry out, all issues of spiritual importance are discussed at meetings. Various sub-committees are created from time to time to deal with specific matters such as sickness and poverty.

The Christelike Jongedogtersbond is an association similar to the Sustersbond but membership is open only to unmarried women. The Kinderbond is really a junior Christelike Jongedogtersbond with a membership of girls of school-going age. We see, therefore, that in the realm of local church associations, women are organised into three groups based on age and status, unlike men who do not form voluntary associations, stratified or otherwise, except in some parts of the Reserve where they form the nuclei of burial societies. The Studente Christelike Vereniging is a branch of the Students' Christian Association of South

12

Africa, and has a membership consisting of high-school students. Its activities are mainly religious, but those who can afford the costs occasionally attend 'camps' in Cape Town during their school holidays.

In addition to the church associations there are five burial-societies which, although independent of the Kerkraad, nevertheless operate in close association with the Church. The first of these societies was formed in 1928 during a serious drought when people were too poor to afford coffins in which to bury their dead or to pay for proper funerals.[10] Prior to the establishment of this society the close kin of deceased people had often to collect money from other relatives and friends to cover expenses. Thus the formation of the first burial-society really institutionalised a practice which was already in operation.

Today five such societies exist, one in each of the main districts. Die Goeie Hoop Steinkopf Begraftenis Vereniging (GHSBV) is the largest, having a membership of roughly 350 women. Only women (usually wives) are admitted as members, for it is argued that, as men are so often away from home, their wives are better suited to represent the family. However, in some of the smaller burial-societies in the districts where conservative people predominate, both men and women are admitted as members, but only *men* are elected to the committees. The initial subscription on joining the GHSBV is £1, and thereafter £1 or more a year until a total of £10 has been paid to the treasurer. Membership entitles everyone in the elementary family to a full burial. The society makes all the arrangements for the funeral, digs the grave, and supplies the coffin. Families who wish to have a more elaborate funeral and a more expensive coffin may do so, provided they pay the additional costs. In the smaller societies subscriptions cover not only the costs of the coffin and the funeral arrangements but also the expenses of the *lykwaak* (wake).

Each burial-society has its flag, which is flown outside the dwelling where the corpse is lying to indicate to the other members that one of their number has died, and also to show people where the wake will be held. During the funeral procession from the church to the graveyard the flag is always carried by an office-bearer. It is not obligatory for members of burial-societies to attend the funerals of their deceased colleagues, but everyone 'tries to attend if he can'.

[10] In the next chapter we shall see how important these factors are in the religious life.

SCHOOLS[11]

The foundations of school education at Steinkopf were laid by missionaries and members of their families, and in the contemporary community the schools have retained close ties with the established Church. The pioneering work in education was extremely difficult, for not only did the majority of the people first have to be taught to understand Dutch, the language in which all instruction was given, but also, as the people were nomadic pastoralists, the boys and young men were needed by their parents to assist in herding, while the girls usually trekked with their families to assist in the domestic chores. In spite of these difficulties, however, there were 165 pupils on the roll in the year 1867 although the average attendance was only 44; and it is significant that of these 165 pupils only 64 were males. In that year there was one teacher, the missionary's wife, and most of her time was spent teaching her pupils to read and write Dutch. About a third of the pupils were taught elementary arithmetic, history and geography.[12]

By 1905 the number of pupils on the roll had risen to 301, while the average attendance was 258. There were 219 pupils in Sub A, 41 in Sub B, 26 in Standard 1, and 13 in Standard 2.[13] No details regarding the sex ratios of pupils or the number of teachers are given. By the third quarter of 1938 there were 330 pupils attending the same school (in the village) which had 11 teachers. Two farm schools had also been established at the hamlets of Gladkop (56 pupils and 2 teachers) and Bulletrap (72 pupils and 3 teachers).[14]

In 1958 there were five primary schools having 21 teachers and a total enrolment of 691 pupils, and one high school staffed by 7 teachers who catered for the needs of 100 pupils. Table XVI below indicates the enrolment and staffing in these schools. The high school and the largest primary school are situated in the Steinkopf village; the rest, all of which are 'farm' schools, are to be found in the larger hamlets.

The primary and the 'farm' schools are administered by the Kerkraad under the chairmanship of the missionary, who is responsible, *inter alia*, for the appointment of teachers and for enforcing discipline over the

---

[11] For a description of the history of education in Namaqualand see J. A. Heese, 'Onderwys in Namakwaland', 1942.

[12] Report of the Superintendent-General of Education, 1867. Cape of Good Hope, G. 1—1868.

[13] Ibid., G. 5—1906.

[14] P. W. Kotzé, op. cit., p. 205. By 1938 the N.G. *Sendingkerk* had taken over from the Rhenish Mission Society.

pupils (and teachers) when necessary. Under its direct control is a school hostel in the mission village providing accommodation for 46 boarders, each of whom is required to pay a fee of £39 a year. In 1958 there were 16 girls and 30 boys in the hostel. The majority of these boarders came from other parts of Namaqualand and the district of Vanrhynsdorp because Steinkopf has the only Coloured high school in the north-western Cape. The Kerkraad also administers the three farm schools at Rooiwal, Vioolsdrift, and Goodhouse, all of which are situated beyond the boundaries of the Reserve and cater for the educational needs of pupils who may have no connexions with the community of Steinkopf.

TABLE XVI

TEACHERS AND PUPILS IN STEINKOPF SCHOOLS (1958)

Schools category	Locality	No. of teachers		No. of Pupils
		Men	Women	
1. High school	Steinkopf Village	6	1	100
2. Primary school	Steinkopf Village	8	6	463
3. Farm school (Sub A—Std. 3)	Eyams	1	—	42
4. Farm school (Sub A—Std. 5)	Gladkop	3	—	90
5. Farm school (Sub A—Std. 3)	Bulletrap	2	—	60
6. Farm school (Sub A—Std. 3)	!Kosis	1	—	36
All schools		21	7	791

The high school is administered by the Cape Educational Department through the school-board at Springbok, while a parents' association (*skoolkomitee*) consisting of five persons represents the parents from whom the members are elected. The function of the skool-komitee is to deal with parental grievances and to submit proposals to the school-board for the improvement of education in general and the administration of the school in particular.

No official statistics are available for the educational standards attained by the whole population, but a sample of 223 persons (see Table XVII) indicates certain significant tendencies among the population over 20 years of age: 20 per cent said they had never received any formal education,[15] 19 per cent stated that they had passed Sub A, Sub B or Standard 1, 38 per cent claimed to have passed Standard 2, 3, or 4, while 23 per cent asserted that they had passed at least Standard 5. A further significant feature of this sample was the fact that slightly fewer women than men claimed to have received no education. Moreover, women showed a marked tendency to acquire a higher standard of education than men. For example, whereas 30·5 per cent of the women passed Standard 5 or more, only 16 per cent of the men achieved this standard. A probable explanation of this phenomenon is that in former years boys were taken out of school earlier than girls to assist in the herding of livestock. Contemporary statistics, however, show that nowadays a much higher proportion of boys than girls are at high school (see Table XVIII) and this indicates how the attitude

TABLE XVII

EDUCATIONAL STANDARD ATTAINED BY PERSONS
OVER THE AGE OF 20 YEARS (1957–8)
BASED ON SAMPLE OF 223 PERSONS

	No. education		Sub A & B and Std. 1		Stds. 2–4		Std. 5+		Total
	No.	%	No.	%	No.	%	No.	%	
Men	27	22·7	27	22·7	45	37·82	19	15·97	118
Women	18	17·14	16	15·24	39	37·15	32	30·47	105
Men and women	45	20·18	43	19·29	84	37·67	51	22·88	223

towards boys' education has changed. The change in attitude towards boys' education and education in general is essentially a function of the rise of the 'new people', whose emergence must in turn be seen partly as a function of the increase in the number and quality of the schools. Two additional farm schools, one at !Kosis, the other at Eyams, were established in 1940 and 1950. The high school was opened in 1950.

Table XVIII, in which the number of pupils in each standard is set out, speaks for itself and resembles the distribution of pupils enrolled in all the Coloured schools of the Cape Province. Approximately fifty of the pupils in Standards 6 to 10 come from outside the Reserve. Three of the six pupils in Standard 10 have their homes in Steinkopf. Figures are not available to show the proportion of children of school-going age who are not at school.

[15] In 1952 I found 31 per cent of the labourers on the Kleinzee Mine to be illiterate. The majority of these men came from Steinkopf.

TABLE XVIII

ENROLMENT OF PUPILS IN STEINKOPF SCHOOLS IN TERMS OF STANDARDS

(December 1960)[1]

School category	No. of pupils			Sub-standards	1	2	3	4	5	6	7	8	9	10
	M	F	T											
High school	72	47	119							33	46	24	10	6
Primary school	216	218	434	185	98	45	49	25	31					
Farm schools	99	91	190	78	44	31	18	15	4					
All schools (No.)	387	356	743	263	142	76	67	40	35	33	46	24	10	6
All schools (%)	52·1	47·9	100	35·4	19·1	10·2	9·0	5·3	4·6	4·4	6·2	3·2	1·3	0·5
% of pupils enrolled in Coloured schools in the Cape Province (June 1954)[2]				40·7	14·7	12·3	10·5	8·2	5·9	4·0	1·9	1·1	0·7	0·2

[1] Figures from Cape Education Department. Those for 1958 were not available.

[2] Report of the Coloured Education Commission (1953–6).

The teachers[16] at Steinkopf may be divided into two categories, the locally born and the aliens. The former received some of their education in the Reserve but trained at colleges in the Cape. The latter received all their education at other centres. In 1958 there were twelve alien teachers, six of whom taught in the high school.

CONCLUSION

We have already drawn attention to the functions of specific aspects of the Church. To summarise let us look at the institution in a broader perspective in order to assess the part which it plays in social life as a whole.

First, the Church of Steinkopf must be seen as an association whose activities reinforce local solidarity, overriding the cleavages and class-distinctions that divide people in narrower circles. For, apart from the small minority who belong to other denominations and those who still regard themselves as Rhenish, all the members of the community have some connexion with the Nederduitse Gereformeerde Sendingkerk. This means that the majority of the population owes its allegiance to one Church, one Kerkraad, and one minister. In Church they pray and sing together, and share the message which the preacher 'gives' to them; and four times a year, those who have been confirmed receive the symbols of bread and wine at the quarterly celebrations of Nagmaal.

Second, the Church plays an important part in education especially through its link with the schools, and may be said also to strengthen the system of local government.

Thirdly, the Church must be seen as an instrument of social control. Not only does it reinforce Christian supernatural sanctions, but the missionary and the Kerkraad have judicial powers over the congregation, whom they have authority to punish.

Fourthly, we must see the Nederduitse Gereformeerde Sendingkerk as an institution which the people of Steinkopf share with other groups of Coloured people and a high percentage of Afrikaans-speaking White South Africans. For though there are differences between the Mission and the Mother Churches, the dogma, the rituals, and the form of government are the same.

Fifthly, the Church provides, through its officers (deacons and elders) the opportunity and means for potential leaders to express their ability and aspirations. And the fact that these leaders hold office for a

[16] See also chapter 10, Table XX.

limited period only, enables a relatively large number of people to hold office in one generation. Even after relinquishing their positions they still retain some of the prestige which they formerly enjoyed.

Sixthly, the various church associations (including the burial-societies) apart from the opportunities for leadership which they provide, enable people who have common interests and share common sentiments to co-operate and form groups that cut across the ties of kinship. Here we should stress also the important part which women play in these voluntary church associations.

In this summary of the function of the Church we have stressed the structural aspects of corporate activities. But the religious life of any people is surrounded also by an elaborate system of beliefs and their accompanying sentiments and emotions. In the next chapter we deal with some of the beliefs which find expression in the institution we have described, and also those outside its jurisdiction.

CHAPTER 9

SUPERNATURAL BELIEFS

THE SUPERNATURAL beliefs which the people of Steinkopf hold are of two kinds: those which have their origin in Christian teaching, and those which belong to the Nama tradition. Neither of these is 'pure' because each has had an influence on the other during the past hundred and fifty years.

After a summary of the main features of local Christian theology we shall be largely concerned in this chapter with the non-Christian beliefs. We shall attempt also to analyse the causes of good and bad fortune, and to show the relation of beliefs in general to the social structure in which they occur.

CHRISTIAN BELIEFS

All the people of Steinkopf are nominal Christians. The majority of the people, however, although they claim to adhere to the doctrines of the Church, are not always orthodox in their individual beliefs. We have already discussed the Church as an association under the leadership and control of the missionary and the Kerkraad. Now we shall analyse the beliefs which the people themselves hold about the nature of God, Jesus, and the Devil.

God (*die Here*) is believed to be the creator of the universe and all that is found on the earth. He is the giver of life and happiness to man, the sender of rain, and the Being responsible for good crops and plenty. God's benevolence, though, is conditional on man's good behaviour. That is to say, God's benevolence continues so long as people conform to the norms of behaviour approved of in Steinkopf. When people are wicked, God punishes them by allowing droughts and epidemics to overcome them. The innocent and the virtuous are thus punished for the sins of wrongdoers, though the latter may be in the minority. It is, in fact, accepted that God normally punishes or rewards the people collectively. Thus, when good rains fall and the crops flourish, God is said to be pleased with the people of Steinkopf. On the other hand, when there is drought and the crops fail, He is said to be angry either with the whole community or, more commonly, with a section of it. On the whole things are never so perfect that some manifestation or other of God's wrath cannot be discovered, and a great deal of time is devoted to discussing in ordinary conversation the possible causes of

His present anger. In the contemporary community the conservative people attribute all collective misfortune to the behaviour of the 'new people' and the manner in which the Management Board, sometimes referred to as *die Satan*, administers the Reserve. These conservative people naturally object to having to suffer for the sins of the other group. On the other hand, the Management Board and those who support it blame the conservative people, who are said to rouse God's displeasure by refusing to accept the new order. It must be pointed out in connexion with the community's ideas of collective guilt, rewards and punishments, that Steinkopf is not seen as including any Whites within its borders. A White person, therefore, cannot be responsible through his sins or his virtues for anything which may befall the *bruinmense*. Thus when an informant remarked, 'White Afrikaners hate Jesus when things go wrong', he stressed that this hatred did not affect God's attitude towards Steinkopf.

God is not only believed to influence the material welfare and happiness of the people collectively; He also stands in an intimate relationship to individuals. It is God, for instance, who brings peace and eternal rest to people after death as a reward for a good life; and conversely, it is God who withholds this peace from people who have lived wickedly or who try to resist death when they are due to die. But even wicked people can attain the tranquillity of the grave if they confess all their sins to God, and obtain forgiveness from those kinsmen and friends whom they have wronged during their lives.

The greatest sin any man can commit is to resent anything which God has 'allowed to happen to him', for everything that happens is in accordance with the will of God. Most people are familiar with the book of Job, which they firmly believe was written exclusively for them, and it is usual for afflicted persons to be consoled and exhorted with the text: '. . . the Lord gave and the Lord hath taken away; blessed be the name of the Lord. In all this Job sinned not, nor charged God with any foolishness' (Job i. 21–2). When things go wrong there is comfort also in the belief that God can alter the things which He has allowed if one prays sincerely to Him. Through prayer, God grants one success, happiness, good fortune, and protection. An example of God's response to prayer in everyday affairs can be cited. A. E. was on a hunting expedition with a friend; they had had no success all day so they prayed to God to make the springbok tame. Their prayer was answered and they shot two, but no sooner had they removed the entrails than a police van was seen approaching them.

The country was flat and the bushes were small, so they prayed to God again to protect them (for they were shooting illegally out of season). They lay down flat behind what cover they could find. Their prayers were answered and the van passed them by at a short distance without the police noticing them. A. E. admitted that they had broken the law of the land and should have been punished, but on that day he said they had found favour with God, who had brought them good fortune and protected them.

To the people of Steinkopf, God the Father is the all-important member of the Trinity. He is a person; people talk to Him and ask His advice and guidance in their daily problems, yet they seldom mention their love for God or His love for them. No satisfactory explanation can be given for this relationship, but an elder of the Church once stated, 'Man cannot love God because He is too far away, and the gap between God and man is too great.' Nevertheless, people do love Jesus, who loves and hates as He is loved and hated by man. He is believed to have died for the sins of the world, but He is not believed to be God incarnate, nor is He believed to be of equal status with God the Father: He is junior to God. Finally, although the existence of the Holy Ghost is not denied, no specific function is attributed to it in the religious life of the people.

The Devil is seldom mentioned in contemporary Steinkopf as the personification of sin, although the missionary frequently gives instruction in church about the Devil and his works. By the people themselves the Devil is regarded not as a person nor as a distinct and separate force, but as the evil nature in man which causes him to sin, and brings down upon him the wrath of God. The manifestations of this wrath, however, are believed to be independent both of God and the Devil. For instance, if a drought or a blight destroys the crops it is considered an undoubted sign that God is angry with the people, but they do not believe that God actually sent these misfortunes as a punishment; He is said simply to have allowed them to happen and their origin remains obscure.

No man is completely free from evil; every man, however virtuous he may appear, has something of the Devil in him. After death, perhaps, a man may become entirely good, but on earth such a state is not possible however hard a man tries or prays for it. In Steinkopf there has never been a saint. Finally, to the members of the community God is their God, the God of Steinkopf, who is believed to define only local norms of behaviour. Those who deviate from these standards are associated with the Devil (*die Satan*), and in those instances where norms differ from one group to another, God is firmly believed by each group to approve of its standard and no other.

So far, we have been dealing with those beliefs which have Calvinist Christian teaching as their basis but which have been more or less modified by the influence exerted upon them by Nama tradition.[1] We turn now to those beliefs which are not founded on Christianity at all, but which are almost entirely derived from the system of beliefs that was present in traditional Nama society. It is important to see these beliefs as complementary to those we have already discussed, for all the conservative people and a large percentage of the 'new people' are agreed that all these beliefs are consistent with the teachings of the Bible.

BELIEFS AND PRACTICES CONCERNING DEATH

Spirits and Ghosts

It is said in Steinkopf that when a person dies his spirit (*gees*) becomes separated from but remains near the body even after it has been buried in the ground. Sometimes the spirit wanders away from its body but it always returns. Spirits (*geeste*) are of two varieties, evil spirits (*bose geeste*) which are black, and ordinary spirits (*gewone geeste*) which are white. *Bose geeste*, sometimes called *spoke* (ghosts), are believed to be the spirits of people 'who have not gone to God', and can usually be seen at night by ordinary people. They terrify everyone because they are said to haunt and harm the living, especially their own families. *Gewone geeste*, on the other hand, are deceased people 'whose spirits have gone to God'. Normally they cannot be seen, but certain individuals claim to have seen them at night near their graves.

It is said that all people would become *gewone geeste* after death if they were able to live a life free from sin, but this is impossible because even the good have a 'little bit of the devil in them'. Therefore, in order to become a *gewone gees*, certain expiatory rituals have to be performed before a person dies: he has to confess all his sins to God through the missionary, or an *ouderling*, or in the presence of members of his family; and must ask forgiveness from the members of his family and from his friends for all his former wrongs. In addition to obtaining absolution from God and forgiveness from man, persons

---

[1] For a general discussion of traditional Khoi Khoin supernatural beliefs, see Schapera, *The Khoisan Peoples*, pp. 357–99.

about to die are often given spiritual counsel by the missionary or by an *ouderling*.

People who become *bose geeste* are said to include those who failed to carry out the expiatory rituals; those who resisted death while they were dying; and those who died suddenly in accidents. A man who has 'resisted death' is generally said to be someone whose death was preceded by a long and painful illness, the degree of resistance being proportional to the length of the illness and the amount of pain suffered; or someone who tried to sit up or writhed and shouted as he was dying. Some people, we are told, resist death so violently that they burst their stomach arteries. But whatever form the resistance takes, they are said to have refused to die. 'Hulle is nog nie dood nie as hulle sterwe: hulle is nog vir die wêreld.' ('They are not really dead when they die: they are still for the world.')

People who die suddenly, such as those killed in accidents, become evil spirits because they do not have the opportunity of confessing their sins and making up their quarrels with their friends and relations. In the three cases of sudden death known to me, the deaths were reputed to have been preceded by some form of family tension. My informants were uncertain whether there was any connexion between the two events (the tensions and the deaths), although all agreed that it was highly probable that there was.

A fourth way of becoming a *bose gees*, but which is beyond the control of the deceased person, is for him to be denied a proper burial or burial in the churchyard. Great care is taken by kinsmen to ensure that these obligations are fulfilled, even if a person dies when absent from the Reserve.

People who become *bose geeste* do not necessarily remain perpetually in that condition, for it is possible, through prayer, for their close kin to ask God to forgive them and grant them the rest He affords others; and it is said that the *bose geeste* occasionally return to their homes to confess and fulfil the obligations which they failed to carry out before they died.

Death Rituals

As soon as a person dies, all his friends and relatives living in and outside the Reserve are notified, and informed when the funeral is to take place. Meanwhile the coffin is constructed and preparations are made for the *lykwaak* (the wake). The *lykwaak* begins the evening before the funeral and continues until sunrise the following morning.

Nowadays, if people die on their farms, the corpse is usually taken to a relative's house in the mission village, but formerly all wakes were held in the homes of the deceased persons.

Anyone may attend a wake, but generally only relations and close friends are present. Wakes are partly religious and partly secular. Prayers are said for the spirits of the dead, portions of the scriptures are read, and hymns are sung the entire night by the women while the men occasionally hum the tune in the background if the melody pleases them. Tea is handed round at intervals, food is served, the largest animal (sometimes two) being slaughtered for the occasion, and there is usually a good supply of strong drink for the men.

A wake is said to be a jolly occasion (*vrolike tyd*), jokes, some of which are obscene, are told, although amongst the 'new people' wakes have, in recent years, centred in solemn religious activity rather than in sport. Formerly a lively personality used to be appointed as official jester to entertain people during the night. The purpose of the wake is twofold. First, it is a gathering of relatives and friends to pay homage to the dead person and to please his spirit, an obligation which must be carried out because the dead expect it. And those who are about to die often say, 'Sing for me that I may go to God and never worry you again' (i.e. that I may become a *gewone gees*). The obligation, therefore, is also important to the kinsmen of the deceased for it is they who will suffer should the departed return to reveal his displeasure.

Secondly, the wake is said to help the bereaved and the other mourners to overcome their grief. It is thus an outlet for pent-up emotion and provides an institutionalised gathering where people can sing and weep and laugh freely without restraint. Indeed people are expected to express their feelings at a *lykwaak*: the bereaved can weep and publicly receive the sympathy and comfort of their kinsmen and friends, while those who are only mildly distressed can express their feelings openly with laughter.[2]

Among the 'new people', the wake is sometimes omitted from the funeral rites, an omission about which the conservative people are greatly perturbed. As one informant said, 'It is all very well for them to say that the wake is nonsense and an unnecessary expense, but what about the mourners, how are they going to overcome their grief, and what will the family of the deceased do if they are troubled by a *bose gees*?'

When the wake ends at dawn the following morning, those not

[2] Cf. William McDougall, *An Outline of Psychology*, 1923, p. 169.

helping with the burial arrangements go home to prepare themselves for the funeral, which begins with a service in the mission church, where the coffin is placed after the wake. In cases where death is due to an infectious disease, or if the corpse has begun to smell, the coffin is placed in the grave immediately.

The church service consists of a sermon (preached by the missionary or, in his absence, by an *ouderling*), hymns, prayers, and a suitable lesson. Frequently, after the sermon, friends of the deceased person also address the congregation, adding their comments to the sermon they have just heard. At the end of the church service, the congregation, joined by late-comers, make their way in procession to the graveyard. The procession, which moves slowly and silently, is led by an official of the burial-society, who carries the flag which was flown earlier at the house where the *lykwaak* took place. The burial-society official is followed by a few members of the Kerkraad and the close kin of the deceased, and the rest follow, men in front, women behind. As soon as the graveyard is reached, the members of the procession break ranks and stand round the grave, and the service begins with a hymn, which is followed by several obituaries and an account of the sort of death the person died. After the missionary or *ouderling* has buried the body according to Christian rites, hymns are sung while the grave is filled with earth, each adult man present (and some women) assisting the grave-diggers in their task.

Graves[3]

The people of Steinkopf talk relatively freely about the beliefs and practices concerning death, but only a few informants were willing to give information about the decoration of graves. Even this information was given with extreme reluctance.

The majority of graves consist of mounds of earth (roughly equal in size to the volume of the coffin), which are decorated with certain objects, the nature of which varies according to the sex and age of the deceased person. For example, babies' graves are usually decorated with babies' bottles, baby-powder tins or other objects (excluding clothing) associated with babies. The graves of adult men, on the other hand, are generally decorated with objects such as teacups and saucers, plates, teapots, ointment jars, and electric torches, while adult women's graves may have on them teacups and saucers, teapots,

[3] Cf. P. W. Laidler, 'Burials and Burial Methods of the Namaqualand Hottentots', *Man*, vol. XXIX, no. 9, Sept. 1929.

plates, perfume bottles, kettles, face-cream jars, etc. But the most common objects are babies' bottles on babies' graves, and teapots and teacups and saucers on adults' graves. In addition to these objects, roughly half the graves in the graveyard have wooden headstones, some in the shape of a cross with suitable epitaphs engraved on them. The graves of some of the Khoi Khoin bywoners are covered with white limpet-shells brought from the sea shore seventy miles away.

During my periods of field-work I constantly asked questions about the significance of these objects but never received adequate information. However, from the information collected, four different explanations were offered. First, there were those who said that the objects were merely for decoration, 'just like you Europeans put flowers on the graves of your dead'. Secondly, there were those who said that certain objects were placed on the graves when there was no inscribed cross, so that relations and friends could recognise the graves of their own people. However, when it was pointed out to these people that most graves which had crosses also had the objects in question, they gave no reply. Thirdly, there were those who explained that these objects were things of which the deceased persons used to be very fond, and it was, therefore, fitting that they should be placed on their graves. Fourthly, there were those few people who agreed with the third explanation but added that very often the last thing a person touched before death ought also to go on the grave. They said the reason for placing these objects on the graves of those people with whom they were associated was that if these were kept, or even disposed of, there was always the risk that the spirits of the dead would come back to collect them. It is not possible to make any definite statement as to the significance of decorating graves, owing to the wide disagreement among informants. Nevertheless, the fourth explanation is preferred since it is consistent with the other beliefs concerning the dead.

MAGIC

The basis of the belief in magic in Steinkopf is the assumption that certain substances, usually derived from animal or vegetable sources, contain mystical powers which can be put to both good and evil purposes. These substances (medicines) can be used by anyone, including those who have only limited knowledge of their properties and efficacy. Most commonly, however, medicines are manipulated by experts: those who specialise in bad magic are known as *blikdraers* (people who carry tins of medicines) or *towenaars* (sorcerers), while those who specialise in good magic are known as *bossiesdokters* (bush doctors) formerly known as *toordokters* (sorcery specialists). Medicines may also be used for protection against bad magic, and to promote success, and most laymen are familiar with the techniques for these purposes. Various herbs are used by most families to cure common ailments, but these practices belong essentially to the art of leechcraft and not to that of magic.

Blikdraers are said sometimes to use their magic for divination but normally they use it for causing misfortune to others. The most efficacious substances for preparing bad medicines are those which have a very strong stench, such as the kidneys of a jackal mixed with the ashes of burnt twine, or the stomach fat of jackals and goats. Occasionally medicines are made from herbs and bushes but only when the other substances cannot be obtained.

Nowadays, we are told that when *blikdraers* manipulate their medicines they do not verbalise spells as they used to in former years; they are said merely to 'think about' the misfortune they are effecting. Sometimes they put medicines in people's tea or food, or on sweets, sometimes they have it on their hands when they greet people, and when they wish to harm all the members of a household they put it under the threshold of their victims' huts; sometimes they 'just keep it in their pockets and stand next to people'; sometimes they 'work on people's nail-clippings'.

It is not always known why *blikdraers* harm people. They are said to do so for different reasons, the most usual of which is simply for their own satisfaction. But a *blikdraer* whose pride has been hurt is believed to retaliate immediately with his medicines. Some are said to use their magic to make people act against their wills.

Sorcery manifests itself in several ways and sometimes it is difficult for people to decide for certain whether misfortune is due to natural causes or sorcery. But sorcery is usually associated with certain special misfortunes, which include madness, unhappy love affairs, paralysis, tripping unexpectedly over things, falling down, spending money unwisely, letting the milk boil over, and constant and abnormal inability to resist sin. Natural causes on the other hand are thought to be responsible for common diseases such as tuberculosis, common colds, whooping cough, measles, etc., all of which may attack a large number of people at one time, and phenomena such as droughts and poverty. These are believed always to be present in the world, that is

13

to say, they are natural, but affect people only if God permits them to operate.

People whose health has been seriously impaired by sorcery claim that the only way to be restored to full health is to visit a *bossiesdokter*, a person with an expert knowledge of good and bad medicines and their properties, and concerned with diagnosis and cure. Cures are effected by making afflicted persons drink, or apply to their bodies, medicines which contain mystical powers stronger than those contained in the *blikdraer's* medicines. Treatment, however, can begin only after the cause of the complaint, that is to say the type of bad medicine used, has been discovered. Thus, if a patient is suffering from paralysis believed to have been caused by bad medicine made from jackal kidneys and burnt twine, the *bossiesdokter* will supply the same formula 'only a little bit stronger'. In practice therefore the difference between the two medicines is that the antidote smells a little bit more (*stink 'n klein bietjie meer*) than the sorcerer's mixture. It is considered most important that the antidote should be made only a fraction stronger, for, if it is too strong in relation to the original medicine, it is thought that the patient will become either worse or, even if a cure is effected, insane.

The one antidotal medicine, however, which if prepared properly can render all medicines ineffective, is the small gecko (*Ptenopus garrulus*). Dried gecko rubbed with kidney fat can be used with perfect safety by anyone to cure the effects of sorcery. But the preparation is exceedingly scarce because most people, including *bossiesdokters* themselves, believe the gecko to be more dangerous than the most poisonous snake, and only certain men are prepared to kill them. In addition to providing a cure for sorcery, the gecko is used in the treatment of snakebites, to immunise people against any kind of danger, and to give strength. The latter two uses of the gecko are rarely found nowadays because local *bossiesdokters* are not properly trained to perform the necessary operation, which consists of making two incisions in the patient's arm, one on the inside of the wrist, the other on the inside of the upper arm, and injecting powdered gecko flesh into the wounds.

Today people do not patronise the services of *bossiesdokters* to the same extent as they did in the past, since more and more faith is being placed in the work of European medical men, who are believed by some to possess even better antidotal medicines than *bossiesdokters*. But when a European doctor fails to effect an immediate cure, the services of *bossiesdokters* are made use of again.

Medicines are also used extensively by laymen, largely for socially approved purposes, but sometimes for causing misfortune to others. According to informants, there are a greater number of laymen using medicines today than in former years, especially bad medicines, and they agreed (to a leading question) that as the number of expert *blikdraers* and *bossiesdokters* decreased, so more and more laymen were 'working with these dangerous things' themselves.

The most general use of medicines by laymen is for protection against sorcery. It is believed that if certain substances are applied to one's person or placed in one's house, one is likely to remain free from the effects of bad medicines. Protective medicines do not have to be as strong as bad medicines because they are used only to ward off the latter before they penetrate the body. But if bad medicine is consumed, all protective medicines (except the gecko formula) are ineffective. Individuals often protect themselves by rubbing their hands with lard or placing strips of bacon in their shoes before they come into contact with other people. They do this because 'pigs have many devils to drive out evil'. As an alternative to lard and bacon, some people wear their underclothes inside out on certain occasions 'because body dirt is full of *toor* (magic) and can drive away bad medicines'.

The extent to which protective medicines are used is not known since only a few people discussed the question freely with me. But one reliable informant stated that most people took precautions against bad medicines when they were in a crowd or any public place. Women, she said, always put bacon in their shoes when they go to the shop, to keep away bad medicines, especially the medicines of the shopkeepers, who use them to make people spend their money on things they do not want. She herself found it safer to carry the bacon in her shopping-bag!

THE POWER OF MEN

Blessings and curses

In addition to the powers which people are believed to have over others through the use of medicines, individuals themselves are believed to be able to cause good fortune or misfortune in others by giving them their blessings or curses.

Blessings and curses are usually, but not always, given by parents to their children. Blessings are always given in private and kept secret, curses are uttered openly. It is customary for blessings to be given at a parent's deathbed, and sometimes they are given at the onset of old age. Occasionally a father or mother may be displeased with the children and give the blessing to another child, or not at all.

Children who violate the accepted standards of behaviour and refuse to mend their ways are sometimes cursed by their parents, who wish them evil and misfortune. But this is a drastic form of punishment and is only resorted to when all other social pressures have failed. To my knowledge the only curses uttered nowadays are by parents whose children marry against their will or without their consent.

The /has[4]

Certain individuals in Steinkopf are believed to be capable of directing the extraordinary activities of the /has, a mythical species of spring hare with large red ears and superhuman powers. There is no specific term for these people and they are merely referred to as 'mense wat die /has het' (people who have the /has). The /has may be described as a familiar, though a person who 'has it' cannot rightly be called a witch since his activities are not regarded as antisocial.

Traditionally, the only people reputed to have this power were women, though nowadays certain men are also said to possess it. It is said that women are 'given' the /has by their mothers or mother's sisters, the general rule being that it passes from mother to daughter. It is not known how men acquire it.

A woman who was reputed to have the /has testified as follows: 'In the old days we used to go inside the /has but we don't do so any more: we just send it. Also, we who have the /has, used sometimes to change ourselves into lions and jackals; in fact we could change ourselves into practically any animal. I can remember when people used to change themselves into animals to prove to those who did not believe us that we had the /has. The way they used to change themselves was like this: they would rub their bodies with buchu powder (kept in a tortoise-shell) and as quickly as a chameleon changes its colour, so also would they change their form. Then the person who had been changed, would say, "Now you can see what powers I have, give me the buchu powder and I will be a human being once more." The old people did this only when others did not believe.'

[4] Probably derived from Nama !õas, a hare. See J. G. Kroenlein, *Wortschatz der Khoi-Khoin*, Berlin, 1889, p. 282. But see Schapera, *Khoisan Peoples*, pp. 369–70.

Informants tell us that the /has may be seen only at night, when it moves from place to place at great speed, screaming like a jackal, and, if it is angry, flapping its big red ears. The /has may be 'sent' for four purposes. First, and most commonly, it is sent to warn people who have offended its sender to mend their ways. Hurt pride is always the factor which makes a person send the /has. A man might steal from or quarrel with someone who has the /has, but provided he does not hurt the person's pride, 'so that he feels it in his heart', the /has is unlikely to be sent to him. Secondly, the /has may be sent to frighten people, and, when necessary, to do them bodily harm if they attempt to retaliate. A serious offence may cause someone who has the /has to send it to frighten people *and* to do them bodily harm, the first time, but most frequently it will be sent to use physical violence only after people have ignored a warning. Thirdly, the /has is sent to spy on people away from home to see that they are behaving themselves, or perhaps just to see that they are safe. Fourthly, the /has is used for protection: friends and relatives of the person who 'has it' (and the person himself) may be protected on long and dangerous journeys by the /has, who dances about warding off wild animals and frightening away people who may attack them. We should note here that formerly the only people who could benefit from somebody else's /has-power were those undertaking a journey, and this protection could emanate only from those who 'had' the /has and no one could ask another, known to 'have it', for protection for himself or his kinsmen or friends. Similarly, requests could not be made to a person, known to have the /has, to warn, frighten or harm an enemy. Nowadays, however, it is common for certain people to advertise the fact that they have the /has and use their power for others in return for a small payment.

The /has is never believed to be responsible for illness, though as we have said, it is thought to injure people physically.

Nearly everyone has either seen or heard the /has, especially when travelling at night, but it is said that only those guilty of misconduct need fear its existence. So, we are told that when a person sees the /has or hears it screaming, 'Hee ... Hee ... Hee ...' he must remain quite calm—never be aggressive—and say, 'Ja, ek het gehoor' ('Yes, I hear you'), and it will go away. Very often the /has is just passing on its way to someone else, but people should always acknowledge the fact that they have seen or heard it, or it may become angry and attack. On the other hand, those guilty of an offence, such as forgetfulness, or theft, or insulting behaviour, or any conduct which might have hurt another's feelings, are said to be greatly disturbed by the presence or scream of the /has. Such people are instructed to make up their minds quickly and to make amends for their error, and then say, 'Ja, ek het gehoor.' Should they not do so, they are believed to be in great danger of being attacked. Very few people are reported to have been harmed bodily by the /has; many are said to have been frightened. Most people, we are told, mend their ways quickly enough after they have been warned, so that it is seldom necessary for the /has to exercise its strength.

In the contemporary community it is necessary to distinguish between the various categories of people and their attitudes towards the /has. Generally the pattern we have described applies only to conservative members of lineage category B, the Namaqua and short-haired Basters, and to the bywoners. The members of the rest of the community on the other hand, regard the belief in the /has more as a 'fairy story' (sic) than as an actual phenomenon, using it to frighten children who misbehave. In fact they pride themselves on not believing in this superstition, referring to it as a 'stupid Namaqua belief'. In practice, however, there are many Basters and Kommers who are unable to reject completely the possibility that some people really do have the /has.

There are reports nowadays of the /has being sent to the mines, and these appear to be associated with people who fail to send money home to their wives or mothers. On the other hand migrant workers are believed to 'send' the /has to spy on or frighten their wives and girl-friends who are unfaithful to them in their absence. Some say, however, that these people, i.e. migrant males, merely 'pretend' to have the /has, and have never received the power in the traditional way. (Of course, as we have stated earlier, it is possible nowadays to pay someone who has the /has to send it on one's behalf.) Yet there is evidence that these pretences are effective since many women admit that they have been frightened by the /has sent to them from the mines.

The chief function of the belief in the /has is clearly the effect which it has on maintaining good personal relationships, by discouraging breaches of etiquette and custom amongst members of extended families and among friends, usually from the same locality. Cases show that there is a connexion between the sending of the /has and the inability or failure to control other people's behaviour or actions.

Thus, women, whose authority is generally considered to be less effective than men's, use the /has to reinforce their jurisdiction over others. Similarly men who send the /has from the mines to spy on their wives and girl-friends do so because they are unable to keep an eye on their activities personally: in a sense their authority is diminished while they are absent from home.

One of the reasons why the belief is so effective as an institution of social control is because no one can be quite sure who 'has' the /has. As one man put it: 'When I hear the /has screaming behind me, I am always terrified because I never know who has sent it, or whether or not it has been sent to me. It may have been sent by anyone whose pride I have hurt, or whom I have antagonised.'

But the /has is used not only to correct improper behaviour; it can, as we have said, be used also to protect people or to see to their welfare. Some people reported that they have often been comforted by the knowledge of the /has's presence because they have known that they were being protected or that it had come to see that they were safe. One man said that every time he goes on a long journey the /has comes to him, and when he hears the 'Hee . . . Hee . . . Hee . . .' he replies, 'Yes, I hear you; I am fine.' Then he knows that the person who sent it will receive the message that he is safe and well.

Perhaps the most unpopular activity of the /has is spying. People say that those who go away from home and get up to mischief, find on their return that everyone in the settlement knows what they have been doing. This they attribute to the /has, who, they say, peeps through the small holes in houses and watches them making love, or sees them drinking, or hears them swearing, and then goes back to their homes to report what it has seen.

The tokoloshe (sic)

Men who have worked on the Kleinzee diamond mine, have returned home with accounts of the activities of a 'tokoloshe'. Some have even complained to the mine authorities about it. Tales about Tokoloshe are common in Steinkopf, but they are generally looked upon as 'fairy stories' rather than as true accounts of active agents. The idea of Tokoloshe almost certainly came to Little Namaqualand from the Bantu-speaking people who have migrated to the towns and mines during the past sixty years. But in Steinkopf it has acquired a special meaning.

The tokoloshe on the Kleinzee mine is reputed either to have been left there by the Ovambo workers who were employed on the mine between 1946 and 1949, or to have been sent by them to frighten the Coloured workers now employed in their place. There are two descriptions of Tokoloshe's physical appearance: some say he resembles a little baboon, others say he is a small black man who wears a large hat, and is eighteen inches tall. Tokoloshe is said to appear at any time of the night (but only at night) through an open door or window and sometimes through the fanlight. He appears suddenly without any warning. He is essentially malicious and always comes to harm or frighten people. Sometimes he bites his victims while they are in bed or picks them up and hurls them with great force to the floor; sometimes he merely comes to frighten people, and on one occasion is reported to have switched off the electric lights while people were dancing at the mine-compound. Deterred by these events a few people sought work elsewhere after their contracts expired. One woman reported that her son had been so terrified by the tokoloshe that he had turned quite *black* and she had forbidden him to return to the mine after his leave.

What precisely is the significance of the tokoloshe as he has been described from the reports of informants from the Kleinzee mine, and why his activities appear to be confined to this particular mine, cannot be stated. But the general belief, as found in Steinkopf, seems to be connected with the local attitudes towards the Bantu-speaking people with whom the people of Steinkopf have only recently come in contact. Children, for instance, are frightened by stories about the tokoloshe and the 'black kaffirs' (*swart kaffers*) who are described as evil and dangerous. It is significant that children are no longer frightened by tales of the Bushmen, as their grandparents used to be frightened by their parents and grandparents, many of whom had themselves clashed with Bushman bands in their childhood. Today it is not the Bushmen who are the rivals but the 'black kaffirs' (i.e. the Bantu-speaking people), who have become economic rivals in the towns and on the mines. Thus the prejudice and antagonism held towards the Bantu-speaking people appear to be symbolised by the belief in the tokoloshe, which characterises also the strength of the new competitors on the labour market.

CONCLUSIONS

One of the problems to be solved in the realm of beliefs is the relative importance of Providential and personal causes of misfortune. Although no adequate answer to this question can be offered, two general observations can be made. First, collective misfortune is normally attributed to the wrath of God amongst all sections of the population. Second, amongst the 'new people' who have progressed (*voortgegaan*), leaving behind them (*agtergelos*) the Namaqua tradition (*outyd se goed*), God is also believed to be the main power responsible for sending individual misfortune as a punishment for sin. The conservative people, on the other hand, usually tend to explain individual misfortune in terms of personal causation, although they believe that God sometimes punishes individuals. To see these differences in belief merely as pagan–Christian differences is misleading, and we must regard them rather in terms of the changes in the conception of God, changes which have taken place during the past 150 years.

It seems that one of the reasons why the early missionaries of the Reformed Churches were so successful in their mission work among the Khoi Khoin was that the latter found no difficulty in grasping new concepts such as 'God' and 'devil', because they already understood them. The missionary George Schmidt, for example, writes about the Hessequa: 'They believe that there is a supreme Lord over all, whom they call *Tui'qua*. They believe also in a devil, to whom they give the name *Gauna*. But they do not care much about him.'[5] The hypothesis offered here, therefore, is that the early inhabitants of Steinkopf merely transferred their conceptions of a supreme being and a spirit of evil to Christianity, preserving also their traditional beliefs in other supernatural powers. Today the supernatural beliefs of the conservative people still reflect the early Christian–pagan pattern, while the 'new people' have transformed it by incorporating into their belief in God the functions of subordinate powers.

Thus, if the hypothesis is correct, pagan beliefs in personal causes of bad (and good) fortune will continue to decrease as more and more conservative people become assimilated into the ranks of the 'new people'. The fact that these beliefs *are* becoming less important than they were in former years, is borne out by the fact that today only poorly developed techniques of divination are found and that people seldom consult diviners. The only diviners are the *bossiesdokters*, who, according to reports, are mere amateurs in the art of divination compared with the old *toordokters*.

Throughout the history of Christian Steinkopf, God has always been

[5] George Schmidt, *Reise nach dem Vorgebirge der guten Hoffnung*, p. 275. Quoted by Schapera, in *Khoisan Peoples*, p. 387.

regarded as omnipotent, and His power believed to be capable of overriding all other supernatural forces. But, whereas God was formerly believed usually to concern Himself with certain matters only, today His actions tend to be seen as being connected with all supernatural phenomena, pleasing and otherwise to man. In more general terms we might say, that although omnipotence has always been attributed to the God of Steinkopf, it has taken contemporary social relationships to effect those changes in belief necessary to remove non-Christian powers from the world of the unknown.

In conclusion let us summarise the functions of the beliefs and practices we have discussed. First, viewed as a system, the majority of beliefs fulfil the function of offering rational[6] explanations for individual, as well as collective, good and bad fortune. Thus individual good fortune, depending on its particular manifestation, may be explained as God's reward for good behaviour; or as due to petitions (prayers) that were made to God for a specific purpose; or as blessings that were given by parents; or as the result of certain medicines used to give power over others; or it may be explained simply as due to luck (*die geluk*) when none of the former explanations seem relevant in accounting for an extraordinary and pleasant event or occurrence. However, when good fortune comes to all, or the majority of people (i.e. is collective), the only explanation is that God is pleased with His children and, as a reward for their good conduct, has blessed them with the fruits of His work.

Individual misfortune, on the other hand, is attributed either to punishment from God, or to sorcery, or to a parent's curse, or to the /*has*, or simply to bad luck (*die ongeluk*). Collective misfortune, like collective good fortune, is attributed mainly to God, who allows droughts, epidemics, and crop-failure to occur as punishment for man's collective wickedness. In addition to God's wrath, we must include sorcery as a cause of collective misfortune, when bad medicines placed under the threshold are believed to have harmed all the people living in a dwelling. But with this exception, collective good and bad fortune are always believed to be due either directly or indirectly to God.

Secondly, we must consider those beliefs which increase a sense of security. These include the beliefs that God answers the requests of those who face danger or uncertainty to watch over and protect them,

[6] 'Rational', as used here, does not refer to the objective reality of the explanation, but to its assumed efficacy.

the belief in the protective powers of certain medicines, and the belief that the /has may sometimes be sent by others to grant one protection. The /has tends also to increase the authority of those who lack it.

Thirdly, we may regard certain beliefs as mechanisms of social control in that they impose either positive or negative sanctions on certain aspects of behaviour. We have seen, for instance, that if all the members in the community display exemplary behaviour, all are rewarded by God, just as virtuous individuals receive His blessing and the blessings of their parents. Misconduct, on the other hand, exposes people to the possibility of having to face the consequences of the wrath of God or the curses of their parents. It may also expose them to sorcery or the power of the /has. And people who fail to carry out their obligations to their dying and recently deceased kinsmen, are likely to receive visitations from evil spirits.

Fourthly, we must emphasise the fact that the beliefs in God unite the whole community through the common sentiments that people hold about Him, even though a subordinate belief (see pages 171–2) reinforces indirectly the sentiments which govern the cleavage between the conservatives and the 'new people'. Yet, in spite of this paradox, God is everywhere, He can do and prevent all things. His existence and power are never doubted.

Finally, the belief in 'the devil in man' gives all men a common basis for their sins. For it is sin that is believed to be responsible for man's eternal failure to please God consistently.

CHAPTER 10

THE SOCIAL STRUCTURE OF STEINKOPF

The greater part of the text in the preceding chapters has been devoted to a discussion of the components of the social structure of a peasant community during the past twenty years, with some space given to earlier periods. In this chapter an attempt is made to give a conspectus of the contemporary social structure and to show also the inter-connexions between the main components. An attempt has also been made to show the way in which certain of the components of this web of internal interactions are linked with associations and institutions beyond the bounds of the community. The analysis of these links is crucial to the understanding of contemporary Steinkopf. For, as Redfield has pointed out, 'If the student of a peasant society is to describe the systems of social relations of that society, he will study those social relations that communicate the higher dimension of civilization to the lower or peasant dimension'.[1]

THE WEB OF INTERNAL INTERACTION

The social structure of Steinkopf is characterised chiefly by a number of primary and secondary groups (which are set out in Tables XIX, XX, and XXI), and certain cleavages and social classes discussed in chapters 5, 6, and 7.

Here the term primary group is used to describe a group of people whose interaction with one another is characterised by intimate face-to-face relationships. The primary group, moreover, covers a wide range of needs and personal gratifications but does not refer to a group organised for a specific purpose or purposes.

The term secondary group, on the other hand, is used here to describe a group that is organised for a specific purpose or purposes and in which interaction is not necessarily intimate and face-to-face. Thus a distinction is made between secondary groups characterised by intimate face-to-face relationships and those which are not.

EXTERNAL INTERACTION

The web of internal interaction may be said to coincide with the widest area of maximum interaction, and this we have called the community. But as a community Steinkopf is neither economically nor socially

[1] R. Redfield, *Peasant Society and Culture*, Chicago, 1956, p. 66.

self-sufficient, for, as we have already shown, a high percentage of its members leave the territory sporadically as migrant workers; government officials, traders, doctors, prospectors and others visit the Reserve from time to time; emigrants from other parts of the country join the community temporarily or permanently; and many of the groups have connexions with institutions and associations outside the Reserve. All these factors inevitably influence in some way or other the web of internal interaction and provide the interactional links with the wider society. Thus a convenient way of illustrating the connexion between Steinkopf and the wider society is to analyse the relationships between local groups and external groups and institutions. The four main channels of interaction may be seen in terms of the economy, religion, government and formal education.[2]

The chief economic links with the outside world are provided by the migrant workers and the consumers' co-operative store. The migrants who leave the Reserve for long or short periods each year not only provide the community with money without which its members could hardly survive, but, through their interaction with persons on the mines and in the towns, are in effect extending the boundaries of the community beyond its generally accepted limits. The consumers' co-operative is the major centre of business and trade, both local and external.

Other economic activities which promote interaction with the wider society include the selling of livestock, meat and hides in Springbok, or to White speculators who periodically visit the Reserve; and base minerals are nowadays also sold by local tributers to agents in Springbok.

It is clear, therefore, that apart from the sale of grain and dates, and the work of the co-operative store, the main external trading activities are carried out directly through the elementary family, although a considerable measure of labour recruitment is effected by the Management Board.

Thus the relatively small local demand for labour and local products, together with the low productivity of mixed-farming and mining, may be said to induce each family to establish relationships beyond the borders of the Reserve. This pattern of interaction occurs without any interference from the local government except in that individuals who leave the Reserve as migrant workers for periods longer than three

[2] Cf. M. Fortes, 'Culture contact as a Dynamic Process', *Africa*, supplement, 1938.

months are required by law to notify the Management Board; and these migrant workers are expected to return to Steinkopf at least once every two years in order to retain their official rights and privileges as members of the community.[3]

Whereas the majority of interactions with the outside world for economic purposes tend to be direct through the family and through the co-operative store, in the realms of religion, and politics, and education, the basis of interaction is mainly through institutions other than the family. The most powerful religious institution is the N.G. Sendingkerk which is closely connected with the four church associations already mentioned, and with primary education. Its local governing body is the Kerkraad under the leadership of the missionary. But local church policy is greatly influenced by a hierarchy of groups (committees) within the framework of the Mother Church[4] — *Die Ring*, *Die Ringsendingkommissie*, *Die Sinode*, and *Die Algemene Sendingkommissie*. Further, the missionary is a White South African who, quite apart from his interaction with other White church officials, provides a very strong link in the community with Afrikaner Whites whose attitude towards colour he largely shares. It is, therefore, not only with regard to church policy that external groups exert a strong influence over the community through the Church, but also through the missionary, who is a most powerful member of the Steinkopf community.

The relatively few members of the two other denominations, Anglican and Roman Catholic, have more direct links with the outside world in that they have either to leave the Reserve in order to attend public worship and receive the sacraments of their respective Churches, or to wait until a priest visits the Reserve. The Anglican Church, however, is represented in the community by the postmaster and his wife, who occasionally arrange services and prepare people for confirmation.

In the political field the Management Board is the local governing body. All its members are registered occupiers, but, as has already been shown, the system of nomination, appointment and election, as well as the other provisions of the Mission Stations and Communal Reserves Act, has effected a political group which is largely an instrument of

[3] See Government Notice no. 2706 of 28 November 1952, section 43. To my knowledge this regulation has not been enforced.

[4] *Wette en Bepalings vir die Bestuur van die N.G. Kerk in Suid-Afrika*. Chapters 3 and 4, and arts. 302–10, *et passim*.

the Coloured Affairs Department. And it is in this capacity that the Management Board provides the *official* link with the mines, the neighbouring Reserves, the Coloured people in general, and the rest of the outside world.

In the field of education, external interaction may be seen in the teachers' relations with teachers elsewhere, especially through the Teachers' Educational and Professional Association (T.E.P.A.),[5] which holds occasional meetings and dances at Port Nolloth or O'okiep; and the teachers' connexion with the Cape Education Department through the circuit inspector and the Skoolkomitee.

Another group through which external interaction takes place is the opposition group to the Church and Management Board, which has contacts with lawyers, members of Parliament, and 'organisations' in Cape Town, and its leaders frequently make journeys to Cape Town to interview their legal advisers.

LEADERSHIP AND POWER

Georg Simmel believed that the most important type of social relationship was that between a leader and his followers, between the superior and his subordinate, and he maintained that without this relationship no social life was possible, since it is the main factor in sustaining the unity of groups.[6] Simmel's ideas regarding groups and leadership have greatly influenced modern sociology, especially in America. In fact, any sociological analysis of leadership must begin by accepting the broad principles of Simmel's proposition, though few sociologists would nowadays accept his assertion that the principles of superiority and subordination constitute the sociological expression of psychological differences in human beings.[7]

In this discussion we shall assume that there are three categories of leadership: natural leadership, official leadership, and outmoded leadership.

Natural leadership corresponds with Homans's extended definition of leadership in a small, relatively autonomous group.[8] Natural leaders

[5] See S. Patterson, *Colour and Culture in South Africa*, pp. 160–1.

[6] Kurt H. Wolff (translator and editor), *The Sociology of Georg Simmel*, The Free Press, Glencoe, pp. 87–303. See especially N. J. Spykman, *The Social Theory of Georg Simmel*, Chicago, 1925, Book II. Spykman gives an excellent summary and interpretation of Simmel's formal sociology, in many ways better than the original.

[7] Cf. Spykman, p. 95.   [8] Homans, p. 188.

may be said to share the sentiments and aspirations of their groups, and in doing so, provided they have other qualities as well, are able to maintain their dominant position and regulate the solidarity of their followers.[9] This conception of the natural leader approximates also to Bertrand de Jouvenel's *dux*, 'the man who leads into action a stream of wills . . .'.[10]

Official leadership exists when an institution like a church or school confers on an individual (or a group of individuals) a status which could not have been acquired merely through the leader's relationship with other people.[11] This type of leadership, it could be argued, approximates to De Jouvenel's *rex*, 'the man who regularises and rules'.[12] A *rex* of course may also be a *dux*, just as an official leader may also be a natural leader, and there may be more than one leader in any group.

The third type of leadership has been termed *outmoded leadership*. It occurs frequently in societies undergoing rapid social change, when the functions or certain of the functions of a particular group are taken over by another group or groups. The most obvious example of this kind of leadership is the somewhat redundant position of an African chief whose political, legal, and religious functions have been taken over in part or in full by the leaders of new associations,

The study of leadership in its various forms is important because it provides a means of gaining an insight into the structure of the groups of which the leaders are an integral part. Thus, in that leaders are the focal points of group structures, it may also be said that a study of them provides us with the indices of collective or group expression. The study of leadership, moreover, enables us to gain an insight into the nature and distribution of power in a society or community.

In terms of leadership (see Tables XIX, XX, and XXI) the contemporary community of Steinkopf is dominated by people who may conveniently be called aliens, in that the majority of secondary groups are led by recent immigrants to the community or by outsiders. Furthermore, certain groups such as the Management Board and the majority of schools, although officially led by registered occupiers, are in fact greatly influenced by alien institutions which exert pressure

[9] Cf. Spykman, pp. 97–101.

[10] Bertrand de Jouvenel, *Sovereignty: an Inquiry into the Political Good*, Cambridge, 1957, p. 21 (Huntington's translation).

[11] Spykman, pp. 101–2.

[12] De Jouvenel, p. 21.

TABLE XIX

STRUCTURE OF MAIN PRIMARY GROUPS IN CONTEMPORARY STEINKOPF (1957)

Primary group	Approx. size of group	Activities of group	Usual leader or leaders	Notes on group membership	Year or period in which group was formed
Elementary families	2–12	Domestic, economic, and recreational	Husband	Husband, wife, and dependent children (sub-groups based on sex are normally found within each elementary family)	Traditional
Extended families	5–35	Domestic, economic, and recreational	Senior male	Usually patrikin and wives (sub-groups based on sex and age are normally found within each extended family)	Traditional
Lineages	20–300	Attending important weddings and funerals; minor economic activities	Senior male or males	Agnates (lineages are often segmented)	Traditional
Adult cliques	2–5	Gossip and local politics	Natural leaders	Usually kinsmen or neighbours who are of the same age group and sex	—
Children's gangs	3–10	Recreation	Natural leaders	Usually of same age group and sex	—

TABLE XX

STRUCTURE OF MAIN INTIMATE SECONDARY GROUPS IN CONTEMPORARY STEINKOPF (1957)

Intimate secondary group	Approx. size of group	Activities of group	Usual leader or leaders	Notes on group membership	Period or year group formed
Kerkraad	32	Church administration etc.	Missionary (alien, age 50–60)	*Diakens* and *ouderlinge*. Aliens have been elected as *diakens* but not as *ouderlinge*	1840? R.M.S.
Sustersbond	30–40	Religious and welfare	Missionary's wife (alien, age 50–60)	Membership open to all confirmed married women in N.G. Sendingkerk. Regular church-goers of each lineage category and social class. (The size of the group refers to effective membership.)	1937?
Christelike Jonge-dogtersbond	25	Religious and welfare	Missionary's wife (alien, age 50–60)	Membership open to all unmarried women who belong to N.G. Sendingkerk. (Size of group refers to effective membership.)	1940?
Kinderbond	50	Religious and recreational	Missionary's wife (alien, age 50–60)	Membership open to all girls of school-going age. (Size of group refers to effective membership.)	1940?
Studente Christelike Vereniging	40	Religious and recreational	Male teacher (lineage category A, 'new person', age 35)	Membership consists mainly of high-school students	1950
Farm schools (4)	30–90	Educational and recreational	School principals (lineage categories A, B, B, and C;	Pupils and teachers	1930's, 1940, 1950

Group	No.	Function	Leadership	Membership	Date
Standards (grades)	10–40	Educational and recreational	Class teachers (mainly 'new people', five belonging to lineage category A, six to lineage category B, twelve to lineage category C, four unknown) all 'new people' except one belonging to lineage category B, who is essentially conservative	Pupils and teacher	—
Management Board	10	Political and administrative	Superintendent of Reserve (lineage category B, 'new person', age 57)	Membership according to provisions of Act No. 29 of 1909 as amended	1913 (formerly raad)
Police	3	Legal and gossip	Sergeant (alien)	All are aliens	1914
Tennis club	9	Recreational	Postmaster (alien, lineage category C 'new person', age 35)	Membership, which is based mainly on merit and interest, includes White police-sergeant	1950
Rugby club	30–40	Recreational	Male teacher (alien, lineage category C, 'new person', age 35)	Membership based on merit and interest	1957
Soccer club	30–40	Recreational	Clerk in co-operative store (lineage category B, 'new person', age 25)	Membership based on merit and interest	1940?
Opposition group to local government and N.G. Kerk	?	Mainly political	Senior male of //are Cloete lineage (natural leader belonging to lineage category A, conservative, age 70)	Membership open to any person who shares sentiments of group. Not all members are consistently antagonistic towards the N.G. Kerk	1936?

TABLE XXI

STRUCTURE OF MAIN SECONDARY GROUPS (NON-INTIMATE) IN CONTEMPORARY STEINKOPF (1957)

Secondary group	Approx. size of group	Activities of group	Usual leader or leaders	Notes on group membership	Period or year group formed
N.G. Sendingkerk	3,125	Worship	Missionary, superintendent of Reserve and other Kerkraad members (see Table XX)	The size of the group refers only to those who have been baptised	1934 (formerly R.M.S.)
Anglican Church	50	Worship	Postmaster and wife (both aliens, see Table XX)	All members of Anglican Church in Reserve	?
Roman Catholic Church	50?	Worship	Priest stationed near Springbok (alien)	All members of Roman Catholic Church in Reserve	?
G.H.S. Burial-Society	350	Funeral and burial arrangements	Founder's wife (lineage category C, age 60) and other active church-going women of different lineage categories; all tend to be conservative.	Membership open to women only (usually wives of villagers)	1928
Other burial-societies	20–50	Funeral and burial arrangements	*Diakens* and *ouderlinge* in each hamlet; mainly conservative	Membership open to anyone living in or near the hamlet for which the particular burial-society caters	After 1945
Consumers' Co-operative	937	Economic	Board of Directors, which includes representatives of all major categories and classes in community	Membership open to all people in and outside the Reserve whose applications are approved by the Board of Directors	1946
Secondary school	100	Educational	Principal (alien, lineage category C, 'new person', age 50) and teachers.	Teachers and pupils (some of the pupils come from outside the Reserve)	1950
Primary school	300	Educational	Principal (lineage category B) 'new person', age 45–50)	Teachers and pupils	1840

directly or indirectly on the official leaders.

Our analysis shows also that in terms of leadership the Baster Pioneers (lineage category A) exert relatively little influence nowadays in the community, and that the majority of leaders of secondary groups are recognised as belonging to the ranks of the 'new people', many of whom belong to lineage category B.

The conclusions related to alien leadership may be further substantiated as follows:

(a) The resident missionary, who is an alien, leads the N. G. Kerk and its Kerkraad, and is the manager of all the primary schools in the community. He is essentially an official leader although his roles are inevitably modified through interaction with the members of the congregation, the Kerkraad, etc.

(b) The members of the Roman Catholic Church are led by an alien, a White priest, who lives outside the Reserve. He is also an official leader.

(c) The members of the Anglican Church are led by the local postmaster, a newcomer (who is only a temporary member of the community), and the Rector of Namaqualand, who is an alien. The postmaster in his capacity may be classed as a natural leader although he carries out some official duties for his Church. The Rector is obviously an official leader.

(d) Three of the church associations are led by the missionary's wife (an alien) while the remaining church association is led by a local school-teacher who works in close contact with the missionary and his wife. The leaders of all these church associations are natural leaders, although they occupy official positions to which they are elected.

(e) The Management Board is headed by the superintendent of the Reserve, who is the official leader of the political community. He is a registered occupier, an ex-teacher, and a well-paid officer of the Coloured Affairs Department, by which he is appointed. This leader, therefore, may be regarded in part as an alien since he owes allegiance to two groups, his own community and the Coloured Affairs Department, which in practice controls the Management Board.

(f) The local head of the police, a White sergeant, is also an alien and an official leader.

(g) Although the majority of primary school-teachers are registered occupiers as leaders of the various schools their roles are modified by the rules of the Cape Education Department. Moreover, the primary school and the farm schools fall under the jurisdiction of the N. G.

Kerk as well. The principal of the secondary school is an alien as are the majority of his teachers. All teachers are official leaders in their schools.

(*h*) The tennis and rugby clubs are led by newcomers who are temporary members of the community. They are both natural leaders.

In these preceding paragraphs we have drawn attention to those groups whose leaders are either aliens or registered occupiers whose leadership is modified by their connexion with alien groups and institutions. The remaining groups in the community—the consumers' co-operative, the various burial-societies, the rather nebulous group of opponents to the Management Board and the Church, the various kinship groups, and the majority of cliques and gangs—have local leaders. Certain of the local teachers' groups, however, have alien leaders. The leaders of cliques, gangs, and the opposition group to the Management Board and Church may be described as natural leaders, as are the leaders of the burial-societies, although in the burial-societies they occupy official positions. Leadership in the consumers' co-operative is essentially official.

The classification of leadership among various kinship groups provides difficulties. Traditionally the leader of each kinship group (viz. elementary family, extended family and lineage or lineage segment) either achieved his position through marriage in the case of elementary families, or acquired it after the death of the person he succeeded by a sort of positional succession[13] in the case of extended families and lineages. Leadership amongst kinsmen tended, therefore, to be institutionalised in a semi-official system. This pattern largely persists today amongst the conservative people but, as has already been shown, there is a tendency for familial authority and leadership to be weakened as the functions traditionally fulfilled by kinship groups shift to associations, cliques, gangs, and the Kerkraad. This change has been accompanied also by a change in the pattern and type of leadership in the family: the traditional semi-official leadership is being superseded by what can conveniently be called outmoded leadership. The head of the elementary family is still conventionally the father, the senior male remains head of the extended family and the lineage or lineage segment, but the traditional functions of these leaders have become superfluous (particularly among the 'new people')

[13] A. I. Richards, 'Some Types of Family Structure amongst the Central Bantu', in *African Systems of Kinship and Marriage*, p. 224.

although each leader still receives the nominal recognition of his former position.

From what has been said regarding the various categories of leaders, certain general statements can be made. First, there is the obvious fact that natural leaders tend to be most common in groups whose activities and interactions are essentially local. Secondly, it is clear that in those groups where interaction with outside institutions and groups is greatest (whether the interaction is voluntary or not), the leaders tend to be aliens, or have strong external connexions. Thirdly, it appears that within the community the existence of voluntary associations is correlated with the weakening of traditional authority (i.e. the outmoding of traditional leaders), and the greater recognition of new natural leaders and official leaders, many of whom are aliens or registered occupiers having obligations to alien institutions as well as to the community. Fourthly, although *natural* leadership is most common in those groups which are relatively unaffected by external interaction *and* external pressure, it is significant that official leadership by aliens is not generally or effectively opposed. In fact, judging from the opinions of a large number of people, the most unpopular leader in the community is the superintendent, who is an official leader but not an alien (although he does have alien allegiances). In other words, there is a strong suggestion that the members of the community tend to favour aliens as leaders of groups that have external connexions.

The implication of the fourth generalisation above does not mean that tensions in the existing pattern of leadership are largely absent. We have already drawn attention to the cleavage between the conservatives and the 'new people', and this cleavage, which has been analysed earlier mainly in terms of conflicting values and sentiments, may now be seen as a function of the pattern of leadership we have been describing. Many of the conflicts implicit in this cleavage emanate from the lesser conflicts which exist between the traditional leaders, whose authority is gradually becoming redundant (i.e. outmoded leaders) and the new leaders (aliens and progressive registered occupiers), whose actions frequently extend beyond the bounds of the local community.

With the weakening of their authority, therefore, the traditional leaders have to find a new basis whereby they can acquire effective leadership. A few, as we have shown, have achieved this by acquiring positions in the Church, the local government or the schools. But an alternative means is open to the outmoded leader, namely, by changing his former primary group affiliations within the community.

Thus Barnabas Cloete, who wields considerable power amongst his followers, does not merely limit his activities to the interests of his own lineage, but is concerned with, and welcomes support from bywoners and others, irrespective of their kinship or class-ties. It may be said, therefore, that only by modifying his traditional role has Barnabas Cloete been successful in leading into action a significant 'stream of wills'. Yet he could not ever hope to attain greater power in the community by the means he has chosen, because he is opposing the two strongest institutions, and they derive the greater part of their strength from their connexions with other institutions beyond the boundaries of the Reserve. It is true, of course, that he and his followers also have links with persons and groups outside the community but their influence is meagre compared with that of the Mother Church and the central government of South Africa.

The three main foci of power in the community are the Management Board, the N. G. Kerk, and the schools. That is to say, the leaders in these institutions have the opportunity of realising their own wills and desires in various collective actions, even against the resistance of others who are also participating in these actions.[14] The leaders in these institutions, therefore, may be said to make the major decisions in the community, and it remains for us to summarise briefly the sociological significance implicit in the distribution of power. Part of the problem has already been dealt with: we have indicated the power which each of these institutions derives from external sources and the way in which the pattern of leadership is influenced as a result thereof. But our analysis would give a distorted picture if we did not appreciate the fact that a great deal of power is derived locally through the interrelationship of these institutions. The most satisfactory way in which this pattern can be explained is by analysing briefly the duplication and triplication of leadership in these institutions. In 1957, for example, there were *three* individuals who, in addition to being teachers or ex-teachers, were also members of the Management Board and Kerkraad; *five* members of the Management Board (including these last three) were also Kerkraad members; and *five* members of the Kerkraad were teachers. These figures do not include the missionary, who is the dominant official leader in the Church and primary schools. In view of this role-duplication and -triplication and the inevitable way in which power is therefore diffused among these institutions,

[14] Cf. Max Weber, *Essays in Sociology*, Kegan Paul, London, 1948, p. 180.

we can speak of this particular pattern of relationships as the 'power complex' of Steinkopf. The Management Board can, of course, theoretically maintain its position by coercion, since it has the backing of the central government, the law and the police, but it is unlikely that it would have been able to achieve its relatively stable position had it not been for co-operation from the schools and particularly the Church. It is significant in this context that one of the main reasons for the unrest and 'disorder' in the Komaggas Reserve during the past thirty years is the fact that in this community the N. G. Kerk as the established Church has never been accepted by the majority of the population. Thus the official separation of Church from State in Steinkopf in 1913 was in practice only partial. Had the separation been complete the relative stability of the present Management Board could never have been achieved.

CHAPTER 11

CONCORDIA, KOMAGGAS, LELIEFONTEIN, RICHTERSVELD

WE TURN now to a brief comparative study of the social structures of the other Namaqualand reserves: Concordia, Komaggas, Leliefontein, and Richtersveld. These may also be classified as Baster peasant communities.[1] By comparing the main structural features of these communities we hope to be able to understand Steinkopf better and gain an insight into the nature of these communities in general. But since we are concerned mainly with Steinkopf, the contents of the preceding chapters are taken for granted in our comparison.

HISTORY

The origin of these communities is basically similar. They were formerly occupied by Khoi Khoin and a few Bushmen, and owe their identity as separate Reserves nowadays largely to missionary influence. But there are certain important variations which must be noted: in terms of their social histories Steinkopf, Concordia, and Komaggas belong to one category, Leliefontein to another, and Richtersveld to a third.

The three communities which belong to the first category were 'invaded' by Basters, the pioneers of the North-Western Cape, who together with the missionaries acquired political power soon after their arrival. Within this category there are minor variations. In Komaggas the Baster 'invaders' appear to have acquired land in exchange for stock from the indigenous Khoi Khoin,[2] and Concordia was part of Steinkopf until 1891, when 'for the better pastoral Evangelisation of the people in Church and School [the inhabitants] found it expedient to divide it into two Communities'.[3] Further, in Komaggas the missionary as chairman of the raad appears to have had the power to veto decisions taken at meetings.[4]

In Leliefontein the original Khoi Khoin did not lose their power to

[1] See Report of the Rehoboth Commission, U.G. 41–1926, pp. 17–44; and J. S. Marais, *The Cape Coloured People*, chapter 3, for a general account of the Basters.

[2] Report on Coloured Mission Stations, p. 54. L. Schultze, *Aus Namaland und Kalahari*, Jena, 1907, pp. 115–16.

[3] 'Mutual Rules . . . of Steinkopf and Concordia', 29 May 1891.

[4] Cf. Report of the Rehoboth Commission, pp. 71–3. Schultze, pp. 116–20.

the Baster pioneers, who tended to settle in the north-east corner of the territory. There seem to be two reasons for this. First, the Methodist missionaries who settled permanently at Leliefontein (after J. Seidenfaden of the London Missionary Society had done the pioneering work[5]) did so at the invitation of the Khoi Khoin and worked among them before going on to the Basters.[6] Thus instead of the two alien elements (missionary and Baster) effecting the disintegration of the Khoi Khoin, the missionaries achieved power by operating within the framework of the traditional society without support from the Basters.

Second, in Leliefontein the missionaries achieved much greater political power (and did so much sooner) than in any of the other communities. In January 1825, eight years after the mission work of the Methodist Church began, the missionary was given power by the government of the Cape Colony to manage and direct certain of the affairs of the community,[7] and the Khoi Khoin chief was told that he had no more power or influence among his people in these respects.[8] Actually these drastic powers which were granted to the resident missionary at Leliefontein by the colonial government had been requested by the missionary himself, Barnabas Shaw, in 1824.[9] The following particulars were specified when the powers were granted:

'(i) Power to receive whom he may think proper as residents.

(ii) To expel any who may be disobedient or unruly.

(iii) To give out portions of land for sowing corn and making gardens.

(iv) To erect substantial dwelling houses, which must be built on the spot and according to the plan pointed out by the missionary.'[10]

But in spite of his new powers the missionary worked through the traditional political framework, although he and not the chief now presided over the monthly meetings of the raad. Cheeseman says:

[5] H. P. Cruse, 'Die Eerste Sendingreis na Groot-Namakwaland . . .', in *Die Kerkbode*, 28 July and 4 August 1937.

[6] Barnabas Shaw, *Memorials of South Africa*, London, 1841, p. 68. Also Shaw's letter to the Committee, 10 October 1816, quoted in *Methodist Magazine*, 1817, p. 233. Melvill Report, G. 60—1890, p. 27.

[7] T. Cheeseman, *The Story of William Threlfall*, p. 74. Shaw, p. 109.

[8] Cheeseman, p. 105. Letter from Governor's Secretary to 'Rev. Mr. Shaw', 24 Dec. 1824. (Cape Archives—C.O. 4852, p. 88.)

[9] Letter from James Whitworth *vice* B. Shaw to Governor, Lord Charles Somerset, 14 Dec. 1824. (Cape Archives—C.O. 230, No. 148.)

[10] Cheeseman, p. 74. Shaw, p. 109.

'[The Raad] was the Namaquas' Parliament, and the missionary being *ex officio* chairman, was by common consent Prime Minister, while the Ministry consisted of twelve Raadsmen—some of whom ranked as corporals—elected annually by the burghers of the Institution. At these gatherings the temporal affairs of the Station were discussed, and many opportunities were afforded the missionary of giving the people just such words of counsel, reproof, or encouragement as they seemed to require.'[11]

No evidence of resentment on the part of the Khoi Khoin towards the missionaries, after the latter had acquired the powers already listed, can be found. And there is a strong suggestion that the Khoi Khoin accepted missionary political leadership in place of their former chief, whom Shaw described as a 'poor, inoffensive, ignorant Old Man'.[12]

The relation of the mission to the Basters during the early period is not known, nor can it be discovered whether the Basters were ever directly represented on the raad as a minority group. Evidence from the contemporary community, however, suggests that the Basters were soon absorbed by the indigenous population and that any cleavage which might have existed between the two groups in the last century was soon eliminated.

Prior to 1844 all mission work in Richtersveld was carried out by visiting missionaries from Steinkopf. But in this year, J. F. Hein, a 'Baster-Hottentot'[13] from Wupperthal, was sent there as an evangelist. Hein was married to a Baster from Steinkopf. Both he and his wife spoke Nama; they lived simply, first in a mat-house and later in a crude, stone cottage. Hein devoted most of his time and energy to evangelisation although he did establish a small school in which he taught. The medium of instruction in both these institutions was Nama. In 1893 he was ordained and became the first non-European minister of the Rhenish Mission Society in South Africa.[14] He died in 1901 and his son continued his work as an evangelist until his death in 1917.

Richtersveld was also formerly inhabited by Khoi Khoin and Bushmen, but from a study of its local history and genealogies, there is a strong suggestion that during the nineteenth century integration

[11] Cheeseman, p. 104. See also J. E. Alexander, *An Expedition of Discovery into the Interior of Africa*, 1838, vol. 1, p. 58.

[12] Cape Archives—C.O. 230, No. 148.

[13] *Berichte der Rheinischen Missionsgesellschaft*, No. 18, 1855, pp. 282–8.

[14] *Ligdraer*, vol. 19, no. 11, 1958, pp. 327–30.

between these two peoples took place to a greater extent than in the other communities.[15] Moreover, although Richtersveld did have its Baster immigrants it was not subjected to a Baster 'invasion' comparable to that in Steinkopf, Komaggas or Concordia. In Richtersveld the Basters seem to have come as isolated individuals or families and, except for a few cases, have tended to lose their identity as a separate category or class.[16] Thus, generally the Baster immigrants were absorbed into the indigenous population. For example, round about 1830, perhaps earlier, the *kapteinskap* was acquired by a Baster named Meyer, who married a kinswoman of the former Khoi Khoin kaptein (who was a woman at the time). This office, which later became the *hoofkorporaalskap*, was handed down patrilineally until 1957, but the members of the lineage are not regarded as Basters, and bear the name of Swartbooi Links. Today the only surviving Baster pioneer family to retain its identity consists of the descendants of Jasper Cloete, a man who acquired great wealth and became a korporaal on the raad, a position which in subsequent years has been held by members of his patrilineage.

A strong rivalry for power between the present Baster korporaal's father's brother (the famous Ryk Jasper Cloete) and the father of the last hoofkorporaal (Kaptein Swartbooi Links) occurred during the first two decades of the twentieth century. Each had his followers and the community was split into two rival factions. The division was closely related to Le Fleur's politico-religious movement which was spreading through the Namaqualand Reserves at the time.[17] Ryk Jasper and his followers allied themselves with Le Fleur while Kaptein Links opposed the movement. The details concerning the activities of Le Fleur in Richtersveld are complex and cannot be discussed here, but it seems clear from the accounts given by local Richtersveld historians that Ryk Jasper thought he could use Le Fleur's movement as a means of usurping the hereditary kaptein's power and so take over the political leadership of the community, which carried with it the right to receive personally all grazing fees collected from the white farmers. This money was supposed to be used for the benefit of the community but it is doubtful whether it ever was.

Le Fleur, on the other hand, wanted Ryk Jasper's wealth and took advantage of the latter's generosity and enthusiastic support.

It is said that civil war almost broke out between the two rival

[15] Cf. A. W. Hoernlé (*nee* Tucker), *Richterveld, The Land and Its People*, p. 12.
[16] Cf. Hoernlé, p. 8.   [17] See pp. 34.

factions,[18] but the police intervened and Ryk Jasper was persuaded to reject Le Fleur. An immediate reconciliation appears to have taken place after Jasper and Links had shaken hands, and the former agreed to accept the traditional political leadership.

Although the early missionaries succeeded relatively easily in converting the people of Richtersveld to Christianity, no missionary ever achieved political power in Richtersveld as they did in the other communities and, largely as a result of this, a wide cleavage between church affairs and local government persists today. We should add, however, that there has been no resident missionary since 1917, although the community has received attention from a visiting missionary except during the eleven years 1917 to 1928.

Nama is still the home language of the majority of Richtersveld's population (except among those recent immigrant Basters living at Stinkfontein), while in all the other Reserves Afrikaans is spoken generally except by some of the older people. This significant linguistic difference reflects the fact that the community of Richtersveld is closer to the Khoi Khoin tradition than any of the other Reserves, a conclusion which can be illustrated also from its social structure. Afrikaans is nowadays the medium of instruction in the schools.

The people living at Stinkfontein are known as the Bosluis Basters. They emigrated from Bushmanland via Steinkopf in 1936, and were granted permission some years later to settle at Stinkfontein (later called Eksteenfontein). In this discussion of Richtersveld social structure I have not included the Bosluis Basters because, although they live in the same Reserve, they really constitute a separate isolated community. Moreover, there is practically no interaction in everyday life between these people and the rest of the population. It is important, however, to note that the Bosluis Basters regard themselves as superior stock. They are very light in colour and do not marry with the indigenous Richtersveld population; and several individuals have made efforts to be classified legally as White in terms of the Population Registration Act. One notable exception to the marriage rule was the marriage of a Bosluis Baster's three daughters and son to the children of the Cloete Baster member of the Richtersveld raad. After the marriage all the couples joined the Bosluis Baster's homestead.

[18] See account of the rivalry given in the Commission on the Rebellion of the Bondelzwarts (U.G. 16—1933), pp. 26–9, which investigated the matter because Richtersveld was believed to be indirectly connected with the Bondelzwart Rebellion.

ENVIRONMENT, POPULATION AND ECONOMY

All these communities share basically the same geographical environment. They have a low annual rainfall, the greater part of which occurs in winter, high summer temperatures and an inadequate water supply. Richtersveld, however, has the lowest annual rainfall in the territory, but this is to some extent alleviated by the fact that livestock grazing near the Orange River have water throughout the year. And parts of Leliefontein receive up to 13 inches of rain annually, which together with the fertile soil in the valleys greatly facilitates the production of grain. Vast tracts of land in Leliefontein, Komaggas and Richtersveld are mountainous and consequently uninhabitable.

Broadly speaking Concordia, Leliefontein and Komaggas follow the Steinkopf pattern regarding the distribution of population. Concordia and Steinkopf, however, are the only two Reserves which have central villages large enough to be classified as small towns or dorps, and Leliefontein has two main villages (Leliefontein mission village and Kharkams). In Richtersveld the two villages (Kuboes and Lekkersing) are sparsely populated and would be difficult to identify as villages in the absence of the churches, shops, and school-buildings. Even the huts constituting homesteads are often separated by distances of up to fifty yards. Actually these villages in Richtersveld resemble very closely the Steinkopf hamlets, although they have recently acquired shops and have churches and schools. Similarly, the hamlets in Richtersveld are less complex than those in Steinkopf: only one has a school, and in size they generally resemble a large Steinkopf homestead, though the huts are more spread out.

The economic systems of all these communities, except Richtersveld, are basically similar and resemble closely the Steinkopf pattern. The members of each community practise mixed-farming; there is communal land tenure; and migratory labour is nowadays an established institution. Steinkopf is the only Reserve with a large date-plantation and a co-operative store, and tributing is not practised in Leliefontein. Plans for the establishment of co-operative stores in Richtersveld and Komaggas were drawn up in 1960 and it is significant that the plans to establish these and the Steinkopf consumers' co-operative were made at the end of periods of extreme drought.

Richtersveld is primarily a stock-farming community, but in recent years a large number of people have found employment outside the Reserve. To my knowledge there is only one family (excluding the Bosluis Basters) which is actively engaged in tributing, although the territory is rich in minerals. There is no regular cultivation although some people claim to produce grain when adequate rain has fallen: little evidence, however, can be found to prove that cultivation has taken place for the past ten years.

Owing to the absence of reliable statistics, it is not possible to make an accurate comparison of income in these Reserves. An attempt, however, has been made to give a rough estimate of the annual income per head of the population in terms of local stock-farming and agriculture. In making these estimates it has been assumed that the annual income per small stock-unit is £0·375[19] and that the value of one bag of grain is £2 12s. 6d.

TABLE XXII

ESTIMATED INCOME PER HEAD OF POPULATION IN NAMAQUALAND RESERVES

(Small stock and grain only)

Reserve Population		A Small stock		B Grain		A plus B
		No.	Income per head of pop.	No. bags	Income per head of pop.	Total annual income per head of pop.
Leliefontein	2,970	40,000	£5·05	7,000	£6·19	£11·24
Steinkopf	4,400	48,455	£4·13	5,000	£2·99	£7·12
Richtersveld	1,336	18,848	£5·29	—	—	£5·29
Komaggas	2,000	14,320	£2·68	600	£0·79	£3·47
Concordia	2,400	14,150	£1·88	500	£0·55	£2·43

Note: The figures regarding the size of the population and the numbers of small stock for these Reserves (except Richtersveld) have been taken from the Commissioner for Coloured Affairs Annual Report, U.G. No. 13 1954, p. 16, and refer to 1953. The figures for Richtersveld in this Report are so inaccurate that I was obliged to use those supplied by the Secretary of the Richtersveld Advisory Board for 1960 instead. Figures relating to grain are the annual average crops (see U.G. 33—1947, p. 53).

The figures in Table XXII speak for themselves, but it is significant that the two Reserves (Concordia and Komaggas) with the lowest

[19] H. A. Kotzè, 'Verslag oor Ekonomiese ondersoek na die ontwikkeling van 'n Voerbank op Goodhouse vir die Kleurling-gebiede in Namakwaland', 1960, p. 12.

income per head also have the highest density of population.[20]

With regard to migratory-labour rates, statistical information is available for two Reserves only. In Steinkopf approximately a quarter of the population (30 per cent of the males and 19 per cent of the females) appear to have left the Reserve temporarily in 1957, while in Richtersveld (Kuboes village and environs) 22 per cent of the population (36 per cent of the males and 11 per cent of the females) became migrant workers in 1960. Inquiries concerning Concordia revealed that the migrant-labour rate was low, and this may be explained by the fact that many people find employment near their homes on the copper mines and in the towns adjacent to the Reserve.

In all these communities migratory labour has now been accepted as an economic necessity to supplement the low income derived from the local traditional economic systems which still operate though in a modified form. Geographical and especially social isolation appear, however, to limit this migration: in Richtersveld and at Komaggas[21] (the two most isolated communities) a large-scale exodus of migrant workers began only six years ago. In 1952 only a few people in Komaggas and Richtersveld entertained the idea of leaving their respective communities to work, and in Steinkopf and Leliefontein there were fewer migrant workers than there are today. Thus there is a suggestion that migratory labour is not only a function of increased poverty, but that it is stimulated also by greater intensity of interaction with the outside world through the advent of new internal institutions which reduce the former centripetal focus and the concomitant conservative attitudes within each community. For example, in Richtersveld and Komaggas the change seems to have been correlated with changes in church structure and church organisation. In Richtersveld there was the extension of the activities of the N.G. Sendingkerk; in Komaggas there was the advent of the Calvin Protestant Church.[22] Both Churches, moreover, encourage their people to leave their communities as migrant workers to augment family incomes (from

[20] See p. 14, Table II.

[21] Schultze, however, points out that men from Komaggas used to work on the Spektakel Copper Mines from December to March. This mine, which opened in 1880, is situated about 20 miles from Komaggas village. It closed in the 1920's. (Schultze, pp. 129–31.)

[22] In 1952 when I visited Komaggas I was told by the missionary of the N. G. Sendingkerk that he was actively opposed to all forms of migratory labour and had urged people not to leave the Reserve.

which the Churches also benefit), and both Churches retain links with those who go to the mines and towns through special church officers.

Mention must also be made of the value attached to belonging to a common territory. Even if individuals do leave their respective Reserves temporarily as migrant workers, they know that they have a permanent home, a place to retire to, or to go back to when they are sick or unemployed. And in this respect they have greater security than the majority of Coloured persons in the towns or on European farms. This attitude to land, moreover, is reflected in the erroneous belief that the territory is owned by the registered occupiers. And the most unpopular Whites featured in the oral traditions are the surveyors, notably those of the last century, who are said to have greatly reduced the former boundaries.

We have shown that in the Steinkopf Reserve migratory labour, in addition to its other functions, appears to have reduced internal land disputes by relieving the pressure on land. No information is available for the other Reserves, but it is significant that Komaggas and Concordia, which have the highest population density, tend to display marked internal tensions and dissensions which are not found in the other communities. There is a suggestion, therefore, that these conflicts may be related in part to local competition for land.

KINSHIP

The kinship systems in Concordia, Leliefontein, and Komaggas all conform to the pattern already described for Steinkopf.

Richtersveld kinship on the other hand varies in striking ways from this pattern, and we record here the main structural differences between them. Firstly, there is a measure of separation of the sexes in Richtersveld, but this is by no means as rigid as the pattern existing in Steinkopf. Husbands and wives, for example, interact closely with one another in domestic affairs, men and women gossip freely together, and girls often assist in herding. This pattern is exemplified, moreover, in the layout of the dwelling units. The cooking hut is built only a few feet away from the living-hut, thus enabling women to join in conversations between the men, who usually sit in the living-hut while the women are cooking or washing up; and courting is not as strictly controlled in Richtersveld as it is in Steinkopf. That the status of women in Richtersveld is higher than in the other Reserves is borne out also by the type of family groupings discussed below, and by the fact that a female kaptein once ruled the community.

Secondly, the types of families forming the homesteads in Kuboes village in Richtersveld and its environs show marked differences from those in Steinkopf. We base this comparison with Steinkopf on the pattern found in the hamlets and farms, since the Kuboes village resembles a Steinkopf hamlet more than it does the Steinkopf mission village. In the Steinkopf hamlets and farms there are two main types of families constituting homesteads: elementary families (42·8 per cent) and patrilineal extended families (52·3 per cent). In Richtersveld (Kuboes) the categories of family type are set out in Table XXIII.

TABLE XXIII
TYPE OF HOMESTEADS IN
KUBOES VILLAGE AND ENVIRONS
(Richtersveld Reserve)

Type of family	Number of families	%	Total number of persons	Av. size of family
1. Elementary families	19	44·2	93	4·9
2. Rejuvenated families	1	2·3	4	4·0
3. *Extended families*				
(a) Patrilineal extended families	4	9·3	36	9·0
(b) Matrilineal extended families	3	6·9	39	13·0
(c) Matrilineal extended families plus other kin (affines and agnates)	4	9·3	93	23·2
(d) Extended families containing affines	9	20·9	113	12·5
(e) Extended families containing affines plus unrelated persons	1	2·3	15	15·0
4. Homesteads consisting of neighbours	2	4·6	21	10·5
	43	99·8	414	9·6

Here it can be seen that in the Kuboes district of Richtersveld, as in the Steinkopf hamlets and farms, the majority live in extended families, but that there is no correlation between the types of extended families in the two areas. It is interesting to note also that the percentage of elementary families is practically identical for the two areas.

In Richtersveld we see that the greatest number of people live in extended families containing affines and that uxorilocality is common.

Moreover, only a small number of people live in patrilineal extended families. Now this is difficult to explain, particularly as it can generally be shown that pastoralists tend to practise virilocal marriage.

Thirdly, we have already shown that in Steinkopf extended families constitute comparatively closely-knit groups, the members of which live in close geographical proximity. But in Richtersveld there is a tendency for the huts constituting an extended family group to be spread out, and interaction between the members of the extended family less. It is significant, however, that two of the four patrilineal extended families at Kuboes follow the Steinkopf pattern in this regard.

Fourthly, in Steinkopf the lineages are clearly defined as they are also in Concordia, Leliefontein and Komaggas. But in Richtersveld the only true lineages are the Links patrilineage down which the hereditary *hoofkorporaalskap* has passed, and the Gwarra Cloetes, light-coloured Basters, whose ancestors used to be extremely wealthy.

Fifthly, the process of getting married in Richtersveld also varies considerably in detail from the Steinkopf pattern. In the first place, as already noted, there are less strict rules regarding courting in Richtersveld although both parents expect to be informed. Second, during the *vrou-vraery*, far from extolling the virtues of the future bride, the member of her family emphasises her shortcomings—'so that the man knows what he is getting'! Thirdly, the day before the wedding takes place, the husband's parents bring a live sheep (or a goat) to the future bride's home. Here they slaughter the animal but are careful not to spill any blood in the course of their work, because every portion of the animal must be handed over to the mother of the bride. This gift of a slaughtered animal is considered essential to all marriages and none takes place without it.

After the marriage the animal is cooked in its own fat if it is in good condition (otherwise in plain water), but the heart is cooked separately. The marriage feast begins with the ritual eating by both families of the meat of the slaughtered animal at the home of the parents of the bride.

The first part of this ritual is known as 'the biting of the heart'. The heart of the slaughtered animal is placed on a separate table in the newly constructed hut in which the new couple will live, and the mother of the bride or her sister or some other kinsman who has 'always lived in peace with other people' takes the heart and bites off and consumes the apex. She then divides it with a knife and gives a half to each of the bridal pair, telling them to eat that their own hearts may be united in love and so live together in peace and happiness. When the couple have consumed their portions, the rest of the family and friends present share the meat of the animal, and enjoy the other food which is also served—cake, bread, rice, beans, tea and sometimes honey-beer supplied either by the girl's or the man's family.

These customs lead us to a better understanding of the type of residence formed in extended families in Richtersveld. An animal, as we have said, is always supplied by the man's family in every marriage for ritual use, but, if virilocal residence after a short period of uxorilocality is to take place, the bulk of the food at the marriage feast is also supplied by them. And informants reported that occasionally the type of residence changed after a long period of uxorilocality when the 'groceries' (sic) had been given by the man's parents to the wife's parents. While investigating the question of uxorilocal marriage in Richtersveld, it was first thought that this might be connected with income, but subsequently the assumption was found to be incorrect. In fact there was a slight suggestion that the more prosperous the people were, the greater was the tendency to practise uxorilocal marriage.

No satisfactory answer can be given to explain the tendency towards uxorilocality in Richtersveld. It is possible that the relatively high illegitimacy rate explains the problem, but the hypothesis suggested is that the practice of agriculture in the other Reserves has tended indirectly to reinforce patrilineal ties through the 'ownership' of arable lands (which are generally patrilineally inherited) and co-operation in ploughing, reaping and threshing by certain patrikin. This hypothesis is only tentative, but it is supported also by the fact that in Leliefontein the cultivation of grain is more rewarding than in any other Reserve, and patrilineal bonds are extremely strong.[23] A possible complementary explanation is that the Khoi Khoin were not as strict about virilocal residence as has been suggested, and that the initial period of uxorilocality was often continued indefinitely.[24]

CLASS-STRUCTURE

In all these communities, except Richtersveld, there is a major cleavage on hereditary class-lines between registered occupiers and bywoners. However, the ratio of bywoner families to registered occupier families,

[23] Cf. Report on Coloured Mission Stations, pp. 50–1.

[24] Cf. I. Schapera, *The Khoisan Peoples of South Africa*, p. 230. See also Hoernlé's 'Social Organisation of the Nama Hottentots', p. 10.

expressed as percentages in these communities in 1945, indicates different trends in the hereditary class-pattern:[25]

Leliefontein	23·6%
Concordia	20·0%
Steinkopf	5·4%
Komaggas	3·6%
Richtersveld	—

The relatively high bywoner ratio in Leliefontein can be explained by the fact that during no historical period has the privilege of *burgherskap* (citizenship) been extended to any newcomer. Bywoners, however, are allowed to cultivate if land is available and they pay fees for grazing their livestock. The same practice appears also to apply in Concordia, although one informant stated that a few newcomers had been admitted to the status of registered occupier. No satisfactory statement regarding the status of bywoners at Komaggas can be made, but, as in Steinkopf, newcomers have in the past been admitted to registered-occupier status.[26]

The only reason that can be suggested as to why newcomers in Concordia have tended not to be admitted as registered occupiers is the shortage of land due to the high density of population, although this is partly invalidated by the fact that Komaggas also has a relatively high population density but (with the exception of Richtersveld) has the smallest percentage of bywoners. In Leliefontein the practice not to admit any newcomers to the community except as bywoners is related possibly to the fact that in this Reserve the missionary, who was given the power in 1824 to control the number of residents and the distribution of land in the community, realised the dangers of over-population, although there may also have been political reasons for their exclusion.

In Richtersveld a class-system is still in embryo. In the first place, there is no bywoner class since all newcomers have in the past always been admitted as burghers after a short period of residence. Secondly, there are no clearly defined lineages except the two we have already mentioned. And thirdly, Baster physical characteristics are not regarded as symbols of high status by the majority of people, probably because those Basters who went to the Richtersveld were largely assimilated by the indigenous population. In fact there are many families whose physical characteristics are essentially Baster but who speak the Nama

[25] Report on Coloured Mission Stations and Reserves, p. 65.

[26] Cf. Report of Rehoboth Commission, p. 73; L. Schultze, p. 119.

language, which is only now beginning to carry a lower status than Afrikaans. There is a suggestion, nowadays, however, that the people living at Lekkersing and its environs have started to regard themselves as superior to those living in Kuboes and its environs. More people speak Afrikaans as a home language at Lekkersing than at Kuboes, and a number of families have left Kuboes for Lekkersing in recent years because 'they were not happy there any more'. All these families are now Afrikaans-speaking and tend to follow the Baster rather than the Khoi Khoin way of life.

We must nevertheless record that even in Richtersveld certain individuals, irrespective of their other social ties, during the course of time have acquired rank. Known collectively as *ampdraers* (office-bearers) these people consist of teachers, Kerkraad members and ex-members, members of the raad, and in recent years shopkeepers and leaders of voluntary associations. Wealth also carries with it high status in the community, but far less prestige than does an 'office' such as one of those mentioned.

All informants agreed that nowadays the person with the highest status in the community was the missionary, but he is a White man who visits the Reserve on church business only. Second in the status hierarchy are the Kerkraad and the ex-Kerkraad members. Third are the members of the raad: 'They are not as highly respected as the members of the Kerkraad because they lean towards the White man's government.' Fourth are the teachers and other *ampdraers*: 'They count a lot today.' Fifth are the prosperous farmers who have large numbers of small stock.

In the previous section we attributed the solidarity of lineages in the other four Reserves partly to the practice of agriculture but, as we have already demonstrated for Steinkopf, lineage and class are also closely connected. Thus in Richtersveld it is significant that the only two lineages which exist are those associated closely with the high status of certain of their members: the Swartbooi Links had the hereditary *hoofkorporaalskap* until 1957; the Cloete Basters have been represented on the raad for two generations and used to be extremely wealthy.

LOCAL GOVERNMENT

All these communities are now classified as Coloured Reserves and fall under the control of the Coloured Affairs Department. With the exception of Richtersveld their forms of local government are similar to that of Steinkopf; they also have similar political histories although in Leliefontein the missionary remained a member of the Management Board until 1959, when he was ordered by the Coloured Affairs Department to vacate his position as church representative on the grounds that he was neither a Coloured person nor a 'registered occupier'.

The Mission Stations and Communal Reserves Act was first applied in Richtersveld in 1957, but here the system of local government is geared to an Advisory Board[27] consisting of 'five ordinary members appointed by the Minister' and one additional member who is the superintendent of the Steinkopf Reserve. The five ordinary members 'hold office for such period as the Minister may determine at the time of the appointment', but should he have 'good reason for doing so', he may terminate the period of office of any member at any time. The duties of the Advisory Board consist of making recommendations to the Minister on matters submitted to it for consideration, and generally to advise him on and to assist him in the administration of the community. But the Minister possesses all the rights and powers and performs all the duties (with certain provisos) conferred or imposed upon a Board of Management by the Act.

'Elections' for the five members of the Advisory Board were held in Richtersveld in 1960 and the results sent to the Coloured Affairs Department. Local investigations, however, revealed that the Coloured Affairs Department did not appoint all those candidates who gained the most votes in the 'election'.

During the years preceding the proclamation of the Mission Stations and Communal Reserves Act in Richtersveld in 1957, the form of local government resembled that already described for Steinkopf during the Baster–missionary period, with the important qualifications that the resident missionary (when there was one) took little part in the political life and that the functions of government were simpler. The political head of the community was the *hoofkorporaal*,[28] an hereditary position following patrilineal succession. He was assisted in his duties by a number of korporale (eight in 1945). The only source of revenue this raad had was derived from the grazing fees paid by the trekboers, other White farmers and a few Coloured people. The burghers paid no taxes and there do not appear to have been any bywoners. The raad

[27] Cf. Coloured Mission Stations and Reserves Amendment Act, No. 35 of 1955.

[28] In 1925 he was still called *kaptein* (letter dated 27 October 1927 from Surveyor-General's Office, Cape Town, to the Minister of Lands).

received no outside assistance from any government department, and apart from occasional police patrols and sporadic visits from the Superintendent of Reserves, it managed all the internal affairs of the community. Its functions were limited owing to the nomadic nature of the people, and in general the form of government was structurally simpler than that described by Schapera and others for the Khoi Khoin,[29] and the raad had very little control over the people.[30]

CHURCHES, VOLUNTARY ASSOCIATIONS, AND SCHOOLS

All these communities, with the exception of Leliefontein, are at present under the official religious jurisdiction of the N.G. Sending-kerk, which, as in Steinkopf, took over the work of the Rhenish Mission Society in the 1930's. Regular mission work was begun at Leliefontein in 1816 by Barnabas Shaw of the Methodist Church and this denomination has remained the official religious body in the community.

In Leliefontein and Richtersveld, as in Steinkopf, these official Churches may be said to be dominant religious institutions, since the majority of each population are active church members in their respective communities. But in Komaggas a strong rivalry exists between the members of the N.G. Sendingkerk (the official Church) and the members of the Calvin Protestant Church, a new denomination which was formed in Cape Town in 1950 by a former Coloured minister of the N.G. Sendingkerk.[31] The moderator and founder of the Calvin Protestant Church was invited to Komaggas by members of the community because they did not wish to be ministered to by the N.G. Sendingkerk and also because they disliked the personality of the resident missionary. They allege also that the majority of the community never agreed to the transfer to the N.G. Sendingkerk after the Rhenish Mission Society had ceased to operate in their Reserve. The Calvin Protestant Church has the largest following, and in 1957 more than 700 adult members of the community of approximately 2,000 signed a letter urging the moderator of the Calvin Protestant Church to establish a congregation in the Reserve and build a church.[32] Neither the N.G. Sendingkerk nor the Coloured Affairs

[29] Cf. I. Schapera, *Government and Politics in Tribal Societies*.
[30] Cf. Report on Coloured Mission Stations, pp. 54–5, and letter to Minister of Lands mentioned above.
[31] S. Patterson, *Colour and Culture in South Africa*, pp. 133, 159.
[32] W. P. Carstens, 'The D.R. Church Militant'.

Department reacted favourably to this request, but in 1958 the Calvin Protestant Church was allowed to hold services once a month in the Reserve. There are also a few members of the Anglican and Roman Catholic Churches in Komaggas.

In Concordia approximately forty members of the community have also joined the Calvin Protestant Church, which has permission to hold services in the Reserve once every three months. Members of the Anglican, Roman Catholic and Methodist Churches are also found in Concordia. Statistics are not available but the total membership of all these Churches, including the Calvin Protestant Church, is unlikely to exceed 5 per cent of the population.

In Leliefontein there are a few Roman Catholics at Spoegrivier, two Anglicans who are teachers, and one Moravian. The rest of the population belongs to the established Methodist Church.

The people of Richtersveld are active supporters of the N.G. Sendingkerk, and some of the ten Roman Catholics worship in the mission church.

The system of church government and church structure found in the Reserves under the religious jurisdiction of the N.G. Sendingkerk has already been described, and it remains for us to draw attention to the fact that the Methodist system found at Leliefontein differs greatly from it.[33]

In the Methodist Church in South Africa little distinction is made between White and non-White congregations, but in practice the various 'racial' groups within the Church worship separately. Thus the Methodist minister at Leliefontein is not a missionary in the community, but the superintendent minister of a circuit. Although the circuit extends beyond the borders of the Reserve most of its work is carried out locally.

The Leliefontein Circuit is divided for the purpose of administration into what are known as societies. Nine out of the total of twenty-one societies in the Circuit fall within the boundaries of the Reserve. Each society is again subdivided into a number of classes, groups of people who are supposed to meet once a week for prayer and Bible study. Thus instead of local church affairs being administered by a single body or committee as in the other Reserves, Leliefontein has a sort of federal administrative framework which provides opportunities for a

[33] Church Government in the Methodist Church of South Africa is laid down in: *A Manual of the Laws and Discipline of the Methodist Church of South Africa*, 4th ed., 1962.

large number of active religious leaders and a system for the greater control of the congregation by the established Church than in the other Reserves.

Each society is administered by a Leaders' Meeting consisting of six deacons nominated by the minister but elected by the full church members, and the leaders of the classes, who are appointed by the minister. The minister presides over all the meetings. The work of all these societies is co-ordinated by the Quarterly Meeting, which is the official body administering the Circuit. All the members of each Leaders' Meeting are represented at the Quarterly Meeting and together with the twenty-five lay preachers in the Reserve and two additional deacons (nominated by the minister and voted into office by the Quarterly Meeting) constitute this body. The Quarterly Meeting is presided over by the minister, who has a casting as well as a deliberative vote in all matters on which a unanimous decision is not reached.

It should be clear from this account of church government in Leliefontein that the minister, in spite of the decentralised system of administration in the community, wields great authority. It is true that he delegates his power to his many church officers but in practice he can be more autocratic than the ministers in the N.G. Kerk, who, by church law, are responsible to their respective Kerkrade, whose members are all elected by the representatives of their congregations.

The number of voluntary associations in any community generally provides a good index of the degree of complexity of social structure. Richtersveld, which is closest to the Nama tradition than any of the other communities we are discussing, had no voluntary association until 1944, when the first burial-society was formed by an alien teacher at Lekkersing. In 1947 the sustersbond was established by the visiting missionary's wife. In 1955 a second burial-society was created (at Kuboes) by a local teacher, and towards the end of 1960 a kinderbond grew out of the sustersbond.

Leliefontein has a complex network of voluntary associations most of which are or were geared to local Methodist Church structure and have been in existence for a long time. In this community there are *seven* burial-societies, one of which has extended its activities to local charity and welfare. They were all founded by the Church but are now independent associations although the majority have leaders who are also church officers. There is a Women's Association which has ten branches, and each of the nine societies constituting part of the Leliefontein Circuit has organisations for young people and a local

Sunday-school. Certain of the nine choirs have recently taken on the character of clubs with constitutions and subscriptions. There is also a sports club which was started in 1958, and this is attached to the Church. An *opvoedings organisasie* (educational organisation) was founded in 1959 to raise funds to send children to the secondary school at Steinkopf.

In Concordia the forms of voluntary associations resemble the Steinkopf pattern although there is only one burial-society and fewer church associations, and the adherents of the Calvin Protestant Church have now formed an association of their own.

In Komaggas, apart from one burial-society, no voluntary association of the Steinkopf type existed in 1959. This appears to have been the result of the disintegration of the N.G. Sendingkerk and the other dissensions within the community. The large number of adherents of the Calvin Protestant Church, however, have formed an association which is beginning to take on the characteristics of a Church in spite of legal difficulties, and the moderator of the Calvin Protestant Church expects his Komaggas congregation to develop burial-societies and other voluntary associations in the near future.

The most significant feature which emerges from this analysis of voluntary associations is that the majority are not only linked with the Churches in the Reserves but that the number of church-linked voluntary associations is connected with the structure of church government and church solidarity in the communities in which they occur.

The pattern of formal education is basically the same in all the communities though there are variations in the number and status of the schools. Steinkopf is the only community which provides education up to Standard 10. In Leliefontein there are nine schools with a total of 23 teachers and 682 pupils, Concordia has four schools with 14 teachers and 446 pupils, Komaggas has two schools with 11 teachers and 391 pupils, Richtersveld has four schools with 10 teachers and 263 pupils. All these figures are for 1960.

It is only in the last ten or fifteen years that the Richtersveld children have received adequate formal primary education by present-day standards. Between 1933 and 1945 there appears to have been only one permanent regular teacher; between 1917 and 1932 no formal education was given at all, and those who received training in the mission school prior to 1917 appear to have been taught only the alphabet, and to count.

In Richtersveld a modified form of the traditional Khoi Khoin girl's initiation ceremony[34] is still carried out, though the custom is fast disappearing. The purpose for which this ceremony is performed is to protect the girl physically in her change to womanhood, since a girl during her first menstruation is believed to be prone to illness of various kinds. It is performed also to test the girl to see whether she will be healthy in later life and if she will be a good and lucky wife; and to instruct her in her proper duties as a wife and mother.

LEADERSHIP AND FOCI OF POWER

If a comparison is made of the categories of people represented on the Leliefontein Management Board with those on the Steinkopf Management Board, one is immediately struck by the differences. In Leliefontein the superintendent is an alien. He was transferred by the Coloured Affairs Department from the mission-station Zoar where he had held a similar position. He is officially a member of the N.G. Sendingkerk, but has tried without success to obtain permission from this Church to transfer to the Methodist Church, which is the only recognised Church in the Reserve. This difficulty has, however, been partly overcome since the local Methodist Church has accepted him unofficially and has made him a lay preacher.

The superintendent is favourably accepted as an official leader by the majority of the population although many of the teachers and educated people feel that he should show more deference towards them. His wife, who is a nurse by profession, is also well liked.

One of the factors which may explain why tension exists between the superintendent and the educated people is that no teachers are members of the Management Board. In Leliefontein the minister (missionary) does not approve of teachers' (whom he appoints) doing two jobs of work and this attitude has prevented them from standing for election or nomination. Paradoxically though, the minister apparently encourages certain teachers to become office-bearers in the Church which in many ways requires more time and energy than membership of the Management Board.

The secretary of the Management Board plus the church-nominated, government-appointed member, the two government-appointed members, and all (except one) of the six elected members are office-

[34] I. Schapera, *Khoisan Peoples*, pp. 272–9. A. W. Hoernlé, 'Certain Rites of Transition . . . among the Hottentots', in *Harvard African Studies*, vol. 2, 1918, pp. 65–82; 'The Social Value of Water', in *S.A.J. Science*, 1923, vol. 20, pp. 523–5; *Richterveld, The Land and Its People*, 1913.

bearers in the Methodist Church. And three of the elected members (who are church officers) are also shopkeepers.

All the Management Board members are prosperous by Leliefontein standards: those who are not shopkeepers or paid officials (the superintendent and the secretary) are successful farmers.

The Church in Leliefontein in spite of its decentralised system of local administration is largely dominated by the alien minister since it is through him that the majority of church officers gain their positions (either by the minister's appointment or by his nomination for election). In practice though, all categories of people in the Reserve appear to be adequately represented on the various church committees and inquiries suggested that the system operates smoothly without any obvious tensions or conflicts between office-bearers or the groups they represent.

Although the school-teachers are not elected as members of the Management Board, they do play their part as leaders in church affairs. But not all teachers become church leaders: only locally born teachers or alien teachers who have been members of the community for a long time tend to fill these positions. This is due partly to the fact that alien teachers are often members of other churches and also, according to the minister, because 'the type of outsider who comes to Leliefontein is usually someone who has been unable to hold down a job elsewhere. They are often drunkards and other immoral persons.' In 1960 only *one* out of the *twelve* alien teachers was a church leader, whereas *nine* of the *eleven* locally born teachers were.

In terms of the number of teachers in each category (alien or local), it can be seen that the education of the young is partly in the hands of aliens and partly in the hands of locally born people. But, as in the case of Steinkopf, the minister, who is an alien, is largely responsible for the appointment of teachers and manages all the schools.

Leadership in the voluntary associations—the burial-societies, the church associations, the choirs, the women's association, the sports club, and the *opvoedings organisasie*—lies almost entirely in the hands of the local inhabitants, most of whom are traditional leaders. In fact the only alien leader (of one of the burial-societies) is a teacher who has taught in the Reserve for many years.

The majority of these voluntary associations fall within the framework of the Church, but even those which do not, viz. the burial-societies and the *opvoedings organisasie* and the choirs, are dominated by leaders who are also church officers.

In Richtersveld, which is administered by the Coloured Affairs Department through an Advisory Board, the official leader in local government is an alien, the superintendent of the Steinkopf Reserve, and he visits the community each month to preside over Advisory Board meetings. The Steinkopf superintendent, however, is not a complete stranger to Richtersveld as he spent several years in the late 1930's at Kuboes, where he was principal of the school. Although the majority of people regard him more as a police-sergeant than as their superintendent, there is no real antagonism towards him. He is seen merely as a government official whose authority they have to accept.

The secretary to the Advisory Board is a grandson of the famous Rhenish Missionary of Kuboes, J. H. Hein, a man of mixed descent. He is also principal of the Lekkersing school, owns the shop and runs the postal agency at Lekkersing, possesses large herds of livestock, and is a deacon in the Church.

Two of the five ordinary members of the Board are traditional leaders, the hereditary *hoofkorporaal*, who has held office[35] since his father's death in 1928, and the Cloete Baster who has been a member of the Board (formerly the raad) since 1930 and is prosperous. The latter's lineage has been represented on the raad since about 1850. The third ordinary member is a brother of the secretary and is involved in his brother's business. One of the remaining two ordinary members represents the Bosluis Basters while the other has no special distinction.

It used to be the practice in Richtersveld for the raad, the Kerkraad, and the schools to be entirely separate institutions. But with the increase in the number of teachers accompanying the development of education and the extension of the Church, close links between church leaders, school-teachers and their wives have been made; and, as we have shown, the composition of the Advisory Board has tended to bring local government into a common orbit with education and the Church. Thus in Kuboes and Lekkersing most of the work of the Kerkraad is done by the two school principals. They hold services on Sundays (except when the missionary or the evangelist visits the main centres), the *biduur* on Wednesdays, they conduct funerals, and prepare people for confirmation. Other teachers run the Sunday-schools and one of the principals organises the church choir. The sustersbond and the kinderbond have executive committees consisting entirely of teachers' wives, although the president of the sustersbond is the missionary's wife. But since she visits Richtersveld so seldom, her role is more that

[35] Legally the hereditary *hoofkorporaalskap* ceased in 1957 (see pp. 207, 217–18).

of a patron than a leader.

The official leader of the N.G. Sendingkerk is the White missionary and, as in the other Reserves, his office carries with it great prestige and respect. But in Richtersveld the main impact which the Church makes on the community is through the teachers and their wives.

The White evangelist, who lives outside the Reserve, is also the manager of the schools. He visits Kuboes and Lekkersing once every month to hold services but his work must be seen as supplementary to that of the teachers and their wives, who are better integrated in the community, although the majority of them are also aliens.

Leadership in the church voluntary associations has already been described. The only other voluntary associations (excluding those at Eksteenfontein) are the two burial-societies. The Lekkersing burial-society, which was first founded by an alien teacher is now under the leadership of a deacon with a committee consisting predominantly of other Kerkraad or former Kerkraad members. At Kuboes a locally born teacher (the founder) is the chairman, but he is assisted by his wife, and the locally born manager of the shop, and an alien teacher. Both burial-societies as in the case of Steinkopf and Leliefontein are independent of the Church.

We should point out also that in 1960 the teachers extended their activities as leaders in the community by being largely responsible for the creation of a consumers' co-operative store at Kuboes. Two of them (both aliens) were elected as senior directors.

Owing to difficulties[36] encountered during field-work, less detail regarding leadership and the foci of power is available for Concordia and Komaggas than for the other Reserves. Discussion is limited, therefore, to certain aspects of their management boards, schools, and churches.

In Concordia the superintendent of the Reserve is a registered occupier and is also chairman of the Komaggas Management Board. His appointment is made on the same basis as that of the other superintendents. In neither Komaggas nor Concordia are teachers represented on the Management Boards, and each Management Board includes only two members of the Kerkrade of the established Churches (N.G. Sendingkerk). During the past four years both Management Boards have had a Roman Catholic as a member, and in the main the majority of councillors have been farmers, none of whom were particularly wealthy.

[36] See Preface.

In recent years the rise of the Calvin Protestant Church in Komaggas has influenced the whole pattern of leadership in that community especially in the field of local government, for it is the aim of members of this Church to obtain a majority vote on the Management Board in order to pass a motion requesting the central government to recognise their Church as one of the established Churches in the Reserve. But in order to achieve a majority vote on the Management Board it is necessary for them to place in office all six of the elected members.[37] This, however, has not been possible because certain of the Calvin Protestant Church voters have for various reasons (e.g. failure to pay taxes before the due date) been excluded from the electoral roll before polling day. But by 1960 they had managed to return four of the six elected members to office, including two of their unofficial church leaders.

As regards the schools in Komaggas all the teachers are aliens and members of the N.G. Sendingkerk, but none are members of the Kerkraad. In spite of their membership of the established Church the majority are said to be secretly sympathetic towards the activities of the Calvin Protestant Church, but in view of the fact that they are appointed by the N.G. Sendingkerk missionary, they are unable either to change their church affiliation or to express their feelings in public.

In Concordia nine of the teachers are registered occupiers and five are aliens. Information regarding the number of teachers who were members of the N.G. Sendingkerk is not available but two (both of whom are registered occupiers) are on the Kerkraad.

A feature of the pattern of leadership in these five communities is the tendency to accept *and approve of* alien leadership in certain secondary groups, notably those groups whose activities extend also beyond the boundaries of their respective communities.[38] An important aspect of the role of the alien leader in this context is that of a go-between between the Reserve and the wider society. This tendency, moreover, appears to be influenced by the system of the local church government, and to increase in inverse proportion to the size of the bywoner-class. Thus the reasons why alien leadership in Leliefontein is less marked than it is in Steinkopf seem to be: (*a*) in Leliefontein the federal administrative structure of the Methodist Church provides a system in which various local 'traditional' groupings of people in the Reserve

[37] See pp. 136–7.

[38] Cf. R. Frankenberg, *Village on the Border*, London, Cohen and West, 1957.

16

are represented; and hence the locally born inhabitants tend to be preferred as leaders in certain church and church-linked associations, and (b) in Leliefontein all aliens are bywoners and consequently have low status in terms of the hereditary class-system, whereas in Steinkopf, which has a small bywoner-class, the intermediary semi-permanent hereditary class of strangers caters for newcomers who are likely to be accepted later to full citizenship. Similarly, it is argued that aliens figure prominently as leaders in the newly formed secondary groups in Richtersveld because of their close relation to the N.G. Sendingkerk, and because of the absence of a bywoner-class in the Reserve.

Lack of details on leadership in Concordia, *which has a large bywoner-class*, and Komaggas, *which has not*, prevents the testing of the modifying hypothesis (relating to alien leadership) in these two communities. But it has already been shown that no alien is represented on the Concordia N.G. Sendingkerkraad, and inquiries did not reveal any alien leaders of other voluntary associations in this Reserve. Moreover, in Komaggas, although the rebellion against the authority of the N.G. Sendingkerk weakens the hypothesis, the inviting of the Moderator of the Calvin Protestant Church to the community shows clearly a desire on the part of the majority of the inhabitants to be served by an alien religious leader, albeit of their own choice.

Finally, we should point out that in these communities local government appears to be most effective when political power is reinforced by religious power, and/or power in education, and/or economic power, or traditional authority when that authority is still accepted by the majority, provided that leadership in the reinforcing institutions is accepted by the majority of people in the community, and that certain of the key men in the political power group also hold key posts in the reinforcing institutions. Thus we have shown that in Steinkopf there is a marked duplication and triplication of power among the leaders in local government, the established Church, and the schools, and that certain wealthy stock-farmers are members of the Management Board. In Leliefontein political power is greatly reinforced by the established Church, the shopkeepers, and the wealthy farmers, but not by the educational system. Richtersveld with an Advisory Board instead of a Management Board provides a somewhat different situation for comparison, but it seems unlikely that the new system of local government would have been so readily accepted and so effective had the status of the members of the Advisory Board not been reinforced by their other affiliations—the school, the Church, traditional authority, and wealth. Moreover, under the old raad the ties between politics, religion and education in Richtersveld were absent and local government was ineffective (e.g. the Le Fleur crisis already referred to).

It is true, of course, that contemporary local governments in all these communities can use force to carry out their duties, but some degree of acceptance is necessary to make political authority effective, and the suggestion made here is that this requirement is satisfied largely through the close association of the local government members with other institutions which are accepted. Hence in Komaggas the system of local government has been ineffective because the Management Board has not been strengthened by the established Church (although leaders and members of this Church hold offices on the Management Board) because the established Church is not accepted by the majority of the population. Moreover, there are no teachers represented on the Komaggas Management Board, nor does it have the support of any other effective source. In Concordia, a similar yet less serious situation has arisen: the Management Board has great difficulty in enforcing certain regulations, and members of the community have on occasions brought their grievances to the Coloured Affairs Department in Cape Town rather than to their local authority. In Concordia also the Calvin Protestant Church is beginning to challenge the former authority of the established Church and as a result the support given by the two Kerkraad members on the Management Board to local government is rendered less effective. The Management Board has no teacher among its ranks, no well-to-do farmer, although there is one shopkeeper.

In these Namaqualand Reserve communities, then, a high degree of integration between the main institutions, either direct or indirect, seems necessary if these communities are to achieve social cohesion and if each of these institutions is to function effectively. This phenomenon, however, is not peculiar to the community-type under discussion, for in all social situations external interaction in the form of co-operation (and alien leadership) tends to reduce the intensity of certain local interactions within each institution. But its importance in the reservation-complex must be stressed, since patterns of social expression are here radically inhibited by the imposition of inflexible systems of administration and the concomitants of racial or minority group discrimination.

The general conclusions drawn from the five Namaqualand Coloured Reserves in this and earlier chapters have therefore a much wider theoretical and political significance. Thus it was not surprising to discover that many of the same principles are operating also in the Okanagan, Kamloops, and Lytton Indian Reserves of British Columbia, in spite of the fact that these Canadian communities are much smaller in size, and that the aboriginal population belong to a different cultural heritage.[39]

[39] My material relating to these communities has not yet been published. See also page 1.

CHAPTER 12

AN ANALYSIS OF SOCIAL CHANGE

IN THE Herbert Spencer Lecture of 1958 Morris Ginsberg explained that the term social change included two things:

(i) 'A change in social structure, e.g.: the size of a society, the composition and balance of its parts or the type of organisation.'

(ii) 'The changes in attitudes and beliefs in so far as they sustain institutions and change with them.'[1]

Here we are concerned mainly with the first of these aspects of social change, since information regarding attitudes and beliefs held in former periods is not always available in a form which can be used for sociological interpretation.

We begin this analysis of social change with a general discussion of an aspect of the colonisation of the North-Western Cape, i.e. the origin of the Basters, who were the Pioneers or Voortrekkers of that part of South Africa.

KHOI KHOIN—TREKBOER INTEGRATION

Steinkopf and other similar communities are partly the result of racial and social integration. The process began, as we have seen, with the fusing together, on the north-west frontier in the early eighteenth century and in later years, of certain Khoi Khoin and early Cape Dutch into relatively homogeneous nomadic groups of Basters.

The explanation of this phenomenon is, I believe, twofold. First, it may be argued that during the greater part of the eighteenth century the Dutch frontiersmen and the Khoi Khoin were dependent on each other for survival and for the satisfaction of certain needs. Secondly, I suggest that certain similarities between the social structures of the trekboers and the Khoi Khoin during this period facilitated interaction between individuals and groups in the two societies.[2]

When the Dutch colonists first entered the north-western section of South Africa they found themselves occupying the same territory as the Khoi Khoin, and since they were also pastoralists it was essential for them to share common grazing-lands with their new neighbours.

[1] Morris Ginsberg, 'Social Change', *The British Journal of Sociology*, vol. IX, no. 3, 1958.

[2] Cf. E. Fischer, *Die Rehobother Bastards und das Bastardierungsproblem beim Menschen*, Jena, 1913, pp. 228–37.

Furthermore they wanted Khoi Khoin cattle and sheep to augment their herds and flocks. They also needed the Khoi Khoin as servants and shepherds, not merely for the work they were able to perform, but also for the companionship they provided on the isolated and lonely frontier. Even today, anyone who visits a trekboer family or an outlying Afrikaans farm in South Africa, especially in the North-Western Cape, cannot fail to be impressed by the part which domestic servants play in providing companionship for the members of the elementary family, notably the women and children. This need for companionship among the eighteenth-century frontiersmen has been noted by MacCrone who states: 'The extreme monotony and loneliness of the lives of many of the women and trying conditions under which they lived may have had something to do with the prevalence of hysterical disorders among them, upon which Lichtenstein comments.'[3]

Co-operation with the Khoi Khoin, moreover, was necessary to obtain additional manpower to swell the ranks of their commandos, which were organised to hunt and annihilate the Bushmen, and thereby to guarantee their own survival. Military service from the Khoi Khoin was necessary also on account of the harsh climate to which the Khoi Khoin were better adapted.

On the frontier there were no medical services, and the trekboers were seldom in reach of European doctors. Thus it was to their advantage to make use of Khoi Khoin leeches and midwives in times of need. Even today the White Afrikaner population of Namaqualand have preserved many of the old Khoi Khoin practices in the treatment of disease. Furthermore, the dwellings of the Khoi Khoin were better suited to local climatic conditions than mud-walled thatch-roofed houses. Mat-houses could be easily and quickly taken down, transported, and assembled; they were well-ventilated and cool in summer, while in winter the reeds swelled during rain and provided excellent shelter. Nowadays it is still common to find White peasants living in traditional Khoi Khoin dwellings,[4] and the remnants of the early trekboers always possess mat-houses in addition to their wagon homes.

But it was not only the frontiersmen who needed the Khoi Khoin;

[3] I. MacCrone, *Race Attitudes in South Africa*, p. 110. H. Lichtenstein, *Travels in Southern Africa in the years 1803–6*, vol. 1, pp. 109–10.

[4] P. J. van der Merwe, *Trek*, chapter XI. P. W. Kotzé, *Namakwaland*, p. 86. See also J. E. Alexander, *An Expedition of Discovery into the Interior of Africa*, 1838, pp. 64 ff.

the Khoi Khoin too were greatly dependent on the trekboers and needed their support to ward off the Bushmen. They also wanted metal goods, tea, coffee, sugar, tobacco, and brandy, which they appear to have been unable to resist.[5] The frontiersmen could supply all these commodities, and some (Engelbrecht[6] for example) were part-time traders.

Apart from these positive factors which stimulated interaction between Khoi Khoin and trekboer, it must also be borne in mind that demographic factors did not hamper or deter association between the two peoples. Most important was the fact that the Khoi Khoin did not check the northerly migration of the colonists, because their population at this time was relatively small in size[7] and widely dispersed. Earlier, wars with Europeans had reduced the number of Khoi Khoin in the Colony and its environs; and imported diseases such as smallpox had decimated their ranks.[8] Thus the relative proportion of Khoi Khoin to trekboer was not so great as to endanger the freedom and security of the latter, especially as the Khoi Khoin were not inclined to guerrilla warfare as were many of the Bushmen.[9]

As a result of this mutual dependence, the Khoi Khoin and the trekboers began to perform common activities together. They began by trading and affording each other protection. In return for livestock and labour the Khoi Khoin received European trade goods; in return for their military service on commandos they received the support of their neighbours and the security provided by guns; and through their daily contacts each group benefited from the culture of the other. Thus it was the existence of these reciprocal necessities which initiated the process of racial and social integration.

But the degree to which the fusion took place seems to have been due to the absence of cohesion in both groups. Neither the trekboers

[5] J. S. Marais, *The Cape Coloured People*, p. 7.

[6] See chapter 2.

[7] Accurate population figures are not available, but Stow in his *Native Races of South Africa* estimated that those Khoi Khoin inhabiting the Cape Peninsula and surrounding country in 1652 numbered between 13,000 and 14,000 people. In 1740, the nominally White free-burgher population was about 4,000 (see Neumark, *Economic Influences on the South African Frontier 1652–1836*, p. 10). Thus in view of the fact that the Khoi Khoin population decreased between the years 1652 and 1740 the difference in the total Khoi Khoin and White population could not have been great.

[8] Schapera, *The Khoisan Peoples*, p. 46.

[9] MacCrone, pp. 101–6, *et passim*.

nor those Khoi Khoin who came into contact with them were strongly unified communities: both were in a state of disequilibrium. The former people had severed their ties with the settlement at the Cape, while the cohesion of the Khoi Khoin tribes and clans had been weakened by earlier contacts with the Dutch, and by Dutch interference and intrusion into the territory which they formerly occupied. Thus, as a result of this general condition of instability and disequilibrium, there were individuals and groups of Khoi Khoin and trekboers who could easily detach themselves from their communities and become the founding ancestors of a new category of people, the Basters. In a sense then, these Basters were the descendants of the non-conformers or deviants of the traditional Khoi Khoin and early Cape Dutch. Among the latter, moreover, it was those who were least affected by the authority of the landdrost or veldkornet, who moved nearest in space to the Khoi Khoin and became closely integrated with them.[10]

The fruits of interaction between these two groups of people can be seen in the extent to which they learned each other's language. And this in turn led to further and more intense interaction and subsequent integration.[11] Concerning the learning of language on the frontier John Barrow wrote: 'Most of the Dutch peasantry in the distant districts speak [the Hottentot language]'[12], and likewise, '[the Hottentots] learn the Dutch language with great facility'.[13] Moreover, James Backhouse, writing specifically about the southern sector of Little Namaqualand, says: 'Notwithstanding the difficulty of acquiring the Hottentot language, many of the Boors, in this part of the country, spoke it fluently, having learned it in childhood, by association with the children of their Hottentot servants.'[14]

[10] MacCrone, pp. 114–18. Marais, pp. 10–13.

[11] Certain of the Khoi Khoin, however, appear to have acquired a knowledge of Dutch from the earliest days of their contact with the Colonists and this must have facilitated the initial interaction between the two groups on the frontier. Cf. *Van Riebeeck Journal*, ed. H. B. Thom, Balkema, Cape Town, 1953, especially vol. 11, p. 89. O. Dapper in *The Early Cape Hottentots*, Van Riebeeck Society, Cape Town, 1933, p. 73. MacCrone, pp. 43–5.

[12] J. Barrow, *Travels into the Interior of Southern Africa*, London, 1801, p. 162.

[13] Barrow, p. 160. See also Marais, pp. 135–6.

[14] J. Backhouse, *A Narrative of a Visit to the Mauritius and South Africa*, London, 1844, p. 526.

THE BASTERS AND THE MISSIONARIES

Towards the end of the eighteenth century, largely as the result of the process of integration we have described, a very marked class-structure developed on the north-west frontier.[15] At this time the population consisted of three main groups of people: the Dutch frontiersmen, the Basters, and those remaining Khoi Khoin who had not yet migrated northwards. The Dutch frontiersmen claimed precedence over both the other groups, and the Basters came to be regarded as an inferior class of European both by their White neighbours and by the government, which had now begun to interest itself in the affairs of the northern half of the colony.[16] As a result of this class-distinction many of the Basters crossed the boundary into Little Namaqualand, where they were free to search for fresh pastures for their livestock without fearing competition from the Whites, who were favoured by the colonial government. Thus, although they left the Colony as inferiors, they entered Little Namaqualand possessing guns, and regarded themselves as superior to the Khoi Khoin with whom they came in contact. It is not possible to state precisely what the Basters took with them in the way of Dutch culture apart from guns, wagons, a European style of dress, a knowledge of the Christian religion, and the Dutch language which had become their mother tongue (although they also spoke the Khoi Khoin language).[17] The fact that they were regarded as an inferior class of European, however, is evidence that they possessed many Dutch characteristics.

Those Baster Pioneers who settled in the territories now known as Concordia, Komaggas, Steinkopf, Leliefontein and Richtersveld found themselves in a position similar to that in which their trekboer ancestors had been earlier, although here the indigenous population was politically more effectively organised. The roles which these people played in their respective territories in subsequent years, however, differed in various important respects. In Concordia, Komaggas, and Steinkopf the Basters soon acquired political power and held it for well over fifty years. And they have largely retained their identity as separate groups, an identity which is nowadays reflected in the lineage- and class-structures. In Leliefontein and Richtersveld, however, the Basters neither achieved power nor have

[15] The north-west boundary of the Colony was extended in 1798 from the Olifants River to the Kamiesberg, roughly where the town of Garies stands today.
[16] MacCrone, chapter 7. Marais, pp. 10–13.
[17] Backhouse, pp. 526, 532, 545–6, 578. Lichtenstein, vol. 11, pp. 301–2.

they retained their identity as separate groups. It is true that in Richters-veld a Baster became kaptein but this was because the female kaptein had no one to succeed her and because this Baster had married one of her kin. Moreover, after his marriage his name was changed to Swartbooi Links and he became a member of the indigenous community whose interests he served.[18] The Cloete Baster lineage to which we have already referred has tended to retain its identity not because of Baster interests but because of its wealth as we have shown.

At the level of comparative analysis the main factor which appears to explain these differences is the role played by missionaries in the communities where the Basters settled. It seems clear that those Basters who received the active support of missionaries[19] achieved political power during the last century in the communities they joined, and this support tended to perpetuate and boost their feelings of superiority over the indigenous people. Moreover, once they had established themselves politically they were able to strengthen their ranks by admitting other Basters as burghers to their communities, although in Concordia the extent to which this took place was limited by shortage of land.

The importance of missionary influence in building up the Rehoboth Baster community has also been observed.[20] Moreover, it seems unlikely that these Basters who crossed the Orange River in 1868 would have retained their unity had it not been for their missionary, who trekked with them. The upper class which Fischer describes were the Basters *par excellence*; they formed the vanguard of the trek and at the beginning of the twentieth century still wielded power in the community.[21]

In accordance with the hypothesis that the Basters in Concordia, Komaggas and Steinkopf achieved power largely through the support of the missionaries, these Basters should have lost their power after

[18] When the Surveyor-General, Charles Bell, visited the Richtersveld in 1854 he took Links to be a 'Hottentot'. Links could not then speak Dutch. *Reports of Charles Bell on the Copper fields of Little Namaqualand*, Saul Solomon, Cape Town, 1855.

[19] Cf. Marais, p. 107.

[20] Fischer, especially pp. 23–31, 228–37. Marais, pp. 88–9, 98–108.

[21] Fischer, pp. 29, 236–7. For an account of the Griqua Basters and their relationship with missionaries see: G. W. Stow, *The Native Races of South Africa*, pp. 316–403; J. Campbell, *Travels in South Africa: Narrative of a Second Journey in the Interior*, 1822, vol. 11, pp. 259–71; S. J. Halford, *The Griquas of Griqualand*; Marais, chapter 2.

the Mission Stations and Communal Reserves Act was enforced. This has been demonstrated for Steinkopf, but I was unable to test it satisfactorily in Concordia or Komaggas because I did not have access to the Management Board minutes. But Mr. J. Fortuin, a former Komaggas Management Board member, proved to me that it applied also to his community.

In the two communities where the Basters did not gain political power and lost their identity as separate groups, we find different circumstances. At Leliefontein it was not the Basters but the indigenous population who had missionary support. This was due to the coincidence which in 1816 brought the missionary Barnabas Shaw to serve the Khoi Khoin people there. On his way to South West Africa he was met by the chief of a tribe of Little Namaqua, who was journeying to Cape Town in search of a missionary to serve him and his people at Leliefontein. The chief, who spoke Dutch, promptly invited Shaw to fill the position. Shaw accepted, and the two travelled together to Leliefontein,[22] where the new missionary was welcomed by the members of the tribe.

It is not known why this chief was so eager to engage the services of a missionary but it seems probable that he needed support in the face of the encroaching Boers,[23] and that he and his people had been impressed by Seidenfaden of the London Missionary Society, who, apart from giving religious instruction, had taught some of the people Dutch during his stay in 1808.[24]

In Richtersveld the early missionaries do not appear to have sided with any one group, and the missionary influence in general has been less than in any of the other communities. The resident missionaries, who were themselves Basters, played no part in politics, contributed little to school education, and even in the field of religious instruction achieved less than those at other stations.[25]

There are, however, other factors which were also responsible for the absorption of the Basters by the Khoi Khoin in Richtersveld. Here the Basters appear to have come as isolated individuals and families, and this tended to facilitate the process whereby they lost their identity, as was also the case in the north-west part of Steinkopf. The extreme isolation of Richtersveld may also have been a contributory factor.

[22] Shaw, p. 68.
[23] Barrow, p. 388.
[24] P. W. Kotzé, p. 204.
[25] Cf. *Berichte der Rheinischen Missionsgesellschaft*, no. 18, 1855, p. 282.

Yet in spite of these additional explanations the comparative material suggests that the missionary factor was the most important.

It is not possible to state what changes the early Basters effected in Leliefontein and Richtersveld. The fact that the culture of the former is nowadays essentially Baster, whereas the culture of the latter tends to be Khoi Khoin, however, suggests that Baster influence in Leliefontein was greater. And since Leliefontein is situated on part of the old migration route to the north, we would expect it to have been greater than in isolated Richtersveld. It would appear, therefore, that Leliefontein's geographical position brought the indigenous population in regular contact with Basters, although few Basters settled there permanently,[26] and that the Basters' way of life was copied. But there is another aspect which must be considered, namely the missionary factor in Baster culture. I have defined the Baster culture historically as a synthesis between two traditions, trekboer and Khoi Khoin, a product of frontier life in the north-west. But very little is known about the culture of these Basters before they settled near missionaries where their way of life was radically altered. Thus it is possible that the Baster way of life, as it can be observed in Leliefontein and elsewhere today, owed more of its character to missionary influence than is generally realised, as Fischer firmly believed.[27]

If we turn our attention to the change from the Khoi Khoin to the Dutch (later Afrikaans) language in these communities (excluding Richtersveld), we see that both the Basters and the missionaries played a part in the process. In 1840 Backhouse visited Leliefontein, Komaggas, and Steinkopf. He tells us that in Leliefontein, 'the people generally use [Hottentot] in conversation', but that most of them had acquired a knowledge of Dutch.[28] In Komaggas, he says, 'The language of the Hottentots] was that chiefly in use', and the fact that the missionary, J. H. Schmelen, used his translation of the Gospels[29] and a hymn-book suggests that few people knew Dutch.[30] And at Steinkopf Backhouse was told that, 'few people understood anything but Hottentot', and

[26] Marais (p. 75) says that Von Rohden reported that in 1840 Leliefontein consisted mainly of Namaqua.

[27] Fischer, pp. 229–31.

[28] Backhouse, p. 526.

[29] *Annoe Kayn hoeaati haka Kanniti Nama-Kowapna Gowayhiihati* (J. H. Schmelen translator), Cape Town, 1831. Schmelen was assisted in his translation by his Khoi Khoin wife (Backhouse, p. 532).

[30] Backhouse, p. 532.

that the missionary generally used an interpreter when he preached.[31] Judging from the names which Backhouse mentions, those who spoke Dutch in Komaggas and Steinkopf were, as one would expect, Basters. It is surprising, therefore, to find that by 1840 the predominantly Khoi Khoin population of Leliefontein had already acquired a knowledge of the Dutch language. But as early as 1808 Seidenfaden of the London Missionary Society had taught Dutch to certain of the Khoi Khoin, as we have already shown. Also, the Khoi Khoin of Leliefontein had been in regular contact with Baster Voortrekkers on their way to the north.[32] Moreover, in Leliefontein interaction with Boers was great and many Khoi Khoin were employed on adjacent White farms,[33] and there is evidence that certain of the Basters were born in the area.[34] The extent to which the Khoi Khoin at Leliefontein understood Dutch in 1816 is borne out by the fact that Shaw was able to preach in Dutch on his first Sunday at the new mission-station.[35] Shaw, who knew no Khoi Khoin, continued to foster the learning of Dutch, and six months after his arrival, 'Jacob Links and three others . . . were able to read the New Testament and several others were exceedingly anxious to follow their example'.[36] And by 1825 interpreters appeared to have been unnecessary.[37] It is not known when Dutch became the home language of the majority of the people in Leliefontein.

In Komaggas, Schmelen's knowledge of Khoi Khoin and the use of his translation of the Gospels may have retarded the learning of Dutch by the indigenous population, but the missionaries who succeeded him on his death in 1848 used only Dutch and increased the amount of formal education in the school.[38] In Steinkopf, Brecher's work in education was enormous and he used only Dutch. In both these communities (and Concordia) the Basters, who gained political power, contributed a great deal to the change in home language from Khoi Khoin to Dutch. It is not possible to determine with certainty when this change occurred, but in Steinkopf it is probable that by 1870 Dutch

[31] Backhouse, pp. 545–6, 578.
[32] e.g. the Griqua. See Campbell, p. 259.
[33] Barrow, pp. 237–9. G. Thompson, *Travels and Adventures in Southern Africa*, 1827, pp. 305–7.
[34] Alexander, pp. 77–8.
[35] Shaw, pp. 71–2.
[36] Shaw, pp. 82–3.
[37] Cheeseman, p. 76.
[38] T. N. Hanekom, *Die Gemeente Namakwaland*, p. 139.

was beginning to be regarded as a second language, and by the turn of the century Dutch was firmly established as the mother tongue of the members of lineage category A and the majority of lineage category C.[39] Fifty years later the whole community spoke only Afrikaans except for the members of a few families in lineage category B who continued to use Nama as their home language.

In Richtersveld (Kuboes), according to informants, Nama was used in the church and the school up to 1917 although some attempts appear to have been made to teach Dutch. There was no school and scarcely any religious instruction from 1918 to 1928. And as late as 1931, when Gert Cloete, who is now superintendent of the Steinkopf Reserve, went there to teach for a few years, he had to give some of his lessons in Nama to make himself understood. He had learnt this language as a child in Steinkopf. It was not until 1937, when the present principal of the Kuboes school arrived from Paarl (near Cape Town), that Afrikaans began to be established as a medium of instruction in school and church. But even today Nama is the home language of the majority. The evidence suggests that at Kuboes the Basters who were absorbed by the indigenous population contributed very little as 'culture agents'. At Lekkersing, in the southern part of Richtersveld, Baster influence on language and way of life appears to have occurred although here also the Basters, with the exception of the Cloete family, have lost their identity. The number of Basters who settled near Lekkersing was probably greater than those who settled near Kuboes.[40]

We have shown that among the indigenous population of Little Namaqualand during the nineteenth century a radical change in language occurred largely where missionary influence was strong and where the Basters were present (temporarily or permanently) in relatively large numbers. But it seems improbable that this change would have taken place had the Khoi Khoin population consisted of large close-knit groups similar to those of the Bantu-speaking peoples in the east. Missionaries were equally active there but did not effect comparable changes in language among the Bantu-speaking peoples; and the influence of the few people of mixed descent was negligible.

[39] Evidence based on information obtained while collecting genealogies.

[40] Hoernlé, *Richterveld, The Land and its People*, pp. 6 and 8. Melvill Report, p. 12.

CHANGE IN THE RESERVES

When we come to ask what have been the general features of social change in the community of Steinkopf during the past century and a half, certain tendencies present themselves. First, it is clear that there has been a gradual change from social and cultural autonomy to a relative social and cultural dependence on the outside world: a change from an isolated to a peasant community.

But our data have shown that not all the institutions in the community have changed evenly or equally. The kinship system, for example, has changed in both form and function but with the increase in complexity and diversity of social life in general, kinship has receded in importance because many of its functions have been taken over by other groups—voluntary associations, schools, churches, and the local government. Yet, paradoxically, the kinship system has also retained many of its traditional forms (with modified functions), while the other institutions, apart from the magical and economic systems, have not. Therefore, while our data verify the hypothesis that there is an inverse correlation between the weight of kinship relationships in a society and the degree of complexity of social structure, they show also that in contemporary Steinkopf many aspects of the traditional kinship system persist because ties between kinship and aspects of the traditional economy and magic still exist. In other words, traditional kinship ties tend to be bolstered up by the retention of certain traditional economic and magical practices. These phenomena represent the conservative aspect of the social life of Steinkopf. But while there has been a tendency to retain aspects of the traditional way of life, there has been a tendency on the other hand to accept readily Western religious and educational institutions, and to a certain extent Western medicine; and although changes in the form of government have been resisted in the past, conflicts in local government are expressed nowadays by the inhabitants largely in terms of internal affairs rather than in terms of antagonism towards the external authority, although the latter is also present. These tendencies represent the new in the social life in Steinkopf, and we have already shown the way in which the 'new people' have achieved and maintain their power over the conservatives. All these phenomena are exemplified in the contemporary patterns of leadership which we have described and analysed: we have seen, for example, that aliens tend to become leaders of secondary groups which have external affiliations.

These tendencies seem to apply also to the other communities, although the degree of external interaction varies from community to community, and in Richtersveld the cleavage between the old and the new is still underdeveloped.

Secondly, there has been a change in the size and pattern of distribution of the population. The population has increased, but more and more people have come to live permanently in the village or settle in hamlets around the farm schools. With this tendency for people to congregate in settlements (especially in the village), the homestead as a permanent isolated local group has tended to disappear. These changes in the spatial distribution of the population began with the establishment of the church, schools, and shops, and the introduction of migratory labour, which has made people less dependent on farming.

All these tendencies apply to the other communities, although in Komaggas, with its simpler village structure and relatively recent acceptance of large-scale migratory labour, part of the population has remained scattered. And in Richtersveld following the expansion of the church and the schools, the establishment of shops, and the pursuit of migratory labour, people are only now beginning to move closer to the centres around which villages and hamlets comparable to those in Steinkopf and the other communities will grow.

Thirdly, there has been a gradual change in all these communities from a relatively simple social structure to a more complex one and a corresponding increase in the variety of types of social groups. These tendencies can be seen in religion, education, economy, medical services, class-structure (although in Richtersveld a true class-structure is still in embryo), composition of the population (less marked in Richtersveld), and in the political system, although, regarding the latter, during the transition from a Khoi Khoin council, to a Management or Advisory Board, judicial and most legislative functions have been lost to the central government. The emergence of voluntary associations, moreover, provides us with a useful index to illustrate these changes, especially as their number and variety have increased during each successive historical period; and there is the very marked connexion between the rise and increase in complexity of voluntary associations and the decline in the functions of the various kinship groups *except those of the elementary family*. The increase in the number of church-linked voluntary associations is essentially a function of church solidarity.

It has been asserted by certain sociologists that an increase in complexity of social relationships is always accompanied by an increase in the degree of impersonality in those relationships.[41] This was found to be true in Steinkopf and the other communities as far as the over-all pattern of relations was concerned. But as relationships have become more complex and more diverse, and as the communities have become less autonomous, so new patterns of interaction have emerged, which are not less personal than the traditional bonds of kinship and locality. For example, we drew a distinction in Steinkopf between primary and secondary groups. Primary groups by definition were said to be characterised by intimate, face-to-face, personal relationships, and were found to exist generally throughout the community; and certain secondary groups were seen also to possess primary group characteristics.

Finally, we may summarise the factors which have initiated the changes we have already described.

First, there are those changes which may be correlated with changes in the composition of the population. In Steinkopf the structure of the original Khoi Khoin community was modified by the arrival of the Baster Pioneers and the missionaries, who came more or less at the same time. The Basters and the missionaries subsequently formed what can conveniently be termed a political alliance and dominated the native inhabitants. The Basters brought guns, they regarded themselves as superior stock to the Khoi Khoin, from whom they held aloof, they spoke Dutch, and were familiar with some of the tenets of the new religion which the missionaries introduced. In addition to the Christian religion, the missionaries introduced cultivation and the plough, European formal education (they used the Dutch language in the schools), some knowledge of Western medicine, and indirectly some of the customs of their own society.

The early missionaries were followed by *smouse* (pedlars), mostly Jewish but also a few Englishmen, who took Baster concubines. As the community grew and became more settled, some of the Jewish *smouse* obtained permanent rights, introduced a greater variety of Western commodities and stimulated the use of money. Then there were the explorers and the prospectors, who in their own ways influenced the people of Steinkopf. And we must also include here the influence which the encroaching Dutch peasantry, the trekboers, and later the doctors, surveyors and other government officials, had on the community.

In addition to the effect which the Baster Pioneers had on the tradi-

[41] e.g. G. and M. Wilson, *The Analysis of Social Change*, pp. 95–8.

17

AN ANALYSIS OF SOCIAL CHANGE

tional class-system, we must also take cognisance of further modifications which were brought about by the admission of the early and recent *kommers* and bywoners to the community.

All these factors operated in Komaggas and Concordia, although in Komaggas there were few prospectors, and in Concordia we must stress again that the effect which newcomers had on the class-structure was different. The importance of the dissimilar roles played by the missionaries and Basters in Leliefontein and Richtersveld has already been discussed. And in Leliefontein, as in Komaggas, the number of prospectors has been few, while in Richtersveld there has been little contact with traders: the first shop was established only a few years ago—by a local inhabitant.

Increase in the size of the population due partly to natural increases and partly to immigration has effected (directly and indirectly) change in the economy. Whereas formerly it was generally possible for these territories to support their populations, today, even in years of plenty, this cannot be achieved without external assistance (e.g. migratory labour), particularly as overstocking and bad methods of farming have resulted in the impoverishment of the soil.

But increase in the size of the population is not the only factor which has effected changes in the pattern of the economy since large-scale migratory labour and external trade were made possible chiefly by the opening up of the copper and diamond mines, the growth of the fishing industry, and the process of urbanisation which accompanied industrialisation. And the development of interaction with the outside world in general through alien institutions such as the Church and the schools has tended also to stimulate people to further and more intense external interaction, and encourage them to achieve a higher standard of living.

Coercion has played a major part in effecting changes in the social structures of these communities. Coercion as a factor in bringing about social change may be defined as any generally unacceptable change effected in the generally accepted social organisation of a particular society or community by an outside power which uses force or the threat of force to impose this change. The Mission Stations and Communal Reserves Act is the main example of coercion as an initiator of change.

In brief, changes in the structures of these communities have occurred as a result of interaction (voluntary or otherwise) with the outside world either by extending the social boundaries of the communities or by the introduction of new elements into the communities themselves. Often both factors have been involved.

It could be argued that the growth of population due to natural increase has not depended on external factors but this would be hard to defend in the light of the introduction of medical services and changes in the economy, which must have affected beneficially the standards of health, as the decline in the death-rate shows.

Those traditional institutions or parts of traditional institutions which have not been directly influenced by external factors have, however, been influenced indirectly, especially when new associations have taken over functions formerly fulfilled by these institutions. I am unable to find evidence of any significant structural changes in these communities, which can be classified as spontaneous changes, that is to say, changes which are not correlated directly or indirectly with external interaction of some kind. Of course spontaneous changes are difficult to isolate in rapidly changing communities because their existence (if they are present) is always blurred by other factors.

Within the framework of each community, therefore, changes are best seen as adaptations to the new—new ideas, new laws, new situations, and new social relationships—whether these phenomena have come directly from outside or are the internal manifestations of external stimuli. The process of adaptation to new phenomena necessarily implies the reorganisation or modification of existing social relationships, because the components of the social structure are essentially functionally interdependent *both in time and space*. We have seen, for example, that European-type education has not merely given new knowledge to those who have received it, but has also been instrumental in effecting changes in the class-structures, etc. The enforcement of the Mission Stations and Communal Reserves Act has not merely imposed alien laws and regulations, but has provided, as we have demonstrated for Steinkopf, channels for leadership among the 'new people'; it has tended also to reinforce *contemporary* patterns of kinship relationships; and by rigidly incapsulating people in a Reserve situation has inhibited the process of emancipation from the peasant migrant-worker complex.

REFERENCES AND RELEVANT WORKS

(*a*) GENERAL

Alexander, J. E., *Expedition of Discovery into the Interior of Africa*, London, 1838.

Backhouse, J., *A Narrative of a Visit to the Mauritius and South Africa*, London, Hamilton Adams & Co., 1844.

Barrow, J., *Travels into the Interior of Southern Africa*, London, 1806.

Berichte der Rheinischen Missionsgesellschaft, 1855–8.

Campbell, J., *Travels in South Africa: Narrative of a Second Journey in the Interior*, vol. 2, 1822.

Carstens (W.) P., 'The Dutch Reformed Church Militant', *Africa South*, vol. 3, no. 2, January 1959, pp. 48–53.

'Basters', in *The Encyclopedia of Southern Africa*, Cape Town, Nasionale Boekhandel. To be published 1967.

'The Community of Steinkopf: an Ethnographic Study and an Analysis of Social Change in Namaqualand, unpublished Ph.D. thesis, University of Cape Town, 1961.

Cheeseman, T., *The Story of William Threlfall*, Cape Town, 1910.

Coloured Affairs Department, Cape Town, *General Bibliography of the Coloured People of South Africa*, 1954 and supplements. Information Service.

Cruse, H. P., 'Die Eerste Sendingreis na Groot-Namakwaland', *Die Kerkbode*, 28 July and 4 August 1937.

Die Opheffing van die Kleurlingbevolking, Stellenbosch, 1947.

Dapper, O., and others, *The Early Cape Hottentots*, edited with an introduction and notes by I. Schapera, Cape Town, Van Riebeeck Society, 1935.

De Jouvenel, B., *Sovereignty: an Inquiry into the Political Good*, Cambridge, 1957.

Dowdle, K., *A Bibliography of Namaqualand*, University of Cape Town School of Librarianship, 1959.

De Villiers, J. J., 'Elim: 'n Gemeenskapstudie van 'n Sendingstasie', unpublished M.A. thesis, University of Stellenbosch, 1948.

Dunning, R. W., *Social and Economic Change among the Northern Ojibwa*, Toronto, 1959.

'Some Aspects of Governmental Indian Policy and Administration', *Anthropologica*, N.S. IV, No. 2, 1962.

Du Plessis, J., *A History of Christian Missions in South Africa*, London, 1911.

Du Toit, J. D., 'Plaasarbeiders: 'n Gemeenskapstudie', unpublished M.A. thesis, University of Stellenbosch, 1947.

Dyason, E. R., ''n Sosiologiese Ondersoek van die Kleurlingbevolking binne die Munisipale Gebied van Kimberley', unpublished D.Phil. thesis, University of the Orange Free State, 1955.

Engelbrecht, J. A., *The Korana*, Cape Town, Maskew Miller, 1936.

Fallers, L. A., *Bantu Bureaucracy: A Study of Integration and Conflict in the Political Institutions of an East African People*, Cambridge, Heffer, for East African Institute of Social Research, 1956.

'The Predicament of the Modern African Chief', *American Anthropologist*, vol. 57, no. 2, 1955, pp. 290–305.

Fischer, E., *Die Rehobother Bastards und das Bastardierungsproblem beim Menschen*, Jena, 1913.

Forbes, V. S., 'The Expanding Horizon: a geographical commentary upon routes, records, observations and opinions contained in selected documents concerning travel at the Cape, 1750–1800', unpublished Ph.D. thesis, Rhodes University, 1958. Published as *Pioneer Travellers of South Africa* (1750–1800), Cape Town, Balkema, 1965.

Fortes, M., 'Culture Contact as a Dynamic Process', *Africa*, supplement, 1938.

Foster, G. M., 'Interpersonal Relations in Peasant Society', *Human Organization*, vol. 19, no. 4, 1960–1, pp. 174–84.

Frankenberg, R., *Village on the Border*, London, Cohen & West, 1957.

Freislich, R., *The Last Tribal War*, Cape Town, Struik, 1964.

Ginsberg, M., 'Social Change', *British Journal of Sociology*, vol. 9, no. 3, 1958, pp. 205–29.

Gluckman, M., *Custom and Conflict in Africa*, Oxford, Blackwell, 1955.

Goodwin, A. J. H., 'Metal Working among the Early Hottentots', *S.A. Archaeological Bulletin*, XI, 1956, pp. 46–51.

Gulick, J., *Cherokees at the Crossroads*, Chapel Hill, Institute for Research in Social Science, 1960.

Halford, S. J., *The Griquas of Griqualand*, Cape Town, Juta, 1949.

Hanekom, T. N., *Die Gemeente Namakwaland*, Kaapstad, N.G. Kerkpers, 1950.

Hawthorn, H. B., Belshaw, C. S., and Jameson, S., *The Indians of British Columbia*, Toronto, 1960.

Heese, J. A., 'Onderwys in Namakwaland', unpublished D.Phil. thesis, University of Stellenbosch, 1942.

Hoernlé, A. W. (*née* Tucker), *Richterveld, the Land and its People*, Johannesburg, 1913.

'Certain Rites of Transition . . . among the Hottentots', *Harvard African Studies*, II, 1918, pp. 65–82.

'The Expression of the Social Value of Water among the Naman of South West Africa', *S.A. Journal of Science*, XX, 1923, pp. 514–26.

'The Social Organization of the Nama Hottentots of South-West Africa', *American Anthropologist*, XXVII, 1925, pp. 1–24.

Homans, G. C., *The Human Group*, London, Routledge & Kegan Paul, 1951.

Horrell, M., *Race Classification in South Africa: its Effects on Human Beings*, S.A. Institute of Race Relations, Fact Paper No. 2, 1958.

Jacobson, E., *The Cape Coloured* (Bibliography). University of Cape Town School of Librarianship, 1945.

Jopp, W., 'Die frühen Deutschen Berichte über das Kapland und die Hottentotten bis 1750', unpublished Ph.D. thesis, University of Göttingen, 1960.

Kirsten, A. J., ' 'n Behuisingsopname van nie-blanke Plaasarbeiders werksaam by 102 Uitvoerdruiweboere in die Distrik Paarl', unpublished M.A. thesis, University of Stellenbosch, 1953.

Kitchingman, J., *Diary* (MS.), 1820.

Kotzè, H. A., 'Verslag oor Ekonomiese Ondersoek na die Ontwikkeling van 'n Voerbank op Goodhouse vir die Kleurlinggebiede in Namakwaland', unpublished report, University of the Orange Free State, 1960.

Kotzé, P. W., *Namakwaland, 'n Sosiologiese Studie van 'n geïsoleerde Gemeenskap*, Cape Town, University of Stellenbosch, 1943.

Laidler, P. W., 'Burials and Burial Methods of the Namaqualand Hottentots', *Man*, XXIX, 1929, pp. 151–3.

Lazarus, Z. J., 'Die Stigting en vroeë Jare van die S.A. Sendinggenootskappe, 1799–1830', unpublished M.A. thesis, University of Stellenbosch, 1949.

Le Roux, W. G., 'Die Kleurling-Jeugbande in Kaapstad', unpublished Ph.D. thesis, University of Stellenbosch, 1951.

Letcher, O., 'Namaqualand, Cradle of Mineral Development in Southern Africa'. Reprinted from *The Mining and Industrial Magazine of Southern Africa*, September 1932.

Lichtenstein, M. H. K., *Travels in Southern Africa in the Years 1803–6*, Van Riebeeck Society, 1928, 1930.

Louw, P. J., 'Pniel: 'n Gemeenskapstudie van 'n Sendingstasie', unpublished M.A. thesis, University of Stellenbosch, 1950.

MacCrone, I. D., *Race Attitudes in South Africa*, London, O.U.P., for the University of the Witwatersrand, 1937.

MacMillan, W. M., *The Cape Coloured Question*, London, 1927.

Mansvelt, N., *Proeve van een Kaapsch-Hollandsch Idioticon*, Cape Town, 1884.

Manual of the Laws and Discipline of the Methodist Church of South Africa, 4th edition, 1962.

Manuel, G., *The Coloured People* (Bibliography), University of Cape Town School of Librarianship, 1943.

Marais, J. S., *The Cape Coloured People, 1652–1937*, London, Longmans, Green, 1939.

Marquard, L., *South Africa's Colonial Policy*. Presidential address to the S.A. Institute of Race Relations, 1957.

Meyer, G., *Die Gemeente te Steinkopf, Namakwaland: sy Wording en Ontwikkeling* (MS.), n.d.

Moffat, R., *Missionary Labours and Scenes in Southern Africa*, London, 1842.

Moodie, D. (compiler, translator, and editor), *The Record, or a series of official Papers Relative to the Condition and Treatment of the Native Tribes of South Africa*, Amsterdam and Cape Town, Balkema, 1960 (photostatic reprint of 1838–42 originals).

Neumark, S. D., *Economic Influences on the South African Frontier*, California, Stanford University Press, 1957.

'Namaqualand's Mineral Wealth', *S.A. Mining and Engineering Journal*, LXIV, part 2, 1954, pp. 889–91.

The Native Tribes of South West Africa, Cape Town, Cape Times, 1928.

Official Year Book of the Union of South Africa, no. 19, Pretoria, 1938.

Oxley, H. G., 'Wyksdorp', unpublished M.A. thesis, University of Cape Town, 1961.

Patterson, S., *Colour and Culture in South Africa*, London, Routledge & Kegan Paul, 1953.

    The Last Trek. London, Routledge, 1957.

Pitt-Rivers, J., 'Social Class in a French Village', *Anthropological Quarterly*, vol. 33, no. 1, 1960, pp. 1–13.

Radcliffe-Brown, A. R., and Forde, D., *African Systems of Kinship and Marriage*, London, O.U.P., for International African Institute, 1950.

Radcliffe-Brown, A. R., *Structure and Function in Primitive Society*, London, Cohen and West, 1952.

Redfield, R., *Peasant Society and Culture*, Chicago, 1956.

Schapera, I., *The Khoisan Peoples of South Africa*, London, Routledge & Kegan Paul, 1930.

    Government and Politics in Tribal Societies, London, Watts, 1956.

Schmelen, J. H. (translator), *Annoe Kayn Hoeaati Haka Kanniti Nama-Kowapna Gowayhiihati*, Cape Town, 1831. The Four Evangelists (Gospels) in the Nama language.

Schneider, D. M., and Homans, G. C., 'Kinship Terminology and the American Kinship System', *American Anthropologist*, vol. 57, no. 6, 1955, pp. 1194–208.

Schultze, L., *Aus Namaland und Kalahari*, Jena, 1907.

Shaw, B., *Memorials of South Africa*, London, 1841.

Smit, H. S., and Du Preez, D., 'The Henkries Date Grove', *Farming in South Africa*, XXX, no. 350, 1955.

Spykman, N. J., *The Social Theory of Georg Simmel*, Chicago, 1925.

Statuut van Namakwase Ko-Operatiewe Handelsvereniging Bpk., 1959.

Stow, G. W., *The Native Races of South Africa*, London, Swan, Sonnenschein, 1905.

Suid-Afrikaanse Buro vir Rasse-Aangeleenthede, *Die Kleurling in die Suid-Afrikaanse Samelewing*, 1955.

Swanepoel, J. J., 'Wupperthal, 'n Gemeenskapstudie van 'n Sendingstasie', unpublished M.A. thesis, University of Stellenbosch, 1951.

Theron, E., *Fabriekwerksters in Kaapstad: 'n Sosiologiese Studie van 540 Blanke en Kleurling Fabriek Werksters*, Cape Town, Nasionale Pers, 1944.

Thompson, G., *Travels and Adventures in Southern Africa*, London, 1827.

Uys, A., 'Plaasarbeiders: 'n Sosiologiese Studie van 'n Groep Kleurlingplaasarbeiders in die Distrik van Stellenbosch', unpublished M.A. thesis, University of Stellenbosch, 1947.

Van der Merwe, H. W., 'Social Stratification in a Cape Coloured Community', unpublished M.A. thesis, University of Stellenbosch, 1957.

Van der Merwe, J. E., 'Saron: 'n Gemeenskapstudie van 'n Sendingstasie', unpublished M.A. thesis, University of Stellenbosch, 1952.

Van der Merwe, P. J., *Die Noordwaartse Beweging van die Boere voor die Groot Trek*, Den Haag, Van Stockum, 1937.

Die Trekboer in die Geskiedenis van die Kaapkolonie. Cape Town, 1938.

Pioniers van die Dorsland, Cape Town, Nasionale Pers, 1941.

Trek, Cape Town, 1945.

Van Vreeden, B. F., 'Die Wedersydse Beïnvloeding van die Blanke, Bantoe, en Kleurling Kulture in Noord-Kaapland', unpublished M.A. thesis, University of the Witwatersrand, 1957.

Van Zyl, J. A., 'Die Kamiesberg en aansluitende Kliprand', unpublished M.A. thesis, University of Stellenbosch, 1957.

Vedder, H., *South-West Africa in Early Times*, London, O.U.P., 1938.

Warnich, P. G., 'Genadendal', unpublished M.A. thesis, University of Stellenbosch, 1950.

Weber, M., *Essays in Sociology*. London, Routledge & Kegan Paul, 1948. (Translated and edited by H. H. Gerth and C. Wright Mills.)

Weiss, A. G., 'The Cape Coloured Woman—within an Industrial Community and at Home', unpublished M.Soc.Sci. thesis, University of Cape Town, 1950.

Westphal, E. O. J., 'The Linguistic Prehistory of Southern Africa', *Africa*, XXXIII, no. 3, July 1963, pp. 237–65.

Wette en Bepalings vir die Bestuur van die Nederduitse Gereformeerde Kerk in Suid-Afrika, 1953.

Wilson, G. and M., *The Analysis of Social Change*, Cambridge, 1945.

17A

Wilson, M., *et al.*, *Social Structure*, Keiskammahoek Rural Survey, vol. III, Pietermaritzburg, Shuter & Shooter, 1952.

Wolff, K. H. (translator and editor), *The Sociology of Georg Simmel*, Glencoe, The Free Press, 1950.

Ziervogel, C., *Brown South Africa*, Cape Town, Maskew Miller, 1938.

(*b*) OFFICIAL REPORTS, BLUE BOOKS, ETC.

Reports of the Surveyor-General, Charles Bell, on the Lands of Little Namaqualand, Cape Town, Saul Solomon, 1855.

Correspondence and Report relative to the Lands in Namaqualand, G. 41–1889.

Report on the Lands in Namaqualand, by S. Melvill, G. 60–1890.

Cape of Good Hope. Votes and Proceedings of Parliament, Appendix 2, vol. II, A. 7–1896.

Reports of the Superintendent-General of Education, Cape of Good Hope.

Report on the Bondelzwarts Rising, 1922, U.G. 30–1922.

Report on the Rebellion of the Bondelzwarts, U.G. 16–1923.

Report of the Rehoboth Commission, U.G. 41–1926.

Report of the Native Affairs Commission, 1927–1931, U.G. 26–1932.

Report of Commission of Inquiry regarding the Cape Coloured Population of the Union, U.G. 54–1937.

Report of the Inter-Departmental Committee on Coloured Mission Stations, Reserves, and Settlements, U.G. 33–1947.

Reports of the Commissioner for Coloured Affairs, 1952–   .

Report of the Coloured Education Commission, 1953–1956.

Communal Reserves and Mission Stations Act, No. 29 of 1909, as amended by Act No. 12 of 1929, Act No. 12 of 1949, Act No. 35 of 1955, and Act No. 32 of 1959. The main regulations subjoining the Act are those promulgated under Government Notice No. 461 of 13 March 1913; those promulgated under Government Notice No. 2601 of 3 December 1948; and those promulgated under Government Notice No. R. 1866 of 18 November 1960.

(*c*) SELECT DOCUMENTS

The Reverend F. Brecher's petition to the Honourable the Speaker and Members of the House of Assembly, 1891.

Short Rules laid down for the Rhenish Mission Institution of Steinkopf, Namaqualand. Unpublished.

Resolution to the Governor-General of South Africa from the Burghers of Steinkopf, 1913. Unpublished.

Memorandum to Native Affairs Commission, 1928. Unpublished.

Letters from the Colonial Secretary to Civil Commissioner and Resident
    Magistrate at Springbokfontein, Namaqualand. Cape Archives, especially
    19 August 1857, 10 December 1857.
Civil Commissioner's Minutes, Springbokfontein.
Village Management Board and Council's Minutes, Steinkopf, Namaqualand.
Appendices in W. P. Carstens, 'The Community of Steinkopf', unpublished
    Ph.D. thesis, University of Cape Town, 1961.

RACE CLASSIFICATION IN SOUTH AFRICA[1]

Prior to 1950 the population of the Union of South Africa was divided for statistical purposes into four main categories officially described as follows:

'1. Europeans—persons of pure European descent.

2. Natives[2]—pure-blooded aboriginals of the Bantu race.

3. Asiatics—Natives of Asia and their descendants; mainly Indians.

4. Mixed and other coloured—this group consists chiefly of Cape Coloured, but includes also Cape Malays, Bushmen, Hottentots, and all persons of mixed race. For considerations of space the name of this group is usually contracted to "coloured".

The last three groups, when combined, form the group referred to as the "Non-European" group.'[3]

None of these 'racial' categories, however, had any legal significance and they were used merely for statistical convenience. For legal and administrative purposes various other definitions of 'racial' categories existed, and these definitions were incorporated into certain Acts passed by the South African government from 1910 onwards. They do not always correspond since each was originally created for a specific piece of legislation.[4]

Not only did these multifarious definitions sometimes conflict with one another but, whether they were designed for statistical, legal, or political purposes they lacked rigidity and it was possible for some people to change their 'racial' categories provided their physical characteristics did not vary too widely from those characteristics associated with the average type in the category into which they were moving. This practice, known as 'passing',

---

[1] For a scholarly discussion of the legal aspects of race classification in South Africa, see A. Suzman, 'Race Classification and Definition in the Legislation of the Union of South Africa, 1910–1960', *Acta Juridica*, 1960.

[2] 'African' is nowadays generally considered to be a more appropriate label to describe the Bantu-speaking peoples. 'Native' is regarded as a term of contempt by the majority of South Africans.

[3] *Official Year Book of the Union of South Africa*, 25—1949, p. 1095.

[4] Cf. Native Labour Regulation Act (1911); Natives (Urban Areas) Act (1923); Native Service Contract Act (1932); Representation of Natives Act (1936); Native Trust and Land Act (1936); Workmen's Compensation Act (1934); Registration for Employment Act (1945); Unemployment Insurance Act (1946); Silicosis Act (1946); Disabilities Grants Act (1946); Asiatic Laws Amendment Act (1946).

is usually associated with Coloured people passing as White, but it was also common among Africans 'trying for Coloured'. In a sense, an African who could pass as Coloured gained even more than a Coloured person who crossed the colour-line since he became free of the whole system of passes, influx-control, registration of service contracts, and the extremely restricted residential and freehold rights.[5]

Thus from many points of view this whole system of classification was unsatisfactory. Moreover, certain of the definitions of the 'racial' categories created difficulties which could prove an embarrassment to the Whites. For example, a large percentage of Europeans could theoretically be classified as Coloured owing to the inclusion of the word 'pure' in the census definition given earlier.[6] The genesis of these discrepancies lies of course in the technical classification, attempts at which are nowadays generally regarded by anthropologists as arbitrary abstractions having little value apart from purely morphological interest. Thus in terms of physical features, European, Coloured and African (Native) categories are approximations only, with the middle category merging into both the others.

In 1950 an attempt to ossify the system we have described was undertaken in the form of the Population Registration Act.[7] This Act abolished the old census classification and reclassified South Africa's population into three categories: White, Native and Coloured. Provision, however, was also made for prescribing and defining the ethnic or other groups into which Coloured persons and Natives are to be classified. According to this Act a White person is defined as 'a person who in appearance obviously is, or who is generally accepted as a White person, but does not include a person who, although in appearance obviously a White person, is generally accepted as a coloured person'. A Native, on the other hand is defined as 'a person who in fact is or is generally accepted as a member of any aboriginal race or tribe of Africa'. A Coloured person is negatively defined as 'a person who is not a white person

---

[5] M. Horrell, *Race Classification in South Africa: its effects on human beings*. Fact Paper No. 2, S.A.I.R.R., 1958, p. 4. This paper is strongly recommended to those interested in the question of race classification.

[6] See G. Findlay, *Miscegenation*, Pretoria News, Pretoria, 1936; Report regarding Cape Coloured Population of the Union, U.G. 54—1937, p. 8; I. D. MacCrone, *Race Attitudes in South Africa*, O.U.P., London, 1937, part 1; J. S. Marais, *The Cape Coloured People, 1652–1937*, Longmans, Green, London, 1939, chapter I; S. Patterson, *Colour and Culture in South Africa*, Routledge & Kegan Paul, London, 1953; M. K. Jeffreys, articles in *Drum*, 1959–60, nos. 102–106, 108.

[7] Population Registration Act, No. 30 of 1950. This Act was amended on 18 June 1956, but these amendments do not affect the present discussion.

or a native'.

In 1962 an amendment to this Act redefined White and Coloured persons as follows:

> 'A white person means a person who—(a) in appearance obviously is a white person and who is not generally accepted as a coloured person; or (b) is generally accepted as a white person and is not in appearance obviously not a white person, but does not include any person who for the purposes of his classification under this Act, freely and voluntarily admits that he is by descent a native or a coloured person unless it is proved that the admission is not based on fact.'

The Act also provides for the issue by the Director of Census and Statistics of identity cards to all persons who have attained the age of 16 years. These identity cards may contain *inter alia* information concerning 'racial' category and in the case of Coloureds and Africans the ethnic or other groups to which they are believed to belong.

Clearly the whole purpose of the Population Registration Act is to provide a rigid system whereby every individual's racial category (with a few exceptions) is determined for him by birth, and in so far as these categories determine status his social position as well. A moral justification for the creation and enforcement of this Act was reported to have been put forward by the Minister of the Interior, who said that many people had lived all their lives in a state of unease because it was uncertain to which racial group they belonged. But now certainty had been given, and the clouds which hovered over them had disappeared. [8]

Theoretically this new system should abolish the flexibility of the older one, but in practice there are still conflicting definitions of racial categories in the existing legislation. This is not surprising, for in spite of the emphasis on racial purity in South Africa, physical characteristics are by no means the only factors that are taken into consideration when determining to what 'racial' category a person belongs, as some of the definitions we have recorded show. Thus the system of 'race' classification in South Africa combines certain biological and social standards, which from the very start complicate the task of those whose business it is to compile the Population Register. The difficulties encountered in classifying people, and the major and minor discrepancies in the definitions under the various Acts, must, therefore be explained in terms of the society in which they occur.

A recent writer on the Coloured people, Dr. Sheila Patterson, [9] in discussing

---

[8] *Cape Times,* 21 February 1958.
[9] S. Patterson, *Colour and Culture in South Africa.*

the question of race classification, maintains that the chief problem of definition is not between Coloureds and Africans but between Coloureds and Europeans, but she has failed to draw attention to the legal difficulties which frequently arise from Coloured-African marriages.[10] Furthermore, her contention has been proved false in recent years by the numerous cases of people who regarded themselves as Coloured but found that under the Population Registration Act they had been classified as 'Native'.[11] It is true, of course, that as far as the Whites are concerned the main problem of classification is between them and the Coloured people because there are many Whites who are more Coloured in appearance than a large number of Coloureds. But the classification of these so-called 'racial' categories provides difficulties at all levels.

To return to Dr. Patterson's argument concerning the difficulties involved in classifying Coloureds: it is her contention, derived from I. D. MacCrone and J. S. Marais, that it is the complex origin and history of the Coloured people and their lasting social consequences which have been largely responsible for the vague and negative content of the legal definitions applied to these people. From the sociological point of view the weakness of this formulation is that it emphasises the perpetuation of former race attitudes in the contemporary society but fails to show clearly the important structural changes that have taken place in South Africa during the past 300 years. It is not difficult to see that in the contemporary society the legal quasi-racial categories that have been selected to classify the population do not necessarily coincide with social reality. The members of the African (Native) category, for example, do not constitute a homogeneous socio-cultural group, but are probably the most heterogeneous aggregation of people in Africa. The Coloured people, moreover, although few in comparison with the African population, are also characterised by their social heterogeneity: roughly 60 per cent live in the urban areas in highly stratified communities, and the remaining 40 per cent are rural people, living on White farms, on the outskirts of small towns and dorps, and on mission-stations and Reserves. Even the White population has a diversity which is far more complex than the linguistic cleavage (usually attributed to White South Africa) displays. Moreover, associational and other structural divisions frequently cut across the legal 'racial' categories, which illustrates that the degree of integration between the members of these 'racial' categories is greater than the would-be classifiers have realised.

Attempts have been made by the government of the Republic of South

---

[10] e.g. *Masholo* v. *Masholo*, Case No. 13 in *Selected Decisions of the Native Appeal Court Cape and O.F.S.*, vol. XVI, part 1, 1944. Government Printer, Pretoria, 1945.

[11] M. Horrell, pp. 57–78.

Africa to classify the members of the Coloured population into their various 'ethnic' groups. For example, a proclamation in 1959 issued under the Population Registration Act defined seven sub-categories (groups) as follows:

'1. Cape Coloured Group:

In the Cape Coloured Group shall be included any person who in fact is, or is generally accepted as a member of the race or class known as the Cape Coloureds.

2. Malay Group:

In the Malay Group shall be included any person who in fact is, or is generally accepted as a member of the race or class known as the Cape Malays.

3. Griqua Group:

In the Griqua Group shall be included any person who in fact is, or is generally accepted as a member of the race or class known as the Griquas.

4. Chinese Group:

In the Chinese Group shall be included any person who in fact is, or is generally accepted as a member of a race or tribe whose national home is China.

5. Indian Group:

In the Indian Group shall be included any person who in fact is, or is generally accepted as a member of a race or tribe whose national home is in India or Pakistan.

6. Other Asiatic Group:

In the other Asiatic Group shall be included any person who in fact is, or is generally accepted as a member of a race or tribe whose national home is in any country or area in Asia other than China, India or Pakistan.

7. Other Coloured Group:

In the other Coloured Group shall be included any person who is not included in the Cape Coloured Group, the Malay Group, the Griqua Group, the Chinese Group, the Indian Group or the Other Asiatic Group, and who is not a white person, or a native as defined in section *one* of the Population Registration Act, 1950 (Act No. 30 of 1950).'[12]

Prior to this Proclamation and after 1936, a distinction was made for statistical purposes only between Asiatics and all other Coloured people. In the 1936 census, however, a very detailed classification of Coloured people was given on the basis of the voluntary returns, which included *inter alia* Bushman, Hottentot, Korana, and Namaqua. In the 1946 Census, although the sub-divisions were omitted, 'the few pure-blooded stocks of Hottentot, Bushmen, Griqua and Namaqua' were also classed as Coloured. Under the Population Registration Act of 1950, however, Bushmen and Khoi Khoin (Hottentots) are

---

[12] *Government Gazette*, 6 March 1959.

classified as 'Natives'. All these factors add to the difficulty of attempting to select suitable criteria for describing the Coloured people, and the fact that Bushmen and 'Hottentots' are now classified as 'Natives' is likely to have serious repercussions when the Population Register has finally been completed. Here it is important to note that the shift of the traditional classification of Bushmen and 'Hottentots' from Coloured to 'Native' was proposed by the Commissioner for Coloured Affairs. In his first Annual Report[13] he states that at an 'Inter-Departmental meeting, which examined possible definitions of the different racial groups, which would be generally acceptable', he proposed certain tentative definitions as a basis for discussion. The definition for 'Native' which he proposed was: 'A person descended from any Native race of Southern Africa—including Bantu, Hottentots, and Bushmen—or mainly of such descent.' Furthermore, he states that he suggested 'that these definitions should be incorporated in some Act and be made generally applicable, preferably in conjunction with the Population Register'.

It is significant that the head of the newly created Coloured Affairs Department suggested that there should be a rigid classification of 'racial' groups, and especially that Bushmen and 'Hottentots' (who had always enjoyed Coloured status in the past) should now be classified as 'Natives'. This change may reflect the attitude of certain middle-class Coloureds, particularly in the urban areas, but also in the rural districts, who no longer wish to acknowledge their 'primitive ancestry'. In a sense, therefore, by eliminating as far as possible the aboriginal element from the Cape Coloured population, the social status usually attributed to Coloureds is increased.[14]

---

[13] Report of the Commissioner for Coloured Affairs (1952), U.G. 45—1952, p. 5.

[14] Cf. chapters 6 and 7; Report regarding Cape Coloured Population of the Union, pp. 13–18; Patterson, pp. 164–5.

INDEX

Laidler, P. W., 177 n.
Land: attitude towards, 42; disputes over, 44–6; surveyors, 212, 225; tenure, 26, 30, 42–6, 117, 212.
Language, 234, 235, 238, 240, 243
Law, 7, 17, chapters 2, 3, 7 and 8 *passim*, 217 ff., 241–5.
Leadership, 103, 142–9, 154–5, 193–203, 223–30, *et passim*
Leechcraft, 15, 232, *see also under* Magic
Le Fleur, The Rev. Mr., 34, 207, 208, 229
Leliefontein, ix, 12, 204–30, *et passim*
Lichtenstein, H., 232, 235 n.
Lineages, *see under* Kinship and marriage
London Missionary Society (L.M.S.), 19, 20, 21, 147, 237

MacCrone, I., 232, 233 n., 234 n., 235 n., 257
McDougall, W., 176 n.
Magic, *see under* Supernatural beliefs
Management Board, 6–10, 29–36, chapters 7 and 10, 217–19, *et passim*; opposition and antagonism towards, 148
Mansvelt, N., 99 n.
Magistrate's court, 138–9
Marais, J. S., 17 n., 19 n., 204 n., 233 n., 234 n., 235 n., 236 n., 238 n., 257
Markets, *see under* Trade and markets
Marquard, L., 134 n.
Marriage, *see under* Kinship and marriage
Mat-houses, 4, 5, 73, 75, 80, 212, 232
Medical services, 5, 8, 232
Melvill Report, 17 n., 26 n., 46, 205 n., 240 n.
Methodist Church, 220–2
Meyer, G., 18 n., 108 n.
Migratory labour, 3, 4, 17, 51 ff., 209–12, *et passim*
Mining, 12, 13, 15, 30, 38
Mission stations and missionaries, *passim*, especially chapters 2, 8 and 12
Missionary—president, 18, 25, 26
Mutual dependence, 231–3

Nagmaal (Communion), 153, 157–8, 162–3

Nama, Naman, Namaqua, *see under* Khoi Khoin.
Namaqualand, 1–3, 10–16, 18–36, 204, 232–45, *et passim*
Natural leadership, *see under* Leadership, *especially* 193 ff.
Native Affairs Commission, 33
Natives, *see under* Africans
Nederduitse Gereformeerde Kerk (N.G. Kerk), 33–6, 150 ff., *et passim*
Neumark, S. D., 233 n.
New-comers, 6, 35, 44, 106, 114, 125
'New people', 7, 35, 103, 113, 130–3, 134, 137, 142, 143, 146–9, 187

Obedience, 90, 104–5
Official leadership, *see under* Leadership, *especially* 193 ff.
Orlams, 11, 18, 21, 106
Outmoded leadership, *see under* Leadership, *especially* 193 ff.
Oxley, H. G., 72 n.

Patterson, S., 72 n., 193 n., 219 n., 256, 259 n.
Physical characteristics, 111, 120, 131, 132
Pioneers, *see under* Voortrekkers
Pitt-Rivers, J., 132 n.
Police, 4–7, 134, 138
Population, 3, 12, 14, 17, 38–41, 44, 47, 51–3, 61, 209–12, 233, 242
Poverty Datum Line (P.D.L.), 63–8
Power, *passim*, but *see especially* chapters 2, 6 and 7. *Also* 131, 193–203, 223–30
Prayers, 88, 156–9, 161, 163, 177
Primary groups, 190 ff., 243

Race classification, 1, 6, 254–9, *et passim*; prejudice, 7, 22, 56, 130, 235, *et passim*
Radcliffe-Brown, A. R., 2, 70 n.
Reciprocal meals, 103
Redfield, R., 190
Registered occupiers, 6–7, 66, 117, 126, 127, 138, 140, 141, 200, 215
Religion, *see under* Supernatural beliefs
Reserves, 1–3, 16–17, 29–36, 204–30, 241—5, *et passim*
Respect, 88
Rhenish Mission Society (R.M.S.), 20, 21, 33, 34, 146, 147, 152, 206, 225